D0035833

LINDA LAEL MILLER

New York Times bestselling author Linda Lael Miller started writing at age ten and has made a name for herself in both contemporary and historical romance. Her bold and innovative style has made her a favorite among readers. Named by *Romantic Times* as "The Most Outstanding Writer of Sensual Romance," Linda Lael Miller never disappoints.

LINDSAY McKENNA

A homeopathic educator, Lindsay teaches at the Desert Institute of Classical Homeopathy in Phoenix, Arizona. When she isn't teaching alternative medicine, she is writing books about love. She feels love is the single greatest healer in the world and hopes that her books touch her readers on those levels. Coming from an Eastern Cherokee medicine family, Lindsay was taught ceremony and healing ways from the time she was nine years old. She creates flower and gem essences in accordance with nature, and remains closely in touch with her Native American roots and upbringing.

The Leopard's Woman

LINDA
LAEL MILLER

White Wolf

LINDSAY McKENNA

Published by Silhouette Books
America's Publisher of Contemporary Romance

SILHOUETTE BOOKS

Copyright in the collection:
© 2002 by Harlequin Books S.A.

ISBN 0-373-48475-5

The publisher acknowledges the copyright holders of the individual works as follows:

THE LEOPARD'S WOMAN
Copyright © 1992 by Linda Lael Miller

WHITE WOLF
Copyright © 1997 by Lindsay McKenna

This edition published by arrangement with Harlequin Books S.A.

® and TM are trademarks of Harlequin Books S.A., used under license. Trademarks indicated with ® are registered in the United States Patent and Trademark Office, the Canadian Trade Marks Office and in other countries.

Visit Silhouette at www.eHarlequin.com

Printed in U.S.A.

THE LEOPARD'S WOMAN

Linda Lael Miller

Dear Reader,

I am delighted to see *The Leopard's Woman* rereleased in this lovely new edition from Silhouette Books. The story is an adventure fantasy set in modern-day Mexico and is a personal favorite with me, having plenty of action and passion, two qualities I love in any book—my own or someone else's. The love scenes are at once wild and tender, and the rugged setting is timeless, part Old West, part contemporary.

Come along with me and share in the escapades of Olivia Stillwell and *el leopardo*, Esteban Ramirez, the dangerous, dark-eyed man who cherished her, the outlaw she was born to love....

With love,

Paula Detmer Riggs

Cave Creek, AZ
October 2001

Chapter One

Olivia Stillwell's wrists were bound behind her, and the filthy, rusted floor of the Jeep bruised her anew with every jostle and bump. In that one small corner of her mind that had not yet gone numb with terror, she reflected that this adventure would surely qualify her for a generous bonus—should she survive to collect.

The fierce Mexican sun pounded down, cooking her, unhindered by her sleeveless white cotton blouse and khaki slacks. Her shoulder-length auburn hair clung to the mixture of sweat and dust covering her face and neck, and she was pretty sure she was going to throw up if she had to travel another mile taped up like a lobster on its way to the boiling pot.

Not that Olivia wanted her abductors to stop. *Or* go on to whatever horrifying destination they had in mind, for that matter.

She closed her eyes, trying to retreat into the darkness inside her head, but there was no hiding place there, either. Scenes from B-movies she'd seen years before played in her mind in vivid color.

Olivia couldn't go forward mentally from there, and she certainly found the present intolerable, so she let her thoughts slide backward to the past.

Until that morning, Olivia's life had gone very well, all things considered.

Her Uncle Errol, who wrote fantastically successful romantic adventure novels for a predominantly female audience, had hired her to work on his research staff five years before, after her graduation from college. She'd loved the job immediately and been good at it. Through attrition and a gradual accumulation of experience, Olivia had eventually earned the right to direct the other staffers and take her choice of the research assignments her uncle doled out.

She'd earned her position through a lot of hard work and innovative thinking, though of course a lot of people didn't give her credit for personal effort. Because she was Errol McCauley's only living relative, because he'd raised and educated her, almost everyone assumed her exciting career had been handed to her on the proverbial silver platter.

Even now, under these desperate circumstances, Olivia yearned for an accomplishment of her own, however modest.

For about the thousandth time, Olivia's right cheek thumped against the Jeep floor. Just then, she thought with desolate wryness, she'd have given her job to anyone who asked for it.

Tears flooded her lashes, and she was relieved to know she wasn't dehydrated to the point where she couldn't cry. She sniffled. Only that morning, she'd dined happily on the terrace of her hotel room, shielded from the cruel sun by a bright red-and-white awning. She'd finished her two-week research assignment—Uncle Errol was writing about a rich American heiress who, after many trials and tribulations, married a matador—and decided to reward herself with a few pieces of pottery from a special artists' colony she'd read about.

Olivia had a potter's wheel and a small kiln at home. In fact, she was quite good with clay, and she had aspirations to sell her own work at art shows and in galleries. As much as she loved her job and the adventures it provided, another side of her nature was developing. She wanted a new career, and a baby, not that one had much to do with the other.

After getting directions from a good-natured bellman, Olivia had set out for the compound in her rented car.

Somewhere in the desert, she'd taken a wrong turn, and

the horrors that had followed would have sent Stephen King rushing for his typewriter, inspired.

First, the small sedan, which had seemed perfectly reliable when she'd left the secluded resort town of San Carlos, had overheated. The radiator had exploded, making hot water hiss against the underside of the hood, and of course there had been no starting the car again after that.

Still, Olivia had not been overly alarmed. After all, she'd been in similar predicaments in much wilder parts of the world—"soaking up atmosphere," as her uncle called it—places like Colombia and Morocco and Nepal. She'd had a canteen and there was sunscreen in her purse, along with a billed cap, and she'd never doubted for a moment that she'd find the artists' colony if she walked just a short way farther.

Someone there would take her back to the hotel.

Olivia had put on her sunglasses, slathered her face and arms with protective lotion, donned her neon-pink baseball cap and set off confidently down the rutted road. Several alarming creatures had scurried across her path, and she'd made mental notes about their coloring and size. The more details she brought home, the happier Uncle Errol would be; he liked to use a lot of vibrant description in his books.

Even after an hour, though, there was no sign of the art colony. All Olivia could see in any direction was desert and cacti and a very distant mountain range. She was doing some serious sweating by then, and her bravado turned rapidly to plain fear.

Then the Jeep had appeared, far off on the dusty ribbon of a road, flinging up brown plumes of dirt behind it.

Presently, the vehicle had come to a lurching stop beside Olivia, and she had seen instantly that these men, with their rifles and leering eyes, weren't planning to help her. She'd turned and fled into the desert, the sand so hot that it burned her feet even through the soles of her sandals, and they'd caught her easily.

Olivia had screamed and fought wildly, certain they

meant to rape her and leave her to die, and the younger of
the two *bandidos* had moved to backhand her. The other
man had caught hold of his partner's wrist, staying the blow,
and shouted furiously in Spanish.

After that, however, they'd pulled her hands behind her
back and taped her wrists together. Her ankles were hobbled
in much the same way, and a gag put on her mouth. Her
cap had fallen off in the scuffle.

Olivia had lost track of how long they'd been traveling;
it seemed like days, but she knew no more than a few hours
had passed, if that.

She turned restlessly, giving a low moan. Her throat and
sinuses burned with bile, and every muscle and bone in her
body ached, but it was the fear that caused her the most
suffering. She couldn't forget those terrible low-budget
movies about young women taken captive in Mexico.

When they came to a jolting, unexpected stop, Olivia's
head crashed into the back of a seat. Her heart seemed to
collide with her windpipe.

The older man came around to the back, his shirt soaked
in sweat, clasped Olivia's arm and pulled her upright. For
a moment he wavered, like a shimmery figure in a mirage,
and Olivia felt herself slipping into the darkness.

Her captor muttered urgently, again in Spanish too rapid
and colloquial for Olivia to understand, untied the bandanna
gag and raised a canteen to her mouth. She drank greedily;
he scolded her and pulled the blessed water away until she
realized he wanted her to sip slowly. She nodded, and the
cool liquid flowed over her tongue again, metallic and sul-
fur-scented and more delicious than ambrosia.

When the *señor* finally withdrew the canteen, he gestured
for Olivia to lie down again. She obeyed, since her options
were so limited, and he covered her with a striped blanket,
the kind sold to *turistas* in the marketplace, along with plas-
ter statues, tablecloths and cheap jewelry. The Jeep set off
again.

The heat underneath that thickly woven cover was excruciating in its intensity, but Olivia recognized a kindness when she saw one. Without that shelter, the brutal sun would literally have broiled her alive.

The trip went on and on, and Olivia began to drift in and out of consciousness. There was so much she hadn't done yet—making a place for herself in the art world, getting married, having babies, winning the Publisher's Clearing House Sweepstakes—she wanted to live! On the other hand, if she was about to be sold into white slavery, as she suspected, death seemed preferable.

As if anybody planned to give her a choice.

There was another water stop, but Olivia was in a dreamworld by then. She was back in Connecticut, in the attic of her uncle's wonderful old pre-Revolutionary house, happily spinning pots and vases and fruit bowls to be offered for sale at local craft shows.

The unbearable Mexican heat gradually went away and was replaced by a growing chill that finally revived Olivia, wrenching her back to bitter reality. She wasn't exactly grateful, but she *was* glad for the blanket.

Beneath her throbbing bones, the Jeep trundled mercilessly along, finding every pothole and rut, occasionally making a sudden swerve so that she was flung against the bolts that held the seats in place. She managed to wriggle enough to peer out from under the blanket with one eye, and she saw a galaxy of spectacular silver stars spread across the dark sky like a banner at some cosmic going-away party.

So long, Olivia. Too bad about all you'll be missing.

The idea of dying made her throat thicken with grief. She was only twenty-six, and the world was entirely too beautiful to leave.

The Jeep climbed, descended, climbed again. When it finally stopped and she heard new voices, all male and all speaking the native language, Olivia passed out.

* * *

When she awakened, she thought she was dead. Practically everything in the room where she found herself was covered in white linen, with the palest pastels for accent, and the place was comfortably cool. Beyond the open windows, turquoise waves capped in iridescent alabaster flirted with a sugar-white beach.

Olivia tried to speak, but her throat was too sore.

She sat up in bed, ran her hands over the coverlet, then the expensive cutwork sheets beneath. She was wearing a loose percale gown, and the skin on her arms was red and peeling, though swathed in some rich, soothing cream.

Despite the luxury surrounding her—there was a carafe of cool water on the bedside table, along with a crystal bowl brimming with fresh fruit—Olivia was terrified. This could not be a friendly place, not when she'd been brought here by *bandidos*. Maybe she was in a sort of halfway house, about to be sent to South America, or maybe somewhere like Libya....

The thing to do, of course, was to find her clothes, climb over the terrace and make a break for it. She'd travel on foot if she had to; if she was lucky, she would be able to steal a car. Fortunately, she wouldn't need a key—she'd learned to hotwire engines as part of the research for her uncle's last book.

Carefully, flinching at the pain of her bruises and sunburn, Olivia pushed back the covers and climbed out of the fancy four-poster bed. Her knees immediately folded, and she barely kept herself from toppling to the white woven rug.

Groping, she retreated back to the mattress. Her head was pounding from even that small effort, and her stomach was queasy. She had to get away—as horrible as her kidnapping had been, Olivia was certain the worst was yet to come—but she didn't have the strength.

She gasped when the door opened suddenly, but the visitor was only a mild-looking Mexican woman in her late fifties or early sixties. Neither fat nor thin, she was wearing a pale pink cotton dress and no shoes, and her smile was reassuring.

If this woman was involved in white slavery, she certainly didn't look the part. She said hello in Spanish—the first bit of conversation Olivia had understood since leaving the hotel in San Carlos—and approached the bed.

Olivia asked haltingly if the woman spoke English, and the answer was a regretful shake of the head.

"Maria," the woman said, indicating herself by placing curled fingers against her bosom. Then she gestured toward her guest in question.

"Olivia," said the captive.

Maria smiled and poured a glassful of water from the carafe, then held it gently to Olivia's lips.

Olivia drank gratefully, her nausea subsiding. She settled gingerly back against the pristine pillows, staring up at the ceiling. There were so many things she wanted to ask about, but chattering away at the well-meaning Maria would merely tax her sore throat and strain her already taut nerves.

She must have slept, for when she opened her eyes again, the sunlight pouring through the terrace doors was thinner, and it met the stone floor at a different angle. There was a rap at the door, and Olivia, expecting the gentle Maria, was not as alarmed as she might have been.

Until the visitor entered the room, that is.

He was the most beautifully built man Olivia had ever seen, standing just over medium height. His hair was rich and dark and slightly too long, and the sides were brushed back sleekly, like the wings of a bird. His skin was like fine sandalwood, and his teeth were improbably white, but it was the color of his eyes that really caught Olivia's attention. They were not brown or black, like those of most Mexican people; they were a deep, arresting shade of violet.

Olivia had every reason to believe the white slaver had

arrived at last, and despite her raw throat, she opened her mouth and gave a croaky cry.

He paused and looked back, as though expecting to see a monster following him, smiled, then closed the door.

Olivia let out another hoarse yelp, scrambled to her knees, groped for the fruit bowl beside the bed and sent a pomegranate hurling across the room. It missed his head and split against the door. "Stay back, you pimp!" she screamed.

He laughed, resting his gloved hands on his lean hips. He was wearing cotton pants with shiny silver buttons lining the outside seams, high black boots and a cream-colored shirt open halfway down his chest. In fact, he looked for all the world like one of Uncle Errol's legendary heroes come to life.

"I'm glad to see that I have bought myself a woman with spirit," he said.

Chapter Two

Esteban Ramirez braced himself for a barrage of fruit, since the bowl beside the bed was still full of apples, bananas, pomegranates and oranges, but nothing happened. His lovely, if parboiled, guest just knelt there in the middle of the bed, staring at him in proud, defiant horror.

He felt a peculiar tightening sensation in a hidden region of his heart and knew he'd turned a corner of some kind, that his life would never be quite the same again.

Esteban brought himself up short. Now he was getting sentimental.

He took pity on the woman, though he suspected pity was the last thing she'd want even under the circumstances, and raised both hands, palms out, in a conciliatory gesture. He sincerely believed he was communicating friendliness and safety.

"What is your name?" he asked in polite, precise English. It was possible, of course, that the combination of her terrifying experience and the relentless Mexican sun had done some damage to her mind, permanent or otherwise.

"What do you care about my name?" she retorted after a moment of blustery hesitation. Her arms were folded across her well-shaped breasts, her chin set at an obstinate angle. Even with blisters and bruises covering her sunburned flesh, she was beautiful in an elemental sort of way, like the varying landscapes of Mexico.

Esteban swallowed hard. He had never encountered such a saucy woman before, even on his frequent trips to the United States, and he was both charmed and infuriated by her audacity.

"I demand that you let me go," she rushed on. "If you

don't, I promise you I will find a way to summon the police!''

Esteban laughed, delighted by her fighting spirit and more than a little relieved. The mind behind those pewter eyes was as sharply cognizant as his own. ''This is a very remote part of Mexico,'' he said, giving the last word its native pronunciation. ''Believe me, you're better off dealing with me than with the *federales*.'' He folded his arms. ''I ask you again, *señorita*. What is your name?''

''What is yours?'' she countered, testy as a cornered scorpion.

He should have been reassuring the woman, he knew that—Maria would have him horsewhipped if she found out he hadn't laid the visitor's fears to rest right at the outset—but he was enjoying the game too much. Just being near this woman was like drinking cold well water after a savage thirst. ''Esteban Ramirez,'' he conceded, lifting one side of his mouth in a smile.

She raised an eyebrow and pushed a lock of beautiful tarnished-copper hair back from her face. ''Esteban. That's a version of Steven, isn't it?'' She looked him over after his nod, as though deciding whether or not the name suited him. If she decided it didn't, he thought, she just might change it to something she thought fitting. ''You're certainly not the kind of guy people would call 'Steve,''' she observed.

Esteban held back a chuckle, but he supposed his amusement showed in his eyes, the dark blue eyes bequeathed to him by his American grandmother. ''No,'' he agreed. ''I don't think 'Steve' would suit me very well.'' He stopped, waiting. Although he was certain he was doing a good job of hiding the fact, she'd shaken him, this fierce invader with hair the color of a tiger's coat.

''Olivia,'' she finally threw out, but grudgingly. ''Olivia Stillwell, though I don't see that it matters. A slave doesn't really need a name.''

"You are not a slave, Miss Stillwell—it is 'Miss,' isn't it?" Esteban asked the question in an offhand tone, with a slight and very Latin shrug, but it suddenly seemed as if the *rancho,* his grandfather's silver mines, everything he owned and had ever dreamed of, everything he *was,* depended on her answer.

Remarkable, he thought. I need to get out more.

"Would you let me go if I were married? Because if you expect a virgin, you've got the wrong woman."

Esteban's heartbeat was irregular. He shouldn't have cared whether Olivia Stillwell had ever been with a man or not, but he did. He hoped she had, and at the same time hoped she hadn't. "As I said before, you are not a prisoner. When you are well, you are free to go wherever you wish."

She narrowed her marvelous gray eyes in obvious distrust. "I was kidnapped, Señor Ramirez, brought here against my will. And you said yourself that you bought me!"

"Yes, I bought you. I thought that would be kinder than letting you be passed on to the next prospect, who might not have been so—" he shrugged again "—enlightened."

"I want to go home."

"And you shall. When you have had time to recover from your ordeal."

"No. I have to leave right now. If you'll just let me call my uncle in Connecticut, I'm sure he'll arrange for special transportation."

She didn't have a husband or a lover, Esteban concluded. If she had, she wouldn't have suggested calling an uncle. The realization filled him with a strange joy, but in the wake of that emotion came a quavering despair at the thought of her leaving.

This conflict, well hidden, he hoped, made Esteban furious with himself. He had his choice of women all over the world, far more sophisticated and beautiful ones than she.

He did not need this inconsequential redheaded snippet covered in freckles and sunburn and bravado.

Much.

"It is one hundred and fifty miles to the nearest telephone," he said, attempting to speak reasonably. He had already assured Miss Stillwell at least twice that she wasn't a prisoner, but apparently she still wasn't convinced.

It seemed impossible, but Olivia's face actually got redder. "But my uncle will be worried!"

"Things move slowly in Mexico," Esteban said.

She was persistent, which wasn't surprising, really. She had survived an experience that would have devastated most anyone else. "You must have a shortwave radio in case of emergencies. You could relay a message that way."

Esteban sighed. "No," he said. "Here we live much as our grandparents did." He saw her glance at the kerosene lamp on the bedside table, then at the ceiling where a light fixture would have been in another, more modern house. Clearly, she registered the significance of that. "There is a generator to power the hot-water heater and the appliances in the kitchen," he finished.

She shook her head in obvious annoyance. "No radio?" she asked like a skeptical tourist. "No telephone, no TV, no fax machine?"

He chuckled, wanting to go to the side of the bed and take Olivia gently into his arms, but unwilling to frighten her. "Sorry. Things are pretty low-tech around here. Maria has a small television set that runs on batteries. Somehow, though, I do not think you would enjoy Spanish-dubbed reruns of 'Gilligan's Island.'"

She scooted backward, her lower lip jutting out slightly, and hid everything but her head under the lightweight covers. "You haven't been a whole lot of help, Señor Ramirez," she pointed out.

He smiled, reaching back for the doorknob. He was through trying to make his case with the woman, for the time being at least. She didn't believe a word he said, and that irritated him sorely, since the trait Esteban most cherished was his integrity. "Haven't I? If it weren't for me, Miss Stillwell, you would probably be wishing you were dead right about now."

Her eyes went wide at the reminder of what could have happened, but then they flashed with silver fire again. "You'll pardon me if I don't thank you for holding me prisoner in this house," she said stiffly.

Esteban sighed and opened the door to leave, even though her slender figure seemed to be giving off some kind of electromagnetic charge from beneath the loosely woven covers. His whole being, flesh and spirit, strained toward her, and it took all his strength to resist. "I would never expect gratitude from a spoiled American schoolgirl with no better sense than to go wandering in the desert by herself," he replied. The words were sharp, uttered out of self-defense.

A second piece of fruit struck the door just as he closed it behind him. He grinned as he walked down the hall.

The *rancho,* as much as he loved it, could be a lonely place. For the next few days, at least, the energetic Miss Stillwell would lend some pizzazz to his normally quiet life.

Maria brought lunch soon after Esteban's departure, a wonderful gazpacho, and her friendly concern made Olivia ashamed of the fruit pieces scattered over the floor. While she sheepishly consumed her soup, the housekeeper cleaned up the mess, her expressive mouth drawn up in a soft, speculative smile.

"I wish you spoke English," Olivia said when she'd finished eating and Maria was lifting the tray from her lap. "Then we could talk. I could tell you about my Uncle Errol and the prizes I've won for my pottery, and you could tell me about your boss. He's plainly a bastard—Señor Ramirez, not my uncle—but I suppose you probably like him."

Maria was listening politely, even though she clearly didn't understand more than a few scattered words. When Olivia wound down, the other woman smiled again and said something gentle.

After Maria left the room, Olivia got out of bed, her legs still incredibly shaky beneath her, and made her way into the adjoining bathroom. At least the place had indoor plumbing; that was some consolation.

Back in bed, she tried to come up with a plan of escape, dramatic or otherwise, but her thoughts were still too muddled—not surprising, after the way the sun had sautéed her brain the day before. She closed her eyes and slept, awaking hours later to find Maria lighting the lamp on her bedside stand. There was a simple meal laid out on the white wicker table in the corner of the room.

"*Buenas noches,*" Maria greeted her.

The lamplight gave the room a cozy ambience, and Olivia could almost forget that she was virtually a captive in this house. Dinner consisted of rice and a not-too-spicy but very colorful mixture of sliced chicken breast, red and green peppers, carrots and onions.

She made a point of saying *gracias* when Maria returned to carry away the empty dishes and the silverware, and the housekeeper beamed.

For a few minutes, Olivia had been able to forget that she was in a strange and dangerous situation, for all the attendant luxuries. After Maria had left again, however, Olivia felt bereft. She enjoyed the housekeeper's company, even with the language barrier between them, and was grateful for the other woman's help.

It had been Maria, Olivia knew, who had bathed her when she'd first come to the *rancho*—she remembered it vaguely, like a scene from a fevered dream—Maria who had treated her abrasions with antiseptic and her sunburn with cooling lotion. She owed her silent friend a tremendous debt.

Restless, Olivia decided to venture out onto the terrace.

Maybe there was a trellis or something, and in a few days, when she was stronger, she could climb down and run away. Maybe she would even discover that the room was on the ground floor of the house, though she doubted that.

She unlatched the French doors and stepped out onto the terrace. A shock of tropical beauty made her suck in her breath almost as though someone had struck her.

This was not the sand-spider-and-cacti Mexico she remembered from before the kidnapping. No, here there were palm trees swaying against a star-spangled sky, and silvery moonlight wavered on water so blue that its color was discernible even in the relative darkness.

Directly below the terrace was a courtyard of brick and marble, complete with an enormous fountain, tropical flowers in Garden-of-Eden pinks and blues and yellows, and white wrought-iron benches. It was all lit by the moon and stars and by chunky candles glimmering inside glass bowls.

Enchanted, Olivia moved along the railing, looking for a way down. There were no trellises or trees; indeed, the only way would be to take a twelve-foot drop into the hot tub, and she didn't feel quite that adventurous.

As she watched, the emerald-colored water in the tub began to bubble and churn. She was completely unprepared for Esteban's sudden appearance; he crossed the tiled deck, magnificently naked, except for the odd shadow, and lowered himself in.

Olivia was mesmerized for a long moment, though she knew she should retreat. Her face ached with color when he looked up, his teeth as white as the snowy orchids that grew in glorious tangles along the edge of the courtyard.

"Would you like to join me?" he inquired.

Mortified at being caught watching a naked man, Olivia took the offensive in an effort to hide her vulnerability. "You bought me. I suppose you could command it."

Esteban laughed, and the sound reached up through the warm darkness like a caress, making Olivia's breasts feel full and heavy and producing a sharp ache in her most feminine parts. "If I commanded you to come down here, would you obey?"

"Of course not."

He spread his hands, still looking up. "There you have it," he said with a sigh of resignation. "It is almost impossible to find a good love slave these days."

Olivia bit her lower lip, glad she hadn't tried taking a dive from the terrace railing. Judging the depth of the water by the fact that it reached just to Esteban's waist, she realized she would have compressed her skull into her tailbone. "I thought you said there was no electricity here," she challenged, desperate to change the subject, because all of the sudden she didn't find the idea of being Esteban's captive all that unappealing.

"This?" He indicated the hot tub. "I told you—we have a portable generator. Several, in fact."

Olivia folded her arms. "I think you're holding out on me, Señor Ramirez. I demand that you release me immediately."

"Be my guest," Esteban said, gesturing toward the great world beyond the edge of the courtyard. "I would advise you to head north, carry as much water as you can and avoid being kidnapped again. You were very lucky the first time."

He was right, and damn, Olivia hated that. The least he could do was be wrong once in a while.

"Yes," she said stiffly. "Well, thank you."

Esteban settled comfortably in the hot tub, resting his muscular arms along the sides. Olivia couldn't tell for certain, but she was pretty sure he'd closed those beautiful, sensual eyes of his, giving himself up to the heat and motion of the water.

"You're welcome, Olivia," he said presently, sounding relaxed and resigned. "Anytime you're staggering through the desert, please feel free to have your abductors bring you here. I will be happy to buy you, though I don't think you would command such a high price the second time.''

Olivia knew Esteban was teasing her, and she wasn't amused. ''Naturally, I will repay you as soon as I can reach my bank—''

She knew he had opened his eyes, felt his gaze even through the stone railing of the terrace and the thin night-gown she was wearing. ''You will indeed,'' he replied formally, ''but I have all the money I need. You'll have to think of some other way to settle the debt, Miss Stillwell.''

Chapter Three

Olivia told herself Esteban was only teasing—surely, even in this backward place, he didn't expect her to repay her ransom with her body—but there was enough uncertainty to unnerve her completely. She fled into her room and pushed the terrace doors shut behind her.

Her cheeks were throbbing with a heat far greater than a Mexican sun could have produced, and she stood there in the dim, romantic light of the kerosene lamps, her hands pressed to her face. Although she wanted desperately to disavow her feelings and the images unfolding in her mind, they would not be denied.

Except for a single, highly forgettable love affair in college, Olivia had no real sexual experience. In fact, the one man she'd been with had left her convinced that the whole experience was wildly overrated.

Now, having met Esteban Ramirez, Olivia was beginning to doubt her convictions, not just mentally, but physically. Even being in the same room with him seemed to send a super-charge through her whole body, and it apparently didn't matter whether the conversation was worthwhile or totally banal. In fact, she wasn't sure it mattered if there *was* a conversation.

She climbed back into bed, but she couldn't stop the torrent of imaginings sparked by the sight of Esteban striding naked across the courtyard below, as dangerously graceful as some fierce jungle cat.

She considered the things men and women did together in Uncle Errol's books—they were certainly nothing like the timid encounters Olivia had had with her idealistic poet back at Northwestern—and was shaken by a hot shiver. It was only too easy to imagine doing those things with Esteban, to picture—and God help her, *feel*—his hard, commanding body settling over hers, claiming hers.

Olivia closed her eyes, trying to steady herself against the tide of desire thundering through her. She sank her teeth into her lower lip and attempted to make her mind a blank, but the scenes kept unfurling. Maybe, she thought, it *wasn't* just fiction, the stuff of books and movies, as she'd always believed. She reached out an arm and clung to the bedpost as though fearing she'd be swept away by some invisible flood. Maybe there really were uncharted parts of her nature, places in her being where only a man like Esteban could take her—

"Stop it!" she hissed, now truly desperate to derail her train of thought. Señor Ramirez claimed he'd bought her only to protect her, but he might be lying. He could be a white slaver himself, a link in a chain of criminals, planning to feed and care for her only until she was in a more marketable condition. Why else would he have refused to help her get in touch with her uncle?

Olivia forced herself to relax, but because she'd done so much sleeping during the day, she wasn't the least bit tired. She lay staring up at the ceiling, once again considering her ridiculous plight.

One scenario, being sold to some filthy man as a plaything, or even forced into prostitution, left her chilled with fear. The alternative vision, lying with Esteban in that very bed, doing some of the things she'd read about, made her break into a sweat.

She figured she'd have pneumonia by morning, what with all these abrupt changes in body temperature, if she didn't figure out a way to get a grip.

Somewhere toward dawn, Olivia drifted off, and her dreams were full of whirling colors and churning emotions. When she awakened in the morning, she felt as though she'd spent the night driving railroad spikes into rocky ground.

Seeing her own blouse and slacks lying across the back of a chair raised her spirits considerably. The garments were mended in places, but they'd been washed and pressed, and her underwear was there, too. The prospect of dressing made Olivia feel less like a prisoner.

She took a quick shower, smoothed on the special aloe-vera lotion Maria had been treating her with and put on her clothes. After brushing her hair and teeth and making up the bed, Olivia ventured over the threshold of her room for the first time since her arrival.

The house had a sort of mezzanine with railings on all sides, and below was an indoor courtyard. There were lush green plants in beautiful pots, along with a fountain encircled by a stone bench. Somewhere out of sight, birds sang a muted concert.

Olivia made her way down stone steps, her mind rolling like a wheel spinning downhill. Descriptions of the house would make for authentic detail in her uncle's current book; she wanted to remember everything until she could find paper and pen to write it all down.

Growing bolder with every passing moment, Olivia began to explore, making all kinds of mental notes as she went. There was a big formal dining room, so Esteban probably entertained, despite the isolation of his house. The study walls were lined with books not only in English and Spanish, but French, as well, which meant, to her, that her host was well educated; the substantial, ornately carved desk said he appreciated fine things.

Olivia progressed to a smaller room, outfitted with all sorts of workout equipment, and smiled to herself. That explained, at least partly, why Esteban was so sleekly muscular. He was into pumping iron.

At the front of the house, facing the shining sea, was a magnificent room with floor-to-ceiling windows. The basic color scheme was a clean, soothing beige, accented by splashes of turquoise and pale peach, and the overall effect was one of the room and the ocean being somehow linked in mystical harmony.

Just being there, mentally getting into step with the silent music of the place, gave Olivia a sensation of being touched, healed. She yearned to capture the sumptuous colors and textures, indeed the soul of Mexico itself, in pottery.

"Good morning."

She jumped, startled by the unexpected voice, and turned to see Esteban standing just inside the doorway, at the top of the three stone steps leading down into the living room. "Good morning," she made herself say, speaking in what she hoped was a calm tone. She didn't want him to know how he frightened her, how he haunted her thoughts and the secret places in her soul that she herself had never visited before.

He was wearing dusty riding pants, black, with the same flashy silver buttons along the outside seams, an equally dusty white shirt opened far enough to reveal a sweaty, well-muscled chest, and a short leather vest.

On anybody else, Olivia reflected, the outfit would have looked silly. On him, well, it inspired dangerous fantasies.

Esteban looked down at his splendidly disheveled frame. "Is something wrong?"

Olivia's face heated; it wasn't the dusty grime that had made her stare and he knew it as well as she did. "I guess it's messy work, running a place like this." She paused. "What kind of place *is* this, anyway?"

He smiled, and the effect was blinding. "I thought you knew," he said, leaning against the doorjamb. "This is a *rancho*. We raise horses and cattle here." He stopped to lift one shoulder. "And there are a couple of silver mines."

It could all be a lie, Olivia reminded herself. A cover for white slavery, or maybe drug-running. She retreated a step at the thought, unable to keep her eyes from going wide.

Esteban looked puzzled for a moment, then assaulted her with another of his lethal smiles. "Relax, Miss Stillwell," he said. "If I were going to drag you off to my bed and use you without mercy, do you really think I would have restrained myself this long?"

Olivia was at once injured and relieved. Naturally she didn't want to be dragged off and used without mercy, as he put it, but she had some very primitive fantasies where this man was concerned, and it hurt to realize he would probably find them amusing.

Since she didn't know how to answer his question gracefully, she simply turned away, pretending to be absorbed in the view. As breathtaking as it was, though, Olivia could think of nothing but the man behind her.

When he laid his hands to her shoulders, she flinched, for she hadn't sensed his approach.

Esteban's touch was incredibly gentle and tender; he might have been a poet, instead of a *bandido* with the heart of a dangerous jungle creature. He turned Olivia, studied her face with mingled bewilderment and defiance in his wonderful violet eyes, and then he kissed her.

Olivia stiffened; nothing in her experience, or even in the night of erotic dreams just past, had prepared her for this. It was like embracing lightning; the power jolted her, making her sway so that Esteban's grip on her shoulders tightened.

He tasted her lips as though they were coated with honey, then persuaded her mouth to open for him. The invasion of his tongue was gentle, but it was compelling, too; for Olivia it was like being conquered, right there in the middle of that sunny living room. Excitement twisted into a tight spiral within her.

When he finally withdrew, her breasts were still pressing against his hard chest, the nipples taut. She was stunned by the incomprehensible force of her desire.

He lifted his hand and caressed her cheek, then moved the pad of his thumb over her lower lip.

"I'm sorry," he said. "You are a guest here, and I should not have taken advantage of you."

Olivia didn't respond; she was too afraid she would burst into tears if she tried to speak. She was still overwhelmed by the force of his kiss, and by the new and frightening awareness that she had crossed a significant personal threshold. In some unaccountable way, Esteban Ramirez had changed her forever. She felt stronger, vibrantly alive, more truly herself than ever before.

He looked at her for a moment, as though studying a stranger he knew he should recognize but didn't, then turned and walked out of the room, pulling on his leather riding gloves as he went.

Olivia stood for a long time, as immobile as the statue in the middle of the fountain in the outer courtyard, simultaneously willing him to return and thanking God that he didn't. The fires he'd started inside her were still smoldering, and the yearning he'd created was so strong that she feared a violent eruption even then. Just walking across the room would have been a risk.

Finally, however, Olivia recovered most of her composure, if not all, and continued her explorations. She encountered Maria in the kitchen, a large and airy place full of light and color, and was forced to eat a breakfast of fresh cornbread, fruit and something that might have been either pudding or yogurt.

After that, Olivia tried to wash her dishes, but Maria shooed her out, waving her white apron and uttering a flurry of Spanish words. Finding a large straw hat lying on a bench on the portico out back, Olivia donned that as protection from the sun and set out for a look at the surrounding terrain.

Esteban and his men were busy over by the corrals, raising dust and shouting. Still sensitive to the glaring sun, Olivia returned to the house. More explorations brought her to the study, where she began thumbing idly through a series of leather-bound albums. The pages were covered with clippings from newspapers and magazines, both in Spanish and English, touting the exploits of *el leopardo*. The Leopard.

Olivia felt a shiver. The scrapbooks were obviously Maria's work, and she soon divined that *el leopardo* was none other than Esteban Ramirez himself. Shaken, she only skimmed a few of the articles that were printed in English, and she made little sense of their contents. All she'd really grasped was that Esteban had another identity.

Discomfited, Olivia left the house again and started toward the white beach. The Leopard. If she didn't know better, Olivia could have sworn she'd stumbled into one of her uncle's stories. It would have been pretty amusing if it hadn't been so scary, and if she hadn't been so attracted to Esteban.

The nickname certainly fit Esteban, she had to admit that. He had the sleek prowess and deadly strength of a leopard. And he might well share other traits. He might be vicious; he might, like the animal, stalk his prey, run it to the ground, tear out its throat.

Olivia made her way along a path lined with thick tropical foliage and onto the beach, her thoughts in even more turmoil than before.

The Leopard. Perhaps Esteban really was a white slaver or a drug lord, as she'd first thought. Or maybe he was simply a *bandido*. He had been quick to assure Olivia that she could go back home as soon as she had "recovered" and, although he'd teased her unmercifully, he had not brought her to his bed. None of which meant that the men who'd kidnapped her hadn't been working for him in the first place.

Olivia had been in some bewildering situations in her life, but this one set a real precedent.

Coming to an inlet sheltered by palm trees and foliage, Olivia sat down on the ground, removed her hat, kicked off her sandals. The sand was so white and fine, she thought, sifting some through her fingers, that she could have stirred it into her tea like sugar.

There was something calming about the little hidden pool, and Olivia's troubled mind began to quiet down. Despite her misgivings, she had a sense of returning to Paradise.

Presently, when she could no longer resist, she took off her trusty blouse and khaki slacks and waded in. The waist-deep water reflected the heart-wrenching royal blue of the sky, and it was so clean and clear that Olivia could see the fine white pebbles on the bottom. The coolness was like balm to her skin, so she slipped under the surface to wet her hair, too.

When she came up, lashes beaded with water, just beginning to absorb the delicious peace of the place, Esteban was standing on the bank, staring at her.

El leopardo, she thought, in that dazed moment before alarm overtook her. He certainly moved with the same stealth as a leopard.

Chapter Four

Belatedly, Olivia folded her arms across her breasts. It was no comfort that Esteban was obviously just as shocked to find her in the pool as she was to see him standing at its edge; the situation was no less perilous for his surprise.

"What are you doing here?" he finally demanded, resting his hands on his hips. He was covered in dust from his magnificent head to the soles of his expensive leather boots.

Olivia's mouth dropped open. She'd been about to ask *him* that question. "I beg your pardon?" she croaked after another few moments of hesitation.

"This is my private place," Esteban said, and once again, Olivia had a sensation of returning to the Lost Garden. She might have been Eve, and the man standing on the shore, Adam.

She bristled. "I'm sorry."

Incredibly, he grinned. "You don't look sorry."

Olivia was still flustered. "I didn't think I had to ask for permission to swim in the ocean, that's all."

He began stripping off his clothes, his motions practiced and uncalculated. "This is not the ocean," he said implacably. "It's a spring-fed pool." He paused, inclining his head as he studied her. "I hope you will not be so foolish as to swim in the sea, Miss Stillwell. The currents are dangerous, and there are sharks."

Sharks and currents were the least of her problems. "Perhaps you could just come back later," Olivia suggested cheerfully, growing more nervous as he shrugged off his shirt and reached for his belt buckle.

GET 2

HOW TO GET YOUR 2 FREE BOOKS AND FREE GIFT!

1. Peel off the MIRA sticker on the front cover. Place it in the space provided at right. This automatically entitles you to receive two free books and an exciting surprise gift.

2. Send back this card and you'll get 2 "The Best of the Best™" novels. These books have a combined cover price of $11.98 or more in the U.S. and $13.98 or more in Canada, but they are yours to keep absolutely FREE!

3. There's <u>no</u> catch. You're under <u>no</u> obligation to buy anything. We charge nothing – ZERO – for your first shipment. And you don't have to make any minimum number of purchases – not even one!

4. We call this line "The Best of the Best" because each month you'll receive the best books by some of today's most popular authors. These authors show up time and time again on all the major bestseller lists and their books sell out as soon as they hit the stores. You'll like the convenience of getting them delivered to your home at our special discount prices . . . and you'll love your *Heart to Heart* subscriber newsletter featuring author news, horoscopes, recipes, book reviews and much more!

5. We hope that after receiving your free books you'll want to remain a subscriber. But the choice is yours – to continue or cancel, anytime at all! So why not take us up on our invitation, with no risk of any kind. You'll be glad you did!

6. And remember...we'll send you a surprise gift ABSOLUTELY FREE just for giving "The Best of the Best" a try.

SPECIAL FREE GIFT!

We'll send you a fabulous surprise gift, absolutely FREE, simply for accepting our no-risk offer!

Visit us online at
www.mirabooks.com

BOOKS FREE!

The Best of the Best™ — Here's How it Works:

Accepting your 2 free books and gift places you under no obligation to buy anything. You may keep the books and gift and return the shipping statement marked "cancel." If you do not cancel, about a month later we will send you 4 additional novels and bill you just $4.49 each in the U.S., or $4.99 each in Canada, plus 25¢ shipping & handling per book and applicable taxes if any.* That's the complete price and — compared to cover prices of $5.99 or more each in the U.S. and $6.99 or more each in Canada — it's quite a bargain! You may cancel at any time, but if you choose to continue, every month we'll send you 4 more books, which you may either purchase at the discount price or return to us and cancel your subscription.

*Terms and prices subject to change without notice. Sales tax applicable in N.Y. Canadian residents will be charged applicable provincial taxes and GST.

Esteban shook his head, sat down in the sand and wrenched off one of his boots. "*You* can come back later," he countered, removing the other boot and tossing it aside to lie akimbo with its mate. He looked mildly irritated. "*Madre de Dios,* you American women are petty tyrants, for all your talk about independence and personal liberty."

Olivia narrowed her eyes, crouching in the water and trying to cover herself with her arms, painfully conscious that the pool was as transparent as crystal. "That was uncalled for. I didn't attack your masculinity, for heaven's sake. I just suggested that you might want to leave your bath for another time. Besides, I can't very well get out with you sitting there gawking at me, now can I?" She took a breath. "Furthermore, I'll thank you not to insult every woman in my country just because you don't like me!"

Esteban stood again and began removing his pants. He flashed her a dazzling grin before she looked away. "I'm hot and dirty and tired, Miss Stillwell," he said. "I've been looking forward to taking a cool bath in this pool all day. Therefore, if you don't wish to share it with me, you'd better get out." Having made his decree, *el patrón* speaking to the *peón,* Esteban splashed into the water.

Try though she did to keep her eyes averted, Olivia's gaze went right to him like a magnet.

Good heavens, even Michelangelo had never sculpted such a man. Only God could have achieved that kind of grace and perfection.

Soon, Esteban stood only a few feet from Olivia, in the liquid crystal of the pool. It was almost as though time had stopped, and the universe had gone still around them.

"You are very lovely." He said the words like an offhand statement of fact, as though he were admiring a piece of art in a museum.

"Stop looking at me," Olivia snapped, but her response

didn't carry the strength of conviction it should have. She was busy struggling to assimilate all the new feelings this man engendered in her.

His laughter was a joyous shout. "Not a chance," he said when his amusement had abated, giving another of his south-of-the-border shrugs.

Olivia edged toward the spot where she'd left her clothes. Then she scrambled out of the pool, grabbed them and delved into the dense foliage, where she began pulling them on over tender, wet skin. It was a frustrating task.

"This is a fine way to treat company," she muttered. "I mean, you'd think, after all I've been through, that I could take a bath in peace, but *no*—"

Esteban laughed again. Olivia couldn't help looking at him, seeing the sun catch in the beads of water in his hair and eyelashes, on his brown chest. "Don't go," he pleaded good-naturedly. "Your virtue is safe with me, I promise."

"Oh, right," Olivia snapped. Her disappointment at being driven from the pond was all out of proportion to good sense. "You're a regular Zorro!"

"Please," he said with a gentle authority. "Stay."

Olivia had fully intended to leave, and in high dudgeon, too, but instead she sank to a sitting position in the warm sand. She wasn't anxious to get back to the real world or, in point of fact, to leave the company of this disturbingly charming and irritating man. Besides, she felt shaky from all that activity.

"I'm not staying because you told me to," she said, lifting her chin. Her clothes clung to her damp skin. "I just want to be here, that's all." The lower half of Esteban's body seemed to waver under the water, like a distorted image in a mirror.

"Of course," he replied, as cordial as Ricardo Montalban

greeting a new arrival on Fantasy Island. "Would you mind tossing me the soap?"

It was a simple request, and the bar he'd brought with him was within reach. Olivia complied, but when Esteban began washing his hair, there was something so intimate in the act that she felt they would always be linked by it.

Her blood heated, and her thoughts alone were enough to ensure damnation.

She let her forehead rest on her updrawn knees, willing her heartbeat to slow down and her breathing to be even again. The trouble was, she kept having these images of herself lying with Esteban, not there on the sand, but in a cool, shadowy room between smooth linen sheets. She should just go back to the house right now, she told herself sternly, but she remained as she was, somehow detached from her normally strong will.

Olivia was not prepared for feeling Esteban settle in the sand next to her, his skin cool and wet from the pool. Out of the corner of her eye, she saw that he was wearing a towel around his midsection, but nothing else.

"Oh, God," she said.

He cupped her chin in his hand, gently turned her face, and kissed her. When his tongue entered her mouth, and one of his hands curved lightly around her breast, the thumb chafing her nipple to attention, Olivia figured the inner tumult he caused her would register at least 9.9 on the Richter scale.

She trembled as he eased her backward into the sand and stretched out beside her. Although she spread her fingers across the roughness of his damp chest, she could not, would not, push him away. The attraction was simply too ferocious, but even so, Olivia knew she was *choosing* to make this tentative surrender.

He moved over her, let her feel the hardness and the

power of his body without crushing her under its weight, but the towel and her clothes remained between them.

Finally, mercifully, he released her mouth, and Olivia gasped with relief, only to give a whispered gasp as he began nibbling at her neck. When he opened her bodice and bared a waiting breast to his lips and tongue, she wove her fingers into his hair and held him close, unable to protest. The feeling of his mouth on her nipple was fiery and sweet, and she wanted it to go on and on.

When Olivia was writhing in the sand beneath him, Esteban turned gracefully onto his back and drew her along, so that she lay with her breast above his mouth like ripe fruit on a vine. He wedged his thigh between her legs and gently gripped her hips, moving her tantalizingly against the steely muscle. All the while, he suckled hungrily at her nipple.

Olivia was utterly and completely lost.

Something was happening inside her, something Olivia had only read about before. Something on a level with the formation of a new universe.

After an eternity of moments, she reached the pinnacle she'd been straining toward with both body and soul. Her body arched in a shattering explosion of pleasure, and she thrust her head back and shouted hoarsely to the sky. Esteban drank from her until the sweet spasms had finally passed and she'd fallen, exhausted, to the sand beside him.

"El leopardo," she whispered, still too dazed to think coherently.

But Esteban gripped her shoulders hard, and wrenched her into an upright position. "What did you say?"

Olivia stared at him for a moment, still drunk on the release, her breasts still bared to his gaze. "I called you *el leopardo,"* she finally said, confused.

"Tell me why," he rasped, giving her a slight shake.

Olivia was bewildered, and she hesitated to mention the scrapbooks she'd seen in the study. She sensed that they were private, and maybe he didn't want her to know about his exploits.

Whatever those exploits had been.

"I came across a reference to the Leopard, that's all," she replied, her body still thrumming from his skillful attentions. "It wasn't hard to guess it was you."

He released his hold on her shoulders, and she was almost sorry that the contact was broken. It had not been painful, after all, but there had been a certain command in his hold that strong women sometimes go a lifetime without finding.

"You didn't hear anyone refer to me by this name?" he asked after a long time, looking not at Olivia but at the dancing blue-topaz surface of the pool. "You did not see men who looked out of place among the others?"

Olivia touched his shoulder with one hand and distractedly closed her bodice with the other. A tentative smile twitched on her lips. "I don't think so—I don't even know any of your men by name," she pointed out quietly. "What's the matter, Esteban? Why does this upset you so much?"

He thrust himself to his feet, snatched up his pants and let the towel drop to the sand, leaving the choice of watching or looking away to Olivia.

She looked away.

"I cannot explain it now," he answered as he dressed. "You must go back to the house, Olivia, and stay there until I tell you it is safe to move about the *rancho*."

Olivia couldn't help noticing how much more formal Esteban's English became when he was troubled. She felt a very primitive urge to comfort him, and yet something inside her balked instantly at this new threat to her already limited freedom.

"I won't do any such thing," she said evenly. "I'm not a mole—I need light and sunshine and fresh air. And you keep saying I'm not a prisoner."

Esteban's glare was as fierce as the Mexican sun. "I have said it, and it is so," he told her. "I do not tell lies."

Olivia rose to her feet and faced him, her hands on her hips. "You're not exactly Mr. Communication, either," she retorted. "You want to keep me here—for the time being, at least—but you refuse to tell me why. Now you're intimating that I might be in real danger, but again, you won't explain. Is that fair?"

"It is expedient," he replied, as though that settled everything. And then he started up the path leading to his magnificent house, his shoulders taut with tension. Olivia followed, not because of any desire to obey his dictates, but because the pool and its lush surroundings no longer seemed like Eden.

Esteban could not shake his uneasiness over Olivia's reminder of his days as the Leopard. The hair on his nape was still standing, and he knew now that there had been a feeling of imminent peril in the air since Olivia's arrival on the *rancho*. All his old instincts, still finely honed even though it had been years since he'd led the raids that had earned him a small but lethal army of enemies, had warned that something wasn't right. In his fascination with the American woman, he had simply chosen to ignore the alarm bells in the pit of his stomach and the deeper chambers of his mind.

This was unlike him.

He looked back at Olivia, who was trudging sullenly along the path behind him, and faced the most difficult possibility he could think of. She might be one of them, sent to the *rancho* specifically to take revenge.

Now you're being paranoid, he told himself, turning his attention back to the path ahead. Still, Esteban had not lived to look back on his days as the Leopard by being naive or by underestimating his foes. He would find out exactly what was going on, face it and deal with it.

In the meantime, he would make sure Olivia Stillwell brought no harm to herself or others.

Chapter Five

When Olivia stormed into her room a few minutes later, she found that Maria had been there before her. A simple midday meal of fruit, salad and small delicate sandwiches waited on the glass top of the wicker table, and on the bed was a long, gauzy, emerald-green dress with flowing sleeves and a ruffled, off-the-shoulder neckline.

Olivia's temper cooled slightly as she thought of the housekeeper's quiet kindness, and she took a closer look at the gown. It probably belonged to Maria, but she had taken in the seams, using tiny, perfect stitches, so that Señor Ramirez's American guest would have something to wear besides her own slacks and blouse.

She went into the adjoining bathroom, leaving the pretty gown where she'd found it, and splashed her face with cool water. She was careful not to look at her reflection, however, fearing her eyes would be suspiciously bright and her skin flushed with an achy backwash of passion.

Olivia returned to her table, with as much dignity as if she were about to dine at the White House with her famous uncle as an escort instead of dining alone in what amounted to a luxurious jail cell. She ate the miniature sandwiches daintily, finished with the fruit salad, and then moved the dress to the empty closet, kicked off her sandals and stretched out on the bed.

She was still bruised and sunburned from her ordeal with the kidnappers, and Esteban's kisses and caresses next to the pond had left her so languid that another burst of anger would have been more than she could manage.

Olivia yawned, closed her eyes and drifted off to sleep. Sometime later, sounds—shuffles and bumps and whispers—began to intrude on her rest. Slowly, they drew her upward, out of the sheltering depths of the dream state, and she sat up, frightened. For a few moments she remembered only the kidnapping, and nothing about Maria's kindness or Esteban's pleasuring beside the turquoise pool, thinking she was still in the hands of her abductors.

Then, when her eyes had finally focused and she'd taken several deep breaths, she recalled where she was. Thus far, despite her doubts and suspicions, she'd been safe in this place, and well treated.

Still, for all the reassurances Olivia offered herself, something new was going on. There were people in the hall.

She went curiously to the door and, after tugging at her blouse and smoothing her hopelessly tousled hair, she clasped the doorknob and turned it.

There were two men in the hallway, dressed like members of Pancho Villa's band, and they both had rifles. Olivia gasped, raising one hand to her chest.

"Where is Señor Ramirez?" she demanded tersely, after gathering her courage.

The guards both spoke at once, babbling in Spanish so quick that the words flew past her like a flock of excited birds. All Olivia knew was that the men had been assigned either to keep her inside the room or someone else out. Neither possibility was very comforting.

"Never mind," she said, drawing on all her bravado. "I'll find him myself." With that, Olivia started through the doorway, only to have the men cross their all-too-real rifles in front of her to make a barricade.

That answered one question. She was being kept in.

Olivia would not let herself panic. She made a stabbing gesture at the floor with her right index finger, hoping it conveyed a certain amount of authority. "Bring Señor Ramirez here!" she ordered loudly, enunciating each word as though that would somehow translate them for her listeners.

The taller of the two men put a grubby hand on Olivia's

shoulder and gently pressed her back from the door. Then, in an apparent afterthought, he took a folded piece of paper from the pocket of his vest and held it out.

"These men are here to protect you. Kindly do not drive them insane," Esteban had written in a strong hand that somehow conveyed a smile. "If you are too frightened, you may come and sleep with me. E.R."

"This situation gets more like one of my uncle's books with every passing moment!" Olivia complained, blushing because Esteban had invited her to his bed and because she wanted so much to go. Then she crumpled up the note and tossed it into the hallway, past the mustachioed faces of the guards.

One of them politely pulled the door closed, and a moment after that, a key turned in the lock.

Olivia was overwhelmed by a barrage of emotions—frustration, anger, confusion, fear. She couldn't think about Esteban, because that stirred unwanted sensations in the innermost depths of her person, so she turned her thoughts to her uncle.

Here she was, a captive in Mexico, with God only knew what kind of fate awaiting her, all because Errol McCauley had decided to write a book about a socialite, a matador and a black-market operation. *He* was safely ensconced in his circa-1750 house in Connecticut, or his condo in Vail, or his beach place on the Georgia coast, no doubt sipping white wine and chatting with his longtime companion. In fact, Olivia would have bet her best pair of Italian shoes that neither of them even knew she'd been abducted along a dusty back road and sold to a man people called the Leopard.

Olivia paced furiously, her arms folded. Even worse, when and if she finally managed to get back to the United States and recount the experience, dear Uncle Errol would almost certainly rub his palms together and ask for an accounting of every detail of every moment. Such things were grist for his mill, and instead of sympathy, he would probably just give his niece a fat bonus and an airplane ticket to someplace where she could get herself shanghaied all over again.

She stopped in the middle of the room. Maybe her uncle was eccentric, maybe he'd always been different, but she loved him and missed him enormously. Fifteen years before, when she'd been a very unhappy eleven-year-old tucked neatly out of sight at a rigid boarding school in New England, both Olivia's parents had been killed in a car crash in France. Uncle Errol had immediately come to collect the numb, confused child, and he'd put her straight into a public school in Connecticut, where she wore regular clothes and went home to a regular house every day when classes ended.

Olivia sighed, reflecting. Sure, her life with Uncle Errol had been unconventional—it couldn't have been otherwise, with him and his friend James sitting side by side in the audience at her piano recitals and school programs—but he'd been more of a parent to her than either her father or mother. She'd felt safe with him, and loved, and the town had been remarkably tolerant because there were so many local artists and everyone knew *they* were different.

She sat down on the edge of her bed, brow puckering into a frown. Olivia had always felt a little guilty for loving Uncle Errol so much, for being so glad to go and live with him. It seemed like a betrayal not to miss her parents more, not to grieve for them, but the truth was that Olivia hadn't really known Jack and Susan Stillwell. They'd put her in boarding school the day she turned six, and afterward neglected to call, write or visit. During those vacations when Uncle Errol didn't come to fetch her, she either stayed at school or was shipped off to some mansion belonging to family "friends," where she was ignored by the adults and usually tormented unmercifully by the children.

So it seemed to Olivia that her childhood, which she thought of as a happy one, remarkably enough, had begun at the age of eleven, when her mother's brother had claimed her and made a place for her in his extraordinary life.

Tears brimmed in Olivia's eyes. Uncle Errol had been there for her when she was eleven, and many times since, but she was a big girl now, and she would have to get out of this one on her own.

The question was, how?

Esteban stood before the wall of windows in the living room, watching the tropical sunset breed fire on the restless sea. He had showered after returning from the pool—the cold spray hadn't reached the blazes raging in his groin— but he had worse problems now than the need to bury himself deep in Olivia's softness.

The past he'd thought he'd buried was back.

A decade before, when Esteban had long since completed his studies in England and progressed to the continent, where he gave a new meaning to the term "prodigal son," his grandfather had summoned him home.

There had been no question of disobeying; Abuelito— Grandfather—wielded a much more profound authority than simply being *el patrón* on a remote, if lucrative, Mexican *rancho*. Esteban's father had been the spoiled second son of a neighboring family and had run away without marrying his rebellious young mother. After she was killed in a riding accident, it had been Esteban's grandfather who had looked after him, with a lot of help from Maria.

Esteban's destiny had always been to become *el patrón*, no matter how he might have tried to persuade himself to the contrary. After he'd seen that his grandfather's health was failing and had a few shouting matches with the regal old man in the bargain, Esteban had, as the Americans said, gotten his act together.

He'd learned everything he needed to know, and much more, about raising purebred cattle and fine horses and the management of his silver mines. The latter produced little now, were all but shut down in fact, but the proceeds had been invested wisely almost from the day Abuelito had discovered the ore, and the profits had grown into vast sums, gathering interest in American and Swiss banks.

The isolation of the *rancho* had been a problem for Esteban, however, especially after his grandfather's death. Even though he loved his work, he would occasionally become so restless that he couldn't eat or sleep.

It was during one of those times, when he'd gone to Mexico City for a little R and R, that Esteban had met the American. He always thought of him by his nationality instead of his name, because even though the man had sworn he was called Tom Castleberry, Esteban had never believed him.

Over the coming months, Esteban had encountered the American virtually everywhere he went. Finally, the older man told him a long and intriguing story about a dangerous foreign government setting up a strategic base of operation in the wilds of Mexico. He produced impressive identification and documented proof, and the long and short of it was that Esteban and a few trusted men were recruited for counterespionage purposes.

Esteban smiled bitterly, standing at his window all these years later, remembering. It had been just the kind of offer that would appeal to a hotheaded young man who longed for excitement and adventure.

God knew, he'd gotten those things and more. After the bad guys had started moving in their equipment, and even small missiles, Esteban had led raids on their camp. They'd fought back, all right—he had the scars to prove it—but after a while they'd given up and retreated into Central America.

All this without formally involving either the American or Mexican governments.

Esteban's code name had been *el leopardo,* and he had not heard the phrase since the last time he'd seen the American in the small *cantina* in Mexico City where they'd agreed to meet. The agent's final words to Esteban had been, "Watch your back. Maybe we won this one, but there are plenty of people around here who would have profited from that little missile project, and some of them know who you are. You've made some dangerous enemies."

The words echoed in Esteban's mind as he turned away from the dying sun. It didn't bother him so much that he had endangered himself—he thrived on trouble, because it gave him an edge and kept his wits sharp—but he had inadvertently involved Olivia, and the thought of anything happening to her filled him with a raging terror.

After a moment, he focused on Maria, who had probably been standing there for some time. She smiled, handed him the snifter of brandy he was just realizing he wanted, and spoke to him in Spanish.

"The pretty Olivia was not happy to discover that she is a prisoner in her room. She's been demanding to see you."

Esteban took a grateful and pensive sip of his liquor. When he'd returned to the house, a messenger had been waiting with a message from the United States. Tom Castleberry, the American agent who had dubbed Esteban "the Leopard" in the first place, had been found dead in a cheap motel room. The circumstances had been mysterious enough that the State Department had felt compelled to notify others who might be a target.

He was not afraid for himself, but when Esteban thought of what those vengeful bastards might do to Olivia, especially if they guessed that he cared for her, he had immediately posted two of his most trusted men outside her door.

He handed the empty glass to Maria, with a nod meant to convey his thanks. "Miss Stillwell," he replied, in the soft, musical language of his birth, "may demand all she wishes. I am still *el patrón* and I do not take orders from a woman."

Maria arched one eyebrow. "I think *this* woman is different," she ventured. "She belongs to this place, and to you, the way the lyrics of a love song belong with the music."

Esteban kissed Maria's forehead; she had been his nurse as a child, and now she was his friend. "You've been watching those American soap operas again," he teased, but secretly he was beginning to imagine Olivia in his bed, at his table, beside him as he rode over the land he cherished. He saw her blossoming with his child, and the longing to feel her beneath him was so intense it was painful.

His spurs made a clinking sound as he crossed the central courtyard toward the front door, purposely resisting the urge to lift his eyes to the balcony as he passed beneath. Even when he'd handled this current difficulty with his old enemies, he thought sadly, there would be no hope of a future with Olivia. She saw him as a captor, and besides, they came from two very different cultures. Two different centuries.

The whole thing was impossible, he decided, and the sooner he put Olivia Stillwell out of his life for good, the better off he'd be.

Chapter Six

Olivia was left to stew in her frustration and helpless anger for several tumultuous hours. Then Maria arrived, bearing a stack of richly bound volumes and a small velvet box.

With graceful charadelike movements, the housekeeper managed to convey that Olivia was to rest quietly for a few hours, then dress for dinner. The box contained a beautiful set of antique silver combs, and the books, expensive classics printed in English, were apparently meant to offer much-needed distraction.

Having little choice and feeling enormously grateful for the books, Olivia agreed to Maria's kindly decree with a nod, and settled down to reread *Jane Eyre.* Mercifully, the beloved story kept her mind off her precarious situation for a long, therapeutic interval.

Later, Olivia donned the loose and ultrafeminine green gown Maria had altered for her, pinned up her rich auburn hair and arranged the lovely old combs for accent. Although the cut of the dress was definitely south-of-the-border, the silver ornaments and Olivia's old-fashioned hairstyle gave her a startling Gibson-girl look.

This woman staring back at her from the bathroom mirror was a stranger, a person she had never encountered until that moment. She was sophisticated and sensual, aware of her power as a woman. Able to accomplish anything she set out to do.

It was alarmingly plain that this fresh facet of Olivia's personality wasn't just visiting; she'd come to stay, bringing along a whole steamer trunk full of bright, shiny new dreams, hopes, goals and wishes.

Olivia smiled and, of course, the image smiled back. "I've been waiting for you for a long time," she said softly.

But there was still the matter of her captivity.

Esteban came to collect her himself, and his glorious violet eyes seemed to melt when he saw her. He muttered something in Spanish, and Olivia felt the words like a caress, even though she didn't understand them. She straightened her back.

"I will not be held captive, Esteban," she said in a firm but slightly tremulous voice. "If you don't trust me, then please don't pretend to be my friend."

He looked spectacular, wearing dark trousers, a flowing shirt and a black leather vest decorated with gleaming silver studs. On any other man, no matter how handsome, the outfit would have looked theatrical; on Esteban it was as natural as skin. "I trust you," he said thoughtfully, "though I'll admit I'm not sure why." With that, he held out his arm. "You look very lovely tonight," he said, escorting her past the guards, who stood on either side of the door, their expressions solemn and vaguely disapproving.

Olivia felt a sweet shiver go through her, but she couldn't let her doubts be dismissed so easily. She needed assurances that things were going to be different. "You will send them away?"

Esteban glanced back over one shoulder and spoke quietly to the men, who immediately abandoned their posts.

"There," he said. "They are gone." He did not lead her down the side stairs, but through a pair of arched double doors farther along the hallway.

The suite, obviously Esteban's private domain, was dimly lit with candles, and even though Olivia couldn't see much, she knew the place was huge and filled with substantial masculine furniture. On the far side, another pair of doors opened onto a large terrace; the piece of sky visible through the opening was studded with stars.

Out of the corner of her eye, Olivia made out the shape

of Esteban's bed, which was large, with thick posts and a canopy of some sort. She swallowed, filled with a sense of delicious foreboding.

She wanted to stay here, this dangerous new Olivia, and give herself to Esteban in the rich Mexican darkness. She wanted to nurture his seed in her body and bear a child as arrogantly beautiful as his father. She wanted to set up a potter's wheel and a kiln, and capture the raw, stunning beauty of the land around her in clay.

On the terrace, where candles flickered and flowers filled the warm air with their lush scents, Maria had prepared a table. There was a bottle of wine in a silver cooler, and various dishes under engraved covers. Two places were set with Limoges china—Olivia had developed an eye for such things because Uncle Errol was a collector—and heirloom sterling.

Olivia let Esteban draw back her chair in the old-world way, feeling like a completely different person. She'd read her fair share of sensational psychology and wondered if all the trauma of recent days had caused her to develop a new personality.

Desperate to break the spell of Esteban and the moonlight and the dark chamber behind them, she said, "You agree, then, that you won't keep me locked up in my room anymore. It's a barbaric thing to do, you know."

Esteban sampled the wine in that ritualistic way of a true expert, then poured a glassful for Olivia. "The word 'barbaric' doesn't begin to cover the fates that can befall a woman wandering around certain parts of Mexico by herself. And this is one of those parts."

Olivia sighed. She no longer wanted to leave this man and his spectacular land, and yet she had very grave doubts that anything real and lasting could develop between them. After all, they came from different cultures, different backgrounds, different *centuries* for all practical intents and purposes. "I'm not sure any of us are safe anywhere," she mused.

Esteban, to his credit, did not pretend to misunderstand. He, too, cherished his freedom; he loved the *rancho,* among other reasons, because he could range from one far-flung border to another, with no more constraints than a nineteenth-century bandit. *"Sí,"* he agreed. "And perhaps it is not a good thing to be safe all the time."

Olivia took a sip of her wine. It was a delicious vintage; Uncle Errol would have raved, then ordered cases sent to all his friends. "Do you live here all year round?" she asked, feeling more relaxed.

"No," Esteban replied, handling his knife and fork with an élan Olivia had rarely seen in men his age. "I have a place in Santa Fe, and I enjoy traveling."

Olivia thought of all the countries she'd visited, all the cities, and sighed again. "I do, too," she said, "but now I feel like stopping somewhere, putting everything I've seen and heard and felt into my art."

"Art?" Esteban looked genuinely intrigued. They were developing a bristly friendship, they'd nearly made love, and yet he didn't know about her passion for pottery.

She told him, in glowing terms, forgetting for a few minutes the unsettling nature of their relationship, all about her prizes and small successes. "Of course I probably won't earn a lot of money, at least not for a while, but that isn't really a problem. I make a good salary and I've saved quite a sum because I haven't had many living expenses."

He smiled. "Tell me about your childhood," he said. "I'll bet you had freckles, and pigtails, and were constantly skinning your knees."

Olivia laughed. "You're right on two counts, at least. I did have freckles and pigtails, but I wasn't allowed to skin my knees until after Uncle Errol came and rescued me from boarding school." She went on to give a condensed but truthful version of her life, and felt a little foolish when she'd finished. Usually, she didn't divulge a lot of personal details to others, because it was difficult for her to open up.

Esteban reciprocated by telling her about his grandfather, and growing up on the *rancho*. He, too, had been sent away to school, mostly in Europe, but the effect had been very different for him. He had, in essence, learned to balance the old world and the new with an easy grace that Olivia frankly envied.

His words were as smooth and elegant as the wine, blending with her blood in much the same way, and it was too late to steel herself against them. Even though she was ravenously hungry, a sure sign that she was recovering from the rigors of her recent experiences, she might have left Esteban's table for his bed, had he suggested it. That scared her more than anything.

He sat back in his chair when the meal was over, looking troubled all of the sudden, distracted. "You must be very careful, Olivia. There are men…"

Olivia's heart beat a little faster as she remembered the clippings in Maria's scrapbooks. How she wished she'd read every word of them. "What men?"

Esteban hesitated for a long time. "Men who are my enemies," he said. "If they've noticed you—and it would be wishful thinking to believe they haven't—they will see you as a perfect means of revenge. They've been waiting a long time for such an opportunity."

Although she felt a chill move down her spine, Olivia felt compelled to argue. "Surely no one could get into the house," she insisted. "The guards would never let them pass."

Esteban thought for a long moment, then conceded, "It is true that I trust my men."

Olivia chewed industriously, eager to reply. "You could always send me back to the States," she said, and it was crazy, how much she hoped he would refuse.

He studied her for a long moment before answering.

"Something is unfolding between us. I want to see what it is."

She looked up at the magnificent array of stars, bright as the fancy buttons on the vests Esteban wore in the daytime, and sighed with pleasant resignation. The moon spilled a wash of silver light over the sea, the tropical foliage, the rugged mountains in the distance. "So do I," she whispered at last.

His hand moved to enclose hers, and the dry strength of his touch made Olivia's blood shout in her veins. His thumb, callused and deft, moved over the delicate flesh on the inside of her wrist. "You will be allowed to move freely about the house," he said, his tone hoarse, as if he was making the offer unwillingly. "But you must not so much as step out onto the terrace without an escort."

Olivia cherished this small victory, but something inside wouldn't allow her to be content with it. She raised one eyebrow, took a sip of her wine and asked, "Aren't we on a terrace now?"

Esteban's magnificent shoulders stiffened. "Obviously, I am with you. Manolito and Luis are in the courtyard below. You would not be safe here if this were not so."

Olivia had no idea how to respond, and her emotions were churning. She honestly didn't know which eventuality terrified her more: being abducted by these mysterious enemies of Esteban's, or falling so deeply in love with the Leopard that she was willing to throw off her life in the twentieth century like a thrift-shop dress. Living here, with Esteban, would be like stepping into the pages of a novel...

...where one or more of the major characters could end up dead. The thought dampened Olivia's romantic thoughts, but her body was still seething with volcanic heat. Every gesture Esteban made, however innocent, stirred things up even more.

In the end, to Olivia's great disappointment and relief, he

did not carry her to his bed. He simply escorted her, wine-dazed and warm, back to her own room.

She slept only intermittently that night; her hungry body, taught to want satisfaction and then denied it, was restless. In the morning, Olivia made a drastic decision.

All her pretty dreams were just that—pretty dreams. She had to get out of this backward country and home to the world she knew but didn't love before she was as addicted to Esteban's lovemaking as others were to cocaine or opium. Her longing for him was already a deep, primordial need that clawed at her insides, and her only hope was to get away.

Forget.

She washed and dressed in her battered slacks and blouse. Since there was no breakfast waiting on the wicker table like before, she concluded that Esteban had not changed his mind about dismissing the guards. She crossed the room to try the heavy door.

It was unlocked, and there was still no sign of the seedy ranch hands who had been posted in the hallway the day before.

Olivia flew down the stairs. She slipped into the study to see if the scrapbooks containing the clippings about Esteban were still there, but they'd disappeared. She chided herself for not reading the English accounts of the Leopard's exploits when she'd had the chance.

Maybe, a cooler part of her mind retorted, she hadn't *wanted* to know the whole truth in the first place.

Olivia went on to the kitchen.

Maria was there, stirring batter in a bowl, and she smiled and gestured toward a table near a sunny window. Seated on the threshold of the open door was one of the men who worked for Esteban. He had a rifle lying across his knees, and he yawned copiously while Olivia sat down to eat her breakfast.

Even after finishing and washing and putting away her

plate and silverware, Olivia lingered. Pretending an interest in the Spanish radio show Maria was listening to while she ironed a pile of cotton shirts that were surely Esteban's, Olivia kept an eye on the guard sitting in the doorway.

Perhaps he had pulled night duty, or maybe he was just plain lazy. In either case, the man kept yawning loudly, and presently he sagged against the jamb. Olivia forced herself to stay calm, knowing Maria was perceptive, not wanting the housekeeper to sense what she was planning.

After a seeming eternity, Maria left the kitchen with the crisply pressed shirts, humming pleasantly. Olivia waited until she'd been gone for at least a minute, lest the woman return for something she'd forgotten, then bolted for the door.

It was easy to slip past the guard, who was now snoring.

Maybe it was feminine intuition that drew her toward the outbuildings—she'd been wanting to explore them. Then again, maybe it was just luck. God knew, she was overdue for some of that.

In any case, when Olivia wrested open the door of the largest shed, she saw an intriguing and very familiar shape under a dusty tarp. Lifting the edge of the canvas, she felt, at one and the same time, a leap of hope and a twinge of very real despair.

Contrary to the impression he gave, Esteban had not totally divorced himself from the modern world. The hidden object was a red Blazer with four-wheel drive and all the options.

Holding her breath, Olivia tried the door on the driver's side, and it opened. To her amazement, the keys were hidden under the floor mat near the gas pedal. She crept back to the door, which she'd left slightly ajar in order to let in dusty rays of sunlight, and peered carefully in every direction.

Then she went back, climbed behind the wheel and, squeezing her eyes shut, turned the key in the ignition.

The Blazer started.

Stunned at her continuing good fortune, Olivia opened her eyes and studied the gas gauge. So much for the benevolence of the gods; the needle rode just a hair above the empty mark.

She shut off the engine and let her forehead rest against the steering wheel while she dealt with her frustration and a vague, nagging sense of joy. She'd found transportation, a vehicle equipped for the rugged Mexican terrain, and the tank was empty.

"Hell and hallelujah," she muttered, for it took both words to cover the broad range of her feelings.

Chapter Seven

If there was a Blazer, not to mention several generators to serve parts of the *casa,* Olivia reasoned, carefully replacing the tarp that hid the vehicle, there must also be a gas pump hidden away somewhere. Unfortunately, she couldn't take the time to search for it, since she was bound to be discovered at any moment.

She looked around carefully before stepping out of the shed. The door was wide enough for a car to pass through, and it opened from side to side. Olivia closed it, drew a deep breath and started back toward the house.

The guard—she'd heard Maria call him Pepito—was still asleep, his big, dusty sombrero scrunched against the doorjamb, but his exuberant snores were turning to snuffles. He was probably waking up.

Olivia slipped past him and took a can of soda from the big generator-powered refrigerator, passing Pepito an innocent smile when he snorted awake, laboriously turned in her direction and gave her a suspicious glance.

She saluted him with the cold drink. "Here's to Los Estados Unidos," she said.

Pepito made a sound that sounded like the Latin equivalent of a harrumph. Obviously, he was no great fan of Mexico's neighbor to the north, and he probably thought baby-sitting a woman was beneath his dignity.

Olivia smiled winningly, turned on her heel and left the room. Unable to face returning to her room, even though it was a pleasant place, she went to the living room and stared out the windows, drinking in the gold-washed turquoise of the sea, the impossibly deep green of the trees, the violent colors of the tropical flowers. She yearned to lie in the white sand beside the pool again, with Esteban's hand on her body, his mouth greedy at her nipple...

She turned, drunk on the view and on her own thoughts, actually uncertain whether she could remain standing or not, and he was there.

"No wonder they call you the Leopard," Olivia said. She'd tried to make the observation sound like a joke, but she knew she'd failed. She had been too weakened by the realization of his presence; her voice was too small and too meek.

Esteban was covered from head to foot in dust, but he was no less regal for the fact. Here was a man who knew who and what he was, and believed in his identity. He looked at Olivia in a way that raised her temperature.

It was humiliating. She'd made herself available, and her wanting was about as subtle as a neon sign in front of a Las Vegas casino. For all of that, Esteban seemed to find her eminently resistible.

"Maria found these things for you and laundered them," he said, tossing a bundle of denim and cotton clothing into her arms. She hadn't noticed that he was holding anything. "Change and meet me in the dining room. We'll have the midday meal and then, after *siesta*, we'll ride out."

Olivia's heart leapt joyously, but at the same time her throat constricted with grief. "Are you saying that you're going to take me back to the United Sates?"

Esteban regarded her for a long moment, his patrician face unreadable, and then shook his head. "No. A band of my finest horses has strayed, to the south we think. I must go after them."

She took a step toward him, then stopped, unsure of her feelings. They were in such a contradictory tangle that she couldn't make sense of them. "And you're taking me along? Why?"

"Because I cannot leave you here."

Olivia swallowed. If only Esteban would do that, she'd have a chance to find the gas pump, fill up the Blazer and make a run for it. "You said yourself I would only be safe within these walls, with guards outside."

He shoved a hand through panther-black hair coated, like the rest of him, with dust. "I would not be able to concentrate on finding the horses if I had to worry about you the whole time I was away. Please. Just do as I have told you."

Ever since Olivia had met this man, it seemed to her, she'd been of two minds. She wanted to escape, mostly to spite the arrogant *leopardo,* she had to admit, and yet the idea of riding with him and his men was like the fruition of a fantasy.

"I'm not a very good rider," she confessed when Esteban was halfway across the room.

He didn't turn around. "I am," he countered and then, as though that settled the entire matter, he strode out.

Olivia went upstairs and untied the string that held the clothes Esteban had provided. There were two worn cotton shirts, long-sleeved, and two pairs of ancient jeans.

She took off her own blouse and slacks and changed into garments that had probably been left behind by some ranch hand who had moved on. He'd been a small man, and though his shirts fit Olivia perfectly, the pants were tight across her hips and the waistband stood out a little in front.

Even so, when Olivia appeared in the dining room ten minutes later as ordered, the expression in Esteban's eyes said he liked what he saw. He rose from his chair, seated her, then sat again.

He'd visited the pool, for the dust was gone from his hair and skin, and his clothes were fresh. Olivia felt envious for several reasons—Esteban had so much freedom, he'd enjoyed the cool privacy of the pond while she'd been sweltering, and she remembered only too well the primitive pleasure of surrendering in the soft white sand.

Maria served a luncheon of sliced fruit, cold cuts and her own newly baked bread, and left the dining room wearing a secretive smile, as though she knew something Esteban and Olivia had yet to even guess at.

"What about Maria?" Olivia asked. "Will she be safe here alone?"

"She won't be alone," Esteban replied, settling back in his heavy, beautifully carved chair to study Olivia with shameless leisure. "I'm leaving two men to keep watch. Besides, Maria is not a target."

After the meal, during which Esteban said remarkably little and yet devoured Olivia with his eyes, Maria came to clear the table. Esteban stood, drew back Olivia's chair and pressed one hand lightly but firmly to the small of her back.

"What...?"

He propelled her through the inner courtyard to the stairs. "It is time for *siesta*," he said. "In Mexico, we rest during the hottest part of the day."

Olivia's heart had stuffed itself into her windpipe. Even the weight of Esteban's hand at the base of her spine had aroused her, as had the sleepy, sensual images the word *siesta* had brought to mind. "I'm not tired," she faltered, testing the waters.

If the brightness of Esteban's grin could have been hooked up to solar reflectors, it would have provided enough power for three states. "You will be," he promised.

He escorted her past her door and through his own, closing and latching the graceful arch of carved wood behind them.

Olivia's cheeks were bright red, and this time she couldn't

blame the sunburn. "I'm not your plaything," she whispered, angry because she would be practically anything he wanted and he knew it.

Esteban pulled her plaid cotton shirt from her jeans. "You are like ripe fruit—a sweet, juicy peach, I think. It was all I could do not to lay you out on the dining room table and enjoy you right then and there."

Olivia yearned to defy him, but some elemental part of her nature had taken over and she couldn't. She gave a soft gasp when Esteban gripped both sides of the shirt and pulled, so that the mother-of-pearl snaps gave way. He pushed the fabric back.

Away.

Because of the sunburn and the fierce Mexican heat, Olivia wasn't wearing a bra. Her plump breasts were bare under Esteban's gaze, their pink tips hardening, reaching.

"Madre de Dios," Esteban rasped, sounding stunned, as if a woman's body were a new invention. Then, his hands tight on the curve of her waist, he bent and, using his tongue, teased each morsel until Olivia was leaning back in his embrace, groaning. Just when she was nearly insane with need, he began to suck, gently at first and then with greed.

Presently, he set her on the edge of the bed, removed her sandals and jeans. When she tried to rise, afraid of the force of the passion she knew he could make her feel, he stilled her, placing his hands on her hips. She whimpered and flung both arms back over her head as he nuzzled her, kissed the quivering insides of her thighs, then boldly conquered her greatest secret with his lips and tongue.

Olivia's hands clawed at the bedclothes, and she tossed her head from side to side, wild in her surrender. "Esteban," she choked out. "Oh...*Esteban!*"

He slid his palms beneath her bottom, lifted her slightly, and continued to enjoy her just as he might have enjoyed the ripe, sweet, juicy peach he'd spoken of earlier. Olivia raised her feet to his shoulders, but not in an effort to push him away. She needed to anchor herself to him, to be touching something other than his tongue and his hands.

He slid her closer, then reached up to grip her ankles hard. Olivia shouted with pleasure as her climax first lifted her body high off the bed, then twisted her from side to side. If Esteban was worried that someone would hear, he gave no sign of it. He stayed with Olivia until the last vestige of ecstasy had been extracted, until she lay wilted and half-conscious on the mattress, eyes unfocused, her breathing fast and shallow.

She was vaguely aware of being moved, of Esteban removing his clothes, stretching out on the bed beside her. His hand moved in soothing circles on her stomach, and his nakedness teased her ultra sensitive flesh like the brush of a feather.

"Please," she murmured moments later. That one word was all she had strength for; Esteban had taken everything else.

Still, he knew what she wanted, and he denied her; she felt the shake of his head rather than saw it. "No, *dulce*. Rest now." His voice was gruff, hypnotic. "Rest."

Olivia's lashes fluttered as she fought to keep her eyes open, and even the dangerous realization whispering in the back of her mind could not bring her to consciousness again. She slept, but the cruel knowledge was there, like a burr in the tender folds of her spirit.

To Esteban, this was all a game. He liked to make her respond to him sexually, but he consistently refused to make a surrender of his own. She was a diversion.

She drifted into a fitful sleep, and in her dreams she wept with disappointment and grief.

Olivia awoke at twilight, a sea breeze blowing over her

body and her eyelashes wet with tears. Esteban's side of the bed was empty, but the sheets still bore his singular scent and the air was tinged with the scent of his cologne.

Sitting up, her arms wrapped around her legs, Olivia let her forehead rest on her knees and sobbed. It was bad enough that she loved the Leopard and had to leave him, but to realize he'd only been playing with her body and emotions was shattering.

He came in as if summoned by her thoughts, and approached the bed silently. She looked at him with red, puffy, defiant eyes.

"Don't touch me, damn you," she hissed, trying to slide away. "You've had your fun!"

He was quick, like the animal whose name he bore, and before she reached the far side of the bed he'd tangled her in the top sheet and dragged her back.

"What is it?" he demanded. "What are you talking about?"

Olivia tried to fling herself at him—in a passion of fury—but she was still tightly bound in the sheet; it was as restrictive as a straitjacket. "You think it's funny, don't you? Making me want you so much, making me cry out because the pleasure is more than I can bear, then walking away without actually making love to me!"

Esteban might have been an actor instead of a rancher. His face drained of all color and he looked stunned for a moment, then coldly angry. "Did I not please you?"

"Please me?" Olivia was positively livid with rage and hurt, but he still had her trussed up like a chicken in a burlap sack. "You weren't trying to make me happy, you were *road testing* me, like a car you might decide to lease for a while!"

Esteban's jaw clamped tight for a long interval; it was plain he was struggling for self-control. "So," he finally whispered, "it troubles you that I have tried to respect your honor. You do not like being treated like a lady." He gripped the sheet with one hand and began unbuttoning his shirt with the other. "Well, my lovely little captive, have it your own way."

Chapter Eight

Deftly, Esteban flipped the sheet that had enclosed her like a cocoon, in the same way a magician might wrench away a tablecloth without disturbing the china and silverware on top. Unlike the wizard's dishes, Olivia was definitely displaced; she did a complete revolution in the air above Esteban's feather mattress and plopped on her back into its softness, naked as truth.

She swallowed, watching with wide eyes as her captor-host removed his clothes again. Honor demanded that she oppose him, even though, on the deepest level of her awareness, she knew she wanted to lose.

"Don't you even *think* it," she whispered.

His eyes flashed. "By the time I have you," he said, "you'll be begging." He stretched out beside her, cupped the back of her head in one strong hand and kissed her. She tried to keep her mouth shut, but his tongue was too persuasive, too expert at pleasuring her. Finally, with a whimper, she opened to him.

"You are a pompous SOB!" she gasped the moment he freed her.

"*Sí*," Esteban replied. He seemed to know her protests were hollow, and he smiled at the game. "You are not a virgin, yes?" He inquired practically, when he had kissed and caressed her into a state of near hysteria.

"No," Olivia admitted, moaning the word.

"Then you will be able to take me inside you without pain, and there will be only pleasure," Esteban replied, his voice sleepy and low. He rolled onto his back in a graceful motion and set Olivia on top of him, her legs parted over his hips.

She felt the size and power of him pressed against her belly, and closed her eyes, overwhelmed.

Esteban lifted her slightly, and she felt his manhood move into place like a rocket rolling onto a launch pad.

"Oh, my," she cried in a hoarse whisper, as she felt him glide slowly, powerfully into her.

"Open your eyes and look at me," Esteban ordered, though not unkindly.

Olivia blinked, wonderstruck, and her expression must have been a dazed one. The last thing she wanted to do then was have a meaningful conversation.

Esteban gripped her hips, raising her along his length with merciless leisure, then bringing her down again. When she'd traveled him once, twice, three times, he finally went on. "What am I doing to you, Olivia?" he asked reasonably.

She trembled as a shock of yearning went through her, bit her lip for a moment, and then answered him in two very intimate words.

He let her just sit, filled with his manhood, while he teased her nipples with expert fingers. "Would it be so good between us if I were only using you?"

Olivia didn't trust herself to speak.

Until Esteban held her hips again and gave her three long, mercilessly thorough strokes.

"No!" she sobbed, the word bursting from her in an explosion of desperation and surrender.

"Why not?" He was rubbing her stomach now, making her wait. Mastering her.

Olivia was wild with the kind of primitive need that had probably enabled mankind to survive through so many millennia. "Oh—Esteban—I don't know—I swear I don't know!"

Esteban raised himself to enjoy one of her pulsing nipples for a long, sweetly torturous interval. "I have taken you. From today forward, you will be my woman."

"Yes," Olivia moaned. There was a wealth of meaning in that common word: surrender, joy, defiance, fury.

He twisted, never breaking his bond with Olivia, thrusting her beneath him, and kissed her again, savagely. When he raised his head, he searched her face with unreadable eyes and then gave himself to her, full force, with nothing held back.

Olivia's fingernails dug into the supple flesh of his back— that was something she'd only read about until this glorious, tragic day in the Leopard's bed. The hard, slamming motions of his hips, the rhythmic invasion of his manhood, all of it conspired to drive her wild.

When it finally happened, when satisfaction overtook her, her body buckled repeatedly while, at the same time, her spirit soared. It was as though she'd just jumped from an airplane and found that her parachute wouldn't open, except there was no fear. She tumbled through the sky, end over end, knowing that when she struck the ground there would be another cataclysmic release, then nothing.

It was happening, she was about to collide hard with the earth. Olivia tensed violently in Esteban's arms, gave the keening cry of a wild thing mourning in the dark, and for several seconds she didn't exist because she'd given everything she had and everything she was to the man she loved.

When she returned to herself, Esteban was just crossing the threshold. His head was flung back, his teeth bared, and the muscles in his chest and upper arms stood out as he balanced himself on his hands and lunged deep.

A string of soft Spanish words escaped him as he emptied himself into her, and Olivia couldn't resist caressing him, murmuring tender words as he confronted an elation that was obviously excruciating.

When at last his lean and unabashedly muscular body had relaxed, Esteban collapsed beside Olivia with a despairing moan and dragged her close to him. His embrace was perfect, firm and protective but somehow not restrictive.

Olivia smiled, even though if anything she was in more danger instead of less, and closed her eyes. The velvety breeze sneaked between the woven drapes covering the terrace doors and flowed over her bare skin like lotion.

He was a fool, Esteban thought, lying propped on one elbow, watching Olivia sleep. He'd made up his mind not to have this American temptress—in his opinion, she needed a spanking more than the sweet, fevered exercise he could provide—but in pleasuring her he had created an undeniable need within himself.

Her nipples were peaked, like inviting confections, offering themselves to him. Esteban swallowed, admiring the rest of her small, succulent body. Her hips were wide enough for childbearing and for receiving him, but not broad. Her thighs were like firm cushions, absorbing the impact of his fervor when he mounted her, and her stomach was flat and smooth.

He couldn't help imagining her swelling, ripening, as his child grew within her.

The idea made him hard—hard enough that he wouldn't be able to ride at sunset when they would leave for the southern part of the *rancho,* seeking the lost horses.

He put the animals out of his mind for the moment, valuable as they were, and traced the outline of Olivia's soft, kiss-swollen lips with his index finger. Her lashes fluttered and she looked at him with those marvelous pewter-colored eyes of hers, and she smiled.

Something bitter and rigid melted deep inside Esteban. He tasted her mouth. "I need you," he said in a throaty voice. He hoped the extraordinary truth of the statement didn't show.

"Come to me, then," she replied. "Let me comfort you." With a small, seductive sigh, she wriggled against the sheets, as inviting as the pool on a brutally hot day.

Esteban felt everything inside him tighten and then vibrate at her words, like a guitar string drawn so taut that another twist would either snap that string or break the instrument. With a groan, he gathered her close to him, settled on top of her, devoured her mouth with his own.

She was ready for him, her eyes dreamy, her womanly place moist and warm. With a soft croon of welcome, she arched her back and received him, and Esteban had a sense of returning home after years of wandering.

When her thoughts were finally coherent again, which was a long time later, Olivia was more certain than ever that she had to escape Mexico the first chance she got. Esteban's power over her was frightening in its scope, and if she stayed until he'd made her pregnant, his hold would be even greater. Plus, Señor Ramirez led a very dangerous life. To stay would be to share that peril and maybe force a child to share it, too.

She watched as Esteban and his men saddled their horses in the twilight. Olivia supposed she could have dealt with all the other stuff—women were coping with worse things all over the world—but the fact that made her dreams impossible was something else. Esteban would never marry her; she would be the Leopard's woman, but never his wife. Men like Esteban only wed women of their own social status and religion; everyone else would be classified as a mistress.

Olivia had had a fairly broad education; her uncle was an adventurous soul and had taken her on safari in Africa, to see the pyramids in Egypt, mountain-climbing in Tibet. She'd had a number of exciting times on her own, of course, doing research for Uncle Errol's books. For all of that, however, Olivia had never learned to ride.

There must have been a lot of trepidation in her face when Pepito rode over on his overworked horse, leading an energetic little chestnut mare behind him. He spat something in Spanish and tossed the reins to her.

Resigned, Olivia gripped the saddlehorn, as she'd seen the others do, put one foot in the nearest stirrup and hoisted herself up. In the process, she dropped the reins.

The mare danced and sidestepped so much that Olivia was really afraid the creature meant to buck her off, so she took a new, white-knuckled grip on the saddlehorn. Esteban rode over and, with a grin, bent to collect the dangling reins and hand them to Olivia. He ran the tip of his tongue over his upper lip, briefly reminding her, and Olivia felt her cheeks burn.

She saved her pride by turning her thoughts from the wholehearted, lusty way she'd responded in Esteban's bed to the prospect of escape. She had a horse now; maybe she would get an opportunity to ride back to the ranch house, find the gasoline pump, fill up the Blazer and head for home at top speed.

One question gave her pause. What, exactly, was she going to do with the rest of her life?

She was pondering that earth-shattering question when Esteban shouted an order. He gripped the mare's bridle to bring her apace with his own fierce stallion, and Olivia shifted uncomfortably on the hard saddle as she drew certain parallels. Soon they were riding across the sand, Esteban and Olivia in the lead, fourteen armed and mounted men close behind.

Olivia bounced painfully for some time, until she got the hang of slipping into rhythm with the horse. She knew she was going to be sore the next day.

Out of the corner of her eye, she watched Esteban, waiting for him to tire, but the night wore on and he showed no sign of fatigue. Finally, when the moon was high and coyotes could be heard howling their mournful concertos, the band stopped at a rustic cabin that backed onto a bluff. There were a few scrubby trees around, along with some grass, and there was a horse trough that would logically be filled from the rusty-handled pump standing at one end.

Esteban said something to the men, who were eager to water their horses and, Olivia suspected, themselves. Then he swung one leg over and slid to the ground; probably, he had been riding as long as he'd been walking, so comfortable was he in the presence of these snorting, head-tossing, temperamental animals.

Raising his hands to her waist, Esteban lifted Olivia down from the saddle, letting her body slide along the length of his before her feet finally touched the ground. His palms lingered against her sides, and for a moment, he looked as though he meant to kiss her. Olivia wasn't surprised when he didn't; that would have been a violation of the macho creed, showing such tenderness in front of the others.

He gestured toward the cabin, which leaned wearily into the side of the bluff like a traveler who could venture no farther. "Go inside," he said. "There is a lantern and a box of matches on the table to your left."

It all seemed pretty high-handed to Olivia, his assuming she'd obey him like a trained puppy. "What if there are spiders and rats in there?" she whispered, folding her arms.

"I'll protect you," Esteban whispered back, his eyes laughing in the bright moonlight.

"So far," Olivia retorted tartly, arms still folded, "you've been a regular Robin Hood." Then she stomped toward the cabin, hoping the sarcasm in her words would distract Esteban from the fact that she was obeying his command.

Chapter Nine

Inside the cabin, the darkness was thick and the air smelled of dust, mice and long neglect. Olivia yearned to bolt back through the rickety doorway and cling to Esteban like gum on the sole of a shoe, but she could not shame herself that way.

After squaring her shoulders and taking a deep breath, she groped for the matches Esteban had mentioned, found them, struck one against the rough timber of the doorjamb. Weak light flared, along with the scent of sulfur, showing the promised lamp, a table with a candle at its center, two flimsy chairs and a bed with a rope frame but no mattress or box spring.

Muttering, Olivia worked the filthy glass chimney from the lamp base and moved to light the wick, only to have the match burn her fingers and then go out. She swore, hearing skittering sounds behind her in the darkness of the cabin, and the raucous, irreverent laughter of Esteban's men.

How much did she really know about this man? she asked herself, as she felt for another match and finally managed to get the lamp burning. Suppose she had misjudged Esteban Ramirez entirely? Suppose there was a drunken party and he turned her over to his men?

She turned to look at the pitiful room, hugging herself, taking particular note of the impossible bed. Surely he didn't expect her to sleep there, but if not, where?

Without a squeak of the ancient floorboards or so much as a clink of his fancy spurs, Esteban entered the cabin. Olivia knew when he was there; she felt his presence prickling against her skin like heat from a fire.

He closed the door quietly. ''As a boy,'' he said in a low

voice full of remembrance, "this was one of my favorite places. I used to hide here when I was angry or hurt about something, and for a time my grandfather would let me think he didn't know where I was."

Olivia turned, catching a fleeting glimpse of the boy before he took refuge once again in some hidden chamber of his soul. "We're not staying here, are we?" she demanded, to hide a rush of tenderness. It wouldn't do to care too much, not when she would be leaving soon and never coming back.

Esteban sighed, though Olivia wasn't entirely sure he hadn't seen through her ruse. He removed his gloves and the round-brimmed hat that hung down his back from a string when he wasn't wearing it. "Yes," he answered gravely and at length. "For tonight, we are staying here. Be grateful—tomorrow night the mosquitoes will have a much easier time getting to us."

Olivia shuddered, and that elicited another smile from Esteban. He adjusted the smoking kerosene lamp to his liking, then went outside again. He returned minutes later, carrying two rolled blankets, a canteen and a pair of saddlebags.

Even though she was afraid, and certain she'd finally stumbled upon her last great adventure, Olivia was glad to see him.

He went to the rope-bed, gave it a shake to dislodge the worst of the dust, then spread one of the blankets over the top. The other he folded at the foot.

"You're actually going to sleep on that thing?" Olivia inquired, hands on her hips. She wasn't feeling obnoxious, exactly, just tired and testy and scared.

Esteban answered with a nod and, "Yes, *dulce*. And so are you—unless you'd rather curl up with the rats."

Olivia raised an eloquent eyebrow and said nothing, and Esteban laughed. He pulled back one of the filthy chairs at the table and thumped it against the floor instead of dusting the seat.

"Here," he said. "Sit down and I will give you some supper."

Olivia wondered what kind of supper she could possibly get in a place like this. Roast prairie dog? But she sat. She was about to topple over from exhaustion and she was very hungry.

Esteban brought fruit from one of his saddlebags, along with two slightly dented American candy bars, a plastic bag containing several of Maria's fluffy biscuits and some canned sandwich meat.

"What about the men?" Olivia asked, feeling guilty about her greed. After all, there were more than a dozen riders outside, and they might have been questionable types, but they were human, with stomachs that needed filling.

Esteban bent to kiss her forehead lightly. "They have provisions of their own, *dulce*," he said.

Reassured, Olivia ate with gusto. There was no telling what tomorrow would be like, and she needed her strength.

In the meantime, Esteban, evidently feeling no need to eat, went outside. When he returned, he found Olivia finished with her dinner and pacing the small expanse of the cabin.

She gave him a pained look when he entered, and he interpreted it correctly, chuckled and held out his hand to her. The men had laid their bedrolls out around a small bonfire, and the horses nickered inside an improvised corral.

Well away from the cabin, Esteban indicated a cluster of bushes. "There," he said.

He waited with his arms folded while Olivia slipped out of sight and did her business. When they returned to the cabin, Esteban immediately disappeared again.

Olivia felt deserted, thinking he would probably play cards with the men all night, but instead he came back carrying an old basin brimming with hot water. He dragged one of the chairs over beside the rope-bed, then set the basin on its seat.

Following that, he crossed the room to blow out the lamp.

The cabin was in sudden, primordial darkness—surely a cloud had crossed the moon—and Olivia, who had been standing near the table, floundered inwardly. It was like being dropped into the utter void at the bottom of the deepest ocean, a place where the fish have no need of eyes.

Then she felt Esteban's arm around her waist. He evidently had the vision of a jungle cat, as well as the nickname, for he took her easily to the bed and gently undressed her.

When she was naked, he began to wash her with warm water and a piece of cloth that was probably a bandanna. He cleansed her face and hands first, but then the bath became more intimate.

Olivia shivered.

"Cold?" Esteban asked, his voice seeming independent of his body in that black room.

Olivia shook her head. "No. You're going to make love to me, aren't you?" she asked worriedly.

"Yes, *dulce*," he answered. "Very thoroughly."

"But…" Olivia began in a wailing whisper, "I'll yell— I won't be able to stop myself—and all those men out there will hear me!"

Esteban chuckled, and continued to wash her. "They already know what is happening in here tonight," he said. "As for your yelling, well, you were doing that on the beach, and then again today during *siesta*. It is no secret that you enjoy your pleasures, little one."

Olivia's cheeks were on fire.

He eased her down onto the rope-bed, which felt like a hammock and swayed in a comforting way, and covered her with the second quilt. She heard quiet splashing while he washed, but still couldn't make out even the outline of his body.

"Why did you bring me here?" she asked when she was no longer strangling on her pride.

"I told you," Esteban replied smoothly, joining her. Instead of stretching out beside her, however, he knelt and straddled her, turned her onto her stomach, then lifted her onto her hands and knees. "I wanted to protect you from my enemies."

Olivia felt the tip of his manhood tease her femininity, sucked in an excited breath and squeezed her eyes shut for a moment. "Who will protect me from you, Leopard?" she asked.

He teased her with an inch or so, giving, then withholding, then giving again. "No one," he replied. He eased in farther, and his hands reached beneath to cup her full breasts.

She made a whimpery sound, a sound of frustration and yearning.

"What do you want, *dulce?*" Esteban prompted, knowing very well what the answer was.

"All of it," Olivia burst out hoarsely. "All of you."

Esteban toyed with her nipples while he rewarded her for her surrender, moving deep inside her, deeper than she'd ever dreamed a man could reach.

She gave a small, strangled sob, but it was pure pleasure and Esteban obviously knew that. He withdrew, then gave her even more than he had before. "I'm going to yell," she fretted frantically, seeking him, bucking under him like a mare under her stallion. "Oh, please, Esteban, I'm not going to be able to help it, I'm going to *yell.*"

"Good," he said. "Let the whole world know that my woman is happy in my bed."

Olivia feared she'd go right through the rope-bed and land on the dusty floor, so hard were Esteban's thrusts and so vigorous was her own bounding and leaping beneath him, but somehow the net held.

Finally, Olivia's journey was complete. In those last moments of thunder-and-lightning bliss, her skin was moist with perspiration and musk. She threw herself back against Esteban in a spasm of passion, delighting in his muffled gasp and the subsequent stiffening of his powerful body, and she was still responding moments later while he held her breasts and kissed the damp ridges of her spine.

"I yelled," she said dismally a long time later, when she could speak.

"I'm afraid so," Esteban replied, holding her close against his side. He didn't sound the least bit regretful.

Olivia used what little energy she had left to kick him in the side of the leg. "Macho creep," she said.

He laughed, wrapped his arms around her and dragged her on top of him. "Be careful, or I will make you do it again. Perhaps at a higher octave."

Having no doubt that he could, and would, Olivia forced her ready temper to subside. She made no effort to move off of him, but entangled one finger in the hair on his chest and let her chin rest on his collarbone. "Do you think we'll find the horses tomorrow?" she asked.

Esteban smoothed her perspiration-damp hair back from her face. "Maybe tomorrow, maybe the day after that. We'll find them."

Olivia sighed and scooted up so she could rest her head on his shoulder, wondering what Esteban would say if she told him she thought she'd fallen in love with him.

It would probably be a great joke.

"Sleep," he said, as though sensing her turmoil. Olivia closed her eyes, and when she opened them again, the first light of dawn had invaded the cabin and Esteban was still lying beneath her.

He smiled. "Convenient," he said.

Olivia stared at him and started to wriggle away, but he caught her hips in his hands and held her. He had her again, with finesse, and she buried her face in his neck to muffle the moans the resultant climaxes wrung from her.

After another basin bath, another trip to the bushes, and a largely unhealthy breakfast, Olivia mounted her horse and rode out with Esteban and the others. She was very grateful for the straw hat Maria had given her before they left, because it not only protected her from the sun but hid her face from the gazes of all those curious ranch hands.

When she dared to risk a glance at Pepito, he smiled, and Olivia was mortified all over again. Her reputation was ruined, if she'd ever had one in the first place. She began to think more and more of escaping.

At midday, when the sun was at its zenith, they stopped at a charming old mission house with a bell and white adobe walls. While the horses drank at the trough and the men rested on the brick floor of the shady courtyard, Esteban and Olivia talked with the priest in his chapel. At least, Esteban did. Olivia couldn't make out much of the conversation, so she just sat at the trestle table, drinking deliciously cold water from a plain cup.

"Did the *padre* know anything about the lost horses?" Olivia asked as they left. The old priest had used only one word she recognized—*siesta*—and she suspected she and Esteban would rest until the glare of the sun relented a little.

"I didn't ask him about the horses," Esteban replied, opening a door that led to a plain room decorated only with a crucifix and furnished with two inhospitable cots.

"Then what was all that talk about?" Olivia asked, selecting a cot and sitting down to pull off her shoes.

Esteban gripped the waistband of her jeans and pulled her playfully back to her feet, then not so playfully against him. "He thinks we should be married."

Chapter Ten

The stone floor of the small room, worn smooth by the traffic of many years, seemed to sway a little under the soles of Olivia's feet. At the same time, her traitorous body was fully occupied in reacting to such close contact with Esteban's commanding frame.

"Married?" she croaked, as though she had never heard the word before. She certainly had not expected Esteban to raise the subject, even after their lovemaking.

He touched her nose. "The *padre* says we will surely burn in hell for all eternity, if we don't correct the oversight right away," he told her.

"Now there's an appealing prospect," Olivia answered, trying to keep her voice light.

Esteban smiled and rested his hands on her shoulders. His thumbs made caressing motions in the hollows of her collarbone. "It was probably not as poetic as some proposals," he admitted.

Olivia swallowed hard. "That was a proposal?"

"Yes," Esteban said with a sigh, as though surprised by his own actions. "Marry me, Olivia. Stay with me. Laugh with me, sleep with me, capture the beauty of the land in your art."

She swayed, swallowed again. Sometimes it was such a dangerous thing, hoping. "Esteban, there are so many problems—"

"We will solve them all," he said, his lips warm and insistent and so very close to hers. "Where is it written that all problems, real or potential, must be worked out before the wedding?" He paused, and his sigh moved against her mouth, sending a fever racing through her blood. "What has begun between us will not be stopped, *dulce*. I cannot keep myself from touching you, and yet I was raised to believe that one woman in a man's life must be cherished, honored above all others.''

Olivia felt tears of happiness sting her eyes, but she was afraid, too. She reveled in the gentle kiss that followed.

Esteban cradled her face in his hands, wiped a tear from her cheekbone with one callused thumb. ''I believe you are that woman,'' he told her.

She was struck by an attack of practicality. ''But we haven't taken blood tests, or gotten a license—''

Esteban's white teeth showed in a cocky grin, and his eyes danced as he scolded her. ''How many times must I remind you, my stubborn little desert flower? This is the heart of Mexico—*old* Mexico. Things happen here that could never take place in any other part of the country, let alone north of the border.''

Olivia's heart was hammering. She thought of Uncle Errol and the delight he would take in this outlandish situation, and of how he'd always urged her to be bold and take chances, to grasp at life with both hands. She decided to reach out for what she wanted. She loved Esteban desperately, and she yearned to be his wife, as well as his woman.

''All right,'' she said. ''But I'm scared.''

Esteban bent his head, nibbled at the fragile flesh beneath her right ear, then confided, ''So am I.''

They returned to the *padre* and were married in the shady courtyard under a carefully nurtured, leafy tree, and while Olivia didn't understand most of the words, she felt their meaning in her soul. The only thing that kept the ceremony from being perfect was the fact that Esteban had never told her he loved her.

Olivia knew from long experience that nothing in life was perfect, and Esteban *had* said she was ''that one woman'' in his life, the one to be cherished and honored. She had sensed centuries of tradition behind his words.

"W-would this marriage be recognized in the United States?" she asked, when they were alone once again in the little room with the stone floor.

Esteban folded his arms and cocked his head to one side, looking smug. "It is recognized in heaven. If you returned to your own country and married another man, you would be a bigamist."

Olivia felt herself go pale. She wasn't particularly religious, but she did believe in God and in the sanctity of wedding vows.

He gave another of his Latin sighs and sat down on one of the merciless-looking cots to pull off his boots. That done, he stretched out, apparently to rest. He shifted and sighed while he made himself comfortable, causing Olivia an embarrassing barrage of sensation, then yawned, laid his hat over his face and, without another word, went to sleep.

Olivia could have killed him.

Presently, she lay down on the other cot, her mind spinning, trying to absorb the fact that she was married.

Some honeymoon this was, she thought. Her groom was already asleep, and their marriage bed would be a monk's pallet.

For all of that, she was happy, too happy to sleep. She rose, crept out of the room and went to the low adobe wall of the mission to look out at the desert. She saw a pink flower blooming on a cactus some distance away, and suddenly had to see it up close, touch it, find out if it had a scent. She wanted to bring that particular shade of pink home in her mind and blend a glaze to match it exactly.

She looked around and saw that the mission was deserted—like the Leopard, his men were indulging in their *siestas*. Olivia decided to climb over the wall and check out the cactus flower. She would be back before anyone even knew she was gone, though fear of Esteban's displeasure was not her reason for hurrying—she knew what the relentless Mexican sun could do to her if she stayed out too long.

The desert blossom was so delicately lovely that Olivia's throat constricted at the sight of it, and her eyes brimmed with fresh tears. She was about to go back to the mission, only about a hundred yards away, when she saw a rock formation farther out. It suggested an interesting new shape, one she wanted to copy in clay, and she wandered toward it.

After that, it was the layers of pastel colors against the distant horizon. Olivia was hypnotized, her brain whirling with wonderful ideas, and she kept walking. It was only when she took refuge from the sun under the teetering roof of an old shed with no walls, that Olivia realized the mission was no longer in sight.

She bit her lower lip, studying the rugged and unforgiving, yet beautiful, terrain around her. All she had to do was walk back that way...

Or was it *that* way?

Esteban stretched luxuriously when he awakened from his *siesta*. In the cool of the approaching evening, he and Olivia and the others could push on in pursuit of the stray horses. He glanced at the opposite cot, expecting to see her curled up there, perhaps delectably naked because of the heat, but the bed was empty.

A cold feeling zigzagged through the pit of Esteban's stomach, but he immediately stemmed the panic rising inside him. Olivia had merely awakened before he had and gone off to find the amenities, such as they were in this isolated place. Or she might be sitting quietly in the garden where the *padre* liked to hide away while pondering great mysteries of the spirit.

Someone had set a bucket of cool well water outside the door, complete with a chipped enamel dipper. Esteban brought the *agua* in, drank thirstily, doused the back of his neck. Then he set out to find Olivia.

Esteban was pleasantly waylaid by the *padre*, who wanted to talk about building dormitories and classrooms at the mission so that children could come to live there and be educated. He had spoken with representatives of an organization up north, in Los Estados Unidos, that would be willing to provide books, supplies and a couple of teachers, but money was needed for the buildings. A great deal of money.

Esteban listened, though the whole time one part of his mind wandered the grounds of the mission, seeking Olivia. He nodded at suitable intervals.

"We could house forty to fifty children here," the father concluded in Spanish. "The lost, abandoned ones who would otherwise be alone on the streets of our troubled cities, living by their wits."

Esteban was feeling a strange pulling sensation, as though someone had tied a string around his soul and was now trying to lead him somewhere. *"Sí,"* he answered. "You know I will help. Have you seen Olivia?"

"Your wife?" Padre Tejada teased. "I assumed she was with you, my son."

Esteban could no longer contain his concern—or his rising anger. She had left him, after promising to share his life. It had all been a lie to her, a way to humor the man she regarded as her captor.

Worse, she had deliberately endangered herself. The fierce desert harbored so many evils, so many unexpected pitfalls, and it was so easy to get lost. She could stumble right into the hands of his enemies, or meet up with those characters who had kidnapped her in the first place.

Esteban pushed his hat back off his head so that it dangled between his shoulder blades and stepped into the shadowy quiet of the chapel. He hadn't set foot in a church since his grandfather had died, but the rituals came back to him easily enough.

He dipped his fingers into the holy water in the font at the back of the small sanctuary, crossed himself, genuflected. There were no statues at the altar—those were for more prosperous parishes—but the crude wooden cross on the wall spoke to him as it never had before.

Esteban knelt at the railing beneath the cross and offered the first earnest prayer of his adult life. *Protect her.* His head was bowed, his hands clasped. *I beg You to protect her.*

Nightfall came and Olivia still had no idea which way to go. She remained where she was, thirsty and scared, knowing she would only make her situation worse by wandering. The desert air, so mercilessly hot by day, was cooling off rapidly, and she knew the night would be very cold.

Her mind strayed back to the one before, when she'd tossed and moaned on that rope bed while Esteban taught her one delicious new pleasure after another. She ached to feel his arms around her again.

By now, she reflected, bringing herself back to the gloomy present, her husband had certainly discovered that she was gone. He would assume she had purposely abandoned him, and he might be so angry that he would simply wash his hands of her and not even make the effort to ride out looking for her.

"Esteban," Olivia whispered, but her soul shouted the name.

It grew darker, and she tried to sleep, hugging herself, shivering against the desert chill. The stars overhead seemed enormous, but counting them, a game that had gotten her through some difficult times in the past, was of no comfort.

She dozed, awoke shivering, and dozed again. And then she dreamed she heard a horse nicker and the jingling of a bridle. Something long and steely hard nudged her chest, and that was only too real.

Her eyes flew open. She looked up in horror to find the barrel of a rifle, clearly illuminated in the bright light of the moon and stars, pressing her breastbone. The stock and trigger were in the hand of a man Olivia had never seen before.

He smiled, but made no effort to withdraw the gun. "Ah," he said. "The Leopard's woman." His English was heavily accented but only too clear. He looked around, somewhat theatrically. "Ramirez is not here," he said with emphasis, even though it was obviously a fact he'd long since decided upon. The stranger sighed. "His horses stray, his woman strays. It is too bad. Could it be that the Leopard is not such a man as we have always believed?" With that, the man threw back his head and laughed raucously.

Olivia's first instinct was to panic, but she wouldn't allow herself the indulgence. The rifle still pressed to her chest, she scooted upright, slowly, an inch at a time. If there were other *bandidos,* they were well hidden, for she could see no one but this one man.

"Who are you?" she demanded, as if there were some way she could force him to tell.

"Pancho," he replied, reaching down to clasp her shirt with his free hand. He wrenched her to her feet with an easy, wiry strength. "Are we going to be friends?"

Olivia glared at him to let him know she wouldn't welcome his attentions. "Yes," she replied evenly. "We can be 'friends.' All you have to do is get back on your horse, ride out of here and leave me alone."

Pancho laughed, shook his head. "Too valuable. There is a man who would pay *mucho dinero* for the woman the Leopard loves." His dark eyes glinted, and he stroked the underside of her chin with the edge of his thumb. "It would please him to have you, and to send word to Ramirez that you are enjoyable."

Olivia's stomach roiled, and for a second she thought she would throw up all over Pancho's boots. In that same instant, it seemed that her personal universe had been wrenched into perspective; the mysteries were solved, she knew what was important.

Love. Esteban. The child she secretly hoped she was already carrying.

"The Leopard loves many women," Olivia finally threw out, falling back on bravado. "He will not miss one."

Pancho shook his head and made a deprecatory sound deep in his throat. "No. Esteban Ramirez cares for just one woman, and that is you. We know. We have been watching. Come, we leave now." He tied Olivia's hands behind her back and hoisted her up onto his horse. They set off through the night toward God only knew where.

Olivia was in shock by that time, sick with fear. Something told her that this new man, to whom she was being taken like so much pirate booty, was nothing like Esteban.

At sunrise, they rode over a rocky rise and then down a verdant hillside to where a relatively small but stately brick house stood. From her perspective, Olivia could see a swimming pool and a tennis court and a corral full of sleek horses.

The ones missing from Esteban's herd, some sixth sense told her.

A tall blond man with startlingly blue eyes approached, looked her over as though she weren't human, as though she couldn't understand what his scrutiny meant.

"This is the Leopard's woman," Pancho announced proudly.

The azure eyes lit up. "I see," he said, and although his English was more cultivated than Pancho's, it was still marked by a thick Spanish accent. He ran a hand over Olivia's leg, clenched his fingers around her ankle in a bruising hold when she would have twisted away. "Very good," he said. "We have only to wait. The Leopard will surely appear."

Chapter Eleven

Olivia was doing her level best to keep her composure, but under the circumstances it wasn't an easy task. "What are you?" she asked her new captor, who had dragged her unceremoniously into his house without bothering to unbind her hands. "A drug dealer? A white slaver?"

The Mexican was standing at a beautifully carved sideboard in his airy parlor, pouring brandy into a crystal snifter. He chuckled and raised the glass in a mocking toast. "Nothing so dramatic. I make my living selling weapons and cooperating with certain governments."

Olivia was scarcely relieved by this announcement. After all, she was in the hands of a man who would sell out whole countries if the price was right, not just individuals. "What is your quarrel with Esteban Ramirez?" she asked, partly to stall and partly because of a sincere desire to know.

The mystery man smiled. He was really very handsome, but his looks were spoiled by the essential vileness of his nature, which pervaded the room like a bad smell. "He interfered with a project that would have netted millions of American dollars. I was nearly ruined, and it has taken me several years to regain my financial footing. My design is quite simple, and it is twofold—I will repay Ramirez for the sufferings he caused me, and make certain he cannot repeat his transgressions."

Olivia felt the color drain from her face. This man meant to *kill* Esteban. The knowledge made her reel inwardly, but on the outside she was deceptively calm. "He will laugh at you," she said, falling into step with her captor's formal, carefully paced English. "I am nothing to him."

The monster ran his eyes over her with mingled contempt

and interest. "Even better. You would lie to save the Leopard. My instincts tell me that he will go still further to save you, *señorita*. I believe he might well be willing to lay down his life for you."

Olivia closed her eyes tightly, fighting for control. She wanted to fall apart, to give way to utter panic, but too much depended on her ability to keep her thought processes clear. Esteban's life, for example, and most likely her own, as well. "You are wrong."

"We shall see," he responded. "In the meantime we must make certain that you retain your appeal." He set the snifter aside, empty, and clapped his hands loudly, causing Olivia to start. "Juana!" he shouted.

A slender Mexican girl appeared almost immediately. "*Sí*, Señor Leonesio?" she said.

Olivia could see, even in her state of quiet terror, that Leonesio didn't appreciate the fact that his name had been revealed. Probably, he hadn't planned on introducing himself.

The master of the house blurted an order in rapid, furious Spanish, and Juana winced. Olivia reflected that the girl was probably as much a captive as she was, and felt sorry for her.

When Leonesio had finished his diatribe, Juana turned to Olivia, who was sitting on a small couch, and uttered a single word that was clearly a summons. Her enormous dark eyes implored the prisoner to obey.

Figuring anything was better than staying in Leonesio's presence, Olivia rose, every muscle shrieking with soreness, and followed Juana out of the room and up an elegantly rustic staircase.

"You must not try to run away," Juana whispered in labored English when the two women were alone in an upstairs bathroom. She was cutting the bonds from Olivia's wrists. "The wind brings Leonesio news of everything that happens."

Olivia stared into Juana's eyes, rubbing one aching wrist. "You speak English," she marveled.

Juana shrugged and began filling the big tile-lined tub with tepid water. "Not much. I listen. I say words to my person until I know them like rosary."

Olivia was touched. "Are you… Do you love Leonesio?"

Juana made a bitter sound. "He says I will be his woman when I am older. I will be trained to make pleasure."

A shiver went through Olivia. She closed her eyes. "Who is his woman now?"

"He has many." Juana looked at Olivia pityingly. "I think you will share his bed for a time."

Olivia shook her head. "I'll die first."

"He will have you whipped if you say refusing," Juana said in her convoluted English.

The image made Olivia sway. "Dear God."

Juana added jasmine-scented salts to the bath and gestured for Olivia to get in. Although she wanted to rebel in any and every way she could, she was covered with dirt and dried sweat and fear, and being clean might do something to restore her reason.

Olivia took off her shoes, her jeans, her shirt, her underwear, and climbed into the bath. Juana hovered nearby, dark eyes averted, while Olivia shampooed her hair and washed her aching body. After she was finished, a huge, soft, thirsty towel was provided, along with a long, gauzy, white gown, a very expensive lace teddy with the price tag still attached, and a pair of sandals.

Juana led Olivia into a luxuriously furnished bedroom, urged her to be seated at a vanity table and began brushing her hair dry. When she'd done that, she said, "I bring food. Make strong."

The last thing Olivia wanted to do was eat, but she saw the sense in Juana's words. She would need physical strength, and it was crucial that she keep herself from giving in to threatening hysteria. Her own life, and maybe Esteban's, could depend on those things.

She meant to make the most of every advantage and every opportunity, however small. When Juana left the room, turning the key in the lock after she'd stepped into the hallway, Olivia rushed to the French doors that led onto the terrace.

There was nothing below except a big brick patio that extended to the pool. The drop was at least two stories, and if she jumped, Olivia reasoned, biting into her lower lip, she would be veined with cracks from head to foot like an old piece of china.

She went back into the bedroom and paced—thinking, planning, plotting. Coming up with absolutely nothing. Olivia didn't like to admit it, being a take-charge sort of person, but unless Esteban rescued her, she was in for it.

"Leonesio," Esteban said, when at twilight, he and Pepito found the place where Olivia had been taken. In times of crisis, he operated on Murphy's Law: If anything can go wrong, it will. Leonesio de Luca Santana was the most devoted, the most ferociously vengeful of his enemies, and one of Leonesio's men stumbling across the fleeing Olivia would have been the absolute worst thing that could have happened. "The rumors are true, Pepito. He's back."

"*Sí*," was all Pepito said in response. At Esteban's insistence, they rarely spoke of the old days and the people they had thwarted.

"Go back to the mission for the others," Esteban ordered quietly. "You know where Leonesio lives when he is in Mexico."

Pepito nodded. "*Sí*, the St. Thomas estate." He paused. "There will be a fight," he finished, with a certain relish.

Esteban thought of a battle, imagined Olivia caught in the crossfire and closed his eyes. "Not if we can avoid it," he replied hoarsely. "All I want is my wife, alive and unharmed."

"Sí," Pepito agreed automatically, but he looked skeptical. Men like Leonesio thrived on conflict, and they both knew it.

Esteban gestured for his *amigo* to ride out, then swung back into the saddle and set off toward the luxurious hideaway that had belonged to several owners over the years. When Esteban was a child, the place had been the home of Enrique St. Thomas, his friend. Rico had had a fiery Mexican mother and an equally temperamental French father, and when Esteban and his grandfather had visited, it had seemed that the whole house was charged with the St. Thomases' passion for each other.

Tragically, the explosive couple had perished in an epidemic of influenza about a decade before. As he rode steadily toward Olivia—she was the focal point of his whole existence, the magnet he could not resist—he wondered where Enrique was now. It would be good to see his old friend again.

The darkness was thick by the time Esteban reached his destination. He tethered his horse well back from the inner edge of the lush palm trees and tropical plants that surrounded the familiar house.

There were guards, of course, but if Leonesio's small army was around, there was no evidence of it. Just three sentinels, one leaning against a gatepost, smoking, two pacing the outer grounds.

It was a trap, of course. Leonesio wanted revenge for plans that had been thwarted a long time ago, and he knew Esteban would come for Olivia. He was waiting.

Esteban sighed. He had vowed never to play this game again, but that had been before that redheaded American woman had turned his life upside down. Having no choice, Esteban Ramirez put off his regular identity and became, once again, the Leopard.

Overcoming the guards proved so easy he was almost disappointed.

* * *

Dinner was served on the patio at an umbrella-covered table next to the pool, and Olivia was ordered to appear.

She joined Leonesio with cool dignity, her manner even and quiet, but she was aware of every cricket and bird sound in the foliage that edged the low stone wall encircling the grounds. Maybe it was just wishful thinking, but she could have sworn Esteban was somewhere nearby—it was as if she could feel his heartbeat thumping in unison with her own.

"You will share my bed tonight," Leonesio announced, after taking a sip of his claret.

"In your dreams," Olivia replied bluntly. "I'd rather sleep with a lizard."

Leonesio threw back his head and laughed. "So much fire. No wonder the Leopard is obsessed with you."

Olivia forced herself to sip her wine calmly and even to nibble at a few bites of the sumptuous food. "You're building yourself up for a big disappointment. Señor Ramirez has already grown tired of me. By now, he's bought himself another plaything."

"He bought you?" Leonesio set his wineglass down and leaned forward, pleased.

"That idea *would* intrigue you," Olivia remarked. "I'll bet your parents spend a lot of time wondering where they went wrong."

Again Leonesio laughed. "I am exactly what they raised me to be," he responded presently, "but we were discussing your statement that Ramirez bought you."

"Two men kidnapped me off the road when my rental car broke down," she answered, as though such things happened every day. "They sold me to Señor Ramirez, and I escaped him as soon as I could. Only to be captured by you, of course." She paused, sighed philosophically, hoping the enemy would believe her lie about escaping.

Then, suddenly, Esteban was there, vaulting silently over

the fence behind Leonesio, and she prayed the knowledge didn't show in her face. "The life of a white slave is not easy, Mr. Leonesio. Or is that your first name? Do you have a nickname?"

The distraction kept Leonesio occupied long enough for Esteban to lock one arm around his enemy's throat and wrench him to his feet.

"*Sí*," Esteban growled, tightening his hold. "This is *el pollo*—the chicken."

Leonesio made a strangling sound and flailed.

Esteban's gaze moved to Olivia, took in her flowing white dress, narrowed. "We will discuss your part in this little adventure later," he said. "For the moment, you will return to the house and remain there until I come for you. Is that clear?"

Olivia wasn't entirely sure that being rescued was going to represent a significant improvement in her circumstances. Esteban was obviously furious, and she could just imagine the blistering lecture he would deliver once Leonesio and his men had been dealt with. She nodded, disappointed that he hadn't embraced her, hadn't even said he was happy she was safe, and went into the house without a word.

She and Juana sat together on the leather sofa in Leonesio's study, waiting. When a gunshot sounded, both women jumped, and Olivia bolted for the door, certain Esteban had been shot, that, for all of it, she'd lost him, after all.

She collided with him in the doorway.

Probably, the shot had only been a signal to his men.

"You do not follow orders very well, *dulce*," he said, his voice gruff.

Olivia hurled herself into his arms, buried her face in his neck. "I'll probably never be very good at it," she said, her voice muffled by his flesh. "But I love you, Esteban Ramirez. And whether you believe me or not, I never want to be away from you again!"

He held her apart from him, searched her tear-glazed eyes somberly. "You will stay? But you ran away—"

"I didn't run away, you idiot. I was looking at cactus flowers and things and I got lost," Olivia blubbered. She drew a deep, shuddering breath. "Before I came to this crazy country and met you, I was living my Uncle Errol's life, not my own. Now, for the first time ever, I'm really *me,* and I don't want to give that up!"

Esteban's smile said he understood. So did his kiss.

One month later...

Uncle Errol was wearing a white Armani suit, perfect for the tropics, and looked as pleased as any mother of the bride.

He'd shipped down Olivia's kiln and potting wheel as soon as she called him from Mexico City and announced that, even though she and Esteban were already married, they intended to have a formal ceremony at the *rancho.*

Olivia smiled, watching him from the terrace outside her room. The whole courtyard was decked out in flowers and ribbons, and long tables groaned under platters of Maria's world-class food. Guests from every corner of the globe mingled, sipping champagne in the late-afternoon sunshine.

Esteban stepped up behind Olivia, slipped his arms around her, kissed the place where her neck and shoulder met. She was wearing a long white dress with an off-the-shoulder neckline, so there was plenty of skin to tempt him.

"Happy?" he asked.

Olivia let the back of her head rest against his shoulder.

"Oh, yes," she answered. "I'm happy."

He turned her in his embrace, gave her a lingering kiss that promised many splendors for the night to come. She was still a little dazed when he linked her arm with his and led her inside so that they could descend the stairs and exchange vows for the second time.

"Just don't expect me to promise to obey," Olivia said.

Esteban chuckled. "I would not believe you for a second, even if you did," he answered. "I love you, Señora Ramirez."

Olivia smiled up at him, with her eyes and her heart, as well as her mouth. "And I love you, my Leopard."

*   *   *   *   *

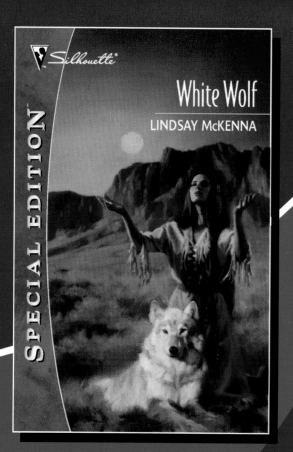

White Wolf

LINDSAY McKENNA

White Wolf

LINDSAY
McKENNA

WHITE WOLF

Lindsay McKenna

* * *

To all my friends at The Medicine Garden.
What a great group of people!

Dear Reader,

The inspiration for *White Wolf* is my own background as a medicine person in the Eastern Cherokee traditions. In our family history, my great-great-grandmother was a full blood Cherokee. Unfortunately, not a lot of information about my great-great-grandmother trickled down through our family. However, we have learned that she was a member of the Wolf Clan (we have seven clans to the Cherokee nation) and that she came from a "medicine" family. And though my great-great-grandmother never spoke of her medicine, her gift came down genetically through my father's side of the family and was passed on to me, his daughter. From age nine onward, I went into training for the gift that she and her family possessed. And I'm glad I have that gift to this day. In fact, I've already passed it on to the next generation of our family.

White Wolf is about the mystical world I live in daily. When I wrote this book I hoped, through the heroine, to give you a bird's-eye view of how Native Americans perceive the world around us. There is great healing in all belief systems, and the Native American model is only now being seriously looked at by traditional medical people. Needless to say, it is a powerful, life-altering and sometimes miraculous paradigm. But read on...and see for yourself. Welcome to my "other" world.

All the best,

Lindsay McKenna

Chapter One

The white wolf was howling again. Hovering between sleep and wakefulness, Dain Phillips heard himself moan as the wolf's lonely, serrating howl cut through him, opening up that gulf of dark fear within. Dying. He was dying. Only six months more to live...

He drifted back to his dream, a hazy, golden colored world where he could see the radiance of the wolf's coat as the animal stood forlornly upon a red sandstone bluff, nose lifted toward the black sky. Again the baying voice stabbed through Dain, tearing at him, making him sweat—making him want to cry out like a frightened little boy.

Oh, God, no! Dain groaned, flailing around on the bed, tearing the sheets from their anchoring points and knocking a pillow onto the floor. Sweat covered him, tiny rivulets trickling down his temples. The urge to scream filled him—to cry out in absolute rage and terror. He didn't want to die, damn it! He wanted to live! *Live!*

In his mind's eye, he stood on the reddish sand and

looked up at that smooth sandstone bluff above him. He watched as the wolf's gold, glittering eyes turned a deep amber with compassion, then filled with an unbridled menace. As Dain groaned, the wolf pricked up his ears and leaped down the cliff—toward him.

Panic set in. If the white wolf got to him, the beast would tear him apart! He'd kill him! Oh, God, he didn't want to die. He had too many things to experience yet, too many things to see. Dain started to run, feeling as if there were weights on his feet, the red sand sucking at his hiking boots.

Breathing heavily, his lungs burning, as Dain ran like a madman across that red desert. Jerking his head to look over his shoulder, he saw the white wolf steadily gaining on him, felt his feral amber eyes burning into his back. Faster! Pumping his arms, he stretched his legs until they screamed in pain and his calf muscles began to knot up. Sweat ran into his eyes, stinging them, burning them. His breathing became erratic and hoarse as he cried out over and over again, *"No, no, no!"*

The white wolf was still gaining on him, steadily, with intent. With savage grace and a primal hunter's instinct, the animal closed the distance between them. No matter how fast Dain ran, no matter how much he pushed himself, the wolf still advanced. Dain couldn't die this way! He just couldn't!

Suddenly, he found himself in a box canyon, the red sandstone cliff in front of him impossible to scale. Whirling around and nearly losing his balance, he sobbed for breath. His knees were like jelly and he lumbered about drunkenly. With the back of his hand Dain tried to wipe away the sweat burning his eyes.

The wolf slowed to a lope, his amber eyes never leaving Dain's blue ones. Standing there, Dain felt helpless. So damned helpless. Wasn't anyone going to come to his aid? Hadn't he prayed to God for deliverance? And then he remembered he'd never prayed to anyone or anything all his life after... So why should God answer his prayers now, when Dain knew He hadn't saved him before?

The wolf slowed even more, stopping within ten feet of him. The animal was barely breathing in comparison to Dain, whose lungs burned. Leaning down, Dain rested his hands against his knees and bent over, trying to think clearly. Lately, his mind was nothing but a damn bowl of mush. *Mush.* The word brought a fresh wave of pain as Dain remembered the horrid stuff he'd eaten as a kid in that damned orphanage.

Suddenly an incredible rage filled him, as if someone were pouring a teakettle of scalding hot water through a hole in the center of his head. He felt the heat settle first in his toes and then move up, filling the cavity of his body. Burning up. He was burning up, and the wolf was standing there watching him. Dain's heart beat wildly and he couldn't steady his breathing. The intent in the wolf's eyes was lethal as he slowly, one step at a time, began to stalk Dain, just waiting for the right moment to leap upon him, grab him by the throat and kill him.

The will to live tunneled up through Dain, thin and fragile, but unmistakable. Slowly he sank to his knees, unable to defend himself from the stalking white wolf. Sinking back on his heels, his arms trembling with weakness, his breathing erratic, he felt the last of his hope burn away as the flood of scalding heat flowed into his head. The wolf was only two feet away and Dain could see every hair on the animal's muzzle, the way his lips lifted to expose large, deadly fangs gleaming with saliva. The wolf's growl reverberated through him, and Dain felt as if he was standing in the middle of a wild, tumultuous thunderstorm.

Resigned to his fate, he tried to prepare himself to die out on that lonely red desert dotted with scraggly sagebrush. A white wolf had howled his name and drawn him into the nightmare in order to kill him. Dain watched, mesmerized, as he saw the pinkness of the wolf's tongue and felt drawn into the animal's gold, narrowed eyes. *Oh, God, I can't fight anymore. I'm too weak. I don't want to die...I really don't...please, let me live, let me—*

The wolf leaped. Too weak to even throw up his arms to stop the huge animal's charge, Dain felt the wolf's powerful body hit him, stunning him. Dain rolled over and over in the sand before he came to a rest on his back, his arms thrown wide, the breath knocked out of him. When he heard the fierce, low growl of the wolf, he opened his eyes and saw the beast hunkered over him. He felt the animal's hot, moist breath against his face, saw the droplets of saliva fall from his muzzle onto his shirt.

There was no time to think. In the next instant, he felt the wolf's fangs sink deep into the center of his chest. In shock and terror, he realized the animal was viciously trying to get to his heart! He felt the invasion of the wolf's massive, powerful jaws, the sound of his own shallow breathing. And then, as he struggled to take one last breath of air into his lungs, he felt the wolf bury his fangs in his heart.

"No...!"

The scream reverberated off the walls of Dain Phillips's bedroom. Abruptly, he sat up, naked and gleaming with sweat, a tangle of sheets wrapped around his legs. Burying his sweaty face in his trembling hands, eyes shut tightly, he desperately tried to get rid of the white-wolf nightmare, of the warm blood flowing across his chest and torso as the wolf wrenched Dain's beating heart out of his body.

"No," Dain rasped, angrily jerking the sheets aside. "Damn him. *No!*" As he got to his feet, dizziness assailed him, forcing him to drop unceremoniously back onto the bed. Dain hated feeling so damn weak. But there was nothing he could do about it, he remembered with anger and resignation. He was dying. Yes, he was dying. A malignant tumor had grown in his brain, too deep to operate on. The doctors said he would die during the surgery, and without it he had less than six months to live. Six lousy months!

Breathing harshly, Dain battled his own weakness and dizziness and forced himself to stand. Anger had always given him power and control over his life. Now he used it as never before, to fight his failing body as he got to his feet. Water. He had to have water. His mouth was dry. He was burning up. The doctors had warned him of a fever coming and going as his body tried to fight off the swiftly growing tumor.

Sweaty, hot and shaky, Dain used the wall to steady himself as he stumbled from the large master bedroom to the bathroom. His mouth was so dry it felt like it was going to crack. That damn white wolf. He hated the animal! He hated the nightmare that plagued him every night!

Cursing, Dain fumbled for the light switch. The resulting glare hurt his eyes. The doctors said he'd be photophobic from now on—sunlight, or indeed, any bright light, would make him wince like he was being struck. Not that a little pain should bother Dain, who'd taken enough beatings as a young kid. One of the matrons at the orphanage had loved to slap the boys across the mouth. Smiling mirthlessly, Dain reached for a glass on the sink. He'd lost count of how many times that old crone had slapped him, but he remembered he'd always had red cheeks. Back then, it was a badge of honor.

Jerking the faucet handle, he felt the cold water spill across his hand. To hell with it. He set the glass aside, cupped his hands and filled them with the cold, delicious water. Leaning down, he splashed it across his face. Yes! The cold always revived him. Helped him. Steadied him. He remembered going to the boys' bathroom to cry after getting a few good slaps from the matron. When his tears abated, he'd wash his face with cold water and make the redness disappear from his cheeks. What a lucky lad he was.

The cold water chased the last of the white wolf's yellow eyes out of his haunted subconscious—at least, for now. Jerking a towel off the rack, Dain wiped his face. Filling the glass, he drank the water in huge gulps, some of it spilling out of the corners of his mouth, dripping down onto his chest and across his still-pounding heart.

Absently, he ran his fingers through the dark mat of hair across his chest, spreading the water over his heated skin. Water always soothed him. Turning, he put the glass aside. Why not take a swim in that Olympic-size pool of his? Indeed, why not? In six months, he wouldn't be here to enjoy it, anyway.

Moving robotically and using his hands to steady himself, he walked through the fifteen-room mansion he'd bought for a mere ten million. It had every convenience, designer this and designer that, artwork from the Old Masters, Ming Dynasty porcelain from China and anything else a man could want with his money.

But money couldn't make this cancerous tumor deep in his brain disappear. Opening the sliding glass door, he walked woodenly toward the pool as the predawn coolness wrapped around his hot, sweaty body. Dain halted and looked up. The lights of New York City glimmered in the distance. His mansion sat on some of the most expensive real estate a New Yorker could buy. But what did his magnificent house mean to him now?

He laughed harshly and glared heavenward. The night sky was light with a nearly full moon. Many of the stars were blotted out because of the moon's pale, radiant light. Scowling, Dain was reminded of the white radiance of the wolf's coat. Shrugging off the image, he turned his attention to the pool, long and rectangular and inviting. Without hesitation, Dain dove in.

Just the act of leaping into the cold depths, chilled by the early September weather, was enough to shock his senses and bring him back into the here and now. He swam with hard, swift strokes, trying to outrun the last of the nightmare, burying himself in the nurturing water, which surrounded him like a lover. He turned over and did a backstroke, moving like an arrow, his legs strong and powerful. Water raced and gurgled around him, healing him.

By the time he'd swum ten laps in the pool, the eastern sky was just beginning to lighten, not quite gray, but no longer inky black, either—a promise of something to come. As he dragged himself wearily out of the pool and wrapped himself in a thick, white terry-cloth towel, he studied the eastern horizon. The sun would edge it in gilt within a couple of hours. A tremor raced through him as he dried the short, black hair that clung to his skull and wiped the last of the rivulets from a harsh, rugged face that few would call handsome, he knew.

Well, he might not be a pretty boy, but he'd carved an empire that no one on the face of this earth could steal from him. After the orphanage had stolen his soul, crushed his heart and destroyed his hope, he'd sworn that once he got out of that hellhole of the damned, he'd insulate himself against the cruelty of the world and make a safe place for himself.

Laughing bitterly, Dain walked to a chair and sat down. His knees were feeling weak again. As he buried his face in the white towel, he closed his eyes and took a deep, shaky breath. *He was dying.* How damned unfair! He was only thirty-eight, one of the richest men in the world, and there wasn't a cure on earth his money could buy to stop this brain tumor from growing, from taking his life.

Looking up, Dain gazed at the moon. Somewhere in this world there *had* to be something that could help him. But where? And what? His money had bought him advice from the world's top specialists and they'd all told him to go home and die. There was nothing they could do for him. Oh, sure, they could operate and more than likely injure the other parts of his brain, leaving him a helpless dullard who couldn't speak or walk.

Dain balled the damp towel in his hands as he studied the white orb in the sky, hanging so silently. It was so beau-

tiful and free. In six months, he'd never see the moon shine
again. And then he thought of the white wolf of his dream.
Wolves howled at the moon. A sad, twisted smile pulled at
his mouth. Well, maybe he was more wolf than he realized.

Laughing bitterly, Dain shook his head. What was he going to do? There had to be *some* kind of healing for his
tumor *somewhere* in this forsaken world! For the last year,
ever since the tumor had been discovered, he'd sent his best
people abroad to find such a medicine and such a person—
and they'd all come back empty-handed because no one in
traditional medicine would tell him what he wanted to hear:
that they could cure him of the tumor.

His mouth flattening, Dain studied the moon's reflection
on the surface of the pool, the water shivering now with
ripples from the morning breeze. There was a wild, animal
restlessness in his soul. This wasn't the first time he'd felt
it. No, when he'd been caged in that orphanage as a young
boy no one wanted, he'd felt just like the white wolf that
had pursued him in his nightmares. Yes, that was it. Maybe
the white wolf that haunted his dreams nightly ever since
he'd gotten the tumor was actually him.

I'm going crazy, Dain decided as he studied the water.
Well, he if he wasn't crazy yet, he would be soon enough.
Toward the end, the doctors said, he'd be drugged and put
away—for his own good—as the runaway tumor began to
make his behavior volatile—even dangerous to himself and
others. That was a joke. He'd made nothing but enemies
growing up and later, while creating his empire. And while
he'd loved many, many women, taken the fruit of their bod-
ies, he'd never married. He'd recognized the greed in
women's eyes when they saw his billion-dollar empire, and
he knew each and every one of them was simply playing
the game to get him, and more important, his money.

Damn it, there had to be something he could do! He just
couldn't accept that he was going to die. His mind churned
as it always did after awakening from the nightmare. Who

could cure him? And where? Hadn't he looked everywhere? His mind was facile and moved like a powerful Indy race car, swiftly closing in on the ever-elusive finish line. Associates had said he had a mind like a hummingbird, always in motion, never resting. To stop meant having time to remember things about himself and his past—memories too painful to contemplate. So he stayed busy. He guessed he was just a Type A personality. And why not? No grass grew under his feet. He had no friends, no wife, no children. Only a worldwide empire, new fields to conquer and money to burn. Yes, he was one of the most powerful corporate raiders of the past two decades—and he'd always gotten everything he'd gone after in the business world. He was a winner.

Wasn't he?

Snorting softly, Dain slowly eased himself to his feet. He pulled the towel across his shoulders. Winners didn't die of brain tumors. He'd overcome so much, so damned much. And now *this!* A stupid tumor was stalking him, just like that white wolf did every night.

As Dain walked slowly around the pool, the coolness of the fall air making him shiver slightly, he had a sudden thought. It came out of nowhere and stopped him midstride. *Yes.* Why hadn't he thought of it before? He'd go see his favorite medical doctor tomorrow, Dr. Sarah Goodwin. He liked her. She'd always been honest with him—and surprisingly compassionate. And Dain had seen enough doctors to know that compassion didn't come cheap. But then maybe it was a game, an act on her part. Maybe she just wanted his money, too.

Well, whatever. Dr. Sarah was into a lot of things medical doctors weren't supposed to be into. She'd hinted he should take vitamins and minerals, get a massage on a weekly basis to stimulate his immune system. Yes, she had some oddball ideas about healing, but for some reason, he hadn't made time to sit and really ask her in depth about these alternative methods she seemed to know something about. A slight smile curved his mouth. Okay, so he'd go see Dr. Sarah and he'd peer into that fine surgeon's mind of hers and see what else she knew. If he didn't take the time now, he'd never have it. Besides, who knew? Maybe Dr. Sarah had a lead for him—something he might want to track down himself. Personally.

Maybe that was the problem, too, Dain decided. He'd spent millions sending his representatives around the world looking for a cure for him, when he should have searched himself. With his body beginning to show the effects of the tumor, it was now or never. Gripping the towel more firmly in his fist, Dain entered his palatial home, closing the sliding glass door behind him. He padded across the thick carpeting to his office to make a note for his secretary, John Hastings, to get Dr. Sarah on the phone early that morning.

Dain didn't believe in hunches, but he chalked up the need to talk to Dr. Sarah as a logical progression, one born out of desperation and a vague memory of her attempts to get him to stay a few more minutes after his appointment to discuss some "alternative" healing methods with him. At the time, he'd pooh-poohed her. He wondered what she would say if he told her about the nightly dream of the white wolf.

"Wolves are about our primal, survival self," Sarah told Dain as she sat behind her huge, walnut desk.

Dain moved restlessly, pacing back and forth as he always did across her spacious office in the city. Early afternoon sunlight slanted through the venetian blinds, filling the room with a sense of warmth. Of hope. "Do people who are going to die get nightmares like this?" he demanded brusquely.

Sarah shrugged and folded her hands in her lap. "Sometimes. I had suggested a good therapist for you to—"

He gave her an angry look. "Doctor, if I wanted a damn shrink, I'd have gotten one by now."

She frowned. "Then why are you here, Dain?"

He halted and placed his hands on his hips, a gesture he'd picked up in his days as an air force fighter pilot. "You mentioned something about other forms of healing. Not traditional ones," he muttered, beginning to pace again and closely watching her thoughtful expression. Sarah was in her mid-forties, with red hair and dark green eyes. She was pretty. And intelligent.

"Oh."

"What do you mean, 'oh'?"

"I didn't think you'd be the type to be interested, Dain."

Anger stirred in him. "Doctor, I'm going to die in six damn months. What the hell makes you think I'd shrug off a good idea that just *might* cure me?"

With a sigh, Sarah stood and slid her hands in the pockets of her white lab coat. She moved slowly, with deliberation, around the desk. "Okay," she murmured. "Last year I attended a conference in Arizona on Native American healing techniques. I talked to this one medicine man, a Navajo from Chinle, who had cured stomach cancer in some of his Navajo patients. I asked him if there were any women healers who could do what he did, and he said yes. I thought a woman healer might be best since I feel you have more trust in women than men, and part of the healing is trusting the healer."

Dain halted a few feet from her. He saw Sarah's green eyes narrow. "And?"

"He became very evasive. Nervous, almost. He muttered something about this woman whose name is Tashunka Mani Tu. She's Eastern Cherokee, but she lives on the Navajo Reservation and the name she goes by is Lakota. It seemed an odd combination to me, but he said she lived the life of a hermit and only those who had the courage to find her would. Apparently,'' Sarah continued, ''those that could find her were healed.''

''Did she heal tumors?''

''This old man said she was *heyoka*.''

''What the hell does that mean?''

''*Heyoka* is a Lakota word for coyote. It means a person who is not what they seem to be. The coyote is considered a trickster. The medicine man said this woman could change shapes, become an animal, a bird or whatever she chose. He said that those people who overcome their fear of her would find her. He said that a woman who had breast cancer, and who had only weeks to live, sought out this medicine woman. When the old Navajo medicine man saw her two months later, the woman was cured, happy and was telling everyone she met of the miracle.''

''Humph.''

''I thought you'd say that.''

Irritably, Dain said, ''She's cured breast cancer. That's a tumor. Where can I get a hold of her?''

Shrugging, Sarah said, ''I don't know.''

''What about this old Navajo medicine man?''

''He died shortly after the conference.''

Angrily, Dain glared at her. ''All right, I'll go to Chinle, Arizona, and ask around about her. *Someone* has got to know about her.''

Smiling tentatively, Sarah ran her fingertips along the edge of her desk. ''Yes, I'm sure someone has heard of Tashunka Mani Tu.'' She paused, studying him intently. ''One word of warning, Dain.''

His hand was already on the doorknob. ''Yes?''

''Take your hard-edged, impatient, angry mannerisms and get rid of them once you step foot on the reservation, will you?''

His brows dropped.

''The Navajo are a very gentle people who believe in living in harmony with nature and with others. If you aggressively attack them, as if they're a corporation to be raided, you aren't going to get anywhere. You've got to cultivate some, er, diplomacy and patience." She leaned down and picked up a piece of paper.

"You need to see this woman—her name is Luanne Yazzie. She's a medicine woman in training. She lives out at Rough Rock, Arizona, about forty-five minutes from Chinle. Take some gifts with you—that might help."

He jerked open the door. "What kind, good doctor?"

"Always bring groceries. Lots of them. Luanne is a councilwoman from Rough Rock and a lot of people from her community are very poor, almost starving. They come to her house and routinely ask for food or money. If you show up with food, it signals to Luanne that you're a man of compassion." The doctor's smile broadened a little. "She's got a master's degree in education, and she's smart as a whip. If you can make her your ally instead of an enemy, I'd bet she could tell you the whereabouts of this mysterious *heyoka* medicine woman." With a shake of her head, Sarah added, "She certainly is a mystery. Tashunka Mani Tu could practice on her own reservation, in Cherokee, North Carolina, but she doesn't. I hope you find her. I'd love to hear about your adventure, Dain. I wish you the best of luck on this. My hunch is if you can find her, she can help you."

Dain saw the sincerity in the doctor's eyes. In that moment all his mean-spirited and paranoid worry about her wanting him for his money dissolved. His mouth softened a bit. "Instinct and hunches. Doctor, you scare me to death. The only thing I believe in is what I can see with my eyes, hear with my ears, taste or touch."

Sarah chortled. "So tell me, why are you chasing down this wild lead? It's about as illogical and nonlinear as you can get."

He shrugged and became pensive. "Did you tell me what her name means? Tashunka Mani Tu?"

Her grin broadened and she leaned her hips against the

desk and folded her arms against her breasts. "The old medicine man said it means Walks With Wolves."

Dain stood riveted to the spot, feeling a bolt of lightning strike him in the crown of his head, rip through his body and exit out his feet. A sudden wave of heat followed by icy cold washed through him like a tidal wave. His hand tightened on the brass doorknob until his knuckles whitened.

"What?" he rasped.

"You heard me," Sarah said crisply. "Her name, when translated into English from Lakota Sioux, means Walks With Wolves." Her eyes sparkled. "Who knows?" she whispered, emotion suddenly choking her voice, "maybe she's been the one all along sending you a dream of the white wolf."

His Adam's apple bobbed. Fear rippled through him, then disbelief. And finally hope. "What," he rasped, "are you talking about?"

With a shrug, Sarah eased away from the desk. She dropped her arms to her sides. "I spent six months at the Chinle hospital working with Navajo medicine people. I saw a lot of things that traditional medicine can't explain, Dain. One thing I heard about again and again was dreaming. Many patients had powerful dreams and the native healers would interpret them. It was commonly accepted that medicine people send dreams to those who are sick, to help them fight off whatever is attacking them. Maybe this medicine woman is already in touch with you, and has been from the start. Maybe she sent the white wolf to you."

His nostrils flared and he gave a sharp, bitter laugh. "Oh, yeah? Then why the hell does that white devil rip my heart out of my chest every night?"

Gazing at him, Sarah whispered, "Go find her and ask her, Dain…"

Chapter Two

She felt his presence. Erin lifted her chin, surveyed her flock of forty sheep, which foraged restlessly across the red sand desert, then narrowed her eyes on the horizon. The megalith known by the Navajo people as Rainbow Butte stood like a magnificent tower rising up out of the surrounding landscape of the high plateau. *He is coming.* Her heart pounded briefly to underscore that knowing.

She smiled a little as she felt Maiisoh rub against her dark red cotton skirt, brushing the heavy material against her knee-high buffalo-skin boots. Looking down, she petted the white wolf's massive head. He, too, was looking toward Rainbow Butte.

"So you sense his coming, my friend?"

Maiisoh whined and sat down, leaning his weight against her right leg.

Erin continued to pat his head. "Is this someone you have been visiting at night, Maiisoh?"

The wolf lifted his muzzle, his huge yellow eyes staring up at her thoughtfully.

Laughter rolling from her lips, Erin said, "You sly old wolf. If you didn't enter people's dreams they wouldn't keep coming here." Her smile turned slowly into a line of sadness as she continued to watch her flock. "The Great Spirit knows what is best," she added with a sigh.

Maiisoh began to thump his big, brushy tail, dirty with red clay and tangled with sagebrush brambles. He had been chasing a jackrabbit, and the old, wise one had led him on a merry chase with no meal at the end of it. Instead, Maiisoh had found himself in huge clumps of sagebrush, muzzle buried in a hole where the old jackrabbit lived. It was an early morning ceremony performed every day by Maiisoh and that old rabbit.

"Oh," Erin said wryly, "and of course, you know best, too. I can see by the pleased look on your face, Maiisoh." Yet a stirring of great sadness overwhelmed her and her fingers tightened briefly on the herder's staff that she always carried. Father Sun was just brimming the horizon and she silently offered prayers of welcome to him and to all her relations, thanking the Great Spirit for the beauty of yet another day being offered to her.

Maiisoh suddenly rose off his haunches and leaped away from her. Being a good guard, he didn't run through the herd, but around it, loping easily toward the east and following a desert track that many vehicles had followed. The rain two days ago had turned the red clay of the desert into slick, slimy goo that no car or truck could traverse—at least, not out here to the middle of the Navajo Reservation. Until it dried, foot and horse traffic were the only kind that could make it to where she lived.

Bothered, but not knowing why, Erin continued to lead her sheep in the direction her white wolf had gone. She watched him work his way around a small hill that wore a crown of dark green Navajo tea brush and sage. Someone was coming. Who? Would he make it to where she lived? Only the Great Spirit knew those answers, and as Erin ambled down the damp red clay already beginning to dry beneath the rays of Father Sun, she hoped in one small compartment of her heart that whoever the visitor was, he would grow weary, give up and turn back.

The bleating of the sheep soothed her worry. Soon she would begin to weave her next rug from the wool she gathered from them in midsummer. Right now, their coats were heavy, growing thick in preparation for winter, which would start in mid-November on the res.

Winter... She loved winter because it meant she would be cut off from everyone—and everything. It was the time of year when she sat cross-legged at her frame and began to weave the strong, soft strands of wool into another magnificent rug. Each rug told the story of the year that had gone before. Erin didn't try and weave as the Navajo women wove; her symbols were Eastern Cherokee, and she wove colorful picture stories across her rugs. They were never shown to anyone; she kept them carefully rolled up and tucked away in a huge old cedar trunk. But the rugs were a living, breathing testament of the last ten years of living in the hermitlike world she preferred. Each rug detailed what had happened to her that had been important to her growth.

As she slowly placed her booted feet upon the ground, she felt the energy of the land, the throbbing quiver reminding her that Mother Earth was very much alive beneath her. It was a soothing feeling, one that opened her heart like a flower, one that calmed her fractious state and made her feel loved and nurtured.

He is coming.

Halting, Erin looked toward the butte in the distance. The only way into her area was a road around the bottom of that spire. Since it had been raining heavily for the past two days, the track was still muddy. Whoever was coming had chosen a very poor time to try and find her. He was doomed to failure, she told herself, her fingers wrapping more strongly around the aged saguaro cactus staff.

Or was he?

He is coming.

A broken sigh tore from her lips. Why did she feel such consternation? Such anxiety? That had not happened before. Oh, she always knew when someone was coming. That was the easy part, for if Maiisoh did not alert her, then that secret part of herself that was connected to the living River of Life energy that glistened and gleamed through and around all things in the colors of the rainbow, would tell her of the approach of her next visitor.

It was a man.

How strange. With a few exceptions, her patients were usually women. Few men had the patience, the perseverance, the utter commitment to find her hogan, to find her. In fact most of her patients over the last ten years had been women. Only two men had made it to her home and asked for help. And they were Navajo, not white men, thank goodness.

She smiled a little as the flock moved energetically along the rutted track vehicles had followed to her hogan. The sheep seemed almost elated and moved quickly—which was unlike them. Sheep foraged slowly. They didn't go trotting briskly down the road, ignoring sparse yellowed strands of grass here and there.

Mystified, Erin picked up her pace to follow the herd, which suddenly seemed to know exactly where it was going. Of course, Maiisoh had already run down this way, because she could see his huge, wide paw prints embedded in the thick, gooey clay. She hurried to keep up.

The tracks led around a small, round hill and then continued to wind around other hills of varying sizes and shapes. Erin knew that a good two miles away, the road dipped down into a wash where many a vehicle had become stuck—but good—after a rain. Keying her hearing, she thought she heard the faint sounds of a car engine in the distance.

He is coming.

The sheep were trotting now, heading straight for the wash. Erin had to trot herself to keep up with her flock. She never allowed them to range out here alone, for fear of coyotes grabbing one of them. There were wild dogs, too, which were more of a danger. The dogs often came from the reservation. Because the Navajo didn't have money to feed them, the animals took off looking for food. Other disowned dogs would find them, and the animals would band together. Erin knew from sad experience that a pack of dogs starving to death would easily claim one of her vulnerable sheep and kill it without a thought. Wild, hungry dogs were a greater problem than the coyotes that owned this land.

He is coming.

Erin heard the grinding gears of a car now. Slightly winded, she saw her flock, as if guided by an invisible hand, continue to trot knowingly along the faint track, which had been washed out during the recent rainstorm. With a shake of her head, she acknowledged the invisible powers that surrounded her. Off in the distance, she saw Maiisoh standing on a hill that overlooked the wash far below. His tail was wagging expectantly and she knew Maiisoh saw the man who was trying to find her.

Well, she might as well surrender to the Great Spirit's demand. Men were not her strong suit, never had been, but if that was what was decreed by the greatest, most loving force in her universe, then she would bow to it and move toward her destiny. That did not mean Erin wasn't afraid. She was. The Great Spirit knew the fear that rested in her heart. Her deep, dark secret of the past still lay open and continued to ooze grief and loss. She had never tended that wound within herself, hoping to cover it, hoping to forget it with time.

He is coming.

"Great Spirit, guide me with this man who comes looking for help. Give me the words, the wisdom, the vision of my heart to see him clearly, so that a healing can take place within him."

How many times had she spoken that reverent prayer with all her soul? Erin had lost count, but she meant each word with every cell in her body as she continued down the slight incline. Less than a mile away was the wash. She knew without even seeing it yet that the man who looked for her was stuck there with his vehicle.

He is coming.

"Damn it!" Dain shouted at the dawn sky as he stood in the wash, his clothes damp with perspiration because the fever was attacking him again, his lips curled away from his teeth. He was ankle deep in red mud, his expensive shoes ruined, his tan chino pants permanently stained. The four-wheel-drive truck he'd bought in Gallup was stuck up to its axles in clay. The owner of the car dealership had sworn this vehicle would make it through *anything*.

"Screw everything," Dain muttered violently, wiping his stained hands against his pants. He'd tried to dig the slimy red mud from the tires of the vehicle, but with every shovelful he'd felt weakness eating at him. He no longer had that magnificent strength that weight training had given him. His legs trembled. His arms felt like so much jelly.

With disgust, Dain threw the shovel into the wash. Sweat beaded along his brow. Damp strands of hair were plastered against his skull. Damn this place. Damn Sarah. Damn the Yazzies. Oh, hell, damn his whole, rotten life! He breathed unsteadily through his mouth, falling back against the vehicle. The walls of the wash were made of sand and clay and rose ten feet on either side of him. The stupid wheel ruts led right through the wash. Why the hell didn't the Navajo build bridges across things like this, as normal human beings would?

Disgust made him snort violently as his gaze ranged across the wash. Suddenly the hair on the back of his neck stood up. Lifting his hand, he ruefully rubbed the area. Tiny, cold shivers ran down his spine—a sensation he'd never experienced before. He wondered if it was another lousy symptom of his brain tumor growing and affecting some new nerve response in his body.

No, this was different. Scowling, Dain began to look around him. This sensation felt like some forewarning of danger. He laughed harshly, the sound muffled by the sand around him. He remembered now—he'd had this sensation as a kid in the orphanage, back when Mr. Gordon was stalking him, the old son of a bitch. Gordon did that to his "favorites." And God knew, Dain had been on the top of the list when it came to Gordon's badgering, beating and name-calling. Yeah, Dain knew this sensation, this feeling. It was one of pure, unadulterated danger. *Something* was stalking him.

Well, old Gordon was dead and gone now, so it couldn't be him. Pushing away from the truck, Dain carefully lifted his foot out of the sucking red clay. He braced himself against the vehicle to keep from falling flat on his face as he moved around to the front of the truck and looked up.

His heart slammed violently into his ribs, his mouth dropped open and his eyes widened in terror. *No! No, it couldn't be!* Dain was positive he was seeing things. *He must be!* Without thinking, he rubbed his eyes, smearing red clay across his face.

There, up on a red-colored hill above the wash, stood a white animal. From where Dain was standing, it looked like the white wolf from his nightmares. Dain's heart pounded savagely in his chest, underscoring the terror he felt and tasted. The hill was a good half mile away, and he couldn't see the animal clearly enough to say whether it might be a white German shepherd, or maybe a husky. Maybe he was just going slowly insane, and this was indeed the white wolf who haunted him nightly.

Dain's mouth grew dry and his limbs froze. The same old terror, the same fear, washed through him. Somewhere within him, on some deep, unconscious level, he *knew* it was the white wolf—even if he wanted it to be anything but.

In the forbidding silence of the dawn, he could hear his heart beating. He could feel it thumping wildly in his chest, in response to the white wolf on the hill, watching him. *Watching him.*

Where did reality begin and nightmares end? As he stood there, he threw out his hand to regain his balance and it struck the hood of the vehicle. The feel of the cold metal beneath his muddy fingers grounded him momentarily. Blinking rapidly, he tried to make the white wolf go away. But it didn't work. The beast stood like a statue on that bloody red hill, watching him, just watching him. Dain found himself gasping for breath. Was the wolf going to chase him, as he always chased him in the nightmare?

He realized that there was nowhere to run. The only way he could escape the wolf's lethal jaws was by climbing back into the safety of the truck. And then what? How the hell was he going to get this thing unstuck and make his way back to Many Farms, the closest community and a good twenty miles south across this damnable desert?

A sound in the distance caught his attention. Dain wasn't sure, but he could've sworn he heard a woman's low, husky laughter wafting toward him in the silence that surrounded him. Where did it come from? Was it in his overactive imagination? He was barely able to tear his attention from the white wolf on the hill, but he did.

Just as the sun's strong, golden rays flowed silently across the land, caressing the Navajo desert like a lover's sleek arms, he saw something out of the corner of his eye. Was it magic? A ghost? Or was it real? Dain suddenly felt his knees tremble violently. He felt as if he was caught in a time warp between reality and a nightmare. He forced himself to move his eyes, very slowly, from the white wolf in the distance, toward the sound, which was much closer, almost on top of him.

It had been a woman's laughter, rich, husky and earthy. The sound had moved through him like the golden sunlight that slowly crept across the desert. Because he was down in the wash, he still remained in the shadows. Dain laughed to himself. He was in the shadows, all right. The shadow of death. What an eloquent testimony! His vehicle was stuck in this dark, shadowed wash—a succinct statement of his life. Normally, he never thought in those symbolic parameters. Maybe because he was muddy, wet and cold, and shaking like a lost, shivering puppy, he was forced to look beyond his normal scope of life. Now that he was completely out of his element, he wasn't sure of anything.

Dain turned toward the welcoming laughter, which seemed to have originated behind him. His eyes narrowed and his heart thumped violently in his chest. Was he seeing things? It was possible—the doctors had told him he'd hallucinate as the tumor grew larger in his brain. Weakly, he lifted his hand and rubbed his eyes. He *had* to be seeing things. Or was he? Dropping his hand, he looked again. No, she was still there.

This time he didn't feel fear, but just the opposite: a powerful surge of hope. On the hill was the white wolf, watching him, making him feel raw fear. To his left stood an incredibly beautiful apparition of a woman. She wore a white deerskin jacket, a red skirt, which fell to her slender ankles, and dark leather boots. Her ebony hair hung to her waist in two thick braids. There was a dark choker around her neck and a dark green sweater beneath her fringed jacket.

In that moment, as Dain absorbed the sight of her standing with that staff in her hand, gazing down at him, the rays of the sun reached her. As the light enveloped her, he gasped. For an instant, he thought he saw a golden radiance flash around her form; scintillating crystals, millions of them surrounded her face and form before disappearing.

Blinking, Dain realized he must be going crazy. He had to be. He remembered that same radiance around the white wolf in his dream. Was this woman real or a figment of his tortured imagination? Suddenly he wished with all the strength left in him that she was real. Staggering along the side of the vehicle, his hand against the cold metal to steady himself, Dain never allowed his gaze to leave the woman. Whether she was real or not, he felt a pulsing, living connection with her.

The golden sunlight embraced her like a familiar lover. Her crimson skirt turned a bright, brilliant red and her fringed jacket glowed an unearthly white. Her once-black hair now danced with brownish-red highlights. And her face! Dain thought for a moment that if he believed in angels, she had the face of one. Her eyes, warm and compassionate, were a light cinnamon color. They were set far apart, almost at an angle, slightly slanted above her broad cheekbones. Her lips were full, promising him that she was a woman of passion.

Everything about her seemed mystical and ethereal in his whirling, dizzied mind and senses. He felt her compassion. *Felt* it! He'd never felt anything except rage, competition and triumph all his life, but at this moment he felt a soft, gentle sensation winding through him, touching his rapidly beating heart and soothing it, soothing him.

He stood there dumbstruck, watching her, absorbing her tall, aristocratic form through his narrowed eyes and gathered her essence into his wildly beating heart, into his withering soul. Was *this* Tashunka Mani Tu? *She had to be,* his brain screamed back at him. Luanne Yazzie had said she was a young woman, probably in her early thirties, though she appeared ageless. Luanne Somers-Yazzie had seen Tashunka on several occasions and was able to describe her.

If her description was correct, then this was indeed Tashunka Mani Tu.

As Dain stood there, fighting the weakness that was overwhelming him from his labors during the last hour, he *wanted* this woman to be the mysterious, magical Tashunka Mani Tu. Turning his head, he looked back at the hill. His heart beat in startled fear. The white wolf had disappeared! Gasping, pain jerked his head back in her direction. Would she be gone, too? Were these things all figments of his overworked imagination? The last of his hope?

To his shattering relief, the woman still stood like a statue, embraced lovingly by the sunlight, watching him in the silence. Gulping, Dain looked around, afraid that the white wolf was coming to get him. He felt like a frightened eight-year-old again, hiding in that old, smelly closet down in the basement, trying to avoid Mr. Gordon, who was stalking him, waiting to prey on him, just like this damn white wolf was doing.

The weakness forced Dain to lean heavily against the vehicle. He swallowed hard, gulped for air and then looked back at the Indian woman, his eyes widening considerably. The white wolf was now sitting at her side! Both of them were watching him.

"I'll be damned," he rasped, angrily shoving away from the car. He utilized his rage to force his body to work for him. Taking staggering steps, he made a violent gesture with his arm.

"Hey!" he yelled. "Get down here and help me! I'm stuck!" He breathed hard, listening to his biting words as they echoed harshly through the wash. The woman stood a good quarter mile away from him and he wondered what effect his demand would have on her. If she was real and not an apparition, she would respond. Or would she? Dain wasn't sure as he stood, legs spread in the clay to balance himself, his hands held stiffly at his sides, muddy fingers curling into fists.

She was too far away for him to see her expression, but
as his echoing voice enfolded her, Dain saw her sway, as if
struck physically by him. For no discernible reason, he felt
bad in that moment. Hadn't his voice been like a verbal fist?
He tried to shake off his remorse. Too bad if he hurt her.
Old Gordon had used his voice like a sledgehammer against
him all the time when Dain was in that orphanage, that
prison. Still, as he stood there expectedly, he felt sorry. It
was the first time he'd realized his voice could hurt another
person, for he saw her sway, catch herself and plant her feet
apart just a little bit more. He also saw the white wolf leap
from his sitting position beside her into a position of pre-
paredness. Even at this distance, Dain could see the wolf's
hackles standing along his spine, raised upward like por-
cupine quills.

The sound that came back to him was a low, warning
growl from the white wolf. It frightened Dain. His gaze
savagely sought out the woman's serene features. Didn't she
hear him? She must have! So why the hell was she still
standing like a statue, staring at him?

Angry, Dain moved almost drunkenly back to the vehicle.
He collapsed, his spine against the cold, hard metal that
supported him now that his knees refused to. Gripping the
door handle, he breathed raggedly, his gaze never leaving
her tall, proud form. Did angels come dressed as Indians?

He laughed harshly at himself. He *was* hallucinating! His
belief in angels died when he was eight years old and Old
Gordon told him Santa Claus didn't exist. It was then that
Dain had stopped believing in angels, God and everything
else—except himself. He'd known even as a child that the
only thing that would help him survive was a strong, over-
powering belief in himself. He learned that if he trusted in
himself, he could do anything and win at it. And this powerful belief—instilled in him by Old Gordon's attempt to
destroy his childhood—had made him the billionaire he was
today.

Fat lot of good it did him now, Dain thought, a reckless grin slashing across his mouth. He looked down at his muddy, wet pants, then at his truck half-buried in the wash. Suddenly, laughter tunneled up from deep within his chest. He rarely laughed, and now he *wanted* to at the ridiculousness of it all. He was stuck! The laughter rolled out, freeing the fear that filled his chest cavity, easing the constricted, suffocating feeling. The unfamiliar sound left his lips and echoed down the wash. Dain himself didn't believe what he was hearing. He was laughing! Suddenly, he didn't care any longer. The fury he'd felt a moment ago miraculously disappeared beneath the deep, rolling laughter that spilled out of him like golden sunlight. He hadn't realized such joy lived within him. He'd never realized it—until now.

Once his laughter had subsided, a rare, careless smile continued to hover around his mouth. For a second, he felt free—and happy—almost joyous. When had he *ever* felt those emotions? Had this woman cast a spell on him? Was she magical, as Luanne Yazzie had proclaimed when he'd gone to her to ask about the elusive Tashunka Mani Tu?

Disgruntled, Dain gathered his waning energy and forced himself away from the vehicle. His knees felt stronger as he sloshed through the thick mud toward the woman. With each step, he felt strangely empowered, like a cold object that has been warmed by the sun.

Would the wolf charge him? Dain wasn't at all sure, but something whispered to him that *she* had full control over that huge, white beast and wouldn't allow it to attack him. As he drew closer, he could see her face more clearly. The sunlight touched her, making her coppery skin glow with a golden radiance and her expressive brown eyes look almost black. It was her eyes that drew him, mesmerized him. He could swear he saw laughter in them—but he somehow knew she was not laughing at him, but simply relishing some funny cosmic joke known only to herself.

As he approached more closely, he heard her speak firmly

in a language unknown to him. Instantly, the white wolf sat down at her side, thumped his tail in a friendly way and looked up adoringly at her. When she placed her long, thin hand upon the wolf's head, Dain almost felt as if she were reaching out and touching *him!* It was a ridiculous thought, but then, maybe this place was magical, as Luanne had warned him. She'd said Rainbow Butte had been a sacred place to the Hopi and Navajo people for thousands of years. Many ceremonies, powerful ceremonies honoring Mother Earth and the Navajo Yei and Hopi Kachinas, had taken place here.

Dain didn't believe in magic, but he couldn't ignore the powerful thrumming now beating through his chest. His racing heart felt light and an unexpected emotion deluged him as he drew within a hundred feet of the woman. That feeling was hope.

Chapter Three

She was breathtakingly beautiful, like a wild animal trapped inside a woman's body. To Dain, she looked more wolf than woman. He couldn't help but smile as he halted, craned his neck upward and simply absorbed the golden radiance of her features. He saw her full lips curve into a smile of welcome—and he felt an incredible warmth come over him, blanketing his head and shoulders, and falling around him like a thick cloak. A security blanket, Dain decided.

He placed his hands on his hips and grinned back at her, feeling like a reckless kid of nineteen again. The sunlight emphasized the ebony quality of her braided hair, and now that he was closer, he could see the details of her clothes and jewelry. A leather thong hung from her neck and disappeared inside the thick, fuzzy green sweater she wore beneath her white deerskin jacket. He saw a huge piece of turquoise-and-silver jewelry wrapped around her right wrist. Drawn to her hands, which were long and expressive, he vaguely wondered if she was an artist. And then Dain recalled that she was a rug weaver. She was taller than he'd expected; probably around five foot ten or eleven inches. He could tell that despite her ethereal radiance, she was a strong woman who could live in this godforsaken desert and not only survive, but probably thrive.

"I'm stuck," he said by way of greeting, gesturing to his vehicle.

"Yes, you are. In more ways than one, I'd say."

Her low, husky voice flowed across him like a lover's caress. Her eyes sparkled with laughter and even though her mouth never lifted into a smile, Dain *felt* her smile. But he knew she wasn't making fun of him. It was a benign, loving thing he felt.

"I'm looking for a medicine woman. Her name is Ta-shunka Mani Tu. Are you her?"

"What do you want with her?"

Dain saw her expression close up, heard her voice lose some of its embracing warmth. The white wolf pricked up his ears in interest, watching him. "They said she could heal anyone. I need a healing from her."

Her lips lifted, the corners curving slightly. "She doesn't cure anything."

His brows fell and he felt sudden anger. "They said she cured cancer."

Not wanting to show her fear, she lifted her hand in a graceful gesture and said, "The only person who can cure you is yourself."

Erin wrestled within herself. Why did he have to be a white man? Anything but a white man!

Thunderstruck, Dain swayed, caught himself and glared at her. The momentary lightness he'd felt in her presence was smashed beneath the tunneling, annihilating anger that surged through him now. Her low, vibrating words were like a slap in the face.

"Just what the hell are you talking about?"

"I'm not responsible for whether you keep or get rid of the tumor you carry." Panic set in and she felt as if she wanted to run—but she knew her duties as a healer, so she remained, even though every shred of her being wanted to flee from this angry white man.

His eyes narrowed and his mouth became a thin line of fury. "Who the hell do you think you are?" he snarled. "They said you cured anything. Well, I want to be cured." He jabbed a finger up at her. Instantly, the white wolf was on his feet. The animal gave a low, warning growl, the hackles on his neck standing up.

"Maiisoh," Erin murmured in her native tongue, looking down at her wolf, "be patient…"

The animal reluctantly sat down and stopped growling. Nevertheless, his amber eyes never left Dain.

Dain had no idea what the woman had said, but when he saw the wolf sit down, he felt less threatened—for the moment. But when he looked at her, saw how she stood there with such a serene look on her face, his anger rose once again. He was dying and she really didn't give a damn! Fury made his voice vibrate. "They said to bring you groceries and ask you to help me."

Erin saw the dark anger in his narrowed blue eyes and felt it all the way to her soul. He was pale, his brow beaded with small droplets of perspiration. A small piece of her felt compassion toward him, but the rest of her simply wanted to run and disappear—as she had done so many years before, from her own reservation.

"Then the groceries are a payment, not a gift of generosity?"

He stared at her. "Luanne Yazzie said to bring you groceries. Do I give a damn whether they're payment for your services?"

"You should," she said as lightly as possible, gesturing toward the vehicle in the wash. "I was hoping you would come with open hands and an open heart." Her experience told her no white man ever had an open heart. Not ever. They were selfish. Self-serving. Why had this white man been sent to her?

"Is that what you want?" he growled. "You want me on my knees, begging you? Well, lady, I don't beg anyone for *anything*. You got that? I followed the rules of this reservation. I brought groceries. Now I expect something in return."

Her lips curved a little more. She couldn't help but smile at his blatant arrogance and self-righteousness. Fine. She'd treat him like all the rest who came to her with this type of belligerent attitude. "Very well, Mr...?"

"My name is Dain Phillips."

"All right, Dain Phillips, you are approaching me with your groceries to buy something from me? Is that correct?"

Suddenly, Dain didn't trust this woman. He heard the lightness in her voice, as if she was teasing him, and that angered him even more.

"You tell me how many groceries you need to cure me of cancer and I'll make damn sure you're supplied with them."

Laughter bubbled up from her. She saw the dark disapproval on his square face, felt the anger aimed at her. She countered his anger with her compassion for his situation.

"I have never been approached with such an offer," she admitted, trying to hide the slight smile that pulled at the corners of her mouth.

"Well," he said waspishly, "though you find this so damned funny, you still haven't told me who *you* are. Are you Tashunka Mani Tu?"

"I am many things to many people," she replied, sobering. Over the years, her fame as a healer had traveled to other reservations. Lakota people who came to see her for help always called her Tashunka Mani Tu, which meant Walks With Wolves. "Who do you need me to be for you?"

"I don't *need* you to be *anything* for me," he retorted.

"Then you must leave, for I cannot help you heal yourself." She turned around.

"Wait!" Dain shouted, lifting his arm.

Erin hesitated and looked across her shoulder. "I cannot heal you. You can only heal yourself, Dain Phillips. Groceries will not force me to support your desire to be well. You come like the coyote, the trickster. Groceries mean only one thing to you—a source of payment for services rendered. I was hoping the groceries were a *gift* given from your heart. A gift without expectations attached to it." In her heart, she prayed he would leave.

"Now hold on just a minute," Dain yelled, struggling up the slick, clay bank as she walked away from him, surrounded by sheep. When he climbed out of the wash, she turned toward him, her hand on the staff. The white wolf was at her side, watching him through wary amber eyes.

Breathing hard, Dain moved brokenly toward her, his legs visibly trembling from the sudden exertion. "Just a minute," he rasped, gesturing at her with his index finger. "Just who the hell do you think you are, lady? What right do you have to judge me or these damn groceries I brought to you?"

Erin felt her heart twinge as a feeling of compassion stole through her. She studied the man before her. Dain Phillips was at least six foot two and weighed close to two hundred pounds. He was obviously in good muscular, if not athletic, condition. He wore a bright red wool jacket over a dark blue denim shirt and tan pants that were splattered with red clay. Once again she felt his desperation and understood it better than he could at the moment.

Calmly, she lifted her hand. "I have not judged you. You have judged yourself."

"What are you talking about?"

She allowed his anger to bounce harmlessly off her. His blue eyes snapped with fury and his otherwise nicely shaped mouth was a thin line of bitterness. "You brought groceries to buy something from me that I cannot give you."

"Dammit, take the stupid groceries then! I don't care what the hell you do with them!"

"There are two elderly Navajo women who live near me. They have no transportation, and with the winter coming on, they can use the food."

"Fine," he rasped, "they can go to them. Now what about you? What's your name? You haven't said whether you're a medicine woman, yet."

"Some people call me Asdzaan Maiisoh. That is Navajo for Wolf Woman. Some call me Tashunka Mani Tu—Lakota for Walks With Wolves. Others call me Erin Wolf, the name listed on documents when I was born on the Eastern Cherokee Reservation in North Carolina. The federal government refused to accept my given Cherokee name, Ai Gvhdi Waya, so my mother chose the name Erin, which is Gaelic, from Ireland. Unlike most white names, which have no meaning, the Irish give as much importance to what a name means as we do. Erin means peace." She frowned. "You may call me anything you like, so long as it's not derogatory." No white man respected Indians and she did not expect it from him.

Ignoring her last comment, Dain studied the woman before him. Peace. Yes, he could see why she was named for that. For a moment, he hated the fact she seemed so damn calm and serene when he felt almost on the edge of losing not only his composure, but his control as well. Her face reflected an inner peace and he wanted to take that from her for himself. The sunlight bathed her, gave her coppery skin a beautiful radiance that was almost unearthly, he thought as he continued to stare at her.

He was mildly aware of the sheep bleating now and then, and the fact that the animals had encircled him where he stood. Out of the corner of his eye, he saw them nibbling at sparse strands of grass sticking out of the red sand, and the sight, combined with the feel of the sun on his back, made some of the inner chill within him abate.

"I'm not very good with Indian names," he began, "so bear with me as I refer to you as Erin Wolf."

Her eyes sparkled with silent laughter. "It will take three days before the wash dries enough for you to drive your car out of there." She gazed up at the clear, light blue sky. "The Navajo rain *yei* have been kind to you. It's not going to rain for at least another week, so you'll be able to retrieve your car."

"What's a *yei?*"

"Navajo for god."

"I don't believe in such things."

She smiled.

Dain glared at her. "Well, what do I do?"

"I'd suggest that you walk back to the road and hitchhike back into Many Farms. Go home, Dain Phillips. What you seek I do not have." Never had she meant her words more than now.

He stared at her as panic set in, eating away at his anger, his strength. "But…" He floundered, opening his hands. "But Alfred and Luanne Yazzie said you've healed many Navajo of all kinds of disease. Why are you sending me away if you can cure me?"

In that moment, Erin saw not a man standing before her, but a scared child. The image of a tousle-haired, freckle-faced little boy in a pair of coveralls and a red-and-white-striped T-shirt crying his heart out flashed before her eyes. The boy stood in the highly polished hallway of some huge, old home and her intuition told her that what he felt was utter abandonment.

Gently, she whispered, "I am not abandoning you, Dain Phillips. You are abandoning yourself." Shaken by what she'd seen and felt, Erin suddenly felt guilty. Her past experience with one white man was coloring her perception of this man. Her parents had taught her that skin color meant nothing—but she knew differently. Inwardly, she wrestled with her own dark prejudice.

Dain was shaken by her words. How the hell did she know that what he was feeling so sharply was abandonment? Flattening his lips, he yelled, "I'm here, damn it! I came in good faith! I bought the stupid groceries I'll give to those two old women! Now, you *owe* me, damn it! You can't send me away. I won't go!"

Erin raised her brows as her heart wrenched in despair. "You won't go?"

"No."

Prejudice stared her fully in the face. The wounded part of herself screamed, *No, go away!* Clenching her hands at her sides, Erin realized the Great Spirit was testing her. She had been tested before and nearly died. This was a test of faith, a trial by fire of the worst sort. Taking in a deep, halting breath, she said, "Then I guess you had better go back to your car, get whatever luggage you have and come with me."

Nonplussed, Dain just stared at her for a moment. "Where are we going?"

"To my hogan." She pointed toward a set of low, rounded red hills in the distance. "We are about five miles from my home. If you are determined to stay, then you need to have enough clothes—and food."

He was feeling weak again, and hot. The fever was beginning to boil up from his toes, calves, and into his thighs. Soon Dain would begin to feel light-headed and he'd have to lie down until the fever passed. He saw Erin watching him expectantly. There was no way he could carry anything five miles in his present condition. Anger boiled through him. He'd be damned before he'd tell her he couldn't make the trek by himself, or that he needed help.

"Just tell me where you live. I'll get there," he snapped.

Erin whispered, "What does it cost you to ask for help?" Her soft, compassion-filled words caught him off guard.

Still, he snapped his mouth shut and glared. "I said I'd get there. Even if I have to crawl, I'll get there."

"You stopped asking for help when you were eight years old."

Shock bolted through him and his eyes widened at her words. For a moment, he hated her for knowing the truth deep inside him. And then he realized there was no way she could have such intimate knowledge of him. His mind raced for answers, but logical solutions eluded him. Dropping his chin, he stared at his muddy, soaked hiking boots.

"Asking for help is natural," Erin continued, her voice wary. "Even animals, when they are sick, will go to a healthy animal to be licked, protected and cared for. Humans are no different." She forced a gentle smile for his benefit. "Perhaps that was beaten out of you long ago, but if you want to heal yourself, you must learn to ask for help."

Pride wouldn't allow him to speak. He drew himself up to his full height, his hands resting tensely on his hips. "I see your game. Your arrogance precedes you, Ms. Wolf—or whoever the hell you want me to think you are. I see through your games. You're no different than a businessman or a board of directors at a corporation. You're manipulating me. Trying to take my power away from me. Well, it's not going to happen. It'll be a cold day in hell when I ask you or anyone for help, believe me."

Shrugging, Erin said, "Fine, believe what you want to believe, Dain." She gestured to the road, mostly washed away by the recent rain. "Your life has been in your hands at all times. I do not wish to take anything from you, but rather, invest it back into you. But you don't see that yet. Follow these tracks. You will go past a series of hills, and then, down below the mesa, is my hogan. I must continue to walk with my sheep so they may find enough to eat today. I will be back at the hogan near sunset." She hoped he would never show up.

Dain watched in disbelief as she turned and spoke in a

foreign language to the white wolf. Instantly, the wolf was up on his feet, herding the sheep along the wash, where there were new sprigs of grass to eat. At first Dain hated Erin Wolf. And then, as he felt the fever and weakness begin to eat away at his anger, he almost shouted out for help. But he didn't. To hell with her!

He stood his ground on locked knees as he watched her disappear from sight down a draw that led into the huge gulch about half a mile away. So what should he do? Turning, he looked at the truck. Should he walk back to the highway and hitch a ride back to Many Farms and leave? Go back to the East Coast? And do what? Die?

Shoving his fingers through his short black hair, he glared in the direction Erin and her sheep had disappeared. What an enigma she was! She'd said she couldn't heal him—that he could heal himself. Snorting violently, Dain turned around and began to clump back to his vehicle. Hell of a thing! Well, no doctor had ever told him that. Just the opposite. They all said they couldn't help him with their drugs, radiation or fancy, million-dollar pieces of equipment. And though some may have inferred they could help eradicate his tumor, they all eventually found out they couldn't.

As he slipped and slid down the wall of the wash, Dain cursed out loud. The words echoed off the walls.

As he trudged drunkenly back to the vehicle and jerked open the door, he felt the fever draining him, as it always did. Out of breath due to his weakness and the six-thousand-foot altitude, he climbed into the truck and laid his head back on the seat, closed his eyes and literally trembled. Exhaustion claimed him, all his anger destroyed in the wake of the fever. He hated the fact that the tumor was controlling him. All his life he'd worked to make sure nothing *ever* controlled him again, and yet this damn tumor was doing exactly that.

Erin's oval face with its high cheekbones danced gently behind his closed eyes. Her light brown eyes danced with such life in their depths—life he wanted for himself. Sitting there, feeling like a rag doll that had had all the stuffing knocked out of it, Dain clung to her serene, beautiful features. Her image haunted him and for a moment, in his fevered state, he wondered if she were really an angel in disguise.

She'd admitted she couldn't heal him. He had to heal himself. How? Intrigued by her challenge, his mind bounced over their conversation. During the last year all he'd heard was how doctors could heal many things—just not his illness. So why was she saying he could heal himself, that she couldn't do it for him?

As he lay weakly against the seat with the warmth of the sun just beginning to strike the top of the truck, Dain tried to understand what Erin had said. If healers didn't heal, just what the hell *did* they do? Medical doctors healed with their shots, their drugs and their expensive equipment. If she was who she said she was, he knew she'd healed others of terrible, encroaching diseases. Why would she lie to him then?

Barely opening his eyes as he felt trickles of sweat winding their way down his temples, Dain cursed. She was an arrogant bitch. Oh, he'd met her type back in the boardrooms and halls of power around the world. Erin didn't fool him. What had thrown him off guard was the fact that she was Indian and a shepherd.

But a voice, barely heard, niggled at him. Was she *really* arrogant? Wouldn't arrogance, true arrogance, preclude her saying something like, "Of course I can heal you of your brain tumor"? And had she said that? No.

"Dammit," he snarled, forcing himself to sit up. Reaching for a thermos filled with water, he unscrewed the cap with trembling hands.

Okay, so maybe she wasn't arrogant. At least, not in the true sense of the word. She'd promised him *nothing*. She'd thrown his disease back into his lap, into his hands, which no doctor anywhere in the world had *ever* done to him.

Something wasn't right, Dain decided as he poured himself some water. He gulped it down and poured some more. Soon the dryness in his mouth abated and he stashed the thermos away. Lying back, he sighed raggedly. The fever was eating at him, making him feel weak as a baby.

He opened his eyes. How the hell had she known about him being abandoned as an eight-year-old? How? Stymied, he tried to explain it with the kind of logic that had made him billions. She lived out in the middle of a godforsaken desert where there weren't any phone or electric lines. And besides, he made damn sure that his life story wasn't privy to any news media, having had things about it sealed up permanently through court injunctions. No, Erin couldn't have known about his young, miserable life—but she had. *How?*

"Damn her," he muttered weakly, closing his eyes again. Because he didn't have a logical answer for her intimate knowledge, he felt a little frightened of her. That was power over him, as far as he was concerned. And yet the look in her eyes when she'd shared that with him had touched him as nothing ever had. He'd seen such love and pity for him in her eyes. He hated pity in any form and he had wanted to hate her in that moment, but the feeling wouldn't form within him. If anything—and Dain fought this feeling violently—he'd sensed he could trust her with his life.

It was a silly, crazy thought brought on by the fever, he rationalized. Or some stupid hallucination of hope that would dissolve when the fever left him in a couple of hours. Trust! Yes, she had a trustworthy face. He liked her voice, even if he didn't like what she'd said to him. It was a low, husky voice laced with honeyed warmth that was undisguised, untainted by anything except…what? Truth.

Well, here he was again with that word and Erin Wolf. Truth and trust. His damnable heart, the heart of that eight-year-old boy, wanted to trust her and believe her truth. The man did not. Not now. Not ever.

So what was he going to do? Hitchhike back to the highway, stay here with the truck or go to her hogan? The prideful part of him said to leave and walk to the highway. The rational part said stay with the truck for the next three days, wait for the ground to dry out sufficiently and then drive back to Many Farms. He certainly had enough groceries in the back to live off of in the meantime.

But his heart whispered that he should go to her hogan and leave everything in the vehicle.

Dain didn't know what to do, so he slept as the fever ate away more and more of his limited supply of energy. He couldn't even think straight. He was crazy to think of going to her hogan. He wasn't going to give the arrogant woman the pleasure of showing up on her doorstep. His pride wouldn't let him.

As he spiraled into darkness, he heard what he thought was singing. It was a woman singing. It was Erin, he realized from the dark embrace of sleep. The song, soft and gentle, was in an Indian language. As he lay there, feeling very warm and safe, the song embraced him and he sighed. Yes, it was a lullaby. He had no idea what the words were, but the song was so beautiful that it brought tears to his tightly shut eyes.

In his sleep, he felt the warmth of tears oozing from the corners of his eyes, trickling down his face. The song was warm and husky, filled with love and hope. And though he had no idea what the lyrics meant, it didn't matter. He *felt* their meaning, felt it vibrating through him, touching his walled-off heart and wrapping him in a sensation he'd never experienced before.

A part of him panicked because he never wanted the song to end, because it fed him, nurtured him like the arms of the mother he'd never known, and he felt as if Erin were invisibly with him, cradling him against her tall, strong and protective body. He swore he could feel his head resting against her full breasts, hear the beating of her passionate heart, which throbbed with such vital life. Feel her arms move protectively around him, drawing him in.

Yes, he was being held and rocked gently as she sang to him. Dain knew she was there even if he couldn't see her in the inky blackness. He could smell the odor of wool, taste the sunlight that had touched her skin, and he heard the lulling bleat of sheep in the background.

A broken sigh slipped from him as he relaxed within her invisible arms. He felt her compassion and it soothed his fevered body and gave him a sense of peacefulness he'd never known. The song continued to flow through him, touching him with the lightness of a feather. For the first time in his life, he felt safe. Safe! The sensation was wonderful to Dain, and he surrendered to it—and to her.

The lullaby continued—haunting, melodic and healing. As he moved deeper and deeper into the darkness of sleep, Dain let go of all his anger, his fears and, finally, his anxieties. He slept the sleep of a baby who was protected by a mother who loved him, a mother who would protect him—always.

Chapter Four

One step in front of the other, one step in front of the other...

Dain kept repeating that litany as he forced his foot to lift, move forward and then land on the damp clay ground beneath him. It was dusk. An all-pervading silence flowed across the land as the sun's rays withdrew from the desert. Looking up, he saw the remnants of the fiery red-and-orange sunset touch the long, wispy clouds high above him.

Those clouds had reminded him of Erin's hair. Even though it had been plaited, he knew that her hair was long, thick and flowing just like those reddish clouds that moved slowly across the darkening vault of the sky.

Trying to take his focus off his own misery, which was considerable, he kept his gaze locked skyward as night descended. Never had he seen stars look so close, or glimmer so brightly, as they now did. He turned to see the bare outline of Rainbow Butte, behind him in the distance. Dain's mouth thinned momentarily as he resumed his slow progress. This land had a raw, primeval beauty about it—just as Erin did.

Erin. Tashunka Mani Tu. Ai Gvhdi Waya. Asdzaan Mai-isoh. Maybe Luanne Yazzie had been right: the medicine woman was more walking dream, a waking miracle…an angel, perhaps, in human form. Many names for a woman who was many things to those who needed her. He sighed. He wasn't sure of anything anymore. When he'd awoken at sunset, he'd felt more rested than he could ever recall being. He'd slept all day! Twelve hours! At first, he'd thought that impossible, because he'd met her at sunrise. But the sun was edging toward the western horizon when he awoke, and that convinced him.

He must have needed the sleep. But the real miracle was the fact that he'd slept without being woken by that white wolf nightmare that always stalked him. Dain had never been able to take naps or sleep during daylight. His days were spent busily plotting new strategies to take over yet another corporation somewhere in the world. His waking hours were war-game hours, and he felt sleep was a waste of time.

All the anger he'd felt toward Erin had disappeared once he'd slowly come out of his protective cocoon of sleep. As he sat there in the truck, which was still warmed from the sun's last rays, he felt two things. First, that he had no anger in him—at least, he couldn't feel any—and second, that he was going to take her up on her offer and walk five miles to her hogan. Her words, softly spoken, still echoed in his head as he walked between two low, rounded hills. *What does it cost you to ask for help?*

With a snort, Dain shoved his hands into the pockets of his leather jacket as he concentrated on staying upright. The ruts from vehicles were nearly nonexistent, and with darkness deepening quickly, the landscape was now becoming indecipherable—like that twilight zone he usually slept in.

He didn't like dusk. It bothered him. Hell, night bothered

him. He felt the calves of his legs beginning to knot and protest with fatigue. Five miles was a damned long way in his condition, but there was something goading, prodding him to move forward in the autumn chill of that high desert plateau.

Somewhere off in the distance of the embracing night, Dain heard a coyote howl—a lonely, forlorn sound. That was how he felt—alone. Abandoned. He compressed his lips, bowed his head and tried to ignore the burning pain in his feet and calves. At least the fever was gone, and for that he was grateful. All he had to contend with was a body that wasn't any longer totally under his control. Because of the tumor, his left leg had a tendency to become tired. His left foot would drag, as it was doing now, and if he didn't re- member to deliberately lift it higher with each step, he would trip and fall.

Asking for help is natural. Even animals, when they are sick, will go to a healthy animal to be licked, protected and cared for. Humans are no different.

Drawing in a deep, painful breath of chilled air, Dain saw his breath crystalizing into a white wisp as it escaped his lips. He had to walk up a slight incline, which for a healthy person would have been easy. But for him it was pure, un- adulterated torture. His legs were getting rubbery. Soon, if he didn't rest, he would fall on his butt. A smile slashed across his deeply shadowed face. Wouldn't his associates laugh at that? He'd been very careful not to let anyone know of his medical condition. When he convened daily strategy meetings, he appeared strong, incorrigible and indestructible to his people.

With a little laugh, Dain halted, threw back his head and gazed upward again. The stars were magnificent here. They shined and twinkled like expensive, multifaceted diamonds he'd seen at DeBeers's operation in Africa, where the stones were mined. The darkness wasn't threatening to him, for some reason. As he stood just below the crest of the hill, he smiled inwardly. His fingers felt warm inside the pockets of his leather jacket. The temperature had dipped drastically when the sun went down, yet he felt amazingly warm under the circumstances. Probably because he'd walked so far.

What does it cost you to ask for help?

His dark brows drew together and he looked down at his mud-encrusted boots. He'd been avoiding the answer every time his mind—or perhaps more accurately, his conscience—asked him that question.

Asking for help is natural. Even animals, when they are sick, will go to a healthy animal to be licked, protected and cared for. Humans are no different.

Grimly, Dain stood there, feeling the soft, black velvet of the night embrace him like a lover. He turned back toward the eastern horizon to see if he could still see Rainbow Butte, but couldn't. Another coyote howled and the land seemed to vibrate, carrying the animal's lonely cry straight to him, straight to his heart. Yes, all right, he *was* lonely in a way that ate at him like acid. And no amount of money, no number of corporate raids, no high-stakes international chess games played to increase his empire, had ever filled that gnawing emptiness deep inside his chest.

The coyote's howl only emphasized how alone Dain felt. Looking around, he chuckled with wry amusement. Well, he sure as hell *was* alone. Wouldn't his office staff howl with laughter if they could see him standing on a high, godforsaken desert plateau out in the middle of nowhere? And they'd roll on the floor with mirth if they ever found out that a woman had made him bend his own inflexible rules.

Well, he hadn't exactly asked for help. She had said to come to her hogan. He would do that—provided he could find it. Perhaps she'd been wrong about the distance. Maybe five miles was really ten. Women were never any good with distance anyway, he'd found out long ago. Still, as he stood there in the darkness, Dain enjoyed looking at the coverlet of the sky filled with incredible diamondlike stars dancing, twinkling as if giving a private show of their beauty to the appreciative visitor who looked up at them from below.

Where he lived, he could barely see stars—just the brightest ones. Here he saw thousands more. The Milky Way wound across the sky like a silent, radiant river of tumbling stars, a magical path. Where did it lead? Dain laughed harshly at himself for his fanciful meanderings. Only a child would see that swath of stars as a path. Only a child would wonder where that path led. Well, his childhood was long gone and he was glad of it.

The burning, cramping pain in his legs had abated enough for him to continue his journey—his *adventure,* he corrected himself. The temperature had nose-dived, probably hovering in the low forties. As he walked, the song he'd heard Erin sing wound gently through him. Without realizing it, he began to hum the tune under his breath. Amazingly, as he crested the incline, it made his legs feel less cramped.

Halting, he looked around the endless, dark landscape that now seamlessly melded with the unseen horizon and the dark blanket of the night. The only way Dain knew where sky ended and land began was to look where the twinkling stars dropped off. He was pleased that he had enough of his own rational logic left to figure that much out. Frowning, he looked around. The vehicle tracks led down—nearly straight down. He was standing on a mesa. Vaguely, he recalled Erin saying she lived at the bottom of one.

Still, where was he? Where was her hogan? He'd seen hogans as he'd driven toward Chinle, one of the major towns on the Navajo Reservation. They were octagonal, made with long, rough pieces of timber, with mud packed between the logs. The roof of the hogan, from what he could observe, was nothing more than dried red clay. Who would live in such a primitive structure? And yet, he'd seen hogans everywhere. They melted into the surrounding soft pastels of the high desert, the reddish clay the same color as the mesas and bluffs so prominent in this part of the reservation.

Squinting, he swept his eyes from left to right. Was there a hogan down there somewhere? Dain thought he saw a glimmer of light as he viewed the darkness below him. Were his eyes playing tricks upon him? And then he remembered that he'd seen no electric poles out here. So if Erin's hogan was nearby, how could he see it if she had no electricity? No light outside her home to guide him?

Frustration ate at him, but the anger, usually simmering just beneath the surface, did not arise with it. Dain rubbed his tired eyes with his fingers and then looked again.

Yes, there. He saw it again—a faint glimmer of light far below him, more than a mile away. Much more. And then the glimmer disappeared. Muttering a curse, Dain rubbed his eyes, and looked again. The glimmer had returned, barely discernible in the distance. He stood there, unsure. Yet what choice did he have? He knew the temperature would dip below freezing tonight, and his thin, leather bombardier jacket wasn't enough to keep him warm. As the tumor had aggressively grown larger in his brain, he'd discovered his body got colder much more easily. The last six months, colds and flu had been frequent in the New York area, and Dr. Sarah had worried that if he caught one, it would develop into pneumonia—and pull from him what little reserves he had to fight off the tumor.

Right now, he wished for a hot cup of coffee, a warm fire and something over his head to protect him from the falling temperature. What if that wasn't Erin's hogan down there? What if his eyes and brain were playing tricks on him, as they had many times before?

There was no choice, so he didn't stand there waffling for long, but headed toward the faint, yellow light in the inky darkness. The slope was steep, and he threw out his hands to balance himself. There were many pebbles and fist-size rocks all around him that he couldn't see. His muscles screamed in protest as he leaned back to adjust to the steepening incline, feeling like a trapeze artist on a high wire with no net below him. Dain couldn't afford to fall. It was the last thing he needed.

As he carefully made his way down the dark incline, he felt his stomach roll once in warning. Groaning out loud, he muttered, ''No! Not now!'' He tried to keep all his concentration on where he was placing his thick-soled hiking boots. Without fail, nausea stalked him nightly—again thanks to the tumor, which affected the vagus nerve leading directly to his stomach. It was a good thing he hadn't eaten anything. Once again, Dain laughed at himself, the sound a bark that echoed eerily through the darkness around him.

Hell, he couldn't eat, because all he'd bought was canned food and he didn't have a can opener. There was a lot of beef, too, but it was raw, and he wasn't hungry enough to force it down. He didn't like sushi, so he imagined raw meat for dinner before he started this little stroll across the desert would have been out of the question. If his damned stomach wanted to revolt, there was nothing that could come up. He smiled ruthlessly as he inched his way downward. For once, the tumor was going to be cheated of its nightly aggression on him.

For nearly half an hour, he descended the washed-out road. Getting to more level ground, Dain saw the yellow glimmer become more steady. It reminded him of his other home—in Wood's Hole, Massachusetts, near the sea. The coast guard station there had a huge lighthouse that sent its powerful, white beam out into the dark ocean to warn ships that land was nearby, and to beware. Well, that little yellow light—whoever it belonged to—was his lighthouse in the night.

The cramping in his lower legs became so severe that he groaned and fell to his knees. He'd have to take time out to massage them in order to get them to work for him again. Sitting down, he rubbed one calf gingerly, and then the other. The nausea became worse. Cursing, Dain knew he was going to vomit. He hated that more than anything.

His mouth began to water in warning. With effort, he rolled over onto his hands and knees. Vomiting was a foul thing. His fingers dug into the damp sand as he tried to anchor himself, to prepare himself. It was impossible. The instant his stomach clenched, he heaved violently. The sounds were terrible.

Exhausted and dizzy, he continued to grip the damp earth. His breath was ragged and his mouth burned with bile. He desperately wanted water to rinse the terrible taste out of his mouth. Sweat beaded along his forehead as the white plumes of breath—mist caused by his gasps—encircled him. The pain in his stomach was severe. Moaning, he drew himself back, resting against his heels, his fingers clawing against his hard thighs.

Why now? Why this bad? His mind spun with questions and no answers. Hell, he'd never vomited as long or as much even when he'd eaten. Maybe that was the key: keep something in his stomach. Hell of a way to learn the lesson, Dain decided. He weakly lifted his head and spat. Oh, if only he'd brought along that thermos of water. Why hadn't he thought ahead? This wasn't like him. He always had everything planned out well in advance.

On the heels of the nausea and vomiting came the headache. Only this wasn't a common, ordinary headache. Groaning, Dain staggered to his feet. He was dizzy, off balance, and he weaved around like a drunk for more than a minute, trying desperately to find his center of gravity. Arms flailing, he finally succeeded in standing still, his legs spread apart. He knew he was in trouble now.

The vomiting and nausea had been a red flag waving in front of his unfocused eyes. Sweat trickled down into them, making them burn. Angrily, he swiped at his eyes with the back of his hand. He had to get to Erin's hogan—or else. How stupid could he be? Where the hell was his sense of survival? As he stumbled forward, his gaze focused on the glimmering yellow light in the distance. He could tell from the first symptoms of his headache that the pain was going to send him right over the edge this time.

The headaches were the effect of the tumor. Why hadn't he thought ahead? He got one every night about this time, but by now, he was usually locked away in his home, alone. There was pain medication he could take to dull some of it, but the drugs never really stopped the worst of the pain. Not by a long shot. This time, he was without medication. He'd stupidly left it back in the truck, too—along with his food.

Desperation fueled his need to reach the hogan. He didn't even know if it was a hogan he saw or if his brain and senses were conjuring that light out of the desert darkness. Dr. Sarah had warned him that the tumor would create hallucinations that seemed as real as he was. This wasn't the time for that to happen. It just couldn't! Dain pushed his body to its maximum. His calves screamed in protest as he began an awkward dogtrot toward the light. His energy was bleeding out of him, eaten up by the headache that was now beginning to throb like hammers inside his brain. He felt his blood throbbing, as if there was too much of it contained within the walls of his skull.

He fell, rolling over and over. Gasping, he shoved himself to his feet, disoriented for a moment before turning around in a panic. There! Yes, there was the yellow light, faint but present. He started again in that direction, his steps ragged and broken. His mouth was so dry, he'd kill for a drink of water right now. He kept pumping his arms forward and back, forward and back, forcing his weakening body to run when all it wanted to do was collapse. No! He would not yield to it! He would not give up or give in, damn it! The yellow light drew closer and closer, a beacon in the night urging him to push beyond the physical barriers created by the tumor and to make it to the hogan.

The throbbing nearly felled him. Dain staggered, his hand gripping his pounding head. The heat, the fire inside his skull made him feel as if he were a boiler that was going

to implode on itself. Groaning, he clenched his teeth, and
with his hands pressed hard against his brow, he began to
run. It wasn't much of a run, more a broken, jagged stride
on wobbly knees. He wasn't sure if he could hold himself
upright any longer, since his legs were screaming for rest.
But something—something intangible inside his chest—
pushed him forward. He reeled, stumbled and fell, but staggered once again to his feet. His eyes never left that yellow
light, which was becoming a more sure, more powerful beacon to him.

He saw it! A hogan, barely outlined by the yellow light,
probably less than a quarter of a mile away. Rasping for
breath, Dain reeled drunkenly. Yes! It was a hogan! Erin's
home! A powerful feeling surged up through his chest as he
stood there, weaving from side to side, the pain almost fell-
ing him once again. And then a sharp, stabbing pain, as if
someone had driven a nail directly into the center of his
head, knocked his feet right out from beneath him.

No! Damn it, no! Dain felt the mud squish between his
hands as he fell, landing in a puddle. The mud coated him,
coated his face. Now he was wet, muddy and mad as hell.
Grunting, he forced himself to his feet. The cold, icy water
dripped off his hands, off his jaw. Clenching his teeth, his
anger hard and strong within him, he forced his legs to
move. Damn this tumor! He wasn't about to let it stop him
from reaching his goal this time.

As he approached the hogan, which sat on a slight hill,
he balled up his fist. The door was made of rough lumber,
severely weathered by hot desert temperatures during sum-
mer, blizzards during winter. Without hesitation, he reeled
forward. Instead of knocking, he fell against the door. His
breath was torn from him, white wisps escaping his contorted mouth. He felt his knees giving out and he leaned
heavily on the door, slapping his hand against it. Surely
someone was inside! What if it wasn't Erin's hogan? What

if it belonged to some old Navajo who wasn't going to answer the door out of fear?

So many wild thoughts, jumbled and distorted by the pain in his head, ran through him. *Please open up. Just open up.*

Dain heard the doorknob turn, a creaky, rusty sound. Shoving himself away from the door, anchoring his hands on the jambs, he waited.

Erin opened the door and her stomach clenched. Dain Phillips stood there in front of her like a muddy apparition. His face was smeared with red clay, his hair plastered to his skull. The wild, dark look in his eyes told her much. He was wet, exhausted and sick. She stepped aside.

"Come in," she invited, her voice belying her disbelief. He'd made it to her hogan. What was she going to do? Erin knew what was right, but it didn't give her solace.

He stood there for a moment, staring at her. He'd never seen her this close before. A sweet scent wafted out of the hogan, one he was unfamiliar with. She wore a dark red velvet, long-sleeved blouse and matching skirt, with a silver concha belt around her waist. To say she looked beautiful didn't do her justice. Her hair, that gorgeous hair, was unplaited, and hung in thick ebony sheets about her oval features, down across her proud shoulders and across her breasts.

"I..." He swallowed hard. Weakly, he gestured at himself. "I'm a little muddy...."

She nodded. "I can see that."

"And you still want me to—"

"I said you were welcome. Come in."

The words flowed like cooling water across his raw, frayed nerves. How many people in his world would let him come into their home like this? And could he even walk? Dain was suddenly afraid that he'd take one step forward and fall flat on his arrogant face right in front of her. He didn't want to do that—he had to salvage something of his tattered pride. So he called up the last of his reserve, straightened a little, threw back his shoulders and took that step into the warmth and serenity of her hogan.

Even though the headache was blinding, he stood on the dry, hard earth within the hogan and looked around as she quietly closed the door behind him. It was warm, deliciously warm, and the chill began to ease from him. In the center of the huge, rounded structure was a large, rectangular wood stove. The stovepipe went straight up to the pinnacle of the roof. The only light was provided by the three kerosene lamps placed on dressers, which sat against the mud-and-timber walls.

Everywhere he looked, he saw Navajo rugs covering the raw earth the hogan was built upon. They were beautiful rugs of many colors and with many designs that he knew meant something to the Navajo, but not to him. He saw the white wolf lying on a rug near a huge wooden loom that was at least six feet tall and four feet wide.

"You make rugs?" It was a stupid question, he realized, too late. Of course she did. Not only had Luanne told him about her skill in rug weaving, he could see the many colors of wool lying near where she worked.

"Yes, every fall and winter I weave a rug." Erin hesitated before reaching out to take his coat. "Would you like to shed your coat and boots here?" Somehow she must put her own prejudice away—once and for all! But she felt as if a war was going on inside her.

He was mesmerized by the graceful gesture of her hand. "Oh…sure," he said finally before he awkwardly got rid of the coat. She took it, opened the door and placed it outside the hogan to dry in the night air.

When Dain bent down to untie his boots, he pitched forward. There wasn't even time for him to get angry at his weakness. He crumpled like a felled ox and found himself lying on the floor. When he painfully turned his face to one side, he noticed some unspoken feeling in her dark eyes as she crouched down next to him.

"Do not move," she counseled, and lifted her palm and placed it on his sweaty brow.

Dain had raised his hands to stop her, but something told him to lie back, relax and stop fighting. He was exhausted. The pain in his head was making his vision blur again. Mesmerized, he watched her closed expression open up as she lightly ran her hand across his hair. It was such a brief, grazing touch that he wondered for a moment if she had actually touched him or if it was his imagination. Whether she did or not, for that instant, the pain disappeared. And then, as she rested her hand in her lap, observing him in silence, the pounding returned.

"Your pain is great," she murmured.

He tried to lift his head, but was too fatigued. With a groan, he muttered, "I left my pain meds in the car." The warmth of the wood fire continued to permeate him as he held her dark, wise gaze. Her velvet skirt brushed his hand. It had to be his imagination, but he swore he felt his fingers tingle where they made contact with her clothing.

"I see...."

Her words came back to him starkly. *What does it cost you to ask for help?* He lay there gazing up at her like young children would stare at someone that they were in complete awe of.

"I hate drugs," he muttered. "I'm supposed to take them all the time, but I don't."

"Why?"

"Because they make me feel like I'm not in control of myself, some damn drug is. I don't like it." He watched her expression grow thoughtful.

"You do not want anyone to have control over you?" Wasn't that ironic, Erin thought. A white man had controlled her, taken her power from her, beaten her until she almost died because she refused to let him rip her selfhood away from her.

"Not ever."

Erin saw tears in his eyes. "Are you crying because you're in pain?" Oddly, some of the fear she felt in his presence became muted. This white man was not her ex-husband, Tom Cramer. She'd never seen tears in Tom's eyes. She'd always seen them in her own, instead.

Dain quickly forced the tears away. He blinked rapidly and avoided her knowing gaze. "I'm not crying," he said, more harshly than he intended. He saw his words, which were like weapons meant to hurt her, strike home. She swayed visibly for just a moment, rocked by his angry response to her gentle question, and the riveting pain worsened. He couldn't hide it for much longer.

Asking for help is natural. Even animals, when they are sick, will go to a healthy animal to be licked, protected and cared for. Humans are no different.

"Look, in a few minutes I'm going to start howling and screaming out of control. I can't help it. Maybe," he joked weakly, "if you have a gun you can put it to my head and put me out of my misery?"

Erin's heart throbbed with fear. Tom had put a gun to her head at one time. She could still taste the terror she had known that night. Forcing herself to focus on the man in her arms, she whispered, "Is that a roundabout way of asking for help?"

He lay there, studying her face. "I—I guess it is," he agreed, stumbling over the admission.

"The Great Spirit has said that if we ask for whatever it is we need, it will be provided." Erin slowly rose to her feet. She had not asked for this white man. Bitterly, she knew it was time for her to mend the deepest of all her wounds and that the Great Spirit had sent this sick man to test her. As far from civilization as she lived, she had not stayed far enough away. As Erin bent and removed one of his muddy boots, she laughed to herself. Leaving the Quallah Reservation, her birthplace and reservation, had been a terrible price to pay to leave Tom and her sordid marriage behind. Easing off the second boot, Erin remembered how she'd hoped that hiding out on a reservation literally out in the middle of nowhere, would keep her from encountering white men ever again. She had deceived herself.

With each touch of her hands, that firm, knowing touch, Dain felt his panic diminish. He felt silly lying here, damn near incapacitated, while she took off his boots. He'd never have allowed this to happen back home. No one knew of his nightly headaches, or heard him shrieking like a wounded animal as he gripped his drawn-up knees to his chest and rocked, just trying to get through another wave of pain.

"There," Erin said huskily, standing. She came back and extended her hand to him. "Can you come over to the fire? It's warmer and you're shivering."

Almost blinded by the pain, Dain reached out. His hand was damp, dirty and trembling. Her fingers were long, warm and strong as they wrapped around his larger hand. He was amazed at her strength as she helped him stand. He wavered, but she moved to his side like a bulwark to steady him, her arm going around his waist.

"Lean on me."

He did, without anger, without embarrassment. He was perhaps four inches taller than her, and he was again dumbfounded by her strength. All he could do to ease her burden was push from his knees to stay upright as she guided him nearer to the iron stove, which radiated wonderful tidal waves of heat. But her strength shouldn't surprise him, Dain realized, for she lived a physical lifestyle out here.

"Lie down on this rug," she told him, helping him ease down onto his hands and knees. "Lie on your back, with your feet straight out from your body."

Just the act of lying down helped. Dain closed his eyes

tightly, the pain gutting him. He barely heard the soft brush of her velvet dress near his ear as she left his side. There was a clink of dishes, the opening and closing of a cabinet door, but he was in too much agony to look. Lifting his hands, he dug his fingers into his skull.

Erin placed the dark green bowl beside her as she knelt near his head. Did she have the strength to deal with him? She wasn't at all sure. And yet the Great Spirit had sent him to her door. As a healer, she knew she could not refuse him. One look at his mud-streaked face, the way his mouth contorted as he fought the pain, the beads of tears gathering on the lashes of his tightly shut eyes, and she knew the answer.

Smoothing her velvet skirt across her knees, she slid her fingers along the sides of his head. "I'm going to ease your head up into my lap," she whispered near his ear. "Take your hands away from your head. I have a herbal salve I will rub on your forehead."

He felt a scream coming on. The instant she touched his throbbing head, his clenched fingers dropped away. He felt her lift his head and neck, felt himself settle against her curved thighs, felt the nubby warmth of the velvet against his hot, sweaty skin. Her words were jumbled in his cart-wheeling mind as waves of pain beat against his brain, made his back arch upward. His mouth opened and he felt the scream coming. *No!* No, he couldn't scream! No one had ever heard him scream with this damnable pain, which tormented the depths of his raw, tired soul.

The moment her callused, work-worn fingers slid across his brow with the salve, the scream abated. With each small, circular motion of her fingers, he began to feel the worst of the pain ease. Oh, God, relief! Nearly instant, grateful relief. The bow in his back relaxed and he fell against the thick wool Navajo rug, his breath returning. Odd sensations sped through him. He felt the touch of her work-roughened hands, which now moved with a knowing sureness across his brow, spreading the fragrant unguent across his closed eyes, down his long, hawklike nose, his tension-lined cheeks, across his cracked and chapped lips to his unforgiving jaw.

The feeling of warmth coming from her hands matched the inner fire burning out of control in his brain. With each light stroke, more and more of the pain receded. Dain lay there somewhere between pain and awe. This was a miracle. A true miracle. He had tried the latest, most powerful pain drugs in the world, and they had only taken the edge off his agony. Whatever she was spreading across him was driving the pain away so quickly that he lay there gasping for breath.

Little by little, stroke after stroke, Dain felt the throbbing in his head reducing. He absorbed her touch like a starving plant that had been denied sunlight for too long, like a thirsty beggar who finally found a source of wonderful, cooling water. He took whatever it was that she was giving him. Even though her hands were like hot irons against his sweaty, muddy flesh, he felt a cooling sensation begin to trickle through him and move inside his head. That cooling energy was like liquid dousing the fire that the tumor had created. Oh! He groaned out of pleasure, out of gratefulness. Her touch was magical. It was healing. To lie in her lap, to feel the quiet strength of her body, the gentle touch of her fingers kneading his flesh, easing away the tension and chasing the pain away, was the most wonderful thing he'd ever experienced.

Erin concentrated on breathing. This man's pain was monumental. Internally, she reeled from it as she saw the dark, churning black clouds that had inhabited his head move up through her fingers and into her arms. She knew from past experience that when that negative energy flowed into her head, she would experience the pain herself. Trying to stay out of the way of the energy coursing through her to him, she attempted to physically and emotionally prepare herself for that coming eventuality.

It was impossible! Her head snapped back. Her lips parted. If not for all her training, if not for her blind trust and faith in the process, she would have yanked her hands away from him, leaped to her feet, screaming. Screaming. The pain was vicious. Tearing. Powerful. She reeled internally from the agony in her head, breathing deeply, breathing steadily. All the while, her hands moved as if they had a will of their own, across his face, across his stubbled jaw. She knew that if she kept breathing fully, deeply and steadily, the violent energy would be forced up and out of her physical body eventually.

Hot tears wound down her cheeks. She tasted their salty warmth as they curved into the corners of her mouth. *Breathe. Just breathe.* And she did. Little by little, the pain eased. It was then that she felt Maiisoh's presence. At some point, the white wolf had come from his sleeping rug to lie beside her. His great yellow eyes studied her and she gave him a wobbly smile. And then, as full consciousness returned to her in those moments, she realized that Dain was finally breathing slowly and deeply.

Her hands stilled on his broad brow. His lips were parted, but not contorted in pain. His eyes were closed, those short, black, spiky lashes lying against his pasty cheeks, but his lids were not shut tight with pain or with tears. She spread her hands against his stubbled cheeks, bowed her head, closed her eyes and whispered a prayer of thanks. Her heart was wide open, and she felt her grateful thanks move through her, through her low, off-key voice, to those who surrounded her on the invisible realms, to those who had heard his request for help, to those who had come to offer their love, their energy through her to him so that he could find momentary solace from the pain he suffered so bravely by himself.

Maiisoh whined.

Erin lifted her lashes and looked down at the man who rested in her lap. He slept deeply, like a child. A tremulous smile touched her lips as she sighed heavily, feeling the last of the energy leave her body. So that was what he lived with. The agony was terrible, more than any she'd ever encountered. As she eased into a more comfortable position, she realized that the fear she'd felt when first encountering him in that wash was of the great pain this man carried. On some level she'd known his agony was so overwhelming that it could destroy her, too, if she chose to try and help him heal himself. Could she withstand the destructive powers that now held him in their grip? Would he trust himself enough to know that he could reach out and trust her, too?

Her hands moved soothingly across his damp hair. In sleep, he looked so young. He was no longer the avenging warrior she'd seen at sunrise today, but like a vulnerable little boy. A boy who had never been allowed to be a child. A painful sigh escaped Erin as she gently eased him off her lap and placed his head on the rug. Rising to her feet, a little dizzy by the transference and removal of that virulent energy, she walked over to one of the dressers. Pulling out two wool blankets and a small pillow, she walked back to Dain.

In the flickering shadows and light created by the kerosene lamps, she saw the hard edges of his face as she knelt down to cover him with the blankets. The one soft thing about him, the only vulnerable thing about his face, was his mouth. It was a full mouth, one that told of his sensitivity, of his feelings. With a shake of her head, she placed her hand under his neck and eased the pillow beneath his skull. The fragrance of the ointment helped steady her own fragmented emotional state.

She quietly got to her feet and stood over him. Maiisoh had moved to the other side of Dain, the wolf's huge, white body parallel to the man's still form. "Yes," she whispered to Maiisoh, "you brought him here. I know you did." Her eyes glimmered with tears and love for her wolf companion.

Maiisoh lifted his broad skull, his amber eyes studying her in the silence.

"Someday, Maiisoh, I will not be able to meet your expectations, I'm afraid. This man is broken with pain." She touched her own heart with her fingers. "How can I help him to help himself when my own heart is still broken and bleeding? This man's heart is shattered. How can I help him mend his, if I cannot mend my own, my friend and teacher?"

The words ebbed and flowed in the silence and warmth of the hogan as Erin stood there, feeling the beautiful, invisible rapport with her wolf. She felt the animal's care and concern, but she also felt his belief in her. She lifted her hand away from her breasts. "*Aho,* my friend. So, I will sleep on it. You've taught me from the beginning to live within the moment, not to worry about yesterday or what will come tomorrow."

Chapter Five

Dain awoke slowly. A slight ache in his right hip had pulled him from sleep initially, then he heard the soft snap and pop of a wood fire nearby. The quiet was comforting as he lay there, the blankets drawn over his shoulders. He felt warm, and a sense of peace flowed through him, a feeling he'd not encountered for… His groggy mind groped to answer the half-formed thought. The kind of peace he was feeling was new in its depth—as if there was a sense of complete serenity within him.

As he gathered his hazy thoughts, Dain remembered the torturous five-mile trek of the previous day. The pain in his hip must be from when he'd fallen, he realized. Then the smell of sheep's wool entered his nostrils and the scratchy quality of the pillow pressing his cheek snagged his wandering attention. He remembered where he was. In a place where there were no ringing phones, no beepers, no assistants running into his office in a panic, no faxes strewn across his massive cherry desk. Just…silence.

Healing silence. Normally, he hated quiet and would turn on a radio or the television just so he could hear another human voice talking in the background and forget how alone he felt inside. Now loneliness didn't seem to bother him. As he lay comfortably in Erin's hogan, the heat flowing from the stove moved in gentle waves across him. He could smell the wood smoke, very light, almost nonexistent, but reminding him he was in a hogan out in the middle of nowhere and not in his Manhattan boardroom running his global empire.

A woman's low, husky laughter, filled with childlike delight drifted into the room. He dragged his lashes open and slowly sat up, the wool blankets falling away. Looking down, Dain realized he was still in the same clothes he'd worn yesterday, replete with dried mud. He wrinkled his nose at his own smell.

More laughter came from outside the hogan.

Who was it? Erin? It had to be.

Dain shoved himself to his feet, feeling every muscle in his body protesting. Rubbing his eyes, he staggered slowly toward the bare window next to the rough-hewn door. Anchoring his hands on either side of the window, he blinked away the sleep that still embraced him.

Outside the hogan in the first light of day, he saw Erin playing with the huge white wolf. She was wearing an old, worn, denim jacket, a maroon-colored skirt and gold deerskin boots. Her hair was braided and she wore a knitted cap over her head to protect her ears from the cold.

Frost covered everything like a coating of white sugar. The sagebrush around the hogan was sprinkled with the glistening confection. Erin's breath came out in small, white clouds as she turn and twisted, a large stick in her hand, while the wolf playfully chased after her. Dain's heart expanded in his chest and he found his mouth lifted in a grin as he gazed intently at her flushed, joyous features. In that moment, Erin wasn't a woman; she was a little girl playing with her dog. Her eyes sparkled with such life that he found himself wanting her, wanting to absorb inside himself the joy she carried.

The white wolf leaped and ran in circles around her as she lifted the stick above her head and pretended she was going to toss it. Laughing gaily, Erin brought the stick down and dragged it behind her, dancing and lifting her feet high. The wolf spun around, lunged for the stick and grabbed it with his teeth as Erin pulled, careful not to jerk too hard and hurt the wolf's mouth or teeth.

Giving him the stick, she ran down toward the sheep pen, her arms spread wide as if she were an eagle ready to take off, her skirt and braids flying behind her. The wolf dropped the stick and raced after her, leaping around her, lunging toward her outstretched arms, but never touching her extended fingers. At the pen, Erin turned and ran breathlessly back up toward the hogan.

Dain marveled at her physical ability, her incredible, breathtaking grace. She ran hard toward the stick the wolf had left on the ground, and without missing a beat, leaned over and scooped it back up. The wolf circled her and leaped many feet into the air. Erin halted, resting her hands on her knees and bending over to catch her breath. The animal came up to her and tried to tease the stick out of her hand. Straightening, she laughed at him and rubbed his head fondly.

Feeling like an interloper, but unable to stop himself, Dain absorbed her every movement, drank in that incredible, husky laughter that was so much like a beautiful song. Her eyes were luminous with happiness, sparkling as she finally tossed the stick to the wolf. Walking down to the pen, she opened the gate. Instantly, the sheep began to spill out, like woolly white tufts of cotton on legs. The wolf put down the stick and began to purposely move the released flock away from the buildings and out onto the frost-coated desert.

Hands on her hips, Erin stood there for nearly a minute,

watching her wolf guide the sheep, before she walked over to a huge pile of wood, leaned down and picked up an armload.

Dain moved away from the window. He didn't want her to know he'd watched her. Suddenly, he was nervous. Him! Of all people! Usually he made others nervous. Well, *he* was nervous now. He went back to the old iron stove and held out his hands toward the warmth, waiting. Waiting for *her*.

The door creaked and opened. Erin entered, the load of wood balanced precariously as she turned and pushed the door closed with the toe of her boot. When she looked up, she saw him.

"You're awake."

He nodded brusquely and watched her drop the wood into a large wooden box next to the door. "Yes."

Brushing the frost from her jacket, Erin unbuttoned it and hung it on a hook next to the door before forcing herself to turn and look at him. She saw the wariness in his eyes and felt his distrust of her as he stood next to the stove. Apprehension flitted through her, making her uneasy in his presence. Last night's events came back to her and Erin chided herself. It was a test to not compare Dain to her ex-husband.

"I woke you?"

He shrugged, not sure he wanted her to know all of what he'd seen. "I haven't been woken up by laughter since—I can't remember."

Halting on the opposite side of the stove, Erin opened her hands, palms outward. "You don't laugh much, do you?"

He scowled, put off by her fearless, direct gaze. He didn't want to talk about himself when curiosity about *her* was eating him alive. He had so many questions to ask about how she'd made his headache miraculously disappear last night.

"Does it show?" he asked instead.

"You don't have any crinkling at the corners of your

eyes. People who laugh a lot have them.'' She felt heat rush to her face and wondered if he realized she was blushing beneath his dark, stormy scrutiny. As ruthless as he appeared, she knew there must be a softer side to him. On the other hand, her ex-husband had the sweet face of an angel and he was hell—her hell on earth.

''Being in a lot of sunlight can cause that, too.''

''That's a moot point. You don't have laugh lines at the corners of your eyes.'' She gestured to his mouth. ''No dimples, either. Instead, two deep slashes at the corners that tell me your mouth is usually tight and pulled inward.''

Uncomfortable, Dain stepped away from the stove. ''Life has a way of marking everyone's face,'' he said irritably. Looking down at himself, he gestured to his clothes. ''I need a shower.''

Erin nodded. ''No disagreement from me. You smell, too.'' A sour smile edged her mouth.

Anger sparked in him. But when he looked up, he nearly drowned in her teasing, light brown eyes. Swallowing his anger because he knew instinctively she was not laughing at him, he rasped, ''Your hogan doesn't have bathroom facilities.''

Looking around, Erin grinned. ''No, hogans are places where people live, eat and sleep.''

''I suppose out here in the middle of nowhere, the rest room consists of a bush outdoors?'' Dain felt cringing at his harsh tone. He hated himself when he got testy and belligerent, and he knew Erin didn't deserve his ill humor. After all, she'd saved his sorry hide from freezing temperatures last night and she'd taken away his headache with those marvelous, work-worn hands of hers.

Moving her fingers through strands of hair that had come loose at her temples, Erin said, ''We're not all that primitive. Go outside and around the back of the hogan. There's a john out there.'' Her eyes sparkled. For a brief moment, she felt a new emotion in her heart—one she'd never felt before. Though she was puzzled by it, Erin relished how delicious it felt. Then, just as quickly, it disappeared. Was Dain the reason for it? Whatever *it* was?

His scowl deepened. He owed her an apology, but he was damned if he'd give her one. He'd stopped apologizing a long time ago to anyone or anything. "I suppose it's too much to hope for a shower?"

"Johns are usually used for one thing. Actually, two things, and no, showers or baths aren't part of their amenities."

He regarded her in the building silence. Automatically, his shoulders had begun to grow heavy with tension, a sensation he usually felt when challenged. Though she was an Indian, Erin had an exceptional grasp of the English language. She was obviously more than what she appeared to be, and he was intrigued. She spoke like a college-educated person, not some medicine woman stuck away in the middle of a desert, deprived and ignorant as he'd assumed she would be.

"My luggage is back at the truck."

"Then," Erin said, moving to one of the cabinets placed against the wall, "I guess you need to wash the clothes you're wearing, dry them and put them back on."

"You're joking."

She turned. "You think *I'm* going to wash your clothes for you? Look around. Do you see a washing machine? A dryer? There's no electricity out here. You are responsible for yourself, Dain Phillips. I'm not. If you want clean clothes, you wash them. Or walk back to your truck and get your luggage. The choice is up to you."

Angrily, he snapped, "You know I'm too damned sick to walk ten miles across this land."

She bent down and retrieved a heavy, black skillet from the cabinet. A part of her, the unwounded part, wanted to nurture him. Erin knew the danger of that. Being a healer was hard work; it wasn't about being a crutch to the one who was sick. "Oh, I don't know. You walked five miles yesterday when you thought you couldn't do it." Straightening, she walked back to the stove and placed the iron skillet on the top of it. "There's a hot mineral springs about a quarter of a mile up the draw behind the john." She pointed to a chest of drawers. "Find yourself a towel and go up there and wash yourself and your clothes. Bring them back here and lay them near the stove. They'll dry soon enough."

What arrogance. He wanted to say that, but bit back the response. She went outside for a moment and then brought in four white eggs. His stomach growled. To say he was hungry was an understatement. He was starving. He knew she must have heard his stomach growl, too.

Putting a dab of bacon grease into the skillet, she spread it around with a spatula. "I have a henhouse out back, too. When you come back from getting cleaned up, you can fix yourself some eggs." Briskly, she cracked the four eggs into the skillet and put the shells in a garbage can. Stirring the eggs frequently to scramble them, she added salt and pepper, then cut up some onion.

The odor was mouthwatering to Dain. He stared at the food, inhaled the incredible fragrance of it. Normally, he rarely ate breakfast, because he was too busy. Looking at those yellow-orange scrambled eggs and onions frying in the skillet, he heard his stomach growl again.

"Oh, no," Erin murmured, quickly lifting the skillet off the stove and going to the table at the far end of the hogan, "you don't get my meal. You fix your own."

Stung, he turned around and went to the nondescript chest of drawers where the towels were kept. "I thought Indians were supposed to be so damned generous."

Erin put the dirty skillet in a pan filled with soapy water. She chuckled as she sat down at the table. "If I were you, I'd leave my assumptions about everything outside that door, Mr. Phillips."

Dain was going to say something smart in return, but he saw her place her hands, palms open, over the food and close her eyes. Only belatedly did he realize she was praying. Disgruntled, he turned and jerked open one of the drawers. The terry-cloth towels were in faded rainbow colors and obviously very old and worn. He took two of them and slammed the drawer shut.

Who the hell did she think she was? The word *selfish* popped into his mind. Along with *arrogant*. Fuming, he stalked toward the door. As he pulled it open, he heard her speak.

"When you get back, I need some wood chopped. No wood, no fire, no food. I think you get the idea."

Lips thinning, Dain moved out of the hogan and shut the door firmly behind him. The freezing weather embraced him. Well, first things first. The john and then this mineral spring. His stomach was so tight with hunger it felt like a hand was clenching at his gut. His anger toward Erin propelled him around the large hogan, where he discovered the john was in a state of disrepair, the door no longer attached, the rusted hinges still hanging there.

Once he stalked away from the john, he realized how incredibly beautiful everything around him looked with a coating of white frost. To the left were two huge, old cottonwood trees, their gnarled limbs clawing skyward. But once he passed the empty sheep pen he noticed several small outbuildings, all in a state of disrepair and obviously in need of not only a coat of paint, but new roofing as well. Erin lived in a junkyard, as far as he was concerned.

Finding the mineral spring was easier than he expected. He followed a narrow path between two small hills that sat below the curve of a thousand-foot, red sandstone mesa that rose above the hogan on its southern side. Noting some barely discernible car tracks, Dain realized that he'd made his way down that steep incline off the flat, tabletop hill to her hogan—in the dark. That was a feat in itself.

Winding his way through the thick scrub, he followed a well-worn footpath between the hills. He climbed to the top and stopped, a little out of breath. But what he saw made his eyes widen enormously. Down below him were four oblong-shaped pools of steaming water. White stones encircled each dark green pool, making them look like emeralds set in the red desert. Steam rose lazily into the freezing air, and the brush a hundred or so feet above the spring was thickly coated with frost from the moisture.

One of the pools was oval, no more than ten feet in circumference. He saw that someone had built a small hitching post out of tree limbs, a good place to hang clothes or a towel. Watching his step as he climbed downward, Dain decided to opt for the oval pool. Kneeling on the flat white rock, he stuck his hand into the water to test the temperature. Perfect. It was probably about a 115° or so.

Suddenly, he was anxious to climb in. Without hesitation, he unlaced his muddy hiking boots and put them aside and then quickly shrugged out of his clothes. As he sat down on the edge of the smooth stone, he saw the sun edge higher in the sky and send its rays racing silently across the land. In the distance, he heard Erin singing. He couldn't see her, but her voice, that joyous instrument that made him want to smile with happiness, embraced him.

As he eased his feet into the water, he realized that the song she sang was the same one he'd heard in his head after she'd left him at the truck. As he slid fully into the spring, the hot water felt like massaging hands on his sore, tired muscles. A sigh slipped from his mouth as his feet found the bottom of the natural well. The water only came up to his waist so he crouched down, completely submerging himself. Rising up again, he began to wash. Scrubbing the mud off his body and out of his hair felt marvelous.

Dain dove under again, pushed himself back on his legs, then threw his head back, gasping for air. Grinning, he gazed down at the water, amazed and grateful. Who would have expected such a marvelous commodity such as this out here? He knew women who paid thousands of dollars a week to go to mineral springs like this in different parts of the world. And here, right behind Erin's hogan, was this incredible hot springs.

With a shake of his head, Dain decided to enjoy the experience, and he sat down, stretching out until his toes touched the other side of the spring. Tipping his head back on the smooth rock, his hands floating naturally out at his sides, he sighed and closed his eyes and let the water do its work on his tired, stressed body.

Much later, after washing his clothes in another pool, Dain wrapped one towel around his waist to cover his nakedness, the other around his shoulders to protect him from the frosty air, and hurried back to the hogan. When he arrived, Erin was nowhere to be found. Just as well, he ruminated, moving into the welcoming warmth of the building.

Spreading out his jeans and shirt, he stood by the stove, absorbing the heat. The sunlight stole brightly through the east window beside the door. At least now he had a chance to look around. His stomach growled, but he ignored it.

Erin's hogan was eight-sided, each mud-and-timber wall flowing into the next. The floor, of hard-packed red earth, was covered with a number of well-worn Navajo rugs. Against the east wall was a table that drew his interest. It was covered with a piece of ragged purple velvet, and on top of it was an abalone shell that was blackened inside. Next to the shell was a large brown-and-white feather. The beadwork on the base of the quill was intricate and beautiful.

He moved to the next piece of furniture. It looked like a chest of drawers, although a small Navajo rug lay across the top of it. There were several framed pictures and he moved closer to study them. Picking up the first redwood frame, he saw an older Indian couple with a young girl in a deerskin dress standing between them. No one in the photo was smiling. In the background stood a dilapidated log cabin, the tin roof in obvious need of repair. There were woods all around them, and the cabin sat in a flower-filled meadow.

Looking closely, Dain thought the little girl looked like Erin, but he couldn't be sure. The other two people were who—her parents? If they were, they were damned old to be having a kid. Maybe her grandparents? That would fit. He set the picture down and looked at the second one. It showed a ceremony of some kind, with a lot of people in attendance. Dain wasn't sure what was going on. There were a lot of Indians dressed in ceremonial garb, with drums, rattles and feathers. Someone was dancing near the center of a circle, someone dressed in what appeared to be a white deerskin dress, but the photo wasn't that good, and he couldn't tell much about the dancer.

A third photo was of a black horse with fiery, large, intelligent eyes. On top of that magnificent horse was Erin. Dain's fingers closed around the chrome frame and he wiped away the dust to see the photo better. Erin was probably in her teens, sitting bareback on the powerful ebony horse. She was holding the reins, smiling triumphantly, her eyes shining with incredible joy.

He stood there, absorbing her young girl's face and those whiskey-colored eyes that shone like the sun itself. Her lips, full and soft, were lifted. She looked so proud sitting on that horse, her bare legs like thin branches draped across that shining animal's back. She was wearing red shorts and a white tank top, her feet bare.

His fingers tightened around the frame. How wild and free Erin looked. There was no question she was free in a way he envied. Free in a way he'd never experienced and never would. Sadness filled Dain as he slowly placed the photo back on top of the dresser. He longed to talk to Erin about her childhood. It seemed like a very happy, secure one—just the opposite of his, that was for sure.

His stomach growled and this time his hunger couldn't be ignored. Feeling stronger and better than he had in months, Dain went back to the stove. In another half hour, his clothes would be dry and then he'd find that henhouse and make himself some eggs.

How the hell did one cook eggs? He had no idea. His mind ranged back over what Erin had done to make herself those marvelous, mouthwatering scrambled eggs and onions. Well, he'd have to do it himself. He'd expected her to share her food with him, or at least make him breakfast. At home he had a butler and a maid, and breakfast was served on a tray at his bedside at six a.m. sharp.

Grinning a little, Dain knew that wasn't going to happen here.

Chapter Six

As Erin rode up on her horse, she saw that the door to her hogan was open. Dismounting and allowing the reins to drop, she lifted her nose and tested the air. Something was burning. She eased the two large clothes bags off her saddle and walked into the hogan. Standing just inside the entrance, she saw Dain angrily jerking the skillet she'd used earlier off the stove. Whatever he had tried to cook, he'd burned—badly.

When he saw her, his mouth flattened. "I burned the eggs."

"I see," she said, as lightly as possible for his benefit. Her heart wrenched with compassion. The helpless look she saw made her acknowledge just how human Dain was—and how dangerous to her unraveling emotions. Walking to the opposite side of the hogan and placing the bags she carried on the floor, she shrugged out of her denim jacket and moved back to where he stood staring down at the burned fare. "Go clean out the pan and I'll walk you through the steps of making it again."

He looked at her ruefully. "Right now, I feel like a klutzy eight-year-old at the orphanage when—" Abruptly, he snapped his mouth shut. What the hell was he doing mentioning the orphanage? No one knew about that part of his life. No one. Then he saw Erin's golden eyes grow shadowed—for him—and the tender look caught him off guard and erased his anger.

"White men are not taught to cook or take care of themselves," she said, reaching out and laying her hand on his arm. "I'll help you learn."

Her touch was electric. Greedily, he absorbed the sensation as her fingers curved around his arm momentarily. It wasn't her considerable strength that he felt now, only the kindness he saw in her eyes and heard in the huskiness of her low voice.

"Yeah, okay...." he muttered, and turned away. His flesh tingled warmly where she'd touched him, and he found himself wanting her to touch him again. He liked her touch. As he put the skillet in the cool, soapy water and scrubbed the hell out of it, Dain admitted that there wasn't much not to like about Erin Wolf, when he heard the hogan door open and shut, then the sound of her puttering around the hogan, he twisted to look in her direction.

"What's that?" he asked as she bent over two large muslin bags.

"I rode back to your truck and opened up your suitcases and stuffed all your clean clothes into them." She turned one bag over and his clothes tumbled out onto the rug.

Stunned, Dain stopped scrubbing the skillet. "You...rode there and got my clothes?" The gesture touched his heart. She had no idea he was a billionaire; she'd only done it out of the goodness of her heart. How long had it been since anyone had done anything like that for him? Dain knew the answer. Grimly, he pursed his lips.

She emptied the second bag. "Yes. After breakfast you'll want to fold them up and put them in this dresser," she said, pointing to her left. "And then I'll show you how to clean and pick up the hogan. It's done every morning after breakfast, before we go to work outside."

A strange contentment stole over him and he grinned a little as he returned to scrubbing out the skillet. "Back where I come from, I have more maids and housekeepers than you can shake a stick at. A butler, too. Housework isn't something I get involved in."

"Every human being has the capacity to be all things," Erin told him with a flash of a grin as she walked over to the stove. Great Spirit help her, but she was enjoying Dain, his closeness, his allowing her to see his wonderful inner being. "Whether it be cook, housemaid, scientist, astronaut or whatever. All possibilities lay within each of us."

Considering her wisdom, Dain found himself unable to deny it. After rinsing off the skillet in a bucket of clean water, he found a towel and dried it. Turning around, he walked back to the stove, his gaze meeting hers. She looked even more beautiful this morning, more radiant, if that was possible. He liked the bold way she fearlessly held his gaze. Not many men could handle his intense stare, but she did—with ease.

"Well, if you choose to stay here," Erin said, holding her hands out over the stove, "then you will become many things simultaneously."

Wryly, he raised the skillet in his hand. "Chief cook and bottle washer?"

"Among them, yes. To survive, everyone must pull his own weight." Erin grew serious. "That's what I love about the Navajo land—it is a place of extremes. It is a land that lives close to life and death." She peered into his narrowing eyes and saw him wince over the word *death*.

"Yeah, well, I'd rather not be somewhere like that." He set the skillet down on the top of the stove.

"Why not?"

"I don't mind living. It's the dying part I don't like." He propped his hands on his narrow hips and avoided her searching look.

"*Death* is a bad word white men use to scare you," she countered. "Among my people, we call it the journey over the rainbow bridge." She gestured down her body with her hand. "We shed only the physical, outer shell we live in for this lifetime, but the rest of us—all our experiences, our memories, good and bad—go with us into the light."

Mouth turning tight, Dain muttered, "I'm not humored by your philosophy. I've got a fast-growing and inoperable brain tumor. I'm going to die in six months unless I can find a way to cure it."

Nodding, Erin rubbed her hands slowly down the sides of her skirt, trying to keep herself from smoothing Dain's disheveled hair. His beard made him look dangerous, and she could see in his eyes that he was a man of immense power and knew it. "I saw your tumor. It looks like a beautiful, iridescent white pearl in the center of your brain."

He stared at her, dumbfounded. "How—"

"Last night, when you were going out of your body with pain, I put a salve on your brow. When I placed my hands on the sides of your head, I saw the tumor."

"That's impossible."

"Nothing's impossible."

"How could you see it?"

She touched an area between her eyebrows. "My invisible eye, which can look into the other dimensions that move within this one where we stand, can see into them. You have one, too. Everyone does, so do not look at me as if I'm the crazy one here." Her lips lifted slightly. "I saw your tumor." She held up her hands and showed him the approximate size of it with her fingers. "As big as a nickel, I would guess. Very beautiful. It reminded me of seeing a pearl exposed in the pink flesh of an oyster after you open it up."

With a shake of his head, he said, "I'm amazed. My doctors showed me the MRI and the CAT scans of the tumor and it's the size you say it is." Looking at her intently, he said, "Who *are* you? Did someone in my corporation give you this information before I got here?"

Laughing softly, Erin shook her head and said, "No one knew you were coming here, did they?"

"Only one person—Dr. Sarah."

"And is she trustworthy?" Erin instantly saw his thawing expression close up. Trust was an issue with him.

"Let's just say that I don't think Dr. Sarah would dial you and tell you I was coming."

Laughing, Erin said, "She couldn't. I don't have a phone!"

Disgruntled, Dain said, "That's right—no phone, no fax, no E-mail, no computer, no *nothing* out here in this god-forsaken place."

"They are distractions."

"Hardly," he snorted. "Why are they distractions?"

She leaned down and rolled one of the rugs up in preparation for the morning cleanup. "Things like that pull your attention away from your inner life, your inner world of being. It disconnects you from your heart, your spirit, and you can no longer hear them speak to you, except through your dreams."

"I quit dreaming a long time ago," he said abruptly.

Erin carried the rug to the door, opened it and placed it outside. She shut the door and went to another rug. "I see many white people who are disconnected from their inner life, their heart."

"So, white men as a group are all heartless bastards in your eyes, is that it?"

Her heart thudded hard, in terror. She leaned down and rolled up the rug. "I stand in judgment of no one. And I didn't say that." Her voice wobbled dangerously, her emotions chaotic. Dain had hit a truth within her, had pried open and seen her raw prejudice. She felt shamed.

"What did you mean by what you said then?" For a fleeting second, he saw stark terror in her eyes before she dipped her head to hide her reaction. What had happened to her? Despite his hardened heart, Dain found himself genuinely caring for this enigma of a woman. For some unknown reason, Erin could touch his heart just as easily as sunlight touched a flower.

Straightening up with the rug in her arms, Erin took a deep breath and pushed her fear aside. In a steadier tone she said, "When you cut the cord from our mother, the Earth, and honor only the contents of your head and belittle the feelings of your heart, that is disconnection. The mind has a voice box through which to talk to the world around us."

She raised her arm and gestured skyward. "But our spirit, that dark, rich inner soil of ourselves, our becoming, does not." She touched the region of her heart. "Our heart is the voice of our inner world of spirit. The spirit speaks through our heart not through sounds or words, but through feelings and emotions. If the cord is not cut, then you have the opportunity to weigh what your mind tells you, as well as what your feelings are saying. You can make an informed decision based on both—a better decision than one made just by your head."

Dain ruminated over her words as she rolled up several more rugs before coming back to the stove. "You are damning Western civilization, then," he said finally.

Her gut clenched. Dain had found her wound again. "Among my people, the Eastern Cherokee, we honor what the heart holds, sees and hears, also. White men do not. They honor the contents of the mind, their brain." She touched her head. "You have universities and colleges for the head and brain, but none for your heart. We find that strange."

"Okay," he replied, struggling to understand her, "you're saying I'm all head and no heart."

"In a sense," Erin said gently. "But just because you have lost your attachment to Mother Earth does not mean you've become a heartless monster, either."

"Glad to hear it. I was worried for a moment." And to his surprise, he *was* glad. Somehow, some crazy part of him wanted Erin to like him, to respect him—even if he was a cursed white man.

"There are heartless monsters among all peoples of the Earth. They have no attachment to their heart, for it was torn out of them either before they came into this life or it was destroyed for them when they were children growing up. A child without a heart-centered world within him becomes unfeeling and cold."

Dain's brows dipped. "I've been called those things plenty of times in my business," he admitted.

"I know."

Again he searched her serene features. Even though Erin looked young, much younger than he knew her to be by the photographs he'd seen on the dresser, she appeared so very childlike. Her face had a radiance to it, her eyes a soft shining quality in them. She had the look of a child who gazed at the world with wonder.

"What else do you know about me?" he asked.

She smiled a little and touched her brow. "When you speak, I see flashes of colored pictures, like photographs, here in my head. They come—" she placed her hand momentarily in front of her eyes "—like a color slide, an overlay. Sometimes they are fragments. Or pieces. Or I may be shown the whole picture. The more I am around the person, the more I feel here—" she touched her heart. "And the more I concentrate on them, the more the pictures will come to me."

"You're a psychic." He said the word with distaste.

"I am me. I am not a set of labels. That is your head talking. What does your heart feel?"

He laughed mirthlessly. "I don't *feel*."

Erin stood there and met his pain-filled smile. "Maybe that is why you have a tumor in your head."

He stared at her, the silence building between them. "Say that again," he rasped, anger edging his tone.

"When something is abused, over time it will break down," Erin explained, opening her hands. "You lost the connection from your heart when you very, very young. You had no mentor, no one to teach you the value of your feelings. You closed down the connection to your heart to protect yourself. You used logic, or worse, rationalization, to tame whatever feelings or emotions you had so that over time, you could not feel. The Cherokee believe that in order to be strong and healthy, you must have balance or inner harmony.

"That means you work with your head and heart, not just one or the other. Disease can be caused by being out of balance or out of harmony with yourself. When people come to me and say they are sick, a question I have to ask is where are they out of balance? Are they too much in their head? Too much in their heart?" She made a cutting motion across her neck. "From here up, you are alive." She gestured downward to her booted feet. "From the neck down, you are dead."

Dain glared at her. "Dead already?" he snarled. "Just what the hell are you mumbling about? I have perfect co-ordination. I'm a squash champion. An international fencer in saber. I'm hardly 'dead' as you put it, from the neck down."

Erin tolerated his outburst. "Dead in the sense that you are not in touch with your body, your spirit. If the spirit is not acknowledged by you, then it slowly withdraws," she said with a sigh.

"And me being out of touch with my spirit caused this damn tumor?"

"I don't know about that. But being out of balance causes disease."

He stared at her, looking uncertain. "You said you couldn't heal me."

"That's right. Only you can heal yourself."

He held her challenging gaze. She held her head proudly, her lips compressed. Something in him wanted to tear her down, tear her beliefs apart and prove her wrong. "Luanne Yazzie said you've cured many people. She's seen it with her own two eyes. How do you explain *that?*"

With a shrug, Erin said, "I don't have to prove anything to you one way or another. The truth never needs a defense. If people want to believe I did something, then that is their choice."

Frustrated, Dain muttered, "Maybe I need to redefine something then. Just what the hell is a healer?"

Her lips twitched. "You asked a good question, Dain Phillips."

Gazing at him intently, she continued, "Last night I helped ease your headache, but you really don't need me to discharge your pain."

He stood there as if considering this for a moment. Then his logical mind went for the most likely solution. "Wait a minute," he said. "You smeared some salve on my forehead. That's what took the pain away."

Her smile broadened. "Really? Do you want to put that to one of your scientific tests?"

"How?"

"You will get the headache again as night falls," she said. "I will give you the salve and you will put it on your brow, and then we will see what happens."

"All right," he said uncertainly. He saw the light dancing in her eyes.

"It is a mixture of chaparral and rock rose petals. Chaparral is a well-known herb that helps to counter effects of disease. Sometimes, if a person has a great enough belief in that herb, it will cure him."

"I didn't know what it was, so how could I know that?"

"You couldn't," Erin said. "But let's find out tonight, shall we?"

He nodded. "Fair enough."

"So, you will stay? You do not want to go back East?" Erin found herself wanting him to stay. It was absolutely crazy for her to want such a thing! He was a white man. But he was different, her heart told her—and with him in her life she felt helpless in a new and wonderful way. No longer was she the medicine woman and he the patient. No, things were changing rapidly. Too rapidly for Erin. She felt off balance, yet hungering more for Dain, for his thoughts and for sharing everything with him. Normally, she was never emotionally entwined like this with a patient. Yes, she had compassion, but with her heart beating wildly every time he gave her that burning look from beneath his lashes, she knew there was something more happening between them.

Rubbing his jaw, he studied her. There was incredible warmth and understanding in her eyes, and he longed to absorb that into himself. He longed to possess that feeling of serenity that always radiated like the sun's rays from her. Shrugging off his feelings, he said, "You haven't said how much this will cost me."

"Medicine people work on a donation basis. I want nothing from you, Dain Phillips. I need nothing you have. If you stay, you stay because you feel worthy inside of yourself to stay and get well. You do not do this for me, but for yourself. But I can always use another body around here, another set of hands. Winter is coming on, and there is much to do, to repair."

Her eyes twinkled. "If you stay, you will earn your keep. We are equals. I do not cook, clean or sew for you. I am not your servant nor am I your slave. Staying means being responsible for every breath you take while you're here with us. You can choose to leave at any time. I have no expectations from you and you should try to place none on me. If you do, I will make you aware of them and ask you to remove them.''

"You sure as hell sound like a bra-burning feminist to me.''

Her laughter was rich and low. "My people are matriarchal. So are the Navajo. Women honor men, but in your world, you generally do not honor women, or what they bring to the table. Here you will. Here you will respect me as I respect you. If you do not understand respect, then I will teach you.''

Ruminating over her words, he shuffled around the stove and picked up the jar of bacon grease that sat on the table. "The only thing I respect is power.''

With a nod, Erin said, "Very well, that is a start. But don't make the mistake of looking at power as power *over* someone or some*thing,* Dain Phillips. White men easily fall into that trap where, just because they are physically stronger than women, they think they can have power over a woman—or a child....'' Sudden images from her own past overwhelmed her momentarily. Erin struggled to control her unexpected feelings as they surged through her.

A sharp pain moved through Dain's heart. He halted midstride and stared at her. The pain of a child. Oh, yeah, he knew that one real well. Too well. Flattening his lips, he rasped, "Don't worry, I won't make that mistake with you. Now, will you show me how to scramble these damned eggs so I can feed myself instead of slowly starving to death around here?''

Chapter Seven

Dain was left to his own devices after he'd managed to make a decent skillet of scrambled eggs the second time around. He was too damn hungry to argue with Erin's laws around her hogan. As he sat at the table and ate the eggs, along with some bread she'd made recently, he'd watched her move around with economical movements. Every Navajo rug, which together created a patchwork carpet over the hard dirt floor, was rolled up, taken outside, hung on the clothesline and beaten with a broom. Once that was done, she brought them in and laid them back down.

He found it fascinating that Erin didn't tell him anything; what he learned about her way of life was from observation on his part. Watching her was a pleasure. At the same time, he couldn't get the memory of her fingers sliding along his face out of his mind—nor did he want to.

"You have a good appetite," Erin observed, coming over to the table after washing her hands.

"Is that good?" He watched as she cut several slices of dark brown bread off the loaf.

"For a man who is supposed to die in six months, I'd say that was a good sign," she murmured, stacking several pieces of cheese in between and wrapping it all up in a cloth.

Dain studied her. "What are you really saying?"

Her mouth twitched. She made another cheese sandwich and then put them into a very old, weatherbeaten saddlebag. "Who said you had six months to live?"

"Actually," Dain said, finishing off the fragrant coffee that had been perked earlier on the wood stove, "Dr. Sarah and her oncology team gave me that determination. They said I had, at best, a year and a half to live. The tumor's inoperable. I was to go home and die. I've spent a year looking for someone or something to help me get rid of this tumor."

He saw Erin's mouth flex in disapproval.

"The only one who can determine when you are going to pass over the rainbow bridge is the Great Spirit, not a human being."

"So," he said, sipping the coffee and watching her intently over the mug's chipped rim, "you disagree with them?"

Erin took a battered thermos bottle down from a shelf and unscrewed the top. "To give you a death sentence was wrong of them," she said grimly, picking up the coffeepot. Very carefully, she poured the hot liquid into the thermos. "How dare they tell you when to die? It is wrong to wound a person's spirit in such a way by planting that information in you."

"Doctors do it all the time," he said, smiling a little. "It's their business."

Snorting softly, Erin put the coffeepot back on the stove. "A healer is supposed to give hope, not death sentences. The person coming to a healer is already confused and frightened." She capped the thermos and glanced at his thoughtful face. "Can you tell me it did your spirit any good to hear their death sentence?"

Chuckling a little, he shook his head. "No, it scared the hell out of me."

"It would anyone," she muttered defiantly.

"So if I had come to you first, what would you have told me?"

She packed the thermos into the other saddlebag. "Nothing."

"Well," Dain murmured, "that would do less damage in one way."

"They had no *right* to take away your hope, your ability to fight back. You looked up to these people and they took advantage of you by playing little gods capable of foretelling the future." With a shake of her head, her voice laced with anger, she added, "I have had people crawl here, literally, on their hands and knees, seeking help and guidance. People who were in far worse condition than you are. I did not take away their hope. I fed it, instead."

"Ah," Dain said, "that's the essence of all this, isn't it?"

"What?" Erin placed the saddlebags across her shoulder.

"As a healer, you give your patients hope instead of destroying their hope?"

She smiled a little. "You catch on fast, Dain Phillips."

"I don't have much time so I have to, Ms. Wolf."

Her lips parted in a smile. "I must go now. I will return before sunset."

"Where are you going?"

"Out with the flock. Maiisoh watches and guards them, but I must ride with them. Too many coyotes around." She gestured to the window, where the large mesa looming above the hogan was visible. "Cougars live nearby, too, and if they don't find a rabbit or wild dog to eat, they go after the sheep."

"So you'll ride your horse with the herd and bring the sheep back at dusk?"

"Yes."

"Can I come with you?"

She shook her head. "You need to rest, whether you know it or not." Looking at him intently, she said, "Do you realize that your body is asking not only for rest, but for more sleep?"

Wryly, Dain said, "Look, that white wolf of yours has been invading my sleep every night, except for last night, for a year. I'd wake up at three a.m. every morning in a sweat from him chasing me."

Erin's laughter pealed out. "So I was right—Maiisoh was guiding you here."

"What do you mean?"

Erin picked up the rifle that leaned against one wall of the hogan and walked to the door. "When I came here, I built this hogan with the help of the Yazzie family. After it was built, I spent the first night here alone and Maiisoh appeared at the door. At first I thought he was a spirit wolf, but when I saw blood on his coat, I knew differently." She rested her hand on the doorknob. "Someone had wounded him with buckshot. He was thin and starving. Because I come from the Wolf Clan of my people, I knew that the white wolf had shown up to become my guardian. So he let me dig out the buckshot along his neck and shoulder, dress his wounds, feed him some mutton stew, and he's stayed ever since. That was six years ago."

"And you think he's the one who showed up in my nightmare?"

Erin nodded. "Wolves have special powers. They are more than what you see with your two eyes. They are wild hearts."

"Wild hearts?"

She opened the door. "Tonight, upon my return, we will talk of this. I must go." When she saw Dain's crestfallen expression, she felt needed in a very special way she'd never experienced before. But then, he was very male, very vulnerable, and that automatically opened her heart.

Once Dain got over his disappointment, a sudden protectiveness overwhelmed him. "Are you going to be okay out there?" Hearing his own question, he wondered at himself. Since when did he care about another enough to worry? Never. Scrutinizing her, he realized he wanted her near him. She made him feel lighter. Buoyant. Hopeful. Never mind the fact that she brought out his very primal, wolflike desire to protect her against the unknown.

With an embarrassed laugh, Erin said, "You are the one I'm concerned about. I wonder if you know how to chop wood. I wonder if you can handle an ax properly without hitting yourself or hurting yourself with it."

Frowning, Dain muttered, "I'm not the city slicker you think I am. I'll be fine." But would she? He'd just found her. He didn't want her torn from his life, too—as all those he'd loved had been.

Erin saw the way he worked his mouth, noticed the sudden shadow of worry in his face and wondered about his feelings for her. An unknown emotion reached out and touched her heart and womanhood simultaneously. Then it hit her like a lightning bolt. She was attracted to him. And she hadn't been interested in a male since her divorce. But despite Dain's hard wall, she could see the soft, inner core of him, the little boy, the man who wanted to reach out, but who was too scared and untrusting to do so—yet.

She smiled at him tenderly. "I'll see you tonight," she whispered, hoping to soothe him—as well as herself.

Sitting at the old, worn, maple table, which was in dire need of refurbishing, Dain moved the thick white mug slowly around and around in his hands. The sunlight of Erin Wolf left the hogan and he felt all his hope, his momentary happiness, leave with her. What was it about her that so mesmerized him? She was an Indian. A woman who didn't take any bull from him—at all. Under ordinary circumstances, in his business world, he'd have destroyed her for challenging him like that.

But this wasn't his world—it was hers. And how vastly different it was—almost like being in a time warp, where he was thrown back into the 1800s, to live. His mind ranged over his corporations and the people he'd left in charge to run them. Well, there was no point worrying about all that now. Looking around the hogan, he was amazed once again that there was no telephone, no fax machine, not even a cellular phone.

Yet he was surviving out here—very nicely so far, as a matter of fact. It was nearly seven a.m. and he felt invigorated and stronger than he could recall being since the tumor was diagnosed. He grinned, remembering Erin's statement that a doctor who was supposed to be a healer had assigned him a death sentence by proclaiming when he would die. Yes, she definitely had something there. Her world wasn't as crazy as his was, by far.

Or, was it the fact that Erin, though she lived so simply, saw things in black and white? She was able to look through all the complexity of a situation and define its essence or root quality. With a skill like that, she'd be one hell of a businesswoman, he decided. There were few people who could look through the mishmash of life and see that important bottom line.

Heat coursed through him as he realized his own personal bottom line. He wanted her—all of her, body and soul. He found himself wanting to meld with her, join together like two hungry flames that had met and mingled. Yes, she was a fire in his heart, and she fed the flames of his desire like no other woman he'd ever met.

Suddenly he was looking forward to the day ahead of him. Glancing around the hogan, he noticed a lot of spider webs hanging here and there where the mud ceiling met the walls. Things needed to be dusted, too. Memories of the past came back, even though he fought them. Memories of working in the kitchen of the orphanage, of washing dishes, scrubbing the floor with a wire brush on his hands and knees, and Old Gordon leaning over him, slapping him on the side of his face, the power of the blow breaking his left eardrum. Blood had flowed out of Dain's ear as he lay on that wet, soapy floor. He'd rolled up in a ball, shrieking in pain, his hands clawing at his ear.

"Damn," he muttered, shoving himself angrily to his feet. Reminding himself that this hogan wasn't anything like his orphanage, he gathered up the dirty dishes and utensils. Instead of allowing the past to ruin his day, he concentrated solely on the moment. He would surprise Erin by doing more than just the menial tasks she'd asked him to share with her. He'd make her proud of him.

Dain tried not to show how eager he was to see Erin and the flock show up. The sun was a fiery red ball on the western horizon, hovering just above the sandstone mesas in the distance, when he saw them coming home. Erin rode on a small, scrawny black horse that trudged slowly behind the flock, the white wolf at her side. She sat proudly on that flea-bitten nag, and he grinned. Standing outside the hogan, his hands on his hips, he enjoyed the way light and shadow lovingly emphasized the classic beauty of her exotic features.

Her braids were frayed where small strands had escaped during the day. The jacket she'd worn was tied behind the cantle of the saddle. The bleat of the sheep was soothing to him. The soft snort of the horse from time to time added to the natural symphony.

Moving down to the holding pen, Dain dragged the gate wide so that the sheep could funnel into it. He saw Erin raise her hand in thanks. Stepping aside, he watched as the white wolf ran forward and guided the head of the flock, a big ram with curved horns, toward the gate.

After the sheep were in the pen, Dain pushed the gate

closed and hung the baling-wire loop over another post. He turned and impulsively walked to her horse and wrapped his hands around her waist. The shock on her face was evident, but she automatically clasped his arms as he lifted her off the animal. He saw a flush color her features as he slid her against his body and brought her to the ground. Her fingers were strong on his arms, work-worn, yet sending tiny shivers of desire up through him to his heart. Then he felt her hands sliding upward, curving around his neck.

Time stood still. When Dain felt her small breasts beneath the velvet of her blouse, an ache gathered in his lower body. She lifted her chin and her lips parted—lips sweet and ripe for the taking. Her sun gold eyes seemed mesmerized by him. Leaning down, Dain took her mouth. He took her. The world suddenly came to a halt as his lips met and molded to hers. Somewhere in his spinning senses, he felt her stiffen in his arms, and just as suddenly capitulate. She swayed fully against him and he felt her fingers move of their own accord into his hair, the touch fiery, goading him on. Her mouth tasted of fresh air, the tartness of the sage that surrounded them. As she met his exploration, she returned his ardor heartbeat for heartbeat. Soaring like an eagle on a current, Dain felt heat gather inside him, and suddenly his heart opened like a flower after a cold, hard winter.

Yes, Erin was his sunlight. His hope. He felt her mouth soften beneath his hungry, searching onslaught. The beat of her heart against his chest was rapid. Wild. Her breathing was irregular and matched his in intensity. She clung to him with her body, with her lips, and the sweetness of life made him giddy with fiery need. She not only tasted of life, she *was* life. Under ordinary circumstances, Dain would have reared back and run the other way. Not now. Not with Erin. He felt her become pliable beneath his hands and he traced the curve of her breasts, her rib cage and womanly hips. She was strong and soft in all the right places. Her breath was moist and warm against his cheek. He felt her fingers curving across his skull, caressing him. Absorbing Erin was like absorbing sunlight on a cold winter's day. He ached to take her, here and now, to lay her down and become one with her. They were like two wolves, hungry for one another, and about to meld together.

Suddenly, he felt Erin stiffen. He released her mouth and drew away, puzzled. She'd enjoyed their kiss as much as he had, no question. What was wrong? Frowning, Dain saw the terror in her eyes as she backed out of his embrace. Her fingers were pressed to her wet, glistening lips as she stared up at him. He saw awe, desire and fear in her eyes. Why fear? What had transpired between them was clean and good. It was life. They were celebrating life!

Awkwardly, he reached out. "I guess I got a little out of hand," he rasped. "I'm sorry...but maybe I'm not..." He stood there, feeling very vulnerable as he watched a myriad of emotions cross her very expressive face. "I didn't mean to scare you, Erin—that I am sorry for. But I'm not sorry for wanting to kiss you." His mouth twisted a little, into a little-boy smile. "You scare me to death on one hand, and the other, I've wondered where you've been all my life...." He caught himself. He'd said far too much, but this woman had the ability to drag the unvarnished truth out of him. What kind of magic did Erin wield over him? He'd never met such a powerful woman in his life. And yet Dain felt safe with her—and maybe he even trusted her enough to allow himself to feel.

Erin took another step back, not because she was afraid of Dain, but because she was afraid of herself and her own boiling reactions to him as a man. She hadn't expected to kiss him! She shouldn't have kissed him! But how could she help herself? His mouth was so male, so provocative. At the same time, it seduced her, gentling her as if she were a wild, wary she-wolf who had gone too long without her mate. Confused, Erin whispered, "Let's just forget this happened. Please...." She saw the hurt in his eyes and felt terrible. "It's me, not you...." *My past*—but she didn't dare say that, either. "Bring that rabbit from the saddle. It's our meal for tonight." Turning away, Erin hurried to the hogan.

Dain stood by the horse. He unsaddled the animal, put the saddle over the fence and let him go. Picking up the rabbit that had been tied to the back of the saddle, he stood there giving himself time to come down from the euphoria still inhabiting him. She was right—the kiss shouldn't have occurred. Hell, he hadn't been consciously thinking of kissing her. It just happened. The joy thrumming through him wouldn't go away, though, because he realized as he slowly trudged back to the hogan that Erin had enjoyed their unexpected kiss as much as he had. But something was scaring her. What was it? Him? No, he didn't feel that. And then he grinned like a little boy. The world was afraid of him— except for this woman who had such fiery spirit and graciousness of heart. She wasn't afraid of him at all. With a shake of his head, Dain wondered if something in her past was making her fearful. He promised himself that at the appropriate moment, he would try and find out.

"You have a good day at the office?" he teased lightly, hoping to make her feel less tense as he approached the sink outside the hogan where she stood washing her hands with soap and water.

Erin turned at the gentle inquiry. She saw Dain trying very hard to make her feel comfortable after their unexpected kiss. Her heart lurched, and her gaze went directly to his mouth—that warm, masculine mouth that had breathed such life into her as a woman.... All she wanted to do was kiss him again. Somehow, Erin had to get her unraveling emotions under control. She tried to smile, but it was impossible, and she gave him a nod instead. "It was a hot day. Hotter than I expected. But in September, we can have frosty mornings, burning days and thunderstorms all within twenty-four hours." She watched as he placed the rabbit on the counter.

He stood there, his hands resting on his hips. Lord help him, he enjoyed her closeness. "I've had rabbit under glass at the best of restaurants. Just haven't seen the 'before' of what it was like," he noted ruefully.

Erin managed a slight smile. "Unless you don't want anything to eat, that's our food for the night." When she saw his quizzical expression, she said, "I have no electricity, no refrigerator. I'm not a vegetarian and I don't think you are, either, so any meat I get is what I find when I'm out with the flock. We were lucky today. This rabbit gave up his life so that we might live."

Dain stood there watching as she rinsed her face, arms and hands. Droplets of water clung to her braids and eyelashes, the last of the daylight catching them, making them glimmer like pearls. There was an incredible naturalness to Erin, to her world.

"I wish I'd thought of doing that earlier today," he admitted, moving to one side and leaning against the counter.

Straightening, Erin wiped the water from her eyes with her fingers. "What?" Her heart beat hard in response to his continued nearness. She wanted him close, but at the same time feared her own loss of control. No man had ever unstrung her as Dain had done.

He gestured to the woodpile near the hogan. "When I was chopping wood, I was hotter than hell and wishing for a cold shower."

He handed her the threadbare towel and she hesitantly took it. Their fingertips met briefly. Tingles arced up her hand, and her heart pounded. Trying to find her voice as she patted her face, she murmured, "The best learning comes from observing another."

He chuckled indulgently. "Cold showers come in many forms," he agreed. He could tell from her quizzical expression that his comment was lost on her. Right now he needed to put out the fire he felt in him. Trying to be more reserved, he said, "So things went okay at the office today?"

Erin looked up at him. She saw less tension in Dain's face and realized he had a mild sunburn. He hadn't shaved, his beard giving him an even more dangerous look than before. "My office is the desert," she agreed, "and I love being on horseback, watching my sheep."

"No cougars?"

"No, not today. Maiisoh chased off a coyote, that was all."

"Maiisoh?"

"The white wolf. His name is Navajo for wolf."

"Appropriate." As they approached the door, Dain pointed to the left. "Think I chopped enough wood?"

Erin stopped and looked. "There's enough wood for three days." She looked up at him and grinned. "Thank you."

Her praise felt like a wash of sunlight through him. He tried not to feel it, fighting the powerful sense of pleasure it gave him. But it was impossible when gold flecks danced deep in her brown eyes. He not only saw the sincerity and gratefulness in her gaze, but the sudden catch of surprise and then happiness in her voice wrapped around him like a loving blanket.

"You're welcome," he said as lightly as possible. Anxious to distract her, he held up the rabbit. "What about this guy?"

"I shot him. You skin him."

Dain was nonplussed. "Skin?"

"Unless you want to eat him fur and all?"

He regarded the animal. "No, but…"

"First," Erin said briskly, gesturing for him to follow her, "we must pray for his spirit." She took Dain to the small, dilapidated barn made out of plywood with tar paper siding. Opening the door, she went in and started searching about on a shelf, finally picking up a knife.

"Bring one of those bundles of dried sage wrapped with red yarn, and some matches," she said, pointing to a small wooden box in the corner. Then she led him back out to the huge cottonwood chopping block that was used to split wood on.

Dain watched intently as she lit the sage, blew out the flame and watched the thick, white smoke purl upward.

"This is called smudging," she told him. "This is sacred sage that I've ceremonially gathered. What that means is that I've gone out on the desert here, asking a sage plant to give me the gift of some of its branches. I explain that giving its limbs will enable me to use it in a sacred way. I give the plant a gift of cornmeal before I ask. And even if the plant denies my request, I present a gift of cornmeal a second time. Eventually, I find a plant that is willing to give me a part of itself."

She held up the sprigs of sage, the stem ends wrapped tightly with red yarn. "Red symbolizes a woman's moon blood, honoring the plant as well as its spirit. We never take anything's life without asking it to give its life so that we may survive." Erin waved her hand to move the thick white smoke across the entire jackrabbit, stretched out across the chopping block.

"Sage is sacred to all Indians, and we use it like you might use soap and water—it cleanses things it touches." She then leaned down and waved the smoke against Dain's feet, slowly moving it upward to the top of his head. "Inhale this and understand that I am cleansing you. This smoke chases away any negative or bad thoughts, so that you are now clean and sacred like the rabbit."

She put the stick of sage into the sand nearby and came back and picked up the knife. "Now we pray to the Great Spirit to release this rabbit's spirit so that it may go over the rainbow bridge and find new life."

Dain didn't pray, but he watched as she laid her hands reverently over the jackrabbit and crouched down beside the block. Bending her head, she closed her eyes, her lips moving with silent prayer. When she was done, she lifted her face and gazed up at him. There was such sacredness to her act, it moved him.

"All life is precious," she whispered as she eased herself to her feet. "This afternoon, as I sat upon my horse, I sent a prayer to the Great Spirit and asked that an animal be sent to me who would surrender her or his life, so that we might live." She gestured to the rabbit. "A few minutes later, this rabbit hopped out in front of me. He told me that he'd come because he'd heard my prayer. I thanked him and told him I would take his life quickly, so that he would feel no pain."

Dain avoided looking at the rabbit's bloody head, where the bullet had entered and left. "Yeah," he muttered, "that's nice." He gave a wry grin. "I think I prefer having the chef bring the final product to the table."

Taking the knife, Erin nodded. "You're spoiled. Now watch me carefully. I will show you how to skin this rabbit. The next time, I will expect you to do it." Just the act of doing something helped her stabilize her wildly fluctuating emotions. She was grateful to be in charge once again—in control. Erin knew that where Dain was concerned control wasn't guaranteed at all—and that both scared and drew her. Her feelings were a double-edged sword, but she knew she must confront them—for his sake as well as her own.

Dain didn't want to watch Erin, but there was a grisly fascination to it all. His mouth went dry and he put his hands on his hips, tension thrumming through him. With the first clean stroke of the knife, it was obvious she'd skinned rabbits all her life. Within a few minutes, she'd skinned the animal. But when it came time to gut it, he turned his head, his lips curling away from his teeth.

"Watch," she commanded.

He snapped his head back and met her dark gaze. "This is sickening."

"I don't know why," she said, gutting the animal. "You go to the supermarket and buy beef, pork and chicken. Someone is doing this for you. Doing what I'm doing."

His nostrils flared as he watched. To his disgust, Maiisoh waited eagerly at her side. She tossed him the entrails, which the wolf quickly gulped down as if they were dessert.

"Why is this a bad thing?" Erin asked. Once the rabbit was clean, she took it over to the water trough. There was a galvanized bucket nearby, and she filled it with water and washed the carcass.

"It's disgusting."

"Why?" she asked calmly, lifting the rabbit from the bucket and walking toward him.

"It just is," he muttered, turning away. He didn't want to look at the damned thing, and his appetite was gone.

With a shrug, she handed the carcass to him. He hesitated, but finally took it. Taking the pail of water, she rinsed the chopping block of blood and fur. "I clean up everything afterward, and later I will clean the skinning knife with soap and water." She took the rabbit fur and smiled. "Tonight I will stake this out on a board to dry. It will make a useful fur for a coat I am making. This winter I'll tan the skin, when I'm forced to stay inside because of the blizzards."

"Nothing goes to waste," he observed distastefully.

"No," Erin agreed genially as she headed up the small knoll. "Maiisoh has his meal, we will have ours and I will have one more skin for a coat I need very badly this winter."

"Why not go to Chinle and buy yourself a coat? Wouldn't that be easier?"

Erin opened the door to the hogan. "I very rarely have money."

He gave her a strange look.

She laughed. "The people who come here to heal themselves are very poor. Many times they bring only themselves. Sometimes a sheep. Or a piece of jewelry from their family."

"You can pawn the jewelry for money."

"I do," she said, entering the hogan.

"So, you've got money to spend on that coat you need," he said, following her in.

"You do not understand," Erin said, going directly to a plastic dish filled with cool, soapy water. "There are many elderly people on this reservation who would starve to death if I did not buy them groceries. In the winter, I try and reach all these old ones in my pickup." She pointed to a small box on the floor nearby. "That is my pawn box. I save the turquoise-and-silver jewelry my patients bring, and each October I drive to Gallup, New Mexico, and sell it for cash. With the money, I shop for groceries, mostly canned goods, and bring them home. Then I deliver the bags of groceries to the old ones who live nearby."

Dain set the rabbit on the table and watched her scrub the skinning knife and then wash her hands. "How the hell do *you* survive then?" he asked, genuinely concerned.

With a chuckle, Erin dried her hands on a thin towel hanging on the side of the dresser. "One day at a time."

"No kidding." Dain frowned, wondering how often she went hungry.

"That is why," she said very seriously, pointing to the rabbit, "that I'm grateful my prayers are answered. On some days, they are not."

"And then what do you do? Starve?"

Laughing, she shook her head and took a butcher knife, quickly cutting the carcass into four quarters. "You saw the huge garden in back of the hogan when you went to the hot springs?"

"Yes."

"I raise root crops like potatoes, yams and carrots." She gestured to the right. "There is an apple tree over there, and each fall she gives me a wonderful stock of her fruit. There is a root cellar there," she said, gesturing in another direction, "where all my food supplies are kept in baskets. The winters are hard around here, and getting a fine jackrabbit like this for a meal is rare." She pointed to the large iron skillet. "Put some bacon grease in it and I'll dredge these quarters in flour and then we'll fry them." She grinned. "It will be a fine meal we'll share tonight."

Dain wasn't so sure. It bothered him that she lived like this. He stood next to the stove and watched her closely because he knew that she expected him to be able to do this the next time. Now that he knew meat was a special commodity and not to be taken lightly, he paid attention.

"I guess," he groused, "I took a lot for granted around here."

Erin gingerly turned the rabbit over and over in the hot skillet. "Out here," she said softly, "*nothing* is taken for granted. Ever."

Rubbing his jaw, he eyed her as she cooked the rabbit. "Have you ever…gone hungry?"

"What is hunger? There is the hunger of the stomach for food. Then, more important, there is the hunger of one's spirit." In a quieter tone, she continued, "The hunger of one's heart…"

Dain saw a special look in her eyes as their gazes connected briefly. "I know how you feed a stomach," he said, pointing at the frying rabbit. "The heart—yeah, that's important, too." Then he rubbed his chest because he could still feel the warmth of Erin's kiss inside.

She smiled a little. "If our heart is happy, we never get sick. Sometimes, when a person opens up his heart, it can be healed.…" She spoke not only for him, but for herself. Dain's kiss, despite its suddenness, made her feel good in a way she'd never experienced. Although Erin had sworn off men in general, she was not about to discount the healing that Dain had just shared with her, for it worked both ways. Wanting to acknowledge in some way how much his presence in her life meant to her, she said, "Thanks for taking care of things around here today. The hogan looks wonderful."

Heat moved up Dain's neck and into his face. He was

blushing like a pimple-faced teenager, of all things! He dipped his head, unable to meet her shining eyes and acknowledge the pleased look in their depths. Him, blushing! How many years had it been since he'd done that? He honestly couldn't recall.

Erin saw his face flush a dull red, and to her, it was becoming. "You are not used to praise?"

Shrugging, he turned away and jammed his hands into the pockets of his pants. "I try not to let people's feelings— whether their anger, their hatred or their praise—get to me."

"Why?"

"Because," he said, turning back toward her, "I don't *care* what other people think of me."

Chortling, Erin shook her head. "Oh, Dain Phillips, you coyote! You have tricked yourself into believing your own lies!"

Scowling, he moved back to the stove. "What are you talking about? I'm not lying."

She heard the anger in his voice and saw it in his eyes. "My grandmother, Howling Moon, told me a long time ago, 'Erin, don't ever lie to yourself. You might lie to others, but know that you are lying. Don't ever lie to yourself.'"

"What the hell does that mean?"

"It means," Erin said calmly, turning the rabbit over in the skillet, "that you are lying to yourself when you stand here and tell me that what a person thinks of you doesn't matter to you."

"It doesn't," he snapped.

"Then," she said, holding his belligerent gaze, "why did you just blush when I praised you?"

Compressing his lips, he saw the merriment in her golden eyes, felt the warmth and honesty she exuded. "I don't know."

Her laughter was husky. "Yes, you do! You see, you've lied to me twice now."

"I haven't lied to you!"

Shrugging, the smile still shadowing her lips, she said, "Very well, continue to lie to me and to yourself, Dain Phillips. Just know that I know, that is all. Lies can only exist if one or both parties believe in them." Her smile dissolved as she held his mutinous look. "I honor your spirit more than you do at this point. Your spirit knows the truth of you, all of you—your hurts, your grief, those things that give you joy and pain. If you must lie to me, so be it, but *never* lie to yourself. Be honest with yourself—no matter how much it hurts."

"Yeah? Well, let me tell you something," he said heatedly, "I don't like being called a liar by you or anyone." Despite his harsh words, Dain was wrong and he knew it. Erin had caught him red-handed, but his stiff-necked pride wouldn't let him admit it to her just yet. There was no anger in her expression, only compassion, and that made him even more prickly.

Erin allowed the silence to stand between them for a good two minutes before she spoke again. She could see he was angry, but she didn't take it personally because it wasn't hers to take. "Tell me," she began gently, "has the fever come to stalk you today?"

Shaken by the sudden turn of the conversation, he stared at her for a moment before he could reply. "Fever?"

"Yes, your fever comes every afternoon. Did it hit you today?"

Thinking for a moment, Dain eased his hands out of his pockets and draped them across his hips. "Why, er, no, I don't think it did."

"Good," Erin murmured.

He studied her for a few moments, trying to make sense of this turn of events. In the silence, his stomach growled and the odor of the frying rabbit made his mouth water. He saw Erin grin knowingly—she must have heard his stomach clamoring for food.

"You are more wolf than you realize," she teased with

a chuckle. "Get the plates out of the cabinet and put them on the table. We're almost ready to eat."

Moving toward the table, Dain found his mind whirling with shock. Why hadn't the fever come to stalk him like it did every afternoon? He hadn't even thought of it—at all. And he'd chopped wood all afternoon. By the time he was done, his knees were weakening, but he'd felt invigorated by the hard, physical exercise. Reaching for he plates in the cupboard, he shook his head.

"I've had that fever ever since they diagnosed the tumor," he told her as he put the plates on the red-and-white-checked oilcloth.

Erin lifted the skillet from the stove and brought it over to the table. She put half the rabbit on his plate and half on hers. "How do you explain that it did not come today?"

He put flatware on the table as she slipped the skillet into the soapy water, causing a sizzling sound and rising steam. "Damned if I know." Without thinking, he pulled out the chair for Erin to sit on. He saw her eyes light up with thanks and that soft, shy smile appear on her lips. Again he felt heat crawling up his neck into his face. Damn it, anyway! Avoiding her gaze, he turned and went to the opposite side of the square table, jerked out his chair and sat down.

As she placed her hands over her portion of the meat, he knew that she was once again praying. Looking down at his share, he felt grateful himself in a way, because he hadn't realized there wasn't a whole lot of food for them to depend on. He waited until she was done and then picked up the fork and knife.

"So," Erin said, slicing off a thick, juicy piece of the meat, "why did the fever not come today?"

"Maybe it was the fresh air and sunshine. Who knows?"

"You did many things different today than you would if you were back East?"

He laughed shortly and savored the chickenlike flavor of the rabbit. "Just a little."

"So what was different?"

"My normal day goes something like this—I get up at six a.m. I have breakfast, swim twenty laps in my pool, and then I take a helicopter into Manhattan, to my office. By eight a.m. I have ten assistants giving me verbal reports from my companies around the world. I look at the faxes that have come in, then start the telephone calls and appointments for the day. This goes on until about one p.m., when I have a business lunch with someone. By two-thirty I'm back in my office until eight, when I usually have a business dinner planned, or some other business function."

Erin's eyes widened. "You never get outdoors?"

"Oh, on weekends," he said casually. "I take fencing lessons three nights a week, and I play in squash tournaments on weekends. I get plenty of exercise."

"But you never see Father Sun or inhale fresh air."

He held up his forearm, and the thick, dark hair on it gleamed in the lamplight. "I got sunburned a little today. I got so hot chopping wood I took off my shirt." He grimaced. "That was a mistake."

She smiled slightly and chewed her food thoughtfully. "There is much healing benefit to being out in fresh air and allowing Father Sun's rays to embrace you."

"Obviously. But maybe it was that salve you put on my head last night that kept the fever away. Or," he murmured huskily, "your touch." *Or your kiss,* he wanted to add. *Your hot, open, giving mouth against mine....*

Flushing, Erin avoided his dark, intense look. She cut up more of the meat with her knife and fork. "Do not give your power away to me," she warned seriously.

"What do you mean?"

"You are putting greater stock in my touching your head last night than in any of the other reasons why your fever may not have stalked you this afternoon. Neither of us can say for sure what helped. Whatever it was, it worked because your spirit gave you permission to allow these good things, like fresh air, sunshine and chaparral salve, to help you. A fever only comes if the body is unable to fight off what attacks it. It's not important *what* did it, only that it happened. If you try and say my touch did it, you are giving your power away to me, and that is not good.''

"Doctors take my power all the time, then,'' he said with a chuckle, finishing off the first piece of rabbit and hungrily cutting up the second.

"That is not good.''

"Let's say your touch did do it.'' Though he didn't suggest it, he really wondered what her kiss had done for him, for he certainly felt healed and more open because of it.

"Then,'' Erin said slowly, "you must understand that your spirit gave permission to allow my touch to in some way help you.''

His grin widened. "Humility. Man, the doctors I know could learn a thing or two from you.''

"If people set themselves up to say they are a doctor or a healer, they have the responsibility to understand their part in this beautiful miracle. They are not the miracle worker. They are only a physical tube through which the life-giving energy flows to the patient.'' She shrugged and lifted her hands. "How can I claim to do anything when only you really understand what is happening?''

Picking up the saltshaker, he sprinkled the meat. "True humility. How about that?'' He set the shaker down and held her perplexed look, understanding that Erin honestly believed what she was saying. "You see the healing dynamic very differently than the doctors I've been going to. I don't know that I believe as you believe. It's too early to tell.'' But he was amazed by her intelligence and perception. She was a woman of many facets and layers, and that drew him even more to her.

"Yet your fever is gone.''

"For today,'' he stressed grimly. Glancing at the gold

Rolex on his right wrist, he said, "In about an hour, my headache should start coming on."

Sighing, Erin said, "Perhaps." She saw the merriment in Dain's eyes for the first time, and the upward curve of his very masculine mouth sent fire streaking through her. She had to stop responding to him woman to man. How? Helplessly, Erin realized that Dain had unknowingly tipped over her apple cart of control, and she was scrambling emotionally. His presence was a blessing and a curse to her. She had to work through the fact that *he* was her teacher, too, and that the white wolf had brought Dain here for many reasons—among them, her own need to begin her healing journey with men in general, and to work through unresolved fears from her past. Dain was as much a catalyst to her as she was to him. Did she have the strength, the bravery it would take, to take on the challenge this rugged man presented her with?

Looking at him, her gaze dropping to his mouth as he relished the rabbit, she felt her body throb with memories of pleasure that had been carefully stored away and ignored—until his kiss.

Chapter Eight

"**W**hy do you live out here instead of back on your own reservation?" Dain asked as they dawdled over coffee after dinner. He watched her expression closely, and saw pain come momentarily to her light brown eyes, muting the gold flecks that often danced in them. Her long, strong fingers wrapped around the old, chipped white mug.

"It is a long story, and not one I wish to speak of," she said in a strained tone. The last thing Erin wanted was to discuss her sordid, nightmarish past.

"Ah," he murmured, "I'm supposed to be an open book, but you're not?"

She gave him a wry smile. "You? An open book? I do not feel or see that—yet."

"I make it my business to know who I'm dealing with."

She shrugged and tried to appear nonchalant. "Look around you. There is nothing hidden about me." She held his searching, intense gaze. "You hide behind a mask, like many people do."

"And you don't?"

"I try not to, although sometimes I do." At least it wasn't a total lie. But Erin didn't like telling him a half-truth, either. Right now, her life, her problems, weren't the focus—Dain was—as it should be. She tried to calm the sense of panic she felt at his probing.

"What's your definition of a mask?" he asked before taking a sip of his coffee.

"A mask is a shield we put in place to protect ourselves from this world around us. It can be used to hide a deep wound that is still open and bleeding within us. The more vulnerable we feel, the larger the mask. And—" she studied him "—the harder it is to take off when we don't need it."

He met her steady gaze. "You think I'm one of those people."

The corners of her mouth flexed slightly. "It's something I *feel*. It's something I have observed in you. The real question is do you know you're wearing this mask? What is the mask composed of? Can you take it off and put it on at will? Do you know when *not* to put the mask on?"

"Give me an example." He felt a frisson of panic, but it quickly disappeared because on some level, since their unexpected kiss, he trusted her. Right or wrong, he was beginning to have faith in her—and that scared him more than anything else.

"I see fear in your eyes. Why?"

His mouth quirked.

"What are you feeling?"

"Right now?" He snorted. "I feel as if you can look straight through me and see me, my fear."

"Perhaps," Erin said slowly, "you are afraid of me seeing your vulnerability? That little boy in you who was abandoned?"

His gut clenched. He stared at her, the silence heavy and brittle around them. Working his jaw, he rasped, "I *never* talk about my past."

Erin's heart lurched unexpectedly at his husky admission. A deluge of terror cascaded around her—his terror. Her heart opened to him, despite her fear of him as a white man who might hurt her. She reached out, placing her fingers over his as they clenched the mug. The tension in his hand, the whitening of his knuckles, told her how much he was hurting. She moved her fingers in a soothing motion across his flesh. "A child who is deprived of touch, of hugs, of loving embraces, will put a powerful mask over himself to hide what was rightfully his and never given to him."

She hesitated, trying to deal with the overwhelming terror she felt and saw in his face. "When a human or animal is not nurtured by its mother, not held, licked or nuzzled, the infant is never allowed to form that invisible tie to its biological mother or its real mother, the Earth. The mask these people put in place shields them from life's many hurts, and they learn that to attack with anger, to assault first before they are assaulted, is the best form of defense."

Dain stared down at her hand. He felt the roughness of her fingers against his skin, felt the tiny prickles of heat that emanated from the contact. Swallowing hard, he absorbed her softly spoken words, words that were filled with incredible compassion. And though some of his fear abated, other fears reared up, and he wanted to jerk his hand away from her. But his heart wanted, needed, her continued touch.

Erin felt desire leap within her. Desire for him alone. It wasn't a proper feeling, but it was there nonetheless. The look in his eyes changed, too, when she made contact with his hand. Trying to deny her own need, she stumbled on. "During lambing season, which begins in March," she whispered, continuing to move her fingers lightly across his hand, maintaining the contact, "some mothers die. I then have to find another mother that will take that lamb. Usually, they won't, and I end up with six to ten lambs here in the hogan that I have to bottle-feed if they are to survive. When a lamb nurses, it butts its head against my breast, snuggles and wants to be held and coddled. I noticed many years ago that if I did not do that, if I did not embrace the lambs, pet them and love them while I nursed them with the bottle of warm milk and honey, that they became loners. They would not follow the flock. They would wander off by themselves, because they had never bonded with the herd or anyone. But when they wandered off, they were often killed by coyotes waiting in the brush.''

Erin gave him an imploring look. ''Your mask is large and powerful. You wear it to protect your vulnerability, because you feel a great loss, of contact with your mother. A good defense is a good offense, and that is what you put out there. It is a frightening mask that I'm sure scares off most people.''

Erin lifted her hand from his and touched her breast. ''Masks may protect us, but they also stop genuine love, care, affection and laughter from entering through it to the vulnerable you hidden beneath. A mask will stop the life energy from penetrating to the core of you, no matter how wounded you are. Little by little, over the years, the mask cuts off this outer energy that is available to everything and everyone. Little by little, like a plant not getting rain from Father Sky, you die. Your spirit, which thirsts for this rain from others, from the things that are around you, begins to shrivel and get smaller and smaller, until it is only a flicker of a candle flame in the darkness of your inner world.''

Anger sizzled through Dain. He felt the white-hot blade of fury thrust up through his gut, through his knotted stomach as he glared at her. ''Who told you about my past? That I was an orphan?''

''No one,'' Erin said quietly, her heart lurching. Gone was the desire in his eyes, replaced by raw fear.

''You're lying,'' he growled, shoving away from the table, his hands flat on it as he looked at her serene features.

She looked back at him, feeling his fury, his shock over her placing her finger on the most vulnerable part of himself, on his worst secret. "I will not hurt you with that information. In order to heal, if that is what you truly want to do, you must own your past. You were abandoned by your mother. You were given up. She did not, in your eyes, love you enough to keep you—"

"Shut up!" As soon as he uttered the cutting words, Dain was sorry. His rage mingled with his need—need of Erin as a woman.

She sat very quietly, seeing the terror in his glazed eyes, in his contorted mouth, in the fists that were balled up at his sides. She felt the brittle rigidity in him, and saw the defensiveness in the way he hitched his shoulder upward, as if expecting a physical blow.

"You asked for an example of your mask. I have given you one. Why do you aim your anger at me when it was you who asked for it in the first place?" Erin knew that whatever trust may have sprung up between them with that unexpected kiss could be destroyed by her probing of his past. And though it had to be done, she lamented it.

Suddenly Dain felt trapped. His nostrils flared and he spun away from her. His breathing strangled, he had to open his mouth and take in several gulps of air.

"Someone's given you that information on me," he growled, whirling around again and jabbing his finger at her. In that moment he hated her as she sat relaxed at the table, her face mirroring such peace—a peace he certainly didn't feel.

"Healing means opening up."

"My past is not up for discussion. You got that?"

"Then," Erin said, slowly rising and picking up her plate and flatware, "you will choose to die."

Shocked, Dain assimilated her words as he watched her go to the sink and place the plate in soapy water. Gathering his scattered thoughts, he strode over to where she stood washing her dishes.

"What the hell right do you have to say that to me?" he demanded harshly.

Erin looked up at him and held his stormy gaze. "You have chosen to live under my roof, in my home. You came here in order to make a choice between living and dying. It was *your* choice. It still is." She slowly resumed washing the plate with the dishcloth. "It is not my place to force you to stay or force you to go."

"This is so much manipulation!" Dain shouted. Then he walked angrily around her, jerked opened the door and slammed it behind him as he left.

Erin cringed as the door slammed. She felt as if he'd physically struck her, and memories of her own past slammed into her. With a sigh, she rinsed off the plate and flatware and put them in the dish drainer to dry. Hurt animals always tried to snap and bite the person who was trying to tend their wounds. What else did she expect? She knew better. Dain's mask of anger and assault were well in place and he was attacking her because she'd identified the core of his wound.

Her heart ached with hurt for him. Even though he was a man—and a strong, confident one—she saw the innocent little eight-year-old boy standing in that great big empty hall—alone. She saw the terror in his face, the destitute look in his eyes. She held on to that recurring image because that's who she was really dealing with—not the rich corporate mogul, but a wounded child who was hurting so much. Tears dampened her lashes as she sensed once again just how much.

Her mother had taught her there was a danger in being an empathic healer because the healer had to take on the wounded person's pain and all his emotions. So Erin had learned how to transfer the pain outside herself. But still it was necessary for her to feel it, even if briefly, and this was her path in this lifetime—the wounded healer who must experience others' pain before she could heal. She was a sounding board, a whipping post and, as such, she had to stand solidly in her own truth, in her own harmony, so that the sorrows of others didn't knock her out of balance.

Her hands trembled slightly as she dried them on a towel. She wasn't that solid herself, she decided. He'd brought up her past and she'd refused him entrance—just as he was refusing her entrance into his. With a shake of her head, Erin realized she felt tenuous and unsure of herself with Dain. Meeting him was like meeting herself in some ways—at least, the wounded part of herself that still needed to be healed. Well, didn't the Great Spirit always bring people to her door who mirrored an aspect of herself? An aspect that was still oozing energy in the form of grief, pain or anger?

Yes. This time it appeared to Erin as if she had met her ultimate reflection. Did she have the courage to open herself up to him? Her own wounds had not been healed, so how was she going to help him emotionally, to prepare him for whatever was to be his final destiny? This was a new experience for her, one that she had no previous knowledge about to help her. Worse, she found herself drawn to him as a man. That upset her most—he was a white man and she knew he could rip her soul apart as it had been once before. The kiss lingered hotly in her memory and her lips tingled. One raw, hungry kiss that had breathed life back into both their souls…

Being around Dain was like constantly being out of balance internally—as if she was skating too close to some dark, unexplored level of herself. His anger flayed her more than anyone's she'd ever encountered. His loss scored her more deeply. His pain was pure agony to her. Wiping her tears away with the backs of her hands, she sniffed and went about collecting her shell and smudge stick. It was time.

Going outside, she saw Dain sitting on the edge of the watering trough, facing the setting sun. The western sky was a bright red-orange, the long, spidery cirrus clouds turning brilliant as they caught the light. He was sitting stiffly, fists

clenched on his taut thighs. As she quietly approached him,
she saw the suffering on his face. It was not a pretty face,
but a rugged one, etched and carved deeply with signs of
his quiet struggle with his anguish from the past.

"Each morning and each evening," she said as she
stopped at his shoulder, "I sing a song of welcome and of
thanks to Father Sun. Sunrise and sunset are the most powerful times for us. When the sun rises we give thanks for
being allowed to see another day, and when it sets, we give
thanks for what we've been given that day." She set the
abalone shell on the red sand and crouched down to light
the sage.

"Would you like to join me?" When she looked at him,
she saw the anger and hurt burning in his eyes, but she also
saw he wanted to be with her. Dain flexed his fingers, re-
laxing his fists. She ached to have those long, strong fingers
caressing her again, awakening her once more. Just the
thought of it caused a throbbing to begin in her lower body.

"What do I do?" he growled. How desperately he wanted
to reach out, catch her hand and squeeze it and say he was
sorry for his roughness toward her. But despite his desire,
he just couldn't do it.

"Nothing. Just be. I will smudge us with the sacred
smoke of the sage. It cleanses us of all our bad feelings, our
thoughts and negativity. Then I will offer a song to Father
Sun, a prayer of thanksgiving for allowing us to live this
day on our mother, the Earth."

"Fine," he muttered, slowly rubbing his hands up and
down the taut material covering his thighs. He had to do
something to keep from reaching out for her—reaching out
and kissing once again those full, soft lips that tasted of the
earth and the sunlight.

Leaning down, Erin waved the thick, white smoke across
Dain's feet and legs, up across his body and over his head.
Then she did the same for herself. Placing the wand of sage
back in the abalone shell, she moved to his shoulder and

faced the setting sun with him. Opening her hands, palms outward, she lifted her chin and allowed the ancient Eastern Cherokee song to flow from her heart.

Dain closed his eyes as he heard Erin begin to sing. A shiver of longing ran through him. She stood only inches from him, her hands outstretched in supplication, her voice low and warm. And though he didn't understand the words she sang, it was obvious from her sweet tune that her song was one of gratefulness and thanks. The last of the fiery, golden orb of the sun dipped behind the darkened line of bluffs in the distance and all the anger, all the fear he felt, dissolved with her song, with her nearness.

How could he hate her in one moment and need her so desperately the next? His head spun with so many questions and no answers. He didn't *want* to need Erin. He'd never needed anyone. Besides, he disliked her staunchness, her ability to stand nakedly and without defenses within her truth. She saw him clearly—too clearly—and he didn't feel safe around her. He wanted to run away, and yet he panicked at the thought of leaving her. How could he feel like this? He'd never felt like this in his life.

Was she controlling him? Was it a subtle form of manipulation she was using on him? He wanted to believe that was it. She was, after all, a medicine woman, someone who knew how to manipulate a person's reality and could probably nail his hide to a wall. Damn! He closed his eyes and compressed his lips into a single line of frustration. Then he remembered that she never attacked him back. Never got angry with him. What gave her that kind of patience with him? *What?*

As the sun dipped further behind the bluffs, he felt the coolness of the evening steal upon him. Erin finished her song of thanksgiving and he opened his eyes. Watching her out of the corner of his eye, he saw a soft smile appear on her mouth, saw the awe, the thanks, in her eyes. The sense that he had been a part of a miracle flowed through him.

Yes, there was magic in this land. Erin was magic. Her voice was an incredible instrument that moved him as nothing had ever done before—except for her physical touch. When she'd reached out at the table and run her fingers over his hand, he'd nearly leaped out of his skin. Her contact had been completely unexpected. No one ever touched him. Everyone was afraid of him and wouldn't dare think of touching him in such a manner. Yet she had, as effortlessly as a sheep nuzzled another, or a horse rubbed another horse's neck.

"Each day is a gift to us," Erin whispered, sitting by his feet in order to remain near him, wrapping her arms around her drawn-up knees beneath her skirt. "A day brings lessons to us. My only question to myself is can I see the lesson? Will I recognize it? If I do, will I be able to learn from it?" She turned and looked up at his features. He seemed contemplative now, no longer burning with anger. But there was raw desire in his eyes, causing her body to throb with need.

She desperately tried to remain impervious to it. Lifting her hand, she said, "The Great Spirit brings people, situations and things to our doorstep for us to recognize, to learn from." She gestured gracefully toward the desert, which was growing more shadowed. "I know that if I do not learn the first time, the same lesson will come to me again and again, in different forms, until I do learn from it."

"And once you learn from it, then what?" Dain demanded darkly, meeting and holding her luminous gaze. In that moment, the shadows were deep across her face, emphasizing the cleanness of her high cheekbones, the slight tilt of her eyes, the vulnerability of her parted lips. He had an overwhelming urge to lean down, to cup that beautifully exquisite face in his hands, to place his mouth against hers and drink her life into him.

Erin saw the change in his eyes, felt the change in him. A new, startling sensation wound through her, like a molten ribbon touching the core of her womanhood. It was a pleasurable sensation, one that she'd felt when he'd kissed her, and she welcomed it back like an old, wonderful friend. She saw his desire for her burning in his eyes—man to woman, not patient to medicine woman. For a moment, it caught her off guard, for her patients were always just patients—not potential lovers. But Dain was both, her heart whispered to her.

She ached in response. How long had it been since she'd been touched physically by a man? Too long. Much too long. The throbbing deepened within her, primal and hungry. It took all her strength to place a lid over that boiling cauldron. When she spoke, her voice was slightly breathy.

"Once one lesson is learned, the Great Spirit places another one before me. Before all of us." She turned and broke contact with his gaze, absorbing the masculinity he exuded. Gesturing toward the darkening sky, she said, "That is why each day is so precious to me. Sometimes I know when I've learned a lesson, and I'm very happy. I don't always learn the lesson the first time. I make many, many mistakes, but that is acceptable. What is important is that I try." She looked up at Dain over her shoulder. "You must try, too."

Her gentle smile went straight to his aching heart. "Tell me something, do you have a Ph.D. in psychiatry you didn't tell me about?"

Her laughter was strong and rich. Getting slowly to her feet, she dusted off her hands. "I don't even have a high school education." Her voice lowered with pain. "I never finished school on my reservation because something happened—and I left before I graduated."

Dain studied her in the twilight and felt her pain—rather than his own this time. That surprised him, because he made it a point to steer clear of other people's emotions. But he wanted to take on Erin's pain—to ease her burden. He was just about to ask why she'd left the reservation when the first, sharp stabs of his headache pulled him back into his own painful reality.

"Damn," he snarled, standing, "the headache's coming back."

"Then come inside," Erin said, reaching out and sliding her fingers along his elbow. "Let us see what you can do to move the pain away."

Her touch was incredibly warm and alive. He tried to focus on that contact, but the pain was coming like waves crashing onto the shore. "That chaparral salve?" he asked as he walked with her toward the hogan. He was glad she kept her hand on his arm. He needed her close contact right now to help him through his devastation. He had thought that because the fever hadn't come today, there would be no headache. He'd been wrong—there had been no progress made. Was his strength today only temporary? A figment of his desperate imagination?

"Here is the salve," Erin said.

After lighting the hurricane lamps, she brought over the small jar of salve. Dain looked defeated as he took it from her hand.

"Do not give up," she said, gesturing for him to sit on the rug near the stove. "First, hold the jar in your hands, close your eyes and thank the spirit of the chaparral for being here with you. Then ask that spirit to help you."

He stared at her in disbelief.

"Ask."

Grimacing, because the headache was getting worse by the minute, he muttered, "I have a real problem with asking for help."

Chuckling, Erin said, "I know. So ask."

Closing his eyes reluctantly, Dain mentally did as she instructed. When he was done, he opened his eyes to find Erin had come and sat down a few feet away from him, her legs crossed, her hands resting in the lap of her skirt. Her face was very grave, the dancing, flickering glow of the kerosene lamps emphasizing her large, cinnamon eyes.

"Now open the jar and place the salve across your brow."

He did as he was instructed. Erin took the jar from his hand, screwed the lid back on it and set it aside.

"Good," she praised. "Now lie down."

He took one of the small pillows, placed it beneath his head and lay down on his back, his hands clasped across his belly. "Now what?"

She grinned. "How did you know there was more?"

He grinned back, his smile weak because of the pain, but he couldn't help but respond to the pleasure in her eyes. "With you, I'm finding there's always an addendum." As he looked at her, his heart opened like a flower, and he felt an incredible warmth spreading across his chest and into his arms and hands.

Tilting her head, Erin said, "I do not know the word."

"A lawyer's word," he muttered, "for a list, another item to be added."

"Ah, yes…" Her smile widened and she felt an incredible joy course through her. Now she was seeing the real Dain—the man without his mask. "Close your eyes and take three deep breaths into your belly." She placed her hand over his. "Breathe in through your nostrils, pull the breath all the way down to where my hand rests and hold it there." She saw him struggle and then felt his abdomen rising beneath her palm. "Good. Now slowly release that breath through your mouth." She felt his abdomen begin to deflate. Nodding, Erin said, "Do this three times."

Dain wasn't sure what was going on. All he knew was that he was wildly aware of her firm, stabilizing touch on his body. The singsong huskiness of her voice soothed his panic and, for some reason, the pain in his head was no longer increasing. Was it the chaparral salve? The breathing exercise? *Her?* Her healing touch? Dain reminded himself that he wasn't to assume that it was Erin healing him—but himself. Though he wasn't yet sure how, he was giving himself permission to make the headache go away. She was merely the catalyst.

It was a struggle, because a huge part of him wanted to transfer this miracle of healing to Erin, or secondarily, to the salve. Confused, he concentrated on her continuing touch, her voice and his breathing exercise.

Lifting her hand from his abdomen, she whispered, "Good. How is the pain?"

"It's not getting any worse," he mumbled, his eyes still closed. How badly he wanted her to touch him again! He almost said it aloud, but stopped himself. A long time ago, he'd sworn he'd never ask for help again from another human being.

Getting to her feet, Erin said, "If the pain starts to come back, then do this breathing exercise again."

"Yeah…okay…" He heard the brief rustle of her skirt and knew she'd gotten up and left his side. A shattering sense of abandonment moved through him and the pain suddenly intensified. Wrestling with his need for her to return, he went through the breathing exercise again. Miraculously, the pain receded. Amazed, he wondered if the pain would go away entirely if he kept up the breathing method. It was worth a try. In the background, he heard Erin moving quietly around. Some of the sounds she made he could identify, others he could not. A sense of safety came over him. Even if she wasn't touching him, she was nearby, and for now, that was enough. More than enough. A strange new feeling moved through him. It was a sense of serenity—something he'd very rarely felt in his life.

As he lay there next to the warmth of the stove, performing the breathing exercise, Dain finally figured out what the feeling was that moved like a warm ribbon through him. It was hope. And love.…

Chapter Nine

Dain awoke to the soft sounds of Erin talking in Navajo to a man with a deep voice. For a moment, Dain was disoriented, until he heard the pop and snap of the nearby fire. The sensation of being wrapped in a warm, protective cocoon was overwhelming, and he longed to be there and just absorb the feelings of serenity, warmth and—did he dare use the word?—*happiness*. With that, Dain forced his lids open. He was lying on his side, his knees slightly bent, facing the stove. Several blankets covered him and sunlight washed brightly through the east window of the hogan.

He must have fallen asleep shortly after sunset last night, while doing that breathing exercise to eradicate his headache. As his body slowly came awake, he realized with shock that his headache was gone. He almost felt like his old self before he'd been diagnosed with the tumor. Again he heard the sound of voices. Had someone come to visit Erin?

Slowly, Dain eased over on his back and sat up. He

rubbed his face with his hands and then looked toward the kitchen area. A cowboy, probably in his late thirties, dressed in a white cotton, long-sleeved shirt and faded denim jacket, with a red bandanna around his thick neck, sat with Erin at the table. The cowboy had a hard, uncompromising face that was heavily lined and worn like bedrock from the harsh weather conditions.

Who was he? A lover? Suddenly, Dain felt jealousy toward the man who sat opposite Erin, a mug of coffee between his large, scarred hands. His hair was short and dark brown; his dusty black felt hat sat beside him on the table. Both he and Erin looked at Dain.

"Morning," Dain said gruffly as he got to his feet, the blankets falling to the floor.

"It is," Erin said. "You slept long and deep. This is Sam McGuire. He's the foreman of a cattle ranch down near Sedona. Sam, meet Dain Phillips."

McGuire nodded brusquely in his direction. "Howdy."

Dain did the same, but said nothing in return. It was on the tip of his tongue to snap at Erin, "Is this your lover?" In turmoil, he ran his hand through his hair to tame it into some semblance of order. "I'll grab a cup off coffee and leave you two alone," he muttered to Erin. Turning, he picked up one blanket and began to fold it.

"You're welcome to stay if you want, Dain. Sam's an old friend of mine," Erin said, sensing Dain's sudden discomfort. What was he so riled up about?

"No, I'm going to the hot springs to bathe." He eyed the coffeepot sitting on the edge of the stove. "I can see you're busy, anyway." His emotions were in turmoil and the cool look of the cowboy made him even angrier.

Erin smiled a little, wondering if he was jealous of Sam. Why would he be? It didn't make sense. "You're not in the way. Because the roads are drying up, people will be driving here to see me almost every day."

Though the news was unsettling, Dain digested it as he walked drowsily over to the dresser that contained the towels. He picked out two, took his cup of coffee and left quietly.

As he shut the hogan door, Dain was blinded by the sun's rays spreading silently like golden arms from the east. The air was cool, but not nippy. Right away he noticed there was a mud-encrusted Chevy pickup down at the bottom of the hill next to Erin's truck. It must belong to McGuire. So he was a friend? Was that all? How desperately Dain wanted to believe Erin. He felt so close to her that waking up to find a man with her shook him. To hell with it—and her, he decided, moving his shoulders to rid them of the collected tension.

Off to the right, he saw that the flock of sheep was gone, and he figured the white wolf was with them, guarding them. Both horses were still in the corral. Sipping the coffee, he was amazed at the shadows and colors of the silent desert around him. Somewhere off in the distance, he heard a raven cawing. There was no breeze, just that wonderful, safe stillness that he was coming to appreciate more and more every day.

The coffee tasted delicious to him, and as he walked slowly around the hogan toward the hot springs, Dain wondered if his five senses had sharpened. Was it his imagination or was he indeed appreciating the beauty of this land more this morning than ever before? He laughed to himself as he took the narrow trail between the two hills toward the hot springs.

His day here was a far cry from a typical one in the city. Briefly, he wondered how the people he'd put in charge were handling his worldwide conglomerates, and then, surprisingly, he dismissed the idea. Worry just didn't seem to be part of this magical, mystical place.

Once he arrived at the hot springs he washed the clothes he'd worn yesterday and spread them out on the white rocks to dry while he bathed. Then he climbed into a fresh pair of jeans and a white, long-sleeved shirt.

By the time he got back, he noticed two more pickups

had arrived. Rounding the hogan, he saw a tall, thin, elderly
Navajo man wearing a black felt Stetson waiting patiently
outside, along with a short, plump woman who Dain assumed was his wife. Another family, six in all, stood quietly
next to the elderly couple. As he approached the door, Dain
nodded to them.

"*Yahtehey,*" the elder said, nodding his head deferen-
tially toward Dain.

"Morning," Dain muttered, not knowing what the Navajo had said. The old man grinned, displaying nearly tooth-
less gums, his dark brown eyes sparkling with unabashed
warmth.

Dain felt the elder's sincere response and suddenly felt
cheap and hypocritical. His own response was given out of
habit—something someone said when meeting a stranger—
a social grace that carried no emotional weight with it. The
Navajo, he could tell, *meant* his greeting. Dain saw in the
old man's weathered, lean face and deep-set eyes the candor
that spoke of many years of experience linked with wisdom.

Everyone else murmured the same thing. Dain found himself nodding back to them as a group, thinking that in some
ways, they were like the Japanese he dealt with in the way
they bowed to one another. He could see that the gesture
was a sincere acknowledgment of him, a way of letting him
know he was important to them, even if he entered their
world only momentarily.

Well, back in his world, the expression "have a nice day"
was often used by people too busy with problems in their
own lives to be sincere. Dain hated going through the social
pabulum, though he would initiate it when necessary. Usually, he didn't have to because of his power and money—
he'd just cut to the bottom line and bluntly tell the other
party what he wanted. And nearly every time, that other
party caved in and gave him what he demanded.

Uncomfortable with the affable crowd gathered outside,
Dain hurried into the hogan. He closed the door and turned
around. Erin was standing behind Sam McGuire, who sat in

the chair. Her hands were on the cowboy's head, her eyes were closed and her booted feet slightly spread apart. McGuire's eyes were closed, too, so Dain felt like a fly on the wall as he watched with curiosity.

Erin wore a long, dark blue cotton skirt and a pale pink blouse with puffed sleeves. Nothing unusual, but something was different about her today. As he mercilessly assessed her, Dain realized her hair was still loose and unbraided. He liked to see her with that mane of hair down. She was breathtaking. Then he realized that McGuire had arrived so early, Erin hadn't had the time to properly braid her hair. Suddenly, he didn't want McGuire to see her that way. Didn't the people outside know she had a life of her own? That they shouldn't come at all hours of the day or night?

He smelled the fragrant odor of recently burned sage and saw the abalone shell with the smudge stick on the table, a thin wisp of smoke spiraling lazily upward. His gaze moved back to Erin. There was an unearthly radiance to her face— the same glow he'd seen when he saw her for the first time—the same glow that was always around that white wolf in his nightmares. Blinking rapidly, Dain thought he was seeing things, but the radiance did not leave Erin's features. There was an incredible serenity about her as she stood behind the cowboy, her body leaning lightly against the man's head, the straight-backed chair a barrier between them.

More than anything, Dain liked to look at Erin's hands. They mesmerized him. Her fingers were long, slightly large knuckled, but so expressive. Her touch was so gentle, Dain realized, and the compassion on Erin's face moved him. How could he have doubted her? McGuire was obviously just one more patient and not the lover Dain had first thought him to be. Warmth expanded in Dain's chest. He was so taken aback by the sensation that he scowled and placed his hand against his heart. What was he feeling? And then a memory from his past flashed before him, unbidden.

Dain remembered his foster mother, Luella. He'd been

probably no more than four years old at the time, and Luella,
with her dyed blond hair frizzy around her plump face, her
blue eyes dancing and her laughter surrounding him, had
watched him as he stood at the shallow edge of a swimming
hole, his thin arms wrapped around himself. Luella had
come forward, laughing, a towel in her hands. He'd expected her to throw the towel around him so he could dry
off, but she surprised him by folding the towel around him
and drawing him forward into her awaiting arms.

Closing his eyes, he recalled how much he'd loved
Luella's plump body surrounding him. She was only about
five foot three inches tall, with large breasts and fleshy hips,
but Dain would snuggle in her arms, burying his thin little
form against her, absorbing the feel of her body, the kisses
she'd drop across his brow, inhaling the lilac perfume she
always wore.

He allowed that memory to swirl gently around him as
he slowly opened his eyes. How much he'd been loved by
Luella and Frank Fairfield, his foster parents who had lived
in Phoenix. And he'd loved them. Fiercely. Forever. But
forever was a short time, as he'd discovered. By age eight,
he was in an orphanage—alone. Abandoned. And now he
was "home"—back in Arizona once again. The ties with
this land were in his blood, somehow.

Erin's murmuring broke into his thoughts and Dain took
a deep, shaky breath. Quietly, he moved across the room
and put the towels on a couple of brass hooks to dry. He
didn't have much of an appetite for breakfast, and since he
felt like an interloper, he left the hogan. Without acknowl-
edging the Navajo people waiting for healing, he went
around back, to the dilapidated chicken coop where about a
dozen hens were living.

Today was turning out unexpectedly, and he found himself begrudging the Navajo who had come to Erin for healing. He felt angry over the intrusion into his idyllic experience with her. He wanted Erin's attention—one hundred
percent of it. But he figured in the meantime, he would make

himself useful. Going to the small barn, he located a hammer and some nails. He found some tar paper and roofing material, too. It was obvious to him that without a man around here, Erin's outbuildings and corral were going to hell in a hurry in these harsh desert conditions.

He didn't know what else to do with himself, so he began to repair the roof of the henhouse, which badly needed to be replaced. Finding a rickety ladder, Dain climbed up on the not-so-stable eaves and tore off the remaining shingles and the rest of the tar paper. The building had been put together haphazardly. Having earned a degree in engineering, he studied the structure and shook his head in dismay.

"You need some help?"

Looking down, Dain saw Sam McGuire standing there, hands propped on his hips. The black Stetson hat was drawn low over his eyes.

Keeping his surprise at the cowboy's unexpected offer out of his voice, Dain muttered, "I'm not sure this thing can be helped."

McGuire grinned, his teeth large and white against his dark, weathered skin. "One of my adopted Navajo uncles built this for Asdzaan Maiisoh many years ago. At the time, my uncle Chee was still hitting the bottle. One day," McGuire continued with a chuckle, "Chee got drunk and fell off the roof and sprained his ankle. Asdzaan Maiisoh came hurrying out, saw my uncle lying out here and went to help him. She gave him hell for being drunk and trying to work. My uncle tells the story to our family to this day, how she put her hand on his swelling ankle and it healed. He was so shocked that it scared him dry. My uncle never took another drink after that." McGuire's grin broadened. "So you'll see half of this building is built solid, the other half flimsy. The sober side and the drunk side."

Dain grinned and made his way across the roof. "I can see the half that's pretty rickety."

"Uncle Chee was in pretty rickety shape until the medicine woman fixed him up. He used to come out here every fall and fix things up for her. She doesn't have a man so me and my adopted family like to make sure she gets help before the winter snows come. That's why I dropped by today.''

"Everything around here is in sorry shape."

McGuire removed his hat and scratched his head. "She's a busy woman. All of the Bad Water Clan come to her for healing. And there's a lot of us. Even though I'm a white man, I was adopted into their family." He smiled slightly. "Never a dull moment, let me tell you."

Frowning, Dain pointed to the tar paper. "No argument from me on that one. You can hand that up to me if you want.''

"Sure."

As Dain began to work side by side with McGuire, he felt relief. Sam was a friend of Erin's, adopted by the local clan. He wasn't her lover, after all. Dain had never felt so much joy over anything. Erin was his—all his....

It was early afternoon before Erin found herself alone once again. She knew Maiisoh was with the sheep, and though she wasn't out on the range with them, they'd be safe enough. Sam McGuire had left an hour earlier, explaining that he was due back at his ranch. Hearing the pounding of a hammer, she left the hogan and wandered around it. She saw Dain up on the roof of the chicken coop, on his hands and knees, pounding nails into shingles.

It was hot, probably in the eighties, and he'd taken off his shirt. She marveled at how beautifully built he was, his skin slightly reddened from being unprotected in the sun too long. Moving to the pump, she took a dark blue plastic glass that always sat there, and filled it with water. Walking to the henhouse, she called up to him, "You're getting sunburned. Here, you want something to drink?"

Startled, Dain looked down. He hadn't expected Erin, yet there she stood, smiling, a glass of water lifted up toward him. Sweat was running in rivulets from his temples and his hair was plastered against his skull. Despite his sorry state, his heart opened and he felt that same, strange sensation he had earlier today. Stymied, he put down the hammer and nails and moved to the edge of the coop. Hanging his long legs over the edge of the roof, he leaned down. Their fingers briefly touched as he took the glass from her. The feeling was electrifying. He saw her eyes go soft with longing for just an instant, before she hid her reaction. Longing for him? Did he dare hope?

"Thanks," he murmured, meaning it.

"You need to drink lots of water when you're out here doing stuff like this."

He smiled, tipping the glass to his lips and drinking deeply. In a few gulps, he'd finished off the water. Giving the glass back to her, he said, "I guess time got away from me. McGuire was out here helping me for a while."

"Oh." Erin smiled and nodded. "Sam's an adopted relative. Yes, he's a wonderful person. Over the years he's been my guardian angel of sorts. Sam is as honest as the day is long. It was good to see him again."

Dain studied her expression. If anything, Erin looked happy, her smile making him want to smile in return. "Why did he come to see you?" he said finally, wiping the sweat off his brow with the back of his hand. He felt his skin smarting and knew he should protect it from the sun's powerful rays. Leaning over, he grabbed his shirt and shrugged it on, but didn't button it.

"Two reasons, really. He usually gets up this way in the fall to help me with odd jobs around here before the snows come. And—" she sighed "—he was thrown by a green horse he was trying to break last week and got a mild concussion. He was having nonstop headaches and said I could do a better job than aspirin for the pain. Now he's fine."

"I thought he was more than a friend to you." Dain watched her face closely for reaction.

Shrugging, Erin said, "No man would have me. I'm too independent." She smiled a little. So Dain *was* jealous of

Sam. He must have thought Sam was her man. "Sam's heart has belonged to Kate Donovan since way back when he was a teenager. He still loves her even though she left at age eighteen and never came back to the ranch."

"A teenage crush that never got resolved?" Dain found that hard to believe.

"Kate Donovan left because of her father. Sam was heartbroken. Sam used to work as foreman on the Donovan ranch until three years ago, when Kate's father fired him. Now he works at the neighboring ranch. He told me that Old Man Donovan got killed by a drunk driver recently. Now the Donovan ranch is in dire straits. He contacted Kate, asking her to come home if she wanted to save her family's homestead."

"Will she?" Dain asked curiously.

"Sam said she was coming home. He sounded hopeful, but he knows that he and Kate have both changed a lot since age eighteen."

"Hmm, a lot of water under the bridge?"

Looking worried, Erin nodded. "There are three Donovan daughters—Kate, Jessica and Rachel. Sam says that it will take all three women to save the ranch, if it can be saved. It's nearly bankrupt because of the father's mishandling of finances over the past few years. Their mother, Odula, was Eastern Cherokee and a medicine woman also. When Kelly Donovan died, it was Sam who took on the responsibility of contacting the sisters, which took some time. Kate is finally coming home tomorrow, and Rachel and Jessica will be there within a week." Erin rubbed her hands against her skirt. "Sam's happy but scared. He'd like to reestablish a relationship with Kate, I think."

"You think he can?"

"I don't know. Kate sounds very scarred by life events. When people get hurt like that, it's hard for them to reach out and try to love again." Erin realized she was speaking for herself, too. When she looked up at Dain, though, her heart whispered that she could have a second chance at loving once again if she could overcome her own painful past.

"Seems like the past haunts all of us," Dain murmured, looking down at her upturned features. She still hadn't braided her hair, and the soft breeze played with the thick, dark strands. The sunlight brought out reddish highlights and he ached to tunnel his fingers through the silky mass.

"Yes," Erin said bleakly, "the past is usually the key to us and our future…"

To hell with it, Dain decided, bending down and gently threading his fingers through her hair. He saw surprise, then pleasure flare in her eyes. Closing his own eyes, he slid his hand alongside her face, memorizing every contour of it. Her skin was sunlight warm and firm, yet inviting. So damned inviting. As he bent over more to rest his hand on her shoulder, he opened his eyes. Her lashes lay against her cheeks, her lips slightly parted, begging to be kissed. There was such naturalness between them. He'd never had that with a woman. But the roof of a chicken coop wasn't exactly a safe place for a continued exploration of her. What Dain wanted to do was kiss her breathless. Kiss her until her breathing combined with his own. Unwillingly, he slid his hand off her shoulder.

Her eyes opened slowly, gold burning in their depths.

"Touching you," he rasped, "is like capturing sunlight." He tried to smile and failed. It was obvious she liked his touch. Maybe even wanted more. If only…

Erin stared up at his hard, sweaty face, those burning eyes that held wolflike hunger in them—for her. Her senses spun. Desire to climb up the ladder and touch his face and kiss him again shocked her out of her state. "Sunlight?" she whispered. Oh, how she ached to kiss him!

Laughing with self-deprecation, Dain nodded. "You bring out the poet I didn't know was hiding in me, Erin."

Climbing down the rickety ladder, he gestured for her to follow him. "Your patients think you walk on water," he said, going over to the trough. Leaning down, he scooped up handfuls of cold water and bathed his head, face and neck. He needed something to cool himself down with because right now a fire was blazing in his lower body. Straightening, he languished in the effect, feeling the water stream down across his chest and soak into the denim at his waist. How good he felt! Opening his eyes, he saw Erin sitting on the wood block studying him, a serious look on her face.

"You are feeling better today?" she asked a little breathlessly, trying to forget how his touch still affected her.

Shaking the water from his fingers, Dain walked around the trough and sat down on the edge of it, a few feet from her. "I feel like I felt when I was in my twenties." He wanted to add, *Because of you,* but he didn't dare.

"What is that like?"

"I feel strong, good...."

She nodded, still nervous in his powerful, masculine presence. Did Dain realize how he was affecting her? "Anything else?"

He shrugged lazily, holding her probing gaze. Then he went to the pump and poured himself another glass of water, gulping it down before setting the glass aside and sitting once again. "I feel fine."

"You look happy." She gestured to his face. "Your eyes are lighter in color, and I can see them smiling." Was it because he'd touched her hair? Touched her?

He grinned sourly, resting his hands on the aged trough, feeling the roughness of the splintery wood. "Like I said, I haven't felt like this in a long time."

Erin brushed several strands of hair behind her shoulder. Right now, Dain looked joyous. "Your face is free of tension, and your smile comes easily. I feel lightness around you."

"Well," he said with a laugh, "it's been a damn long time since I've been out in fresh air and sunshine, wielding a hammer. Usually one of my assistants hires carpenters and roofers to fix whatever needs to be fixed."

"So, you do not do these things for yourself?"

"No. I'm too busy."

"Busy with what?"

"My corporations. Running them. I don't have time for this stuff."

"Yet," Erin said, "you enjoy it. I see the happiness in your eyes, I see it in your face and hear it in your voice."

He studied her in the ebb and flow of the playful breeze, hearing the bleat of sheep in the distance. "I'm beginning to catch on to how you're working with me."

Her eyes lit up with teasing. "Really?" She thrilled to that smoldering look he gave her. Helplessly, she responded to it.

"Really." Dain stood and rested his hands against his hips. "It must be an Indian thing to do. Always giving comparative examples?"

Opening her hands, she laughed. "There is much power in allowing *you* to discover what is missing in your life. If I were to say, 'Dain, you need to get back to basics, back to things that made you happy,' I would be taking the power of your own discovery away from you." Her smile disappeared as she held his amused gaze. "My desire is to empower you, not the opposite."

Digesting her comment, he nodded. "You're a very intelligent lady, do you know that? You'd give most therapists a run for their money."

She felt heat flood her face at his compliment. "Being a medicine person means understanding what makes people stay in harmony with themselves, but it also means identifying what makes them lose their balance, their personal way of walking through their life."

With a shake of his head, his voice reflecting amazement, Dain murmured, "I'd like to send all therapists to whatever school you went to."

Laughing, Erin stood up. There was no denying that Dain Phillips was a beautiful man to look upon. His body was tall, strong and in good condition. The careless smile on his mouth, the laughter dancing in his blue eyes touched her gently, deeply, and she took a ragged breath. There were so many fine lines to walk with this man. Personal involvement was out of the question. She had to maintain a certain distance with him in order to keep him focused on himself.

Still, it didn't hurt to enjoy his rugged good looks, so Erin allowed herself to open up and absorb his male beauty, the unexpected, carefree moment he was sharing with her. "Come, I will help you finish putting on the new roof."

It shouldn't come as any surprise, Dain told himself, that Erin would know how to use a hammer and nails. As he walked easily at her side, he lifted his face to the breeze, the water drying on his skin. "This place is magical," he whispered.

She glanced over at him and saw peace on his face for the first time. "Perhaps," she said softly, "the magic is really in you, and that no matter where you live, it is there, waiting to be given permission by you to be released so that you can experience it."

With a shake of his head, he smiled down at her. "My world on the East Coast isn't like this. It never could be."

"Why not?"

"Because it's work."

"Why can't your work be play? Why can't you follow the feelings you now have in your heart and take them with you wherever you go?"

"Because," he teased, "my world isn't about putting roofs on chicken coops."

She grinned as they halted at the henhouse. "No, but you could transfer the feelings you have in your heart now and take them with you."

Dain picked up the hammer and gave her a sack of nails. "I'd like to see you in my world," he said seriously. "I wonder if you'd stay serene. Peaceful. If that same look that's on your face now would stay there if I took you to my office." With shock he realized he'd like her in his life on a daily basis. He looked hungrily for her response.

"It would." Erin thought about his statement. What would it be like to see Dain every day? Her heart pounded briefly as she explored the idea. The thought gave her a warm, good feeling—completely unexpected, but desired by her.

He climbed the ladder and stood up on the roof. "I don't think so," he challenged, holding out his hand to her as she climbed up after him.

Giving him the sack of nails, Erin stood up on the roof beside him. "My people believe that your inner harmony, your balance, is always with you." She swept her hand toward the pastel colors of the desert around them. "It is true that some places open up your heart and reconnect you with your inner harmony, but once your heart is awakened, the feeling is something you always take with you no matter where you go."

With a sigh, Dain got down on his hands and knees. "You're a hermit who lives in damn near total isolation. My world back in New York City is total insanity twenty-five hours a day."

Kneeling beside him, she handed him some nails. "So how long have you lived that way?"

A bark of laughter rolled from him as he pounded the nail into a shingle. "Ever since I got out of the air force, which was when I was twenty-eight. I'm thirty-eight now. Ten years of insanity," he muttered to himself, taking another nail she proffered.

"So is it any wonder that your lifestyle might further throw you out of harmony?"

He glanced up at her, enjoying her closeness, her attention. "You're saying I was out of balance before I went into this Type A behavior?"

"Yes, there is always a root cause—a shock to your heart, your body—that makes it go out of kilter. If you do not recover from it, then other life choices may make you move further out of harmony."

"And that's when you leave your body open to disease, and things like this damn tumor in my head can begin?"

She nodded, holding the sack of nails in her lap. "Exactly."

"You're smart, like a fox, Erin." And more, much more... An ache centered low in his body. What would it be like to love Erin? To hold her lush form and feel her response? To feel her mouth pressed hungrily against his own once again?

A tingle ran through Erin. It was the first time Dain had called her by her name, and the sound had rolled off his lips like a caress. She compressed her own lips and held his wry look. "Oh?"

"The question I should really be asking is, what originally threw my harmony out of balance?"

She rewarded him with a sunlit smile. "And you are smart like a wolf who sees the heart of the matter." She touched her breast with her fingers. "All winged ones and four-footed ones, those that crawl or slither, possess what we call a wild heart."

"Wild heart?"

"Yes," she murmured, giving him a few more nails. Touching him, she noticed his hands were soft and obviously not used to such outdoor work. "Animals do not allow their minds to take over the instincts that keep them alive, that keep them in balance with themselves and others."

"So," he said as he pounded in a nail, "you're saying I've lost my wild heart, my instinct to survive?"

"Perhaps..."

"And to help get rid of this tumor, I have to be a wild heart, not a tame one?"

Laughing gaily, Erin said, "First, we must discover what has thrown you out of balance with yourself, because when it did, you pushed away the whisperings, the knowings of your wild heart. You shoved it aside and buried it, like you did your spirit. The spirit—" she held up her hands, palms facing one another "—and your wild heart are one. They are inseparable. A wild heart, like the wolf, knows his calling and follows it unerringly, like a scent on the soil of Mother Earth. Nothing can pull a wolf off this scent, for he will honor what it is and honor himself in knowing that he must follow it without being distracted or detoured by anything around him.''

''Like a laser-guided rocket,'' Dain said grimly, recalling his days as a fighter pilot. ''Once that sweetheart was locked and loaded, the destination punched in by computer, and I flipped the trigger switch and pressed it, that rocket went for its objective. Nothing could pull it off track.''

''Yes. Only a rocket is a piece of metal, with no heart, no soul or feelings.''

''Much,'' he said wryly, ''like me, I suspect.''

Chortling, Erin took the hammer from him and began to methodically nail on the shingles. ''Oh, you like to *think* you are an unfeeling piece of metal, but you are not.'' His kiss had told her otherwise.

Her laughter pealed over him joyously. He was seeing Erin in a completely new light—that of a self-sufficient woman who was earthy, alive and so very, very loving. He wanted that love—he wanted her. The ache in his loins intensified to a painful degree. Trying to shift his focus, Dain sat back, noticing that his knees were beginning to feel weak. And then he remembered he hadn't eaten anything all day and realized the weakness he was feeling presently was probably due to lack of food—instead of the tumor. Or was it? He would find out.

''I'm starving,'' he told her. *For you,* he thought, but Erin didn't seemed to catch his double entendre.

''I made you a mutton sandwich,'' she said, looking up from her task. ''It's on the table. Go eat and then come back, and we can finish this roof before nightfall.''

In that moment, with the dark curtain of her hair framing her face, she looked incredibly beautiful to him. How many women did he know who would go up on a roof and lay shingles with him? And in a skirt! Grinning recklessly, he reached over and framed her face with his hands. "You're one of the most generous people I've ever known," he whispered, and he leaned down, sliding his lips against hers.

Erin's breath jammed. The sudden wolflike look in his eyes, his hands capturing her face, had caught her off guard. But as the wind and sunlight swirled between them, her heart pounded. And when his head came down, his eyes holding hers captive, the ache in her body intensified, and artlessly, she lifted her hands and slid them along his sun-warmed arms. How badly she longed to kiss Dain! Leaning up to meet his passionate embrace, Erin acknowledged that she had never wanted anything more.

Sunlight and shadow met and mingled as their lips slid against one another's. She felt his maleness. His power. Her mouth opened like a blossom and moist heat caressed her face. His mouth was strong. Assertive. She responded in kind, eager to drink of him also. The roughness of his beard scraped against her softer skin and caused tingles everywhere. His fingers drew her more surely to him. Her breasts brushed against his chest. The world stopped moving, suspended in the magic of their mouths touching. There was such strength combined with gentleness in Dain that it drove tears into Erin's closed eyes. Her fingers opened and closed spasmodically against his broad, strong shoulders. He took her hungrily, exploring her, asking her to open more to his quest. She did willingly, sinking against his lean body, the pulsing beat of his heart hammering against her own.

Realization broke through Dain's heated haze. What was he doing? He broke the kiss, breathing raggedly. When he saw her hand go to her lips, he realized he'd hurt her!

"I'm sorry," he said huskily, touching her soft, glistening lips. "I didn't mean to cause you more pain...."

"No...you did not hurt me...." Just the opposite, Erin thought as she took a deep, unsteady breath. She saw the blatant, tender concern in his eyes. His hand caressing her cheek was nearly too much for her to absorb in that golden moment. In her heart, she knew Dain was opening her up, asking her to heal, too. He was not a coward, nor would she be. Sliding her fingers through his, she allowed the joy to awaken in her, allowed herself to remember the feelings she'd tried to ignore over the years.

Dain studied her intently in those brief moments. What was going on inside her? Did she enjoy the kiss as much as he had? Then why was there pain in her expression? He blamed himself for her hurt, and so he pulled himself from her arms and said, ''I think I'd better go get that sandwich. I'll be right back.''

Feeling lost as he drew away from her, Erin wanted to cry out, to ask him to remain with her. She saw the real Dain slipping away from her, the man with such a large, giving heart. The man who held such tenderness at bay—except with her. Reaching out as he climbed down the ladder, she called, ''Bring me some water?''

''Yeah, no problem,'' he replied, without looking up again.

The earth felt solid and good beneath his feet as he stepped off the ladder, the sensation so light and carefree. Her kiss had sent him spinning, like a jet powered and climbing straight up into the deep blue sky. When he'd seen the hurt in Erin's face he'd discovered he wasn't very sensitive to other people's needs, wants or desires—he only thought of his own. He realized now the extent of his selfishness. But that would change, because he'd also discovered he liked making Erin smile. He appreciated her thoughtfulness and wanted to reciprocate in some way. Maybe that shared kiss would tell her in another language—his language—just what she meant to him.

As he walked into the hogan, he found it cool in comparison to the outdoors. Sure enough, on a chipped white plate were two slices of that thick brown bread Erin had made, with an even thicker portion of cooked mutton in between. She had set out a jar of mustard, a jar of sweet pickles and a table knife. On another plate was a huge piece of homemade chocolate cake.

Shaking his head, he found himself even more grateful for her thoughtfulness. When he saw a bunch of grocery bags as he sat down, he realized that the Navajo who had come for healing had paid Erin for her services with food. As he hungrily eyed the slab of chocolate cake, he knew someone had given it to her—and now she was sharing it with him.

He munched on the thick, juicy piece of meat, relishing the incredibly delicious taste—better than the five-star-restaurant food he ate routinely in New York. In fact, everything he ate since he'd come here tasted amazingly good. Stymied, Dain wondered if it was just him. Or maybe it was the place, or Erin. A combination of all the above? He wasn't sure.

As he finished off the chocolate cake, he chuckled. Maybe it was his wild heart coming to life again and he was beginning to get back in contact with all those senses Erin had talked about earlier. Or maybe it was her kiss that inspired his wild heart to come out of hiding and not be afraid any longer. Being around Erin was like being around a wolf. And was he her mate? Did that explain all the magic that was happening?

Chapter Ten

The chicken coop roof was finished by late afternoon. As Erin carried the hammer and leftover nails back to the shed, Dain walked at her side.

"The day's work did not hurt you, did it?" she asked as she laid the articles on a shelf.

The kiss had, but he had the good grace not to say that. "I feel pretty good." He patted his stomach. "Either I was more starved than I realized, or you're better than a five-star chef, because that late lunch tasted like it came from heaven."

She smiled and dusted off her hands as she turned and walked back toward the hogan with him. "When a person begins to reconnect with our Mother, their senses become more alive." Erin glanced up at him with a pleased expression. "And you look happy." Was their shared kiss the cause? She thought it might be. She herself felt as if she were a cloud barely grazing Mother Earth. The joy Dain had released earlier simmered brightly, like a sunrise, in her heart.

"Don't tell that to my assistants. They only see me scowling, growling, cursing or yelling."

"Perhaps it is the life you lead back East that makes you that way. If you abuse an animal or a human long enough, it will turn into what you just described."

"I'm afraid I chose my abuse, then," he told her lightly. They halted near the hogan. "The road looks pretty dry. I'd like to take your truck and drive back to that wash and see if I can't get that vehicle out of there." He looked at her. "What do you say?"

Shrugging, Erin gestured to her old Ford. "That is a good idea, but my 1979 pickup is sick."

"What's wrong with it?" The truck had once been green with white sides, but the rust had eaten away the bottoms of the panels and the windshield held a spider-web array of cracks across it. Other than that it appeared to be in running condition.

"I think it's the carburetor," she said, walking with him down the slight incline to where the truck sat.

"Well, I may sit in an office all day, but I'm pretty sharp when it comes to mechanical things." He lifted the latch on the hood and it yawned open with creaks and squeaks. As Dain looked at the engine, he saw Erin come around to one side to watch him. For once, he felt confident, because this was something he was good at. And he wanted to do something for her, to pay her back in some way for all she was doing for him.

As he tinkered, taking off the dusty air filter and handing it to her, he decided this was a good time to ask some questions of his own.

"I see those Navajo left you a lot of groceries from their visit."

"Yes. I was planning on riding over to some of the hogans of the elderly tomorrow to give them the food."

"You ever save any for yourself?" he asked, reaching down into the dusty, dirty engine.

"No. In October I will take the jewelry I've gathered to Gallup and there I will buy what I need."

"And distribute the rest," he said. Frowning, he examined the carburetor. "And you live out here. All alone."

"Yes," Erin said, holding the air filter. She liked to watch Dain work. His face became intense, his mouth set, his eyes narrowed. He had wonderful hands—workman's hands. She found it hard to believe that he was a businessman and not a rancher or farmer instead.

"And no man in your life?" He said it teasingly, but inside, his gut clenched a little because he was afraid she'd tell him she had someone.

"No..." Erin felt a riffle of panic. "What about you? Surely there is a woman in your life. You have much power and money in your world." More than likely, he also had a woman who cherished his kisses, she thought to herself.

Chuckling, he concentrated on the carburetor. "Oh, there're plenty of women who pretend to be interested in me, but all they really want is money—or power. Or—" he glanced over at her "—both."

For some reason, Erin was glad he wasn't with a woman presently. She didn't look closely at why she felt relief. "Surely you are old enough to have been married and had children?"

His mouth tightened. Trickles of sweat dripped from his temples. It was hot working under the hood of the truck. "No wife. No family." His nostrils flared. "I don't want one."

Erin moved to his side and offered him a clean rag. "Here," she said.

Gripping the cloth, he wiped his brow and temples. "Thanks." He shoved the cloth into his back pocket and resumed his work.

"Family is important," Erin said softly, remaining close to him and watching his progress.

"Maybe to you, but not to me."

She heard the flatness in his voice. Fingering the dusty grillwork, she said tentatively, "You do not like marriage? Or children?"

Making a frustrated sound, Dain muttered, "Who the hell would put up with the likes of me and my temper? You see how I am. Most of the time I'm one miserable son of a bitch. And if I'm not miserable, I'm irritable."

"So," Erin queried, trying to understand his reasoning, "you protect a possible mate from your bad side?"

"I don't," he said grimly, "trust people. Marriage, to me, is about the ultimate trust between a man and a woman."

"What don't you trust a possible mate with?"

"Me."

She smiled and nodded. "It is natural to want to have a mate. Sometimes I see Maiisoh longing for a she-wolf to come to him."

"Your wolf has a better chance of finding a mate than I do."

"You do not trust women." Her heart ached. He would not trust her, either. The thought made grief move through Erin.

Glancing over his shoulder, he saw the perplexed look on her face. She was having a tough time grasping how he lived his life. Ordinarily, he'd never discuss something this personal with anyone, but oddly, he knew he could trust Erin with the information. "I don't even know why I'm telling you this," he said. "Maybe because I know you don't have any ulterior motives toward me or my money. I trust women about as far as I could throw this truck with my bare hands."

Frowning, Erin moved to the side of the pickup, her hands resting on the fenders. "Then a woman broke your trust?"

Grimly he said, "Yeah, you could say that. How about

you? Who broke your heart?" He saw her eyes flare with shock and then fear. More gently, he continued, "Come on, this isn't a one-way conversation, you know. If I share some of myself, it's only fair you do the same." And he honestly did want to know why she was out here alone. No man in his right mind would let a woman like Erin live by herself. She was too vital. Too full of life. Too loving...

Fumbling with one of the tools, Erin shrugged and avoided his gaze. "We all carry secrets," she began, her voice strained. "Mine has to do with a bad marriage to a white man. I was too young to marry. My mother warned me, but I did not listen." She smoothed the grease off the tool with her fingers. "The color of his skin does not really matter. He was a two-heart and I did not know that when I married him."

Dain braced his arms against the truck and watched her closely. He felt her pain and her reluctance to speak about it. "What's a two-heart?"

She sighed and looked out over the desert. "Someone who is a liar. My husband lied to me. He—he beat me. I am ashamed to admit this to you—to anyone. I let him beat me and I should have left, but I was so young. I thought this was part of love." With a painful shrug, she barely glanced at him. The look on his face was one of anger and tenderness. "As I got older, I realized the mistake I'd made. I got out before he killed me." She laid the tool on the fender, unable to meet his eyes. What must he think of her?

The suffering in her face affected Dain as little else could. Flexing his fist, he realized he wanted to hit the man who had hurt Erin. But he saw she needed his sympathy, not his anger. "Beatings. Yeah, I can relate to that," he said.

"I am ashamed of myself. I should have known better."

Wiping his hands on the rag, he shook his head. "Listen, you got out, that is what's important."

Looking up, Erin moved her hand restlessly along the fender. "That is what I came to realize much later."

Silence engulfed them. Dain longed to reach out to her, but wondered if his touch would only cause her more pain. To control his impulse, he went back to tinkering. So Erin had been badly burned by a man. And she chose to live alone now. Could he blame her? But what a waste! She was so warm. So alive. So full of *life!* Lips compressed, he began to understand her reluctance to allow herself near him, woman to man. No wonder there'd been such surprise in her eyes after he'd kissed her both times.

"In a way," he growled, "we're like two wounded lone wolves, don't you think?"

Erin nodded, her hands stilling. "Yes, wounded wolves who have lost their pack, who are now alone...."

She waited, seeing his eyes glitter like shards of blue ice. A fine tension went through him, although she doubted he was aware of it. Moving her fingers lightly across the dusty, warm surface of the fender, she murmured, "It must be very hard for you to stay here with me, then. I am a woman. I am a symbol of that broken trust you hold with us."

Snorting, Dain once more took the cloth from his back pocket, rubbed it savagely across his forehead and stuffed it back into his jeans. "I don't have a choice regarding you. I want to get well. Right now, my fear of dying is greater than my distrust of you as a woman. Maybe," he said with less rancor, taking the cloth and wiping some of the components of the carburetor, "I trust you a little." He glanced over and saw the sadness leave her large, expressive eyes, replaced by hope. Laughing harshly, he said, "Don't look so sad. I don't want your pity."

"Don't mistake my look." She lifted her hand and gestured toward him. "Pity is like a crutch. It is unhealthy in a relationship between two people. If I pitied your condition, your close walk with death, then I would allow you to remain in the state you were when I first met you at the wash. To support your anger, to do things for you, to not allow you to make that five-mile walk by yourself, would be pity.''

''Okay,'' he said slowly, understanding her flawless logic. ''So what do I see in those huge, beautiful eyes of yours?''

His husky compliment threw her completely off guard. Once again he had moved beyond that boundary of patient and healer she wanted to maintain—but it hadn't been his fault. She was responsible for her boundaries with others, not him. The compliment made her feel good about herself as a woman. It had been a long time since a man had complimented her, and she found a portion of her spirit starved for that kind of intimacy with a man. Not just any man, either. Somehow, just being able to admit her sordid, shameful past to him was healing her. It was no longer a hot blade of humiliation inside her. Erin was amazed that Dain could do that for her, and in her heart, she knew he could do so much more for her—if she allowed it. If she allowed herself to trust him—a man—once more.

''What you see,'' she said, opening her hands, ''is compassion.''

''Give me an example of compassion,'' he demanded, replacing the parts of the carburetor once they'd been cleaned off.

''Compassion is not a crutch. I knew that if you were serious about wanting to heal your condition, no matter how sick you felt, you would walk that five miles to my hogan. If I had offered to help you, I wouldn't be placing the responsibility for your healing on you—I would be taking it on, instead. So I walked away.''

''Yeah,'' he said. ''I was plenty angry when you left me.''

''I know,'' Erin agreed.

''I thought you were the most selfish person I'd ever met.''

''Except for yourself.''

He lifted his head and met her gaze squarely. Her eyes

did not waver. "You know," he said wryly, "I'm beginning to realize you're a lot more like me than I ever suspected. You don't mess around. You shoot straight from the hip and you're blunt as hell."

Chuckling, she nodded. "It is good to be honest and walk your truth, but you do not always have to hit people over the head with it."

"I think," Dain said, easing out from beneath the hood of the truck, "the saying you're searching for is you can get more out of a person with honey than vinegar."

"I like that saying. Yes, it could apply."

"Hop in," he said, waving his hand toward the driver's side of the truck. "Let's try out this old wolf of yours."

To Erin's delight, the truck fired up after a couple of false starts. She looked up to see Dain standing nearby, grinning boyishly, his hands on his hips. What a change in two days! Gone was the angry stranger. In his place she saw a younger man, one who took pride in his ability, one who received pleasure from being generous with his skill—something that she was sure was a small thing to him, but which was very large in her world. Waving to him to get in, she watched as he lowered the hood on the truck and climbed in.

Dain sat on the cracked plastic seat, which Erin had covered with a frayed old Navajo blanket. The air was refreshing as the truck rattled down the red sand road. He placed his arm out the window, leaned back and enjoyed the sensation. Laughter rolled up his throat.

"Better than walking," he told her.

Erin nodded, holding the wheel with both hands because the truck did not have power steering. "The walk was good for you, though, in many ways."

"Oh, sure," he said, glancing at her out of the corner of his eye. "I crawled more than I walked. It was a new experience for me. Usually, I have people on their hands and knees groveling to me, not the other way around."

Somberly, Erin nodded. "That is not a healthy relationship to have with anything or anyone."

"It works," he said with a shrug. "It gets results. That's all I care about."

She wasn't so sure, but didn't pursue the topic. Soon enough, the wash rolled into view. And Dain was right—the soil had dried out more quickly than she'd thought. Parking the truck, she left it running as Dain made his way down into the wash to his truck. She watched with interest. There were no wasted motions about him. Everything, even his hurried walk, was deliberate. He never looked down where his feet were stepping, just ahead to whatever his goal was. How much he missed by hurrying, by not slowing down to look around him.

Within a few minutes, the vehicle was free. Erin waved and put her truck in gear, and in no time they were back at the hogan. She could see how pleased Dain was as he parked his vehicle and climbed out. Opening the rear, he filled his arms with groceries and began taking them into the hogan. She went to help him and was amazed that the entire rear of the truck was filled with grocery sacks.

Her nose wrinkled as she scooped up two sacks into her arms. The smell of spoiled meat was powerful.

"Here, let me do that," he said, taking the groceries from her arms.

"No," Erin said, holding on to them. "I will help."

He let go of the sack with a shrug. "You and the corporate world would like one another," he muttered. "Everything's teamwork nowadays," he groused, leaning in and getting another armful of goods.

She laughed lightly and walked with him to the hogan. "Why is that so distasteful to you?"

"Teamwork means trust. Remember?"

"Oh, yes, you don't trust anyone." And then she looked up at him. "You don't even trust yourself, so how could you trust another?"

Coming to a halt inside, Dain stared at her. He slowly lowered the sack of groceries to sit on the table. "That's not true. I do trust myself."

Shaking her head, she walked out of the hogan with him once more. "Healthy people rely on their own knowing, their own instinctual wild heart, and they know when to trust a person or situation outside themselves. You do not. You see everyone trying to steal something from you. Not everyone who has crossed your path has been like that."

His brows dipped. He stopped at the truck, resting his hip against the tailgate as he studied her. "I don't trust myself, so I can't trust others?"

"Yes," she said, reaching in for more groceries. She opened the sack that contained rotting meat, took the packages out and laid them on the tailgate. Then, one by one, she opened them and threw the meat out into the desert. "I am saying it is healthy to trust others. Your wild heart will discriminate between those who come as a coyote, a trickster who only wants something from you, and those who are wolves, who are honest and straightforward. Remember, your wild heart lies with your spirit. And right now, both are very small and weak within you. If you trusted yourself, you would have the good instincts and insights combined with your experience from life to know who to trust and who not to. Right now, you see all people as your enemy, never your friend."

Dain watched her get rid of the spoiled meat. "Listen, in my line of work, there's a million tricksters out there," he argued. "Money and power are the two things that run this world. There's a sucker born every minute. I got suckered once and I learned from the experience. So I do question people who come into my life. What are their real motives? What do they want from me?"

She put the empty packages and cellophane back into the sacks. "I disagree that money or power are the most important things in a person's life." She held his dark gaze.

"What about love? The love of a child for his parents? The love of a man for his wife?"

"Well," he snapped, taking two more grocery sacks into his arms, "that's where you and I agree to disagree, Erin. You obviously see love as the greatest force in your belief system. My belief system operates a hell of a lot differently. I *know* what makes this world go round—money and power, not love."

She absorbed Dain's anger as he stalked away, his stride long and uncompromising. Sighing, she followed at a much slower pace. When she entered the hogan, she found him shoving groceries together into one corner to make more room for what was to come. His movements were jerky and she felt his fury.

Placing the sacks she carried on the table, she moved over to where he was working with such savage intensity. "Do you feel," she asked quietly, "that I could do what I do if I saw the world only in terms of money and power?"

Straightening, he glared at her. Why the hell did she have to look so wild and beautiful, her hair hanging in dark sheets around her? "Look," he snarled, "so you're Miss Goody Two-Shoes. You've denied yourself money, I'll give you that. But you sure as hell have power." He stabbed his finger toward the door. "I saw all those Navajo this morning. I saw the hope in their eyes, the belief that *you* could cure them of whatever ailed them. And it's obvious they think you walk on water. That's power, Erin, and don't pretend it isn't."

"It is power."

Tensely, Dain placed his hands on his hips, staring at her. "So you admit it."

"What is there to admit? I told you that power is everywhere, but I try to *em*power a person, not take it away from them, or use it against them or to manipulate them in some way, which is what you do."

Dain stared openmouthed at her for a moment. Snapping

his mouth shut, he stalked out of the hogan and headed back down to his truck. Damn, she could be infuriating at times! But if he was honest with himself, he had to admit that Erin had always tried to empower him, not abuse her position with him. Still, he smarted beneath her truthful words and his pride wouldn't allow him to acknowledge that she was right.

Erin remained in the hogan while he retrieved the last of the groceries. Dain must have bought at least twenty bags of canned food. But she realized his giving wasn't out of generosity; it was payment for something he wanted from her. When he returned, the tension between them remained brittle as they worked in silence. She felt his pain, his fury, his stiff-necked pride and knew he was thinking deeply of their conversation. That was good.

Much later that evening, as Erin sat with him beside the stove, showing him how to mend a leather bridle, Dain's headache began to come back. Without saying anything, he got up, retrieved the chaparral salve and sat down again. Rubbing it across his brow, he brought a pillow over and lay down on his back. By taking deep breaths, he found, the pain would not worsen, and that was a major miracle to him.

Erin sat with the bridle across her lap, her legs crossed. Rubbing oil on the leather with a cloth, she watched him from time to time, dividing her attention between the task of cleaning the desert-dry leather and renewing its luster and watching Dain dutifully perform the breathing exercises.

"I am glad I could share my pain with you today," she told him quietly. "You are one of the few people I have told about my past. It felt good to release that poison." She dipped the cloth into the oil again. "We trusted one another."

Dain made a face over the word *trusted*, but kept his eyes closed and continued his breathing. "You had nothing to be ashamed of, Erin. If the bastard was here right now, I'd punch him out.''

''I'm glad he's not, then.'' She tried to keep the worry out of her voice as she watched Dain cautiously over her cleaning task. ''Sometimes having the ear of someone who cares about you is enough.'' Touching her chest, she whispered, ''My heart does not feel as heavy as before. Thank you for listening and caring.''

Grimacing, Dain opened his eyes. In the lamplight, Erin's face was deeply shadowed. She sat nearby, no more than a couple feet away from him, a thoughtful look on her face as she cleaned and oiled the bridle. ''I suppose you're going to tell me I've mended your broken trust with men?'' If only! Dain wanted her trust, he finally admitted to himself. And he wanted the love from her warm, generous heart.

She heard the derision in his low voice. Stilling her hands, she rested them on the leather in her lap. She glanced down at him. ''I allowed my past experience to stop me from trusting again, just like you chose to do.''

''There are degrees of broken trust,'' he replied.

''What experience did you have that broke your trust so completely?''

The pain in his head suddenly increased. ''I can't talk right now,'' he snapped, ''the pain's worse. I want to concentrate on my breathing and keep it away.''

Rubbing the leather slowly, Erin nodded. She saw the panic in his eyes, the absolute fear. In that moment, Dain was not a man, but a small, frightened boy. Resolutely, she knew she must push him toward that major confrontation with his past. If she did not, he would die never knowing how to love.

Chapter Eleven

Sleep was impossible for Dain. Looking at the dials on his watch, he realized it was around three a.m. Outside, he could hear the lonely howl of a nearby coyote—probably a whole pack of them had found the spoiled meat that Erin had thrown out earlier. Then he heard Maiisoh, moving toward the door. The white wolf obviously heard the coyotes, too.

Although his headache was gone, Dain was restless. He kept replaying his conversations with Erin inside his head. Finally, he threw off the wool blankets and sat up, glad that he'd put on his warm, blue-and-white cotton pyjamas this chilly night. Fragments of moonlight filtered into the hogan, and he looked over to see Erin sleeping along one wall. She had her back to him, the blankets drawn over her shoulders against the cold.

Getting up, Dain made his way over to the stove. He opened the door and put a few pieces of wood on the glowing coals. Feeling nervous and jittery for some unknown reason, he placed the old copper teakettle on the stove.

Maybe some tea would help. Padding over to the cabinet, he rummaged around and found a box of teabags and placed them on the table.

Hearing a noise, he looked around. Erin was sitting up, brushing strands of hair from her drowsy features.

"Go back to sleep," he ordered huskily. "Everything's all right." He saw the concern in her eyes as she studied him across the hogan. He knew beneath the blanket Erin wore a flannel nightgown that fell to her slender ankles. She looked fetching in it, he'd decided earlier when she'd returned in it from the hot springs after taking a bath. The pale pink chenille robe she'd worn with it looked ragged with age. Dain had smiled to himself when he saw the collar of her nightgown had tiny pink rosebuds on it. Somehow, living things such as flowers suited Erin. She was about life.

And he was about death. The thought scared the hell out of him. Sitting down at the table, he gripped the chipped white mug, needing something—someone—to hold on to. Maiisoh came over, sat down near the stove and studied him. The wolf's large yellow eyes seemed filled with curiosity. Oddly, since Dain had come here, he'd stopped having the nightmares. Had this wolf been coming to him in his sleep somehow? Dain scoffed at the whole idea, but he had no logic of his own to rebut the possibility.

"You are bothered by something?"

Dain jerked his chin up. Erin was standing sleepily before him, tying the sash on her pink robe. Shaken, he realized he hadn't heard her get up or walk over to him. His eyes narrowed on her drowsy features. Remnants of sleep still lingered in her shadowed eyes, and her mouth was soft and parted. Vulnerable.

"I don't know," he muttered irritably, shoving back the chair and going over to the stove. Picking up the teakettle, he brought it back to the table, dropped a teabag into the mug and poured in hot water.

"Make me some, too?"

Disgruntled, he took down a second cup from the shelf and prepared her tea. Then he joined Erin at the table, watching her as she thoughtfully dipped her teabag into her mug of steaming water.

"Why don't you go back to bed?"

"I was not asleep."

"Really?" He took his teabag out of the cup and set it on the oilcloth. Damn, he didn't mean to sound so angry and sarcastic with her. She didn't deserve this. But somehow she always managed to get inside the walls he'd erected all his life to keep everyone at bay. And that made him uncomfortable. Looking harshly at himself, Dain admitted he was afraid she was going to start asking questions he didn't want to answer.

"I felt your restlessness," Erin murmured, placing her own teabag on the table. She reached for a jar of honey and opened it. Tipping it, she allowed some to spill into her tea. "Something is eating at you." She lifted her head and looked toward the door. "Like the coyotes who are out there eating that spoiled meat right now."

"Yeah, well, they're a hell of a lot happier than I am right now."

She ran her finger along the lip of the jar, then stuck it in her mouth and sucked off the honey. "You look frightened to me," she murmured, placing the lid back on the honey jar.

"I don't know what I'm feeling," he muttered defiantly. In the shadows, Erin looked beautiful, the soft darkness accentuating her clean jawline and high cheekbones. Her hair, which she'd brushed before bedtime until it shone with highlights, was slightly mussed and gave her a very sensual look. He had a maddening urge to reach over and tame some of those soft strands back into place.

Pointing to her brow, she said, "When you speak, I see things here. I see a small boy, perhaps seven or eight, standing alone and looking frightened in this hall made of dark wood.''

Stunned, Dain stared at her. Instantly tension leaped between them.

She closed her eyes, her hands moving slowly around the mug in front of her. ''I see freckles across your face and your hair is short. You are wearing a bright red T-shirt and blue jeans. I see you looking up, but I do not know what you are looking at. There is such fear in your eyes...'' Her voice dropped to a whisper. ''I feel such terror around you, as if you are lost and do not know where you are.''

Opening her eyes, she looked at Dain. His rawboned face was chiseled with light and darkness, emphasizing the terror and anger she saw banked in his eyes. ''Is that where you lost your harmony? In that place? At that age?''

Dodging her searching gaze, he stared down at the mug of tea in his hands. He was gripping the cup so tightly he thought it might break. ''I don't,'' he said in a dangerously low voice, ''want to talk about it.''

Closing her eyes once more, she sighed. ''This place you are standing is very large and has a lonely feeling. The windows have chicken wire on the outside, and I wonder if it is some kind of prison you are standing in, even though it looks like a very old building that is kept in good condition.''

A frisson of fear jagged through Dain; he felt it in his chest, in his knotting gut. His breathing became ragged. ''Damn it, Erin, stop it!'' His voice echoed through the hogan.

Maiisoh sat up, looking at him intently.

Erin studied Dain. ''Then tell me of this scene I am being shown.''

Nostrils flaring, he realized she wasn't going to stop. ''Damn you,'' he snarled, ''you have no right to do this to me!''

"I cannot help what I see," she said firmly. "The Great Spirit has given me this picture."

"Well, it's a damned curse, if you ask me!"

"You were young when you were placed in that house or building."

His knuckles ached. He glared at her. "If you were a man, I'd knock you down right now." Instantly, he regretted his words, because he saw the shock and pain in her expression. And just as swiftly, it was replaced with a look of compassion. He cursed himself. Just today she'd entrusted him with the fact that she'd been abused. Damn it! Sometimes he felt like a rabid wolf, biting at the hand of whoever cared for him.

Erin sat very still, feeling his rage striking at her. She knew all too well what a man's fists were capable of doing, and his anger brought the taste of terror to her. It took every ounce of her escaping courage to ask, "Is that what they did to you? Knocked it out of you when you didn't behave?"

Stunned, Dain reared back as if physically struck. His eyes went wide as he stared at Erin.

"I am being shown a man now," she whispered. "He is not a big man like you, but small and lean. He is funny looking to me—his head is almost bald, except for some gray-and-black hair along the sides, and he wears owl-like glasses on his face."

"That's enough!" Dain snarled, shoving away from the table and sending his chair crashing to the floor. His tea sloshed across his hands, but he didn't feel the burning sensation. Breathing hard, he backed away.

Erin forced herself to remain calm, though she knew Dain was just as capable of hitting her as her ex-husband had been. Dain's chest was rising and falling with hard, ragged breaths, his fists were clenched at his sides and he was hunkered over, as if ready to leap on her and kill her. Maiisoh came close to her and sat down, on guard, his hackles uplifted, sensing Dain's present state. But the terror Erin saw in his eyes was the same terror she saw in the child's eyes. And she knew she had to overcome her own past, her fear of nearly being beaten to death, and reach out to help him.

Turning, she stood and watched Dain. "This man," she began, her voice off-key, "did not make you go out of harmony with yourself, but he frightened you and he hurt you, didn't he?"

Wrestling with disbelief that Erin knew everything he'd tried so hard to bury with his money and power, he snarled, "Stop!"

Wincing, she heard the anger in his voice, but also the plea. Her heart squeezed in her breast. She knew what she must do, for she was a wolf by nature. Closing her eyes, she said, "I see a woman. A big, fat woman with wild yellow hair. She's smiling and—"

"No!" Dain yelled. Moving swiftly around the stove, he was at her side in four strides, his hand snaking out and gripping her upper arm. Without realizing what he was doing, he shook Erin hard.

"Dain!"

Her cry was filled with shock and terror.

Breathing savagely, he blinked. Oh, lord, what had he done? He saw the panic in Erin's eyes as he felt his own terror rise. What was he doing? Instantly, he released her arm and backed away from her.

"I…" he began hoarsely. "I didn't mean—"

"This man did the same thing to you, didn't he?" Erin whispered, shaken as she pressed her hand to her bruised arm. She *had* to go on. She had to reach the core of his wound, but she was scared to death. "He hurt you all the time. He slapped you. I feel pain along my head. My left ear is ringing and hurts with sharp pains."

"My God!" He stood there, hunched over, struggling for breath and staring at her. He saw the tears glimmer in her huge eyes and watched as they trickled down her taut fea-

tures. Her mouth was parted, and as he saw her lower lip
tremble, he was torn between the memories that overwhelmed him and his fear that he would reach out and hurt
Erin again. Of all people, he'd never meant to hurt her—
but he had. Just as Old Gordon had hurt him.

On the heels of that realization, he stumbled toward the
stove. The pain in his head was back—with a vengeance.
Staring at Erin, who was still pressed up against the door,
he felt his knees caving beneath him. He sat down before
he fell down, the past avalanching over the present, burying
him in pain and confusion. What was real? What wasn't?
He didn't know as he rocked back and forth, fingers digging
into his skull as he tried to fight off the memories.

"No!" Erin cried as she moved to him. "No, let those
memories come! Feel them!" She sank to her knees before
him, her hands resting on her thighs. "Close your eyes and
move *into* them, Dain. If you want to live, if you *really*
want to live, you have to do this! Do it because you are
worth saving! Do it!" It was torture to reach out and touch
him, even though that's what she wanted to do more than
anything in the world. She heard Dain whimper as he buried
his head in his arms and rolled into a ball, like a child being
struck repeatedly.

Erin was unable to stop the horrified pictures from coming into her mind. She felt Dain's anguish, heard him sob
and saw what he saw. The pictures were terrifying to her.
The older, balding man was hitting Dain with his closed
fists. Dain lay in a trembling heap on the floor, trying to
escape the blows, but it was impossible. She saw the man
lean down and jerk Dain up by the collar of his shirt. As
soon as he lifted his head, the man slapped him hard against
the side of his head with his open palm. To her horror, she
saw blood trickling out of Dain's left ear. And then the boy
shrieked.

Hot tears blinded her eyes. The cry she heard in her mind
echoed in the room and she was aware of Dain rolling onto

his side, his knees tight against his body, his arms covering his head. She realized belatedly that the horror of his past had caught up with him and he was reliving it—but so was she, simultaneously. Erin could do nothing but watch, feel and try to maintain her own sense of self as the violence assaulted them.

Another picture slammed into her, rocking her senses. She saw the same man running after Dain, only this time Dain was older, perhaps ten. He was racing on small, spindly legs down a long hallway lined with dark, polished wood. She heard the heavier footfalls behind him. It was the same man and this time he had a long baton made out of wood in his hand. He was screeching Dain's name, his voice careening off the walls. Oh, no! Erin pressed her hands to her mouth to stop her own scream as she saw Dain try to enter a room. The door was locked! She saw him turn, terror in his eyes, to face his oncoming attacker. Erin felt the pain of her own abusive past slam into her. Images of the beating she'd taken—the trauma that had nearly cost her her life—ripped through her.

In those split seconds before the man struck Dain with the baton, Erin saw the defiance in the boy's eyes, along with the terror. She felt the first blow of the baton on her left shoulder, the pain radiating outward and shooting down her arm. Dain never whimpered. He fell to his knees, still glaring up in utter defiance of the man. The second blow stunned her as it exploded against the left side of her neck. Erin reeled, feeling faint. She felt a third blow as she saw Dain pitch forward. She heard the awful sound of bone breaking beneath the baton and her left shoulder became fiery, the pain excruciating.

A cry tore from Erin, but she couldn't distinguish it from all the awful, animal-like sounds filling her ears at the moment. Overwhelmed with the confusion of so many painful images, she struggled to maintain her own sense of identification. Somehow she had to withdraw from Dain's memories and not be trapped by them. But the agony of the blows continued and she reeled under them. She was gasping for air. Gasping to stay alive. Dying. Dain was dying. And so was she. The last blow was to her head. Moments later, blackness engulfed her.

Somewhere in that dark state, Erin felt herself tumbling out of control. She called for help and within moments, she saw the spirit of Maiisoh running alongside her as she fell, like a tumbleweed pushed by a violent wind. Thrusting her hand out, she grabbed for the wolf's heavy, thick neck. Her fingers met the fur and she gripped hard. Slowly, every so slowly, her own cartwheeling stopped and she was able to cling to her spirit guide and center herself once more.

The sounds of a fire snapping and popping filtered through her consciousness. Opening her eyes, she saw Dain lying nearby, still in a fetal position, his arms tight against his head, as if to protect him from the blows he'd received. It was then that Erin realized she was crying, the tears spilling down her cheeks. Dizzy, she crawled on her hands and knees to where he lay.

If she touched him, she knew she would reconnect with his nightmare world of the past. She felt her own past savagely stalking her and knew she would be engulfed again. Spreading her hands toward him, but not making contact, she took several deep, steadying breaths. Center! She must center herself or once again be swept up in that tornado of violent emotions Dain was presently enduring. Her fingers trembled slightly. Now!

Placing one hand on his head, the other on his shoulder, she closed her eyes and tried to prepare for the assault he was experiencing. Dain was shaking like a leaf carried by stormy winds. His pajamas were damp, clinging to his body. She felt every muscle in his body go rigid from the blows. He was gasping for breath, moaning, whimpering like a dog that had been beaten to within an inch of its life.

Tears spilled out of her eyes as she moved closer and

leaned over to hold him. Her hair cascaded across his body and she pressed her cheek against him. In a wobbling tone she began to sing a song of healing, and called in her spirit guides to help him find a way out of the memories that still held him a tortured prisoner. His body convulsed with a sob and the sound tore at her, leaving her unable to shield herself from his anguish. Her own terrifying emotions shredded her and she gasped softly before continuing the song, which came out in broken, husky fragments.

Holding him with all of her woman's strength, Erin began to feel Dain release himself from the experience. Little by little, his arms eased from around his head. She surrounded him with her own arms and rocked him slowly. The song came from her heart, from her own wounded soul, and she knew her voice was giving him the strength he needed to move through the experience and on to the other side of it. The melody fed her, too, and she felt the white wolf's familiar strength pressing against her, steadying her, nurturing her.

Dain had no idea what time it was. All he knew was that Erin was holding him, rocking him, with her strong arms. Despite his recent torment, he felt safe. Safe and protected. Her voice, low and husky, provided a sound that he could focus on, follow and trust. His tightly shut eyes stung with tears, which rolled down his contorted face. His breath grew less raspy, and over time, his chest began to rise and fall in unison with hers.

The words of her song were Cherokee, and though he didn't know what they meant, the sound was reassuring, healing and stabilizing to him. Finally, he felt her arms begin to loosen and a new sense of relaxation flowed through him. He panicked momentarily because he didn't want Erin to leave him—he needed her continued touch, the solace she fed him. When the song finally ended, he became aware of the fire warming his body. Still she continued to hold him, and he concentrated on the feel of her hand upon his back, gently moving back and forth as if she was petting a sick animal. Was he sick? Yes, he remembered with pain.

Bitterly, he forced open his eyes. The taste of bile was in his mouth and his stomach felt nauseous, like he was going to vomit. He tore out of her grasp and staggered toward the kitchen. Dropping to his knees, he grabbed an empty bucket and felt his stomach lurch. He felt the viscous blackness inhabiting his gut come tunneling upward. The sounds he heard couldn't be made by him. They couldn't. And just when he felt lost and alone again, he felt Erin's trembling hands settle gently upon his shoulders, holding him. He continued to heave, his body convulsing, but she steadied him with her own body, her hands gripping his shoulders, helping him. The white wolf stood against him, supporting him.

Finally, he was done and he knelt there on the floor, shaking and trembling. He felt a cool, damp cloth being pressed against his face and belatedly he realized that Erin was wiping away the beads of perspiration and cleaning his mouth.

"Here," she whispered, pressing a cup of cool water to his lips, "drink this and then spit it out into the bucket."

He did as she instructed. Soon his mouth felt cleaner. Erin crouched down, her arm around his shoulder, and provided him with another glass of water, this time to drink. The cold water tasted sweet and good. It tasted of life, not terror, not death. He was still shaky, barely able to hold the glass, so she placed her hand around his and guided the water to his lips so he could drink as much as he wanted.

Wrapped in the pain of the past as well as the physical misery of the present, Dain felt utterly helpless. He had no idea what had happened, he only knew *something* had happened. Never had the memories been so violent. Never had he felt like this. He felt Erin rise, and with all her strength, pull him to his feet. His knees were like jelly and he leaned heavily upon her as she guided him back to his pallet near the stove and sat him down. Then she brought blankets and wrapped them round his shoulders, before sitting next to him, her body strong and stabilizing against his back, her arms around him, simply holding him. The white wolf looked at him with those wise, golden eyes of his before he lay down at Dain's feet.

Closing his eyes, Dain tipped his head back and felt her smooth, warm cheek against his. He turned his face to her thick, silky hair and buried it in the clean strands. Erin smelled of life. And he smelled of death. Oh, God, how many ways were there to die? How many times had he already died? His voice was raw when he finally spoke.

"Old Gordon," he said unsteadily. "That was his name. Old Gordon. That's what all the orphans called him. Everyone was afraid of him. Oh, God, I learned to be afraid of him. We all were terrified when he looked at us with that wild, insane look on his face. We knew he was going to beat us until we screamed for mercy."

Dain choked and took a few deep breaths. He felt Erin's arms tighten momentarily, as if to encourage him to continue talking. He had no choice as far as he was concerned. If he didn't talk, he was going to die of the pain he'd held inside so long. The warmth of her cheek pressing to his was the one thing he clung to.

"He was a schoolmaster at the orphanage where I was put. I didn't want to go there, but Luella, my foster mother, died suddenly of a heart attack, and no one wanted me. I was too old for adoption, so I got put in this orphanage. I was so scared. So scared. I loved Luella. She was my mother. Even if she didn't give birth to me, she was the mother I loved and—" He choked, pressing his face hard against Erin. "Anyone I loved was torn from me."

The admission was so terrible that Dain had never been to verbalize what he'd always known, until this moment. He felt Erin sigh, felt her damp cheek against his. She was crying, he realized dimly—crying for him. That shook him as nothing else ever had. No one had ever cried for him— until now. Gasping, he tried to breathe and found it impossible. A sob constricted his throat, and he could no longer hold back his own tears for the little boy no one had loved. No one had wanted him once Luella was gone. He wasn't worth being loved anymore. He wasn't worth keeping alive.

Tears burned in his tightly shut eyes, and he forced his words out. "I remember going to the orphanage, being dropped off by Luella's husband, who was still in shock over her death. He was partly paralyzed, he couldn't take care of me by himself. I remember sitting in that car with him, and him holding me and telling me he was sorry. He cried and cried. I cried because I didn't want to be let go. When I saw Old Gordon standing in front of our car, and I saw his insane eyes, I clung to my dad. I begged him not to give me away. I told him I'd do *anything* if he'd let me stay, but Old Gordon opened the door and pulled me out of his arms.

"I'll never forget that. I remember Old Gordon's hands being like claws sinking into my arm. I remember my dad crying and apologizing as he shut the door. I tried to get away, to run after my dad's car when he left, but Old Gordon yanked me by my hair and dragged me into that orphanage."

The pain kept rolling out of him in dark waves. Dain could feel the harsh memories flowing up and out of him as he put them into words. He wanted Erin to understand why he'd nearly hurt her, and God knew, she was the last person on the face of this earth he'd ever want to hurt. Somewhere in his cartwheeling mind and shattering heart, he understood that Erin had been a lightning-bolt catalyst to him, helping him rip away the lid he'd kept over all his emotions and memories. Miraculously, he felt cleaner and better now, but he didn't know why.

"I lived in that godforsaken orphanage until I was eighteen. I swore that I'd get out of there, and I did. I made good grades and I got an appointment to the Air Force Academy." He sighed raggedly. "When I left that day, I vowed to never look back.'' Opening his eyes, he looked up at Erin. "And I didn't, until tonight."

He was so close to her, his face mirroring his raw, vulnerable state. Erin eased away just enough to hold his tear-filled gaze. Her lips trembled as she said, "Now I understand why you became what you were." She reached out and gently pushed some damp strands of hair off his brow. "But you do not have to stay in that little boy's unhappy state anymore. You had the courage to walk through those memories from your past. You no longer ran from them or tried to bury them, Dain. You turned and faced your monsters."

He smiled then. Erin's hair was soft against his cheek, her mouth inches from his own. He felt her strength, her incredible compassion as her arms continued to embrace him. "There was only one monster in my past—Old Gordon."

Erin didn't have the heart to tell him there were more. He'd gone through enough hell, enough of a healing crisis already. Right now, Dain needed to be supported and protected. She knew she could give him that. A miracle had occurred, she realized humbly as she stared down into stormy blue eyes that searched hers so earnestly in the gray dawn.

"You need to sleep," she whispered, and she guided him to lie down on his side. Drawing up the covers, her hands coming to rest on his shoulder, she leaned over to see that he'd already closed his eyes. This time there was no tension in his facial features, no rigidity left in his body. By reliving the past, he'd released the virulent poison that had inhabited him. Easing her fingers through his hair, she felt sleep begin to overtake Dain. Sleep was healing. And that was good.

Looking up, she watched the gray light of dawn playing against the windows in the hogan, as she thought about all he'd been through, all she'd been through as well. Releasing a soft breath, Erin realized she could not tear herself from

Dain's side. Instead, she slid down beside him, aligning her body against his, pulling the blankets over herself and wrapping her arm around his chest. She felt such peace lying with him. Her own violent past seemed so distant as she lay there, her face pressed against his shoulder. Was she doing this for his need or her own? There were no easy answers and she was too exhausted to try and discover the truth of her actions.

There was much to be done in preparation for when Dain awoke. He would be in a very raw state and in need of nurturing. That was one thing she could give him, and willingly, from the depths of her soul. For in the midst of this storm, though it scared her as nothing else could, she realized her love for him.

Chapter Twelve

Dain had awakened sometime in the middle of the afternoon and Erin had told him that what was needed was a ceremonial sweat. And though the sweat was hot and stifling, he was relieved to take the cure because he was too embarrassed to talk about what had happened last night—how he'd leaned on her during that horrible time. His gut still ached from all the violent heaving and sobbing episodes.

Erin's low, husky voice filtered through the moisture of the sweat lodge, soothing as well as nurturing. Wearing only a towel around his waist, Dain sat cross-legged on the damp earth, staring dully at a mound of red, heated rocks that had been placed in a hole dug into the floor. He could barely make out Erin's form as she sat opposite him, a bucket of water and a wooden ladle nearby. The steam was cleansing, in a way. Sweat poured off him in continuous rivulets.

He'd lost track of time, and really, he didn't care, because he was still hurting so much from the memories. The red stones dimmed as more water was poured on them, and the lodge darkened. Wiping his hands across his face, slick with perspiration, he heard Erin begin to talk.

"We sit in the womb of our mother, the Earth. Being in a sweat is like being a baby held in your mother's body once again. It is moist, warm and safe. It is here that we constantly renew our tie with our true mother. If you place your palms against her skin, you can feel the pulse of her heartbeat through them. In the darkness, there are no distractions from what is looking back at us. It is a good time to speak of what lies in our hearts and minds."

The silence deepened and Dain knew she wanted him to speak. He didn't have the strength to fight her request, all the struggle having been taken out of him last night. Leaning forward, his brow resting against his hands, his elbows digging into his thighs, he sighed heavily.

"I never wanted to feel the fear I experienced last night," he said huskily, his words swallowed up by the steam surrounding him. "Old Gordon was as mean as they came. All the kids lived in absolute fear of him."

"You challenged him."

Her words were soft. Squirming, he grimaced. "Someone had to."

"Why?"

"Because nobody cared, that's why. Sure, we got fed, we got clothed, we got an education, but so what? Old Gordon had been there longer than anyone and nobody was going to challenge that bastard."

"You must have gone to the hospital that day he beat you so badly."

A strangled sound came from Dain's throat. "Yeah, that was the final round between us."

"There had been others?"

"Oh, yeah, but not as bad as that one."

"Did he not get in trouble for beating you like that?"

Chuckling, Dain said, "He got put out to pasture on that one. They didn't fire him, they just retired him so he could collect his thirty-year pension."

"And he was never punished for what he did to you?"

"Never." Dain dully realized that Erin had seen what he'd gone through. He closed his eyes. "You saw it all, didn't you?"

"Yes. It was very painful to watch…to feel what you suffered." To feel her own past once again.

"That makes two of us." Dain knew it was a poor joke and one even he couldn't laugh at.

"What did you learn from Old Gordon?"

The question took him off guard. *"Learn?"* The word exploded from him and he lifted his head from his hands. Even though he couldn't see Erin in the darkness, he stared in her direction. "Learn?"

"All people, all situations we're placed in are to teach us. What did he teach you?"

Grinning savagely and feeling his anger rise, Dain snapped, "I learned never to trust adults."

"And when you grew up and became an adult yourself?"

"I never trusted anyone after that."

"Do you trust children?"

He considered the question for a long time before answering. "Children are always innocent. They're vulnerable. They have no way to defend themselves against the world in general and adults specifically."

"And so you learned to become a lone wolf, without a family or pack, to make your way through life?"

"You could say that."

"Is this a way of life you like?"

"Like?" His lips lifted in a snarl. "I didn't like Old Gordon beating me. I didn't like the fact that the staff let the bastard get away with it. I didn't like the fact he molested the little girls. He was perverse. I hated him. I hated what he did to us."

"You said 'us'?"

Dain glared through the darkness. "I suppose lone wolves don't use the word *us?*"

Erin laughed gently. "Even in the darkness of the womb,

you see your own truth. That is good.'' How badly she wanted to hold him, but to do so right now might stop the flow coming from him and it was necessary he give words to his pain.

He felt pleased by her compliment. ''Okay, if I'm not a lone wolf, what the hell am I? I'm sure you already think you know.''

''It is not my place to tell you what I see, think or feel. It is your responsibility to walk your own path of discovery and claim it for yourself.''

Ruminating over her words, he sat quietly for a long time. Erin continued to pour water on the stones, making the sweat hotter and causing perspiration to pour off him. Somehow, the whole process was cleaning him out. No longer did he feel as if a monster was lurking inside his gut, howling out his pain where no one could hear him.

''I can see that everything I've built in my life was to keep me away from people as much as possible,'' he muttered almost defiantly. ''And yet you're right—I was always running interference for the other kids, especially the girls that Old Gordon had his eye on, trying to somehow protect them. I never could. I tried and failed.''

''There is no shame in trying,'' Erin said. She felt his anguish at being unable to protect the little girls who had been stalked and harmed by Old Gordon. After a few minutes of silence, she asked, ''And in your world of business, do you do that now?''

''No.''

''What do your businesses do to make money?''

He shut his eyes. ''They take. I'm a corporate raider. I stalk my quarry—some company—and then I attack it and destroy it and absorb it into one of my larger corporations. I get rid of anything weaker than me.''

''Do you replace the people who are caught in this change?''

''No.''

''Then are you behaving like Old Gordon, in a way? He

always took from you, from the other children, and never gave back anything positive.''

Squeezing his eyes shut, Dain ran his hand over his damp face. "No," he muttered, the word barely audible. He waited to hear censure from Erin. Instead, all he heard was water being poured over the stones, the hissing sound that followed. The thought that he was like Gordon scared the living hell out of Dain. And yet, what did he do with his corporations? He took, he raped, he pillaged—without remorse, without conscience—just as Old Gordon had. To rub further salt in his wounds, he realized he was getting rewarded for it, too.

"My God..." he whispered with horror. "I've become what I hated the most."

That evening Dain sat near the sheep corral, alone. The sun was nearly hidden behind the red bluffs in the distance. Maiisoh had just brought the flock back from a day of foraging on the desert, and bleating sheep filled the rickety old corral. Even though he wore a denim shirt and jeans, he felt naked. It was an odd feeling, one of being stripped of all protective walls and left wide open. Vulnerable. He'd been relieved when Erin went about her daily business after the sweat. He'd gone down to the hot springs and bathed, and then dressed. Now he remained outside while she was in the hogan, making bread and mutton stew for tonight.

Maiisoh came up to where he was perched on the railing. The white wolf sat down and looked up at him with those huge, wise, amber eyes of his. Dain grinned a little, reaching out and sliding his hand across the wolf's broad head. It was the first time he'd touched the animal. Maybe the reason he could was because he'd faced all the horror and terror of trying to survive the orphanage and had found the white wolf in himself. Dain was no longer sure of anything anymore. Inside he was a mass of writhing emotions that refused to be ignored any longer.

"You like being a lone wolf?"

The animal studied him.

"Me, neither." Frowning, Dain eased himself off the rail, his boots settling into the red dust. He saw Erin come out of the hogan. She had changed clothes and was wearing a maroon velvet skirt and pink, long-sleeved blouse. Her hair had been frizzy when she'd crawled out of the sweat, but now it was brushed and hung like a dark curtain. As she drew near, he saw a white smudge of flour on her right cheek.

"Did the bread get the best of you?" he teased, motioning to her face as she drew near.

"Oh…" Erin rubbed her skin. "There. Is it gone?"

His smile widened and he walked up to her. Without thinking, he captured her chin and gently brushed the smooth slope of her cheek. "There." Her skin was firm and soft. He saw her eyes change, saw the surprise flare in them and then saw them become a velvet luster. How beautiful, how natural she was, he thought as a hunger began gnawing at him. He wanted her—desperately. This wasn't just need, this was a hot, burning desire he'd never experienced before. He needed her! Like air to breathe, he needed her. Shaken by the discovery, he reluctantly released her.

"Are you going to sing down the sun?" he asked.

Stepping away, Erin nodded, her heartbeat quickening with longing. How desperately she wanted to love Dain, all of him—to give back some of what he'd had torn from him. She could do that for him, Erin realized, and it would not hurt or destroy her. In order to do it, though, she'd have to trust him—fully, without reserve. She wasn't sure she could do that yet. Or could she? Torn, her hands knotted, she replied, "Uh…yes, I was. Do you want to join me?"

Dain nodded and stood facing the setting sun with her. It was a nice little ceremony, he thought, as she opened her palms outward and began to sing. He was coming to appreciate the day's activities as never before. What did it hurt to give thanks for living through another day? Or praying over their food each time they ate, thanking the animals for giving their lives so that they might live?

As he stood there, bathed in the disappearing red-orange

rays, Dain closed his eyes and absorbed her husky voice. There was such feeling in the words Erin sang, for she sang from her heart. Without realizing it, he was humming the tune.

When the song was completed, Dain opened his eyes and looked at her. There was such pride in her profile, a natural sense of confidence about her. "I've been thinking," he began quietly, "about my corporations and how they parallel what Old Gordon did to me...to us."

Erin lifted her chin and looked up at his shadowed eyes. Her heart leaped at the word *us*. Did she dare hope? The love she felt toward Dain was so fresh and new. And frightening. "Yes?" she asked, barely able to conceal the trembling in her voice.

Placing his hands on his hips, he murmured, "There are many things I know have to change in my life back East. There is too much that is wrong with the way my companies are run—with the way I treat people. I know it means listening to my heart—my wild heart—but I'm not sure I really know how to hear it."

Erin pressed her palm to the center of his chest. "Feel it." The joy of getting to touch him spiraled through her like the breath of life itself. She saw his eyes change, a flame appear, and heat uncurled deep in her body. She absorbed his burning look, a look that was filled with desire—for her. Oh, how had this happened? When had her compassion turned into a haunting, aching love for Dain?

Erin's touch was so gentle, it brought tears to Dain's eyes. This time he didn't try to fight them or hide them from her. He saw tears glimmering in her own eyes, and he lifted his hand to her face. "That's all I've been doing lately is feeling," he told her wryly, with a slight, embarrassed laugh. How badly he wanted to taste her lips, savor the womanly strength of her mouth, trace the full roundness of her breasts and find solace within her. It was a bittersweet desire that tunneled through him, for how could she ever possibly love a monster like him?

"That is what a person's wild heart does best."

He didn't want to stop touching her. But it was the wrong time and situation for lovemaking. Gripping her hand momentarily, he squeezed it and released it. "Tears are part of the wild heart?"

"Very much so. So is laughter."

"I notice you do a lot of both around here."

She wiped her eyes and said, "To feel without apology, to laugh, to cry openly, are signs of a wild heart. You owe no one an apology for how you feel. Our connection to our mother is through our feelings, our heart." She gave him a proud look. "You have reconnected, Dain. I honor your courage."

He watched Erin walk back to the hogan, her shoulders squared, her chin lifted with natural pride. There was a wonderful swaying motion to her hips, a seductive rhythm to the way she moved. He ached to capture that rhythm with his own hot, hard body. She reminded him of a willow tree at the orphanage he used to watch sway in the breeze. Erin was willowlike, full of life, and she was able to transfer her love of life to others.

Was that what medicine people did? Transfer their own qualities to their patients? Perhaps. Dain thought about it as he walked slowly back to the hogan.

The mutton stew on the stove sure smelled good. Mouthwatering, in fact. And the odor of bread baking embraced him as he entered. Erin had lit the kerosene lamps, the soft yellow color fusing with the darkness that would soon cover the red desert around them. She took the bread out of the oven and set it on the counter.

Once she'd taken off the oven mittens, Dain placed his hands on her shoulders and gently turned her around to face him. When she lifted her chin, he whispered, "I need you." He'd expected rejection. Instead he saw huge tears welling up in her guileless eyes. Her look tore every last vestige of distrust out of him. "Don't cry, sweet woman of the earth," he whispered huskily, removing the tears with his thumbs.

Wordlessly, he took Erin's hand and pulled her over to his pallet. Sinking down to their knees, they faced one another. Everything was so tenuous. His heart was beating so hard in his chest he thought he might die of a cardiac arrest. It didn't matter. With his hands he followed the curve of her thick, dark hair all the way down to where it covered her breasts. Her eyes closed as he cupped her breasts and molded them with his hands. Erin leaned forward, a sigh escaping her parted lips. That was all he needed—a sign of trust. A sign of surrender.

He undressed her slowly in the dim light, mesmerized by the golden color of her flesh, the soft firmness of her breasts as the blouse fell away. She wore no bra, and her breasts were shadowed and beautiful, beckoning to him. He leaned down and brought her against his body, closing his lips over one hardened nipple. Suckling her sent a shaft of lightning through him. He felt her arch and curve against him, heard her moan in pleasure and felt her bury her face against his neck. She tasted of life. Of rich, sweet honey. She drew such gentleness out of him. Treasuring her, he made a slow exploration of the contours of her body. In time, they lay naked on the pallet together, facing one another, their arms and legs entangled.

The first time he touched his lips to hers, she opened to him. The sweetness of her mouth, combined with the strong, pulsing warmth of her body pressing against his, melted any lingering fear. For once he wanted to give, not take. For once he wanted to convey his deep love, the love he kept so carefully hidden from everyone. Opening her mouth even more, he felt her tremble, and he moved his other hand knowingly down her hip. Rolling Erin over on her back, he felt her thighs part and he couldn't believe the warmth awaiting him, beckoning him and inviting him within her.

Each moment was excruciatingly beautiful to him as he moved on top of her. He loved the way her halo of hair framed her glowing features, the way her half-closed eyes gleamed with gold, the way her thighs closed about him and drew him into her. The moment was like splintered sunlight against the glaring brightness of ice for him. Erin was warm, open, inviting and pulsing with life. He could not stop his forward movement, nor did he want to. In those wild, delicious moments, he realized he was mating with the woman he'd waited for all his life, had dreamed of, but never thought truly existed. Now he knew she did. Here and now. With each undulating movement, he was pulled deeper and deeper into her, a spiraling cauldron of heat and need.

Eyes shut, Dain felt more animal than man in those magical moments. Erin was his mate for life—a wild wolf like himself, once hurt, but surviving. And now, as they moved with the ancient rhythm of the earth where they lay, a pulsing heat scalded his loins and made him take her savagely. Without restraint. He thrust hard and deep into her, taking, giving and sharing. Euphoria embraced him in a wave of heat as, tense and rigid, he felt her arms come around him, felt her hips moving in a timeless rhythm. She held him as he surrendered to the softness of her form, her lips against his and her arms surrounding him. As he gave in, he felt her stiffen and arch against him. He held her, prolonged her ecstasy and caught her small cries of pleasure in a smothering kiss, sharing each wild, untrammeled movement of her body.

How long he lay on top of her, his fingers entwined in the thick strands of her damp hair, his mouth against her cheek, his heart beating in wild unison with hers, Dain did not know. His body burned with pleasure when he saw her swollen lips, marked by his passion. Dain couldn't remember ever sharing anything like this with a woman. As he raised his head slightly, he met her slumberous eyes, filled with happiness and satiation. More than anything he'd wanted their lovemaking to be good for Erin, and it had been. The corners of her lips curved ever so slightly and he smiled down at her as he gently caressed her smooth, damp brow. As he brushed his fingers through her hair, he realized he had never felt so fulfilled. Or happy. Her hands sliding across his back, caressing him, made him feel nurtured and loved. He felt like he was a starving man who had been alone for too long.

But was he the man for Erin? He was more monster than human, he realized with bitterness. Dain frowned and looked into the dim light of the hogan. How could he give Erin what she needed and deserved? He wasn't whole. And hadn't he seen the monster within himself just last night? How could she even consent to make love to him? How? As he gazed down at her, Dain had no answers, just an awful sense of dread. He may have caught a beautiful butterfly, but he knew he was capable of crushing and destroying that beauty. Yes, he'd do to her what he had to everything else—he would destroy Erin. Was that what he wanted? Was that what she deserved?

Gently, he left her side, covering her with the blanket. "I'm going to the hot springs. I'll be back a little later," he promised gruffly, and rose to his feet.

As Dain stood washing up the dinner dishes after the delicious, filling meal, he asked Erin, "Do you think my brain tumor began because of all those emotions I experienced as a kid?"

Erin slowly dried the dish he gave her. "I do not know," she answered softly. Her body still tingled from their lovemaking. Dain had returned an hour later and she could tell he was deep in thought. She felt the fragility of their connection, but knew she must not speak of it yet. "A tumor is nothing more than a sack that holds poisons that the body does not want spread throughout it," she told him, placing the plate on the shelf in front of her.

He rinsed off the bread pan and handed it to her. "So the real question is how do I free myself from my own poisonous sack, right?" But Dain had his answer. He knew it was probably too late for him to be cured. But he also knew that whatever life he had left would be glorious if it was spent with Erin. But he wasn't worthy of her in any way.

She gazed up at his serious, shadowed features. "Listen to what your wild heart needs."

"I don't know what that means," he muttered, frustrated.

Erin slowly dried the pan with the dish towel. "If," she said softly, "you could reconstruct your life and do things differently, if you could have your dreams come true, what would you do?"

Rolling his eyes, he laughed acidly. "Dreams? There you go again, Erin, talking about fluff and stuff." His dreams were of *her*. As compassionate and understanding as Erin was, Dain knew she wouldn't accept the fact that she was *his* dream. Especially now that she knew the truth about him—the monster he'd become.

"Dreams are not fluff and stuff. They are the energy, the beginning of what will become real for us if we desire it strongly enough." Erin saw a war going on in Dain's eyes. She felt his angst as clearly as she felt her own. There was so much she wanted to speak to him about. So much! And yet she was afraid.

His hands stilled in the warm, soapy water. "Dreams. Okay, I had them as a kid. But I'm a man now—and my needs are different."

Dain tried to tell her just what those needs were, but the words wouldn't come out. He was scared to death of telling Erin the truth—that all he needed in his life was her. But what life did he have left? He was slated to die in six months. What kind of life could he give her? She was rich in ways his money would never be able to buy.

She smiled at him. "You have to remember what made you happy."

I was happy making love to you, Dain thought, though the words remained locked in his head. He gazed at her, devouring her, absorbing her warm smile and her faith in him.

When they awoke before dawn she was disoriented. Sitting up, she saw Maiisoh near the open door to her hogan. Then she heard a car door slam. What was going on? Dread filled her as she pushed the covers aside and stood up. Nervously smoothing her nightgown, she moved toward the door, almost running out. Dain.

Automatically, he reached out, his strong hands curving around her arms. "Erin…"

An immediate need clamored through her. Whispering his name, she looked up…up into his shadowed face and a gaze that consumed her soul. "What—?"

"I'm leaving, Erin. I—I realize now I have to. God knows, I don't want to, but I realized a lot about myself while being here—things I need to change," he said. He saw her eyes go wide with shock and then with understanding. She was so close to him that he could feel her body heat, and fire ignited within him. Her lips parted, but no words came. Dain knew she understood why he had to go. If he stayed, she would become a crutch to him. And that wouldn't help him heal. Whether he outran this tumor or not, he had his life back East.

"I'm not good with words," he said harshly, reaching up and cupping her face and looking deeply into her shadowed eyes, now filled with tears. Tears of compassion? Tears that he was going to leave her? God, how he loved her! But how could she ever love a monster? Oh, how he ached to ask her that very question, but it was too soon and it was unfair to Erin. They needed time. He needed to know he could live without her in order to know if he was the man for her. "There's so much to say, so much that needs to be said, and…" Helplessly he gazed down at her.

Tears tumbled from her eyes. Dain groaned and swept her into his arms. To hell with it. He *needed* her mouth on his. He needed to convey his love to her somehow. Would she resist? Would she push him away in disgust? Never had he felt so scared of being told that he was not wanted—or loved. And he knew he loved her because he'd never felt like this in his life. Erin had drawn it out in him—her heart, her goodness.…

Erin's lashes closed automatically as his mouth descended

upon hers. She moaned in surrender, feeling a need so great that it almost overwhelmed her. When his mouth met and melded with hers, she placed her arms around his neck and clung to him. How easy it was to fuse into a oneness! She felt the hardness of his body against her. Felt his mouth moving insistently on hers. Her breath snagged as she spiraled into a haze of fire, a blaze that exploded between them. Her fingers tunneled into his hair and she arched against him. His arms were like bands capturing her, pressing her to him.

The salt of their mutual tears mingled, and a sob caught in her throat as he tore his mouth from hers. His eyes were glimmering with fierce desire—there was no question that Dain wanted her. In that instant, Erin had never felt happier— or more frightened. She knew why he was leaving.

"Go," she whispered unsteadily, placing her hand against his chest. She could feel his heart pounding beneath her fingertips, could see him struggling for breath. His eyes were narrowed, reminding her of Maiisoh stalking a quarry. But it gave her a good feeling, not a bad one. She felt his fingers dig into her arms, as if he was fighting himself.

"I understand," she said quietly.

Dain gulped hard and forced himself to release her. The white wolf came to Erin's side and gazed up at him with sad amber eyes. Awkwardly, Dain took a step away. "I—"

Erin shook her head. "Don't say anything, Dain." Tears in her eyes caused his shadowed form to blur.

"I want to come back to you, Erin," he said huskily.

Her heart pounded hard. "We both have dark pasts to work through and resolve within ourselves before that can happen," she said, sobbing softly. "I am just as wounded as you. I know you know that."

He shoved his fingers savagely through his hair. "Yes, only I haven't helped you like you helped me...."

"Yes, you did," she said unsteadily, wiping her eyes. "You've freed me, too."

"I've got to go...."

She ached to tell him to come back to her—but to do so

would be selfish. Instead she nodded her head once in agreement with his decision.

Dain opened the door and moved quickly toward his truck. Vaguely, he could see the gray silhouette of Erin's form in the doorway of her hogan. "I'll come back, Erin. I'll come back once I can straighten myself and my life out."

Erin stood there, hands clasped against her heart. His words did not give solace, but instead more pain. Though she'd heard the hope in his voice, she knew as well as he did that there was no way of knowing what the Great Spirit had in store for Dain—whether he would live or die. She watched the lights of the truck stab into the darkness as he drove away. And soon enough, the desert night swallowed him up.

She felt Maiisoh brush against her with a whine and her hand fell upon his massive head. Hot tears tumbled down her cheeks. "Oh, Maiisoh," she quavered. "My heart is breaking...."

The wolf licked her hand gently.

Erin cried harder. She pressed her fingers against her tightly shut eyes and let all the fear and hurt from her own painful past tunnel up through her. Dain had been her healer as well—and now she wasn't sure she'd ever see him again. Never had she felt so uncertain. More than anything she needed Dain, man to her woman. His leaving only made her realize how different his world and hers were. Erin could see no way to make such a relationship work.

Slowly, she turned and moved back into the hogan. Never had her heart felt heavier. Would she ever know if Dain survived his tumor? Would she ever see him again if he did?

Chapter Thirteen

The cold, biting wind of February tugged at the heavy rabbit fur coat Erin wore as she rode her horse down the hill. The last of the sheep entered the pen—a good thing, because soon it would be dark. The high desert plateau was spotted here and there with patches of white snow. The snow had started three months ago, shortly after Dain had left.

Her heart clenched as it always did when she thought of Dain. Since his departure she'd heard nothing. Was he dead? Alive? There was no way to know. Even now her heart ached. Erin dismounted, gave the horse a well-earned pat on the neck and unsaddled the animal.

The evening sky was pale pink tinged with lavender and peach—her favorite colors. Maiisoh whined and rubbed against her before standing attentively, looking down the rutted road.

"What?" she teased, ruffling his neck fur. "Another patient is coming at this time of day?" Most of her patients left well before sunset.

After feeding the horse its ration of alfalfa hay, Erin hurried to the hogan, glad to get inside. Her hands were chapped and cold. After making a fire in the wood stove, she fixed herself something to eat.

Maiisoh sat next to the door, his big white tail thumping happily, his full attention on whatever he heard outside. Erin groaned inwardly. It *had* to be a patient. And right now she wasn't emotionally stable enough to deal with someone's sickness. Today had been a day of grieving—for Dain, for so many crazy hopes about what might have been and never would be. It had left Erin feeling drained and sad. She could no more stop loving Dain than she could stop loving her family. Grief had its own healing time, and she was still going through the pain of losing him.

She had just set her bowl of mutton stew on the table when she heard a truck drive up. The engine was turned off, and she heard the cab door open and close. Maiisoh pawed eagerly at the floor near the entrance to the hogan. That was unlike him. Frowning, Erin went to the door. Somehow, she would put her own pain aside and deal with this patient's problems.

She opened the door. The dusky light settled on the tall figure of a man.

"Dain!" It was more a cry of surprise than anything else. Erin gripped the door and stared up at him. How strong and fit he looked! She saw a careless smile pull at his mouth— a mouth she had so many times dreamed of kissing.

"I'm not stuck this time." Dain reached out, briefly caressing her cheek. How beautiful Erin looked. His heart lurched in his chest as he saw tears come to her eyes. "May I come in, Erin?" Swallowing hard, he fought the desire to sweep her into his arms. How he wanted to do that and much more. *Patience,* he warned himself. *Give her time to adjust to me being alive.* Being back in her life—as he'd promised.

Her heart galloped wildly as she stepped aside. "Y-yes, please, come in...."

Maiisoh leaped happily around Dain. Laughing joyfully, Dain knelt down in the middle of the hogan and roughed up the wolf's fur with great affection.

"His hair has grown thicker since I last saw him," Dain murmured, looking up as Erin came to stand near him. In the yellow glow of the kerosene lamps he could see that she was thinner than before. Guilt ate at him. Patting Maiisoh's massive head one more time, he reached out to her. Tentatively, he slid his hand around her fingers. He could feel her work-worn flesh, the roughness of her skin. She worked so hard.

"Come on, let's sit down. Looks like you were just going to have dinner." He guided Erin to the table and pulled out a chair for her. She sat as if in a daze, her eyes never leaving his face. Pouring himself a cup of coffee, he sat down opposite her.

"You are alive," she said with wonder.

He grinned a little. "Thanks to you. A lot has happened, Erin. I figured it was time to tell you what's been going on."

How rested Dain looked! Nothing like the man who had come here a few months ago. Erin saw the relaxation in his face now. His mouth was no longer a harsh, hard line. His eyes were dancing with life, with robust vitality—not like before, when they had been flat and haunted. His hair was a little longer, though still neat and businesslike. He wore jeans, a long-sleeved chamois shirt and work boots, and his skin was deeply bronzed from being in the sun. Her gaze moved to his hands—callused and scarred now from outdoor work—and she ached to have those fingers touch her. Love her.

"And your tumor?" she asked.

"Practically gone." Dain sipped the coffee and smiled. "When I left here, I went home and had my doc look at it.

It was already shrinking, Erin.'' He reached out, lacing his fingers with hers. ''The doctors are amazed, of course, but I'm not.'' He sobered and held her soft, luminous look. ''You're an incredible woman, you made me believe in miracles. I have to be careful when I talk about you to others to keep them from putting you up for sainthood.''

She smiled a little, the warmth from his strong hand feeding her aching heart and hungry soul. ''But it was your belief that did it.''

He squeezed her hand gently at her generous comment, then he sighed and looked around. ''God, I've missed this place.'' His gaze moved back to her. ''And I've missed you.''

Her fingers tightened briefly on his. ''My heart has been hollow since you left.''

''Hollow?''

She blushed a little at his warm teasing. This was a side to Dain she'd never been privileged to see before. And oh, how she loved him even more for being able to share it. ''Hollow as in empty.''

''So,'' he said carefully, ''you missed me?''

''I missed the man I knew you really were. Not the one who came here originally.''

He put the coffee aside and rested his other hand over hers. Moving his fingers lightly across the back of hers, he asked, ''Missed? As in?''

Her heart galloped at his touch, the heat of his gaze upon her. Erin closed her eyes, tears matting her thick, black lashes. ''Missed you,'' she whispered brokenly, ''as in a part of me was like a wolf without her mate.''

Dain looked down at Maiisoh, who lay under the table between them. ''Wolves mate for life.''

''Yes,'' Erin whispered, opening her eyes, absorbing his touch. Absorbing him into her starving self.

Frowning, Dain stared hard at their hands. ''I—I...this is hard for me to say, Erin, but I need to say it to you.'' Fear shot through him, but he'd learned to never let that stop him. "When I first saw you, my heart did a lot of funny things it had never done before. I saw you standing up on that hill above the gulch I was stuck in and I thought, at first, with the sunlight backlighting you, that you were an angel. And when I got closer and I saw your face, I wanted to cry—with relief. It was as if I already knew you."

He slanted a glance beneath the table. "And this white wolf of yours was showing up regularly in my dreams, so when I saw him at your side, I knew. I knew that something magical was happening. I fought it. I fought you. I fought myself." He moved his gaze back to her, his voice growing husky.

"You've taught me so much—*so much*. I give myself credit for taking it and running with it when I got back to New York. I stopped being Old Gordon. I got some therapy to help me sort out who I was instead of letting the past live inside me."

She placed her hand on his. "I'm so glad for you." And she was. How much Dain had changed! Erin had to stop herself from gawking at him.

He smiled a little and enjoyed simply looking at her fresh, natural features. Her long, dark hair framed her face, emphasizing her beautiful cinnamon-colored eyes, now glimmering with tears. And her mouth. How many nights and days had he recalled taking that mouth, kissing it? Drawing her breath, her life, into his lungs? Into his heart and shattered soul? That one twilight of lovemaking had sustained him, made him hope when he shouldn't have hoped at all.

"I wanted to come back to you sooner, but I had to get myself together, Erin. I had to discover who the real Dain Phillips was before I could come back to you. I didn't want the ghost of the past standing between us when I returned."

Erin nodded, understanding only too well what he meant. "The ghosts of others inhabit many of us."

"Yes," he said carefully, "and you had a ghost of your own to exorcise…didn't you?"

She managed a partial smile. "You showed me that a man could be kind, showed me that I could trust again and not be hurt by it. There is more to tell, though."

Dain's hands tightened on hers. She felt shame and could not look into his eyes. Her voice dropped.

"I'm here to listen this time," he murmured, holding her tear-filled gaze.

Erin nodded and took a deep breath. "I was nineteen when I became pregnant. And that was when he began to act insane. I lived every day in fear of dying. When I was three months pregnant, he beat me so badly that I lost our baby and I nearly died."

"My God," Dain whispered.

Erin shook her head. "I ran away. I ran back home, back to my parents' home. My mother helped me file for a divorce. When Tom came looking for me, my family protected me from him. He wanted me back. I—I lived in such terror of him kidnapping me. For years after that, he stalked me. The men of our nation knew who to look for, so if they saw Tom drive onto our reservation, they would send him packing. But I couldn't leave without him waiting to stalk me."

Taking a deep breath, Erin looked around. "That's when I decided to disappear. I talked it over with my family. My mother had friends among the Navajo people. Luanne Yazzie was one of them. She made me welcome here, and it was her family who helped build this hogan and gave me a place to live—and hide." Erin looked back at Dain and found his eyes soft with understanding, not incrimination. How much he had changed. Her mind spun and her heart opened like a flower toward him.

"And Tom never found you out here?"

"No…never." She took a quavering breath. "I'm not

proud of my past, Dain. I knew I wasn't walking with my fear, I was running away from it.''

''Somehow, I brought all of this back to you when I came, didn't I?''

She marveled at his wisdom, his insight. ''Yes, you did. I had to try and separate you from Tom, but you had so much violence and rage in you because of Old Gordon that I fought myself daily.'' She looked around the softly lit hogan. ''Every day was a challenge for me to work through my prejudice against white men. Every day I fought my fear of your inner rage possibly coming out and hurting me.''

''And yet you hung in there with me. You never let it step between us,'' he said in awe. ''I'd say you've pretty much worked through your own inner ghost, wouldn't you?''

She smiled a little. ''Yes, these past few months have allowed me to heal, too.''

''We were both wounded wolves,'' he agreed. Then he captured her gaze. ''I'm scared right now, Erin. More scared than when Old Gordon was coming to beat the hell out of me.''

''Scared of what?'' she asked, surprised. She saw the wry look he gave her.

''Somewhere along the line, Erin, I fell in love with you. When we made love that night, I knew you were right for me. But I wondered if I was right for you. I was a monster with a past.'' He averted his gaze and looked around the hogan. ''I had to leave you in order to find out if I could get rid of the monster inside of me and find the decent human being instead. This time apart has made me see a lot of things. It gave me a chance to question if I could live up to someone like you, someone who has such integrity, such honesty—and guts enough to trust me, of all people.''

Stunned, she stared at him. Had she heard right? Or was it her pining heart making up the words she'd ached to hear for so long? Another part of her wondered at his description of himself. "A monster? You were never a monster," she whispered, gripping his hand. "How could you say that about yourself? You were badly hurt, that was all."

"I love you," Dain said with emotion, reaching out and cupping her cheek. Looking deeply into her wide, surprised eyes, he continued huskily, "I love you and I was afraid you could never love me in return because I was such a monster." His hands fell away and he clasped them in front of him on the table, forcing himself to hold her gaze. "When you held me that night and forced me to realize Old Gordon was my real problem, all I wanted to do afterward was crawl into your arms, love the hell out of you and sleep with you at my side—forever. I wanted you so badly." He shook his head, his voice turning raspy. "I wanted you for all the wrong reasons. I realized that fact when I woke up that morning and found you curled up beside me, your arms cradling me as I slept.

"I had to leave you, Erin, because I knew my love for you was tainted with my past. I didn't think you could love me in return, anyway, with all I'd done to others in my life. So I left. I left in hopes of being able to live, not die. I promised that if I lived, I'd do everything I could to get rid of the monster inside me and come back to you a man. And that if I could do that, maybe you could see the man this time, not the monster of before, and love me in return. Or," he continued unsteadily, "I hoped you'd at least tell me I had a chance of cultivating a relationship with you over time—that there was some kind of hope for a future with you."

Dain risked a look at her. Tears were tracking down her cheeks. His heart wrenched. Gently, he wiped the moisture from her cheeks. "I love you, wolf woman. Over these past months, I've done nothing but feel that love grow and live inside me like an oak tree. No matter what I've done, you've been there like a guardian angel on my shoulder. Sometimes I'd talk to you out loud, or to myself, and ask, 'What would

Erin do?' in this or that circumstance.'' He grinned a little.
''I had a lot of conversations with you, believe me.

''Tell me,'' he coaxed hoarsely, ''that I have a chance
with you, with your affections, Erin. Or am I crazy? If you
tell me to leave, I'll do it and never come back. What I want
is your love. I want marriage. I want you as my life partner.
I won't settle for anything less and I know that's a hell of
a bold thing to say to someone I've only made love to once.
But I knew the loving that night was returned. I *felt* your
heart in that kiss. I felt our souls touch. Or was I wrong?''
He slipped his fingers through her hair. ''I need to know,
Erin. That's why I'm back. To find out how you feel toward
me and if we have a shot at a future together.''

Stunned, Erin got up and stood looking at him, with Maiisoh at her side. What courage Dain had to say all these
things! She recognized the fear in his eyes—the fear of being rejected again. Opening her hands, her voice barely a
whisper, she said, ''My heart has a mind of its own. When
you first came, I didn't like you because the ghost of my
past stood between us. But later, my heart wanted you in
all ways. I had to fight myself not to touch you the way a
woman touches her man. I had to stop myself so many
times, Dain. I had so many dreams of loving you, of holding
you, of lying here on my pallet, wrapped in the warmth of
a Navajo rug, with you at my side.''

She touched her heart with her hand. ''I knew why you
left. I agreed with your leaving. I knew the ghosts of our
past were still strong and we needed time away from one
another to continue to walk our healing path.''

Slowly, Dain stood and walked over to her. He placed
his hands on her strong, proud shoulders. ''You love me?''
Although her feelings were clear in her honest words, he
dared not believe he'd heard right.

A soft smile shadowed her mouth. ''A wolf mates for
life. Even if the mate leaves, that does not mean her heart

forgets him or wants to forget him. I will always love you, Dain.''

Maiisoh whined and thumped his tail happily.

Dain looked down at the wolf, whose amber eyes shone with joy. ''He looks a lot like I feel at this moment.''

Erin laughed. How easy it was to walk into Dain's arms, to press herself against his tall, strong body. She felt him groan, felt the safety of his arms wrapping around her. The air rushed out of her lungs as he held her hard against him, his face buried in her hair.

''I love you,'' Dain said huskily. ''With my life. With the rest of my life.'' He could smell the scent of the desert in her hair, the sweet, wild fragrance of sage. And he could smell the sun and wind on her skin. Lifting his head, he captured her face between his hands. ''I want to love you, Erin. Right now. Right here. What do you want?''

His body screamed for hers, but he knew this had to be her choice and she had to pace their relationship. He wasn't trying to pressure her, but to let her know he wanted only honesty with her. Her cinnamon eyes shone with joy at his huskily spoken words. ''Yes,'' she whispered. ''I love you, Dain. I've always loved you, and I'm so glad you came back...my wolf mate.''

''My beautiful wild-heart woman,'' he said, leaning down, grazing her tear-stained lips with his own. ''Your wolf is back. And he wants you...''

The moments flowed together for Erin. The golden light that illuminated the hogan became their cocoon. When Dain led her over to the pallet and began to unbutton her dark blue, velvet blouse, she closed her eyes and swayed. Each touch of his fingers grazing her flesh sent a shower of fire through her.

How easy it was to slide his shirt off his strong shoulders. Slowly the articles of clothing fell in a heap beside them. Her fingers trembled as she unbuckled his belt and unzipped his jeans. She could see the proof of his desire and felt her knees go weak with need. How long had it been since she'd lain with Dain? Too long. *Too long*.

Dain saw her eyes grow dark with pleasure as he tugged first her skirt and then her lingerie away from her. When they stood naked before one another, he felt no shame, but rather gloried in this golden moment he'd dreamed of for so long. Running his hands up her arms as she stood so innocently before him, he cupped her face.

"I'll be gentle," he whispered, and pulled her down next to him on the pallet. The scratchy wool of the rug felt good against him, and Erin's silky hair was like a river cascading across her shoulders and breasts. It reminded him of her fertile darkness, the feminine place he longed to be captured within. Easing her onto her back, he allowed his fingers to trail down her cheek and jaw to her slender neck and finely sculpted collarbone. Her eyes burned with desire—for him. The discovery was as heady as it was humbling. He felt her hand range upward across his rib cage, her fingers tangle in the dark growth of hair across his chest. Each touch was like a scalding fire making him want to lose control and take her hard and fast.

Pressing his body more surely against hers, he felt her tremble with longing. Her eyes closed and she arched toward him. Smiling to himself, he molded his mouth against hers and felt her open to him, a hot, liquid invitation. She tasted of life, of love, of a promise he'd never had before in his life.

Everything else ceased to exist except her. His heart opened powerfully as he felt her breasts rub against him. The dreams of the past dissolved into the present. He was here, with the woman he loved so fiercely it defied description. Her skin was soft, firm and velvety as his hand skimmed down her body, to her rounded abdomen and long, curved thigh. He felt her moan reverberate through him as he explored the soft, inner recesses of her mouth with his tongue. The black silk of her hair swirled between them. Their breathing was chaotic, short bursts of urgent need.

As his hand slid between her dampened thighs, Erin gave a little cry. She realized what she felt wasn't fear, but rather pleasure as he sought and found her womanly center. Heat uncurled and moved outward like wings on a bird, fluttering through her lower body, overwhelming her with the pure joy and pleasure that he was giving to her, sharing with her. No longer could she think. All she could do was love him like a hungry wolf who had been without her life partner for too long.

She was no longer shy, but responding wildly to his continuing touch and exploration. His mouth was firm against hers, and she returned that loving strength with her own. The wonderful weight of his body upon hers, his knee moving her thighs apart, sent her into a frenzy of raw desire. As their flesh met, and he thrust deeply into her, her body gave way and allowed entrance. For just a moment there was pressure, but never pain. Of their own accord, her hips moved upward to joyously meet and match the rhythm he was establishing with her. A wildfire spread through her. She felt the hard grip of his arms, his mouth devouring hers as he took her with hard, deep thrusts. She met each movement and gloried in it.

When he leaned down and captured her nipple, she gave a small cry of utter surrender. The throbbing heat built so swiftly that she gripped his damp shoulders and arched against him. A cry tore from her lips. His mouth captured hers again, muffling her joyous cry of pleasure. The world exploded within her, as if a white-hot lightning bolt had struck her, and she felt herself melt in Dain's arms as waves of rhythmic pleasure rolled through her. Mindlessly, she responded, and at the same time heard him growl. He lifted his head, his eyes shut tightly as he gripped her hard. She knew that same white lightning raced through him, and Erin moved her hips in an undulating motion, prolonging his pleasure as he stiffened against her.

Within seconds the searing heat became a profound warmth, like Father Sun heating the cold earth after a winter night. She inhaled Dain's male scent deeply into herself, felt him pull the wool blanket across them. Settling comfortably into the crook of his shoulder, she smiled softly, her arm moving across his chest to embrace him.

"I love you," she whispered, her brow pressed against his hard, unforgiving jaw. "I love you with all my life."

The words were like honey flowing through Dain. He held her tightly against him, feeling her breathe in sync with him. Her breasts were soft against him, her hair clinging damply to her long, beautifully curved back as he ran his fingers absently up and down her spine. "I love you, Erin. You *are* my life. You gave life back to me." He pressed a kiss to her brow and looked down at her slumberous eyes.

Smiling gently, he kissed her slowly, longingly. She was so open, so giving that it sent his senses spinning. Erin was such a woman of Mother Earth. There was no coyness in her. No games. How very different she was from women he'd known before her—like night and day. But then, he hadn't been ready to receive an unconditional love like hers before, either.

"All I want to do now," he said, caressing her neck and shoulder, "is go to sleep with you in my arms, sweet woman of mine. I'm so damned tired. A year's worth of tired."

Erin understood and smiled softly up at him. "Tomorrow we will sing Father Sun up."

How he'd missed her simple lifestyle—her tie to all things. Sighing, he lay back, bringing Erin fully against him. His body sang with completion, his hunger sated, his spirit no longer thirsting or starving. Erin fulfilled him on every level. He loved her with a fierceness he could not even begin to put into words. His world, the rest of his life, was in his arms right now.

"Yes," he whispered against her hair, "we'll sing Father Sun up tomorrow morning."

They sat at the table, sipping coffee. Sunlight poured into the east windows of the hogan, warming it and making brilliant golden paths on the floor.

"I never knew what happiness was," Dain admitted in a husky voice, looking at Erin with pure love. Today she wore a red blouse and a black velvet skirt, bringing out the glorious color of her face and eyes. Her hair had been brushed until it glistened like a raven's wing. After singing up the sun, she had made them a healthy breakfast of fresh eggs, bacon and fry bread. Nothing had tasted better to him. But maybe it was just Erin and his love for her that made food taste this extraordinary.

She smiled shyly. "I didn't, either. It—it's wonderful."

"We're in love for the first time in our lives."

"Yes," Erin said. "I feel as if I'm in a dream. I am afraid I will awaken and you—this—will be gone...."

He leaned over and gripped her hand gently for a moment. "I'm real. This is real. What we have is real."

She closed her eyes. "Never have I wanted anything more."

"I think we deserve this," Dain noted ruefully. "We each paid heavy prices."

"But we had enough courage to walk through our fear. The Great Spirit rewards those who do not let fear stop them."

"It's our wild wolf hearts," Dain said, smiling.

She nodded. "What are your plans? I know you think of these things."

He laughed a little and stood up. Moving around to the back of her chair, he rested his hands on her shoulders. Automatically, Erin leaned her head against his body. He loved her ability to be natural and unaffected with him. "You know me too well," he admitted.

"I should."

"Yes," he murmured, leaning down and pressing a kiss to her brow. "You can have my head, my heart... everything."

"You already have mine," Erin whispered, absorbing his touch, his affection.

Dain straightened and placed his hands on her shoulders again. "These past few months I've done some work to rectify the carnage I inflicted on others with my business dealings, Erin." His hands tightened briefly. "But we need to sit down and talk about your needs. What do you want out of life? Where do you want to live? What do you see yourself doing in the future once you marry me?"

She twisted to look up at him and laughed. "Like a good wolf, you are always looking around."

"Yes, well, it keeps me alive and safe," he teased. Maiisoh, who had been sitting near the door, came over and sat next to him. Dain patted the wolf's head. "So I'll stay in contact with the board of directors I've set up. I've got a cellular phone in the car, a fax and stuff like that. They know I'm coming here. They know whatever decisions that are made will automatically include your needs, your wants and dreams, Erin.

"I want to take a week and explore your dreams and mine. Let's see where we can bring these things together. What we can do as the good team that we are. I'm hungry for your input on a lot of ideas I've got. This past year has been about healing for me—personally as well as on a business level. I didn't want to do anything about a possible future together until I was sure that you wanted me, loved me, as I do you."

Sighing, Erin closed her eyes, content to be held by Dain. "Wolves never jump into anything," she counseled him softly. "They look, watch and listen for a long time. Let us take this time. Most of all, be patient with me—with everything."

Dain gave a lopsided smile. "I have a feeling that you'll be the best counselor a man could ever have. And like a good wolf, I'm going to listen to your heart, to you."

She reached up, her hand upon his. "Beloved, all that matters is that we walk and speak from our hearts. That is what wolves do naturally—follow their instincts. They never walk away from their wild heart. No matter what you do, if it is from that place, it is good and all our relations will be blessed by it."

In that moment, Dain realized just how much truth Erin had spoken. Leaning down, he pressed a kiss to her cheek. "Two wild wolf hearts," he whispered against her ear. "I'm going to love you forever. *Forever.*"

* * * * *

Silhouette

SPECIAL EDITION™
&
SILHOUETTE *Romance*

present a new series about the proud,
passion-driven dynasty

THE COLTONS

You loved the California Coltons, now discover
the Coltons of Black Arrow, Oklahoma.
Comanche blood courses through their veins,
but a brand-new birthright awaits them....

WHITE DOVE'S PROMISE by Stella Bagwell (7/02, SE#1478)

THE COYOTE'S CRY by Jackie Merritt (8/02, SE#1484)

WILLOW IN BLOOM by Victoria Pade (9/02, SE#1490)

THE RAVEN'S ASSIGNMENT by Kasey Michaels (9/02, SR#1613)

A COLTON FAMILY CHRISTMAS by Judy Christenberry,
Linda Turner and Carolyn Zane (10/02, Silhouette Single Title)

SKY FULL OF PROMISE by Teresa Southwick (11/02, SR#1624)

THE WOLF'S SURRENDER by Sandra Steffen (12/02, SR#1630)

*Look for these titles
wherever Silhouette books are sold!*

Silhouette®
Where love comes alive™

FREE
Gourmet Garden Kit!

With two proofs of purchase from any four Silhouette® special collector's editions.

Special Limited Time Offer

YES! Please send me my FREE Gourmet Garden Kit without cost or obligation, except for shipping and handling. Enclosed are two proofs of purchase from specially marked Silhouette® special collector's editions and $3.50 shipping and handling fee.

_____

Name (PLEASE PRINT)

_____

Address   Apt. #

_____

City   State/Prov.   Zip/Postal Code

IN U.S., mail to:
Silhouette Gourmet Garden Kit Offer
3010 Walden Ave.
P.O. Box 9023
Buffalo, NY 14269-9023

IN CANADA, mail to:
Silhouette Gourmet Garden Kit Offer
P.O. Box 608
Fort Erie, Ontario
L2A 5X3

FREE GOURMET GARDEN KIT OFFER TERMS
To receive your free Gourmet Garden Kit, complete the above order form. Mail it to us with two proofs of purchase, one of which can be found in the upper right-hand corner of this page. Requests must be received no later than December 31, 2002. Your Gourmet Garden Kit costs you only $3.50 for shipping and handling. The free Gourmet Garden Kit has a retail value of $17.00 U.S. All orders subject to approval. Products in kit illustrated on the back inside cover of this book are for illustrative purposes only, and items may vary (retail value of items always as previously indicated). **Please allow 6-8 weeks for delivery. Offer good in Canada and the U.S. only.** Offer good only while quantities last. Offer limited to one per household.